"First they ignore you. Then they ridicule you. Then they attack you and want to burn you. And then they build monuments to you."

THE BADGES THAT A CITY FORGOT

– One Cop's Story –

- No Law Enforcement, innocent or decent people were harmed during the making of this story. Unless stated, all mangled, beaten, shot, set on fire or otherwise devastated persons were not handcuffed, and they were resisting or at least able to fight back.

Any similarity to actual characters is coincidental. Characters, names, and events have been changed to protect the lady who cooked the hamburgers at the courthouse, and to keep the guilty parties' real names secret. This measure is both required and unfortunate, because these names should be released, to prevent in-breeding -

Cover design by Renarde Andrews. Some artwork provided by Simon Howden, Boaz Yiftach, Stuart Miles, and Digital Art at www.freedigitalphotos.net

Copyright 2019 - Reynard Andrews / RA - C
Communications

ISBN – 9780979923043

DEDICATION

I dedicate this work with gratitude and honor to all the men and women who serve in the badge, one family in blue; true until the end.

I would like to say I found no greater honors than to serve making the peace as a soldier, and keeping the peace as a cop.

To all the brothers and sisters that have *fallen asleep*, on the 'Job' I will see you soon.

TABLE OF CONTENTS

1.0 It Is All A Game 11

2.0 The Greatest Of All Human Endeavors..........................14

3.0 The Police Academy..17
3.1 The Police Academy 18
3.2 The Offensive Report..20
3.3 The Arrest Report 21
3.4 Verbal Judo 25
3.5 Moot Court..27
3.6 Diversity Training 28
3.7 The Gun Range 29
3.8 Traffic Accident Investigation 31
3.9 Physical Training 32
3.10 The Law 33
3.11 Graduation..36

4.0 Rookies..39
4.1 Rookies 40
4.2 Patrol Training Officers 40
4.3 A Female Perspective 43
4.4 A Less Than Humble PTO..44
4.5 First Encounters Of The Fake Kind....................................46

5.0 Patrol...51
5.1 Walking Patrol 52
5.2 That Bitch? 59
5.3 Balls Were Actually Made For Kicking 61

6.0 Under-Cover Ops 65
6.1 Making The Crew 66
6.2 Prostitution Enforcement 68
6.3 Picking Up Whores 69
6.4 Minister Sling-That-Dick...80

TABLE OF CONTENTS

6.5 Prostitution Stings...82
6.6 Club 'Sticky Twat'..84

7.0 Street Level Drug Enforcement...............................93
7.1 The Drug Sting...94
7.2. Buy Busts...98
7.3 Arr- Robbery...99
7.4 Shotgun In Belly 101
7.5 Kid-Napped?...103
7.6 What Kind of Tactics Are Those 105
7.7 Police, Search Warrant 108
7.8 25th And Overland...109
7.9 Skeletons In The Closet 113
7.10 Is That Dirty?..116
7.11 The Contract 117
7.12 Blue Boys...120
7.13 The Punch Heard Around The World....................125
7.14 NFL Type Crap..129
7.15 Tales of Aspirin 130
7.16 Funniest Crap Ever 133

8.0 The Shooting Review Board2nd Appearance 137

9.0 Smoke Signal..139

10.0 Long-Term Investigations.................................143
10.1 Long-term Investigations.....................................144
10.2 Suspension Days..148
10.3 Operation Venereal Disease.................................150
10.4 Operation Little Big Deal 155
10.5 Desk Jockey..163
10.6 Sometimes Mistakes Happen...............................166
10.7 Enemy In The Wire..175

TABLE OF CONTENTS

11.0 Shooting Review Board[4th Appearance] 180

12.0 The Blue Dick 187
12.1 The Other 'Tick' 190

13.0 Toxic Shock Syndrome 192

14.0 Precinct Detective..197
14.1 Precinct Detective 198
14.2 Who's Screwing Whom? 199
14.3 Habla! Poor Bastards 203
14.4 Are These Bastards Ever Going To Run
     Out of Bullets? 204
14.5 Investigating Family 216
14.6 Club Dog Pound...217
14.7 Weed Anyone? 225
14.8 Polygraph Who?...231
14.9 Where You Ever A Lawman?...234
14.10 KPG Gate 244

15.0 Look What We Have Become 245

16.0 Saddle Tramp...249

17.0 Prologue 253

PREFACE

This story was from the time before my life changed. Now I am a librarian hiding in the 'Former Police Who Are Now Ashamed of What the Law Enforcement Industry has Become' Witness Protection Program.

Even though the city forgets badges, may our kids forgive us for what we are now.

Renarde Andrews

"Most people are like sheep, nice, harmless creatures who want nothing more than to be left alone so they can graze. Then of course, there are wolves, who want nothing more than to eat the sheep. There is a third kind of person; The Sheepdog. Sheepdogs have fangs like wolves. But their instinct isn't predation. It is protection. All they want, what they live for, is to protect the flock."

1.0
IT'S ALL A GAME

The hallway yielded many echoes, I thought, while waiting outside the Chief's Office yet again. While I sat on the cheap plastic bench, looking at the familiar yellowing walls and the fluorescent light bulbs flicker, a young officer approached and stood near me, poised to plop down on the bench. He stood about 5'10"; 195-205 lbs, standard cop hairstyle, held in place with mousse, and had a medium build. You could tell he was a younger officer, he did not have bulging pockets full of keys and gum and a wallet line in his hip pocket. His gun belt and all the components matched, and were in good shape. His weapon had a butt-plug and the pommel was not covered in dust and deodorant. His breast pocket bore the silhouette not or a small writing pad but instead of a Smartphone.

"Hey man," he said, "You're one of the Tuna Row guys aren't you?"

I laughed hard at his question. I laughed so hard that my clip-on tie popped loose. The tie popping a loose was ok; it was too small anyway, as was the rest of the uniform. Nevertheless, you wear what you have when called to the Chief's Office for a Disciplinary Process Hearing. I was not nervous; this was an all too familiar situation I found myself in, except this time there were no Credits out there to hide behind, for the first time in a very long time I would have to face the music.

"Hey man, how are you doing?" The officer asked when he sat down alongside. "I am new to this process; I'm Walters, nice to meet you." Now I had company sitting in the hallway waiting for disciplinary hearings.

"What are you here for?" I asked.

Walters replied, "I did not put a seat belt on my suspect when I transported him." I wanted to laugh when he made the statement, but I knew he was serious.

I moved over on the bench so he could sit down. "I think I know you," Walters continued. "You came to my academy class and taught some undercover stuff. Aren't you one of the Tuna Road Boys?"

"Yeah, I guess so," I replied, still amused.

"Where is Tuna Road anyway and why are you up here?" He inquired further.

I laughed a chuckle at first, then a hard laugh, "Tuna Road? Well hell, son, sit back I will tell you. I was walking my assigned post at a crappy extra job when the storeowner ran up shouting in some Middle Eastern language. He was excited about something, actually more upset, and he kept pointing to a white dude walking quickly away from his store. I was not sure what the hell he said but he was serious. I radioed my partner and we started chasing the dude. Dude ran down the stairs and out into the mall. My fat, lazy, ignorant ass, partner fell at the bottom of the stairs, I left his dumb ass sliding on the floor. Honestly, who falls off the bottom rung of a staircase?

Most idiots who can traverse a staircase can figure it out but no not his dumb ass. Dude ran a lot faster now; it was obvious he intended to evade apprehension. I ran faster, and his ass ran even faster. We got out into the parking lot, and he jumped over the wall to the lower stage. I did not want to take the risk but I was not about to let him get away. I tried to curse when I hit the ground and my knees bounced past my belly and into my chin. I got the word 'SHI' out but then I bit my damn tongue, so it came out 'SHI…!' Now I was mad, I fully intended to throat stomp this guy before I took him anywhere near the jail.

Finally, I caught up with the skinny dick head. He fell on the ground begging me not to stomp on his head. It really sucks when you chase one that does not want to fight when caught. You have all this adrenaline, a massive erection and, no one to screw. I snatched butt hole up and we took the long-ass walk back to' Ali-Baba' or whatever his name was.

When we got back to the store, I asked the kid what he did and he said, 'I wasn't paying dude for that duce I dropped.' I looked at him, and shook my head, not because of what he did but because I chased him for nothing, *shoplifter - dammit I thought.*

'Ali-Baba 'showed up speaking in his native dialect. I looked at him and said, English, please. This bastard, took a crap in my store, and stunk up the whole store. All the other customers left. I told him he owed me the $20 because he ran the other customers away. Instead of just paying me he ran.'

After his story, I wished I had continued to let him speak in whatever the language he was speaking. What did he steal?" I asked. "I lost money because of his smelly ass, that's what he stole money out of my kid's mouths; I want it."

I stood still for a moment, kind of in a fog of disbelief. This was the first time in more than 20 years; someone used the word crap in a sentence accurately. I looked at 'Ali-Baba': for the record I am not a racist, "You stupid, Gyro eating terrorist," were the first words out of my mouth, "How the heck did your dumb ass get past immigration?"

I unhand-cuffed the 'mighty pooper', and then walked out of the store with him. That is when I knew my life as a cop was over, I had become the lowest form of human I could think of a mall security guard. I was ready to quit the job, without delay, and not turn in my police gear. They could come to get their radio from 'Ali-Baba's' trashcan.

"All the way home, I looked in the mirror, pondering. *Mirror, mirror on the wall what the crap happened to it all?* I used to be on a team of great people, we did great things, and made a difference: now; I literally am a crap kicker. If I were not so lazy, I would probably slit my wrists. Instead, I just went home and watched "Gun smoke; at least Matt Dillon never gave in and became a security guard."

"Of course, there were no malls then," the young patrol officer jeered.

"Screw you!" I said, "You get the point," we both laughed.

"Sounds like they are screwing you, as long as you have been on they hang you up for this crap. I heard you did all kinds of jacked up things."

"A bad decision is a bad decision, I made a few, and I learned many lessons. Hell yeah, I done a lot worse, but things were different then, less political, they were building something then. Life is a dream. We wake up when we die." I decided to tell him my whole story; we had time, Walters more so than I did.

2.0
THE GREATEST OF ALL HUMAN ENDEAVORS

"It was not always like this Walters, years ago, I helped change the world, and lay the groundwork that helped change the face of a City. A merry band of misfits painted a City bright and made it safer. The fires we set lit the City for years and laid a path for many to walk safely against the darkness. Until the light faded; until the City changed; the City forgot who we were, now they say that we were not true to our calling, and did a disservice." I looked at him, "I will let you decide."

My career began a long time ago. I came on 'The Job' (joined the Police Department) upon realizing that the world needed me because it was screwed up. Society is full of people, people are full of crap, and as a result, society is full of crap. The fact is that the world has become a dirty, crass, inhospitable place to live. One man can make a difference, for good or evil, one man can make a change. Was I that man? I sought to represent change; Good from darkness, justice from vengeance, peace from war. I sought to join the ranks of Spartacus, Wyatt Earp, George Washington, Genghis Kahn, Gandhi, Malcolm X, and others who placed themselves in harm's way to better humanity.

I am a cop, I thought, when I was new like you; damn this is so awesome. I planned to kick asses, take names, wreck cars, and shoot the crap out of people...what could be better? I was going to be a one-man army, just like Batman. No caves no screwed up mask, and no idiot sidekick; just a tall, handsome man with an attitude and the skills to make the world a better place. No one ever said that the job was going to change me more than I was going to change the world.

It is no wonder the name of Wyatt Earp's gun is the Peacemaker. Occasionally, you have to shoot a few assholes; more often than not, you beat the crap out of someone with your service weapon (so choose a good one). The most common use of a cop's firearm is just to point it in the bad guy's direction, and remind the piece of crap that there is something bigger, stronger, and nastier than they are. This is how you make (a) lasting peace; destroy evil's will to live."

I looked down at my uniform, I scrubbed the brass forever; it took at least 7 minutes. I hated brass buttons and belt buckles they tarnish so quickly. The mirror at home confirmed for all time that this polyester uniform is the cheapest crap I ever wore. It is flame retardant because there is nothing natural in the cloth to burn. I stood in the mirror this morning for 15 minutes trying to get this gun belt on atop this brass under-belt. The blue costume used to fit; now, like me it is old, worn, broken, and too small. I do not know why we call it a gun-belt; there is only one gun, and fifteen other ignorant pieces of equipment. There is enough crap on this belt to make Batman jealous. The Whole-Lot-Of-Unnecessary-Crap-Belt made more sense as a moniker. The uniform was too tight and one of the Training officer stripes was falling off. I was a training officer this week, so I probably should have looked better, but I looked the way the job made me feel; like crap. I used to iron my uniform, now I barely wash it, times changed, the department changed, I changed and none for the better.

"I have the Shooting Review Board this morning. If you want to fill the room with a bunch of stupid, inept, judgmental idiots, shoot a criminal. It is amazing how many uninformed buttholes come out of their coffee filled cages to judge cops for doing police work. Given the chance, I could make the world a better place by shooting the board members. The guy I shot was just one single solitary piece of crap: look how many other pieces of crap came here to judge my actions, what a department we could have been if it was all cops and no brass. Somebody once asked me if good people do enough bad things do they become bad? I told them that is the definition of a good person; they do not do bad things. I used to be a good person until I became a cop. It changed me in ways I never thought possible. Policing is what the man must have referred to when he said it was the best of times; it was the worst of times.

Plato had a republic, which was because he was small and insignificant. We have the power, authority, and bullets to make a world, screw Plato; judge us for what we do. Talk never changed anything; I decided it was time, time for action, and time for me."

He looked at me, not sure what to say, so he listened.

"I learned many lessons while I policed, you mind if I share a few as we sit here sucking up taxpayers money?" He shrugged his shoulders, as he looked as his cell. I was unsure if that was lack of interest, or just this generation's lackadaisical manner of communicating. Besides, that was not a no.

The long, outdated hallway gave an ominous backdrop for life lessons, but a blank canvas sat in front of me. I was determined, not to leave these halls today without making some sort of impression on this blank slate.

"The first thing I learned, is lofty, its cerebral but if more people adhered to the basic principle, what a city; what a world we would have. The purpose of life is not to be happy. It is to be useful, to be honorable, to be compassionate, and to have it make some difference that you have lived and lived well."

3.0
THE
POLICE
ACADEMY

"I know it's become fashionable to depict the police as sadistic Cossack riding down innocent citizens, but I've become well enough acquainted with law-enforcement agencies across the country to know that's just not the case. Of course, a certain small percentage of policemen are irresponsible...but that does not justify the current unjust barrage of propaganda against a tribe of men who are hard working, underpaid and daily risking their lives to protect us. I'm sure there are isolated instances of police brutality, but the rising crime rate and urban violence constitute a far, far more pressing problem."

3.1
THE POLICE ACADEMY

"Becoming a cop is the second-best thing anyone can do, next to being a superhero. In the Armed Forces, I jumped from helicopters, blew up stuff, and wore camouflage. I did not know then how much fun it was, kicking the crap out of guilty, low-lives."

"People make mistakes, they are not all low lives," Walters chimed in indignantly.

I looked at him presumptuously; "Smoking weed is not what I am on about."

 He half smiled, half hung his head, "I try not to arrest anyone for anything I do or did myself, that way I am not a hypocrite."

"People play the parts they dress for young man. The teacher wears a tie to school, then goes out, and drinks all night. The clergyman wears his collar, and then uses it to hit his wife in the face when he gets home. When you are on the job, you are paid to do whatever the hell the rules say to do, not to decide if you agree with the law. Handle that dilemma before you join, if you are going to be a cop."

"So you play the role of Nazi, when you are on the clock?"

"I did a lot of things, but it took me a while to find my way." I resumed my story. "I arrived at the academy for the first day of the rest of my life. An emotion crossed my heart on this the first day. It was not awe, or fear, not even glee; when I looked at the academy, the only thing I could say was, 'What a piece of crap!'

The building looked like a WWII raid shelter or field hospital, and no one cared about weeds, it was obvious. I parked, got out in my Goodwill suit and shoes, and made my way towards the 'outhouse' I was to call home for the next six months. One of the first things I noticed was that I was not the only one that went to Goodwill for my clothes. The difference was I bought these clothes specifically for the 'outhouse'; these screw ups looked like they routinely spent time, if not money at Goodwill. I was glad they had a source of income, so they could buy some clothes, not that police are snazzy dressers anyway but damn!

Upon entering the building, we were ushered into the gym. Maybe they said 'Jim', because it was not worth crap for physical fitness. They gave us the Welcome Story, something about integrity, honesty, and courage. As the hobbits spoke, I listened in awe at the unmitigated stupidity presented in the room thinking, *why the hell are they telling police recruits about honesty, integrity, and courage. Does McDonald's have to tell their new hires that they make hamburgers? When you apply for a job, you should know its requirements. If these people do not know what cops should not be, why the heck did you hire them?* Of course, over the years, I saw that I was right, people you had to tell to be courageous, honest and forthright, do not make good cops; they make up the Administration (Blue Ticks, and Dicks).

After the Idiot Address, they took us to a classroom and issued notebooks and gear, the dance had begun. I looked out the dirty ass window; I knew I could do this. I only had to shut up long enough to survive the academy. Whatever I was not enough of before I started; I was going to be now.

Whatever I was afraid of, I was going to conquer, and whatever ever life wanted to throw at me, had to wait, I was about to get into a blue cocoon, and when I emerged, the bad guys better look out for this butterfly; emerging as the predatory eagle.

The police academy was not like Basic Training, the cops that train at the police academy were not the top 1%. They may have been ok to teach a class, but they left a lot to be desired as cops.

The academy was easy for an ex-soldier. The academics were basic;

1. Remember the rules
2. Learn to apply them

Courtroom testimony practice was a waste of time, and no one cares about traffic accident reconstruction. I graduated after 6 months of listening to The Admin Police holler in my face and many police dispatch 10 Codes tests.

Oh yeah, I almost forgot, someone should have told the academy screw ups that the time to talk was over, in 6 months the class graduated; 6 months after that I will be working with a partner, then off to face the world alone. I was born ready; I was born to make a difference, to be in charge and to have men fear me. I did not need the academy. The world, including the Police Department, needed me. The Blue Trail began."

"You said The Blue trail?"

"Yeah, why not, I believe in the brother-hood of all men, but I do not believe in wasting brotherhood on anyone who does not want to practice it with me. Brother-hood is a two-way street."

3.2 The Offensive Report

"One of the reports police filed regularly by cops is the Offense or Incident Report."

"Um you know we still do that right?" Walters asked incredulously.

I fired back, "Yeah but it's my story. As I was saying, the report serves to catalog all crimes and complaints the police receive or file in the city. There are varieties of categories of reports used in the country; all of them exist to deceive the public. Do the math, how could the number of people in jail increase every year yet the crime rate goes down. The more you arrest the higher the numbers go, jailing them works to stop the crime, not fix the crime rate.

In my mind, the police existed to make the place safer via trash control methods. Stopping a burglary is good, making people afraid to steal is best. Maybe that is why the police often have God complexes, because we try to change the minds and hearts of people: by gut stomping them...just like in the Bible. Even if the crime rate went down (whatever a crime rate is), ask anyone you know if they feel safer?

The guy next to my desk and I were given a homework assignment to write a Robbery Offense Report. We started the report in class and then ran out of time. My idiot partner took the report home. One thing to learn about partners, get a good one, or do it alone, a bad partner is worse than no partner at all. Relying on a person that will not support you is devastating because you use the wrong tactics; Team tactics are vastly different from individual tactics.

When we got back to class the next day, my partner was doing pushups in the hallway. I was ordered by Training Officer 'Zombie' to join them. She earned that nickname from my academy class, because she was a bag of dead rotting flesh. Training Officer' Zombie' was completely useless as a cop; she was also lifeless and emotionless. Training Officer 'Mommy Dearest' a clown of a cop, she was like a slug-sloth hybrid. She slid around the training center, taking up valuable oxygen and sunlight.

Training Officer 'Zombie' then started asking me questions, 'What if that was your brother, what if that happened to you?' I did not know what she was talking about, and I really did not care it was only pushups - breakfast for a Marine.

When Training Officer Zombie told me to get up, I sprang to my feet and looked her in the eye. 'Well,' she demanded. I did not respond. 'Well, what do you have to say?' I replied in the most incredulous tone I could, 'I have no idea what you are talking about.' She had me get the report off the desk and read it thoroughly. I read the report; not laughing in the face of the training officer was a skill needed to survive Basic Training. It came in handy, in the police academy; there was so much and so many to laugh at in the police academy.

The report started with standard info, date, location, type of occurrence. I saw nothing wrong on the face of the report or for that matter for the first three pages. The narrative undoubtedly caught her eye. This was not just a robbery it was a robbery and a rape. The part that aggravated Training Officer 'Zombie,' was that the victim was a guy, and the suspects were all men. Training Officer 'Zombie' got mad because she thought we were being funny, this type of thing happens. How the hell are you going to get mad because you do not like the crime…WTF?

Either way, we survived another crappy day of stupid legal concepts like criminal rights, excessive force, and police brutality. Admin losers take all the fun out of playing cowboy. What idiot decided that keeping the peace was a popularity contest, not even children want to be told what to do. The reality of the fact is throughout history people sought less law and less order so they can do whatever they desire. However, just because people can vote does not make them right.

The single best way to reduce crime is to eradicate criminals. Stupid, selfish people commit crimes; dead bastards just turn to termite food. "That's Machiavellian," Walter retorted as he leaned back on the bench. "Yeah well, no one ever robbed, raped or murdered from the grave." I am a public servant, but I came to serve decent people, rhino-screw the criminals. I think police officers deserve termination for using too little force to make an arrest. I soon learned that words are the source of misunderstandings."

3.3 The Arrest Report

I continued the story. "The term Academy is just another way of saying babysitting for cowboys in training. Today's rather boring, inane class is about arrest reports. The instructor for this segment was Sgt. I'm-A-Complete-Moron. I assumed my usual posture, sitting with my arms propped up bored to tears. I was suddenly roused from my partial slumber by a peculiar sound, one that I did not recognize.

The arrest report is my favorite report; after the Use of Force of course. I like the arrest report, because unlike the Offense Report, I am not just writing down a story, I am making one happen. No matter what idiots say, some people need shooting, some need stoning, others need to pick up crap on the side of the interstate in the hot sun; no matter what sentence they receive, it starts with me putting handcuffs on them and dragging them to jail.

The Court System does not deprive people of their freedom, cops do. No one ever stood before a judge without having been arrested by us first. Cops do not even have to arrest, we have the power to adjudicate on the spot; the legal term is Discretion. Turns out, cops are Lawman, Judge and Jury and many cases. Society creates most of its own problems; this is just one of the twisted paradigms alive in The System.

Sgt. I'm-A-Complete-Moron instructed us in what to put in the arrest report. In the narrative, he stated that we needed to include all the details. This is a Phase 1 failure of the police system. All the details do not usually fit in the space provided on the form, and often if placed on paper, the information would result in disciplinary action against the officer.

I learned later in my career, that much of police work relies on hunches and feelings verified. Cops cannot see through lead, or into the future, but we develop exceptional skills and prejudging of characters. Actionable Intelligence relies vastly on info that is not quantifiable; therefore, the report of self-initiated police work usually is deficient. One simply cannot say;

- Dude looked weird or strange so I walked up to him and lied
- I tricked my way into skirting the law and proved that I was right all along
- I caught the person committing the crime, but he made me laugh, so I let him go
- I took the money from the game and gave it to some kids to buy ice cream

The arrest report also does not provide spaces for stupid, ignorant cops to express their racism, sexism, chauvinism, cowardice etc. What about putting this on an arrest report;

- I arrested the guy because he called me a piece of crap; because I am a piece of crap
- I arrested him because he did not have a job, so screw him
- I stopped the car because the girl getting in the car was gorgeous
- I arrested her because she turned me down for a date
- I first noticed him because he was black
- I arrested him because I hated him from high school

Equally as dangerous and just sheer ignorance, is to put things like profiling on the report. Profiling is legal, racial profiling is illegal, but they are both used every single day in law enforcement. If race does not play a role, why include it in FBI Statistics. Is it anyone's fault that serial rapists and the armed robbery in the USA are more than 51% black?

FBI Statistics indicate male whites and male Hispanics (also categorized as white) are prime suspects pedophiles and juvenile trafficking sex statistics, burglaries and suicide point towards male white? However, we cannot put on the arrest report that we saw a white guy driving and followed him simply because he was white. Nevertheless, if we are looking for burglary suspects, according to statistics it is probable that the persons we need to be aware of are male whites.

The second failure of the arrest report is that cops have to ensure that the method used to catch the criminal does not override the (criminal's) right to commit the crime {4th Amendment crap}. If cops cannot profile crooks, on the way to the bank robbery, the only option available is to wait until after the robberies then arrest them. If you asked victims, they would all agree; they prefer cops get them first, but then what do cops put on my arrest report?

Cops have to word the narrative to justify arresting criminals; this slope leads to the Test-a-Lie."

"Test-a-lie?" The youngster asked.

"Yes, rearranging the time-line to make charges stick. All facts are correct except the sequence. Criminal Trespass and Evading arrest are two of the main culprits. You see a guy walking and he has a bulge, you cannot really use the Terry stop, no crime afoot. Of course, you can talk to him; when he runs, what is he running for except the gun, but the

Supreme Court says you did not know that. So what do you do? If you can get close enough, touch him where the gun is, under the guise of asking for ID. This allows for the Plain Feel Doctrine. Alternatively, once you ascertain that the guy is trespassing, that's obviously why and when he ran on the arrest report.

Crooks can stand in plain sight; the cops that must operate in the grey or via subterfuge to accomplish their task. Many I arrested, I did not want to arrest, their actions were not above board, but some of them had legitimate reasons. I do not always get to decide if they go to jail, even though I know more about the case than the judge does. Sadly, not all problems are solved by arrest; hunger and mental illness are problems society faces, rather that fix the problems; society gives cops the task to arrest the hungry, crazy and homeless for the ultimate crime against society - Worthlessness.

Sgt. I'm-A-Complete-Moron explained how to fill out the arrest report, and asked the class what do you charge a drunk with, a homeless guy pissing against a tree with? I replied, 'Nothing it is not a crime, unless someone asked the tree and it states that it did not want to be pissed on.

'Ok smart ass,' Sgt I'm-A-Complete-Moron replied, 'That is not only stupid, but that will earn you some push-ups.'

"No more stupid than arresting a homeless guy for pissing, and not providing him a port-a-john. Besides, you cannot have a crime without a victim." I retorted.

Sgt. I'm-a-complete-moron doubled the push-ups. That was ok because I never arrested a homeless guy for pissing or anything else related to their condition."

"So we don't have a duty to keep vagrants, and bums away from taxpayers?"

"Yes Walters, we have to keep the haves away from the have -nots, but that doesn't mean that I have to crap on the down trodden at the same time. Run their histories, how many arrests vs how many crimes; hundreds of charges stemming from blocking sidewalks, peeing in public and public intoxication. Yeah, we are making the world safer each time we arrest anyone for being poor."

"They can get help or a job somewhere, and get off the drugs." He was indignant this time.

"Horse crap! How can they work, some asshole keeps arresting them and piling on charges. Who is going to hire someone with 200 arrests?" I pursed my lips up after my reply. I was not mad at Walters, he did not know better; but he should have.

"What I learned from all the reports is that politeness is only one half good manners and the other half good lying."

3.4 Verbal Judo

"The Verbal Judo course comprised a non-physical Confrontation Management methodology. The Verbal Judo course demonstrated how to diffuse situations verbally and the Department provided the recruits with the book called "Verbal Judo." Ironically, professionalism was required at the academy in both behavior and language.

The Department frowned on the use of profanity by officers when dealing with the public. Apparently, the instructor for this course, Sgt Foul mouth, missed both that part of his academy experience and every single memo and General Order governing such. Sgt. Foul mouth' was the most vulgar, vile, person I had ever heard speak let alone instruct a course. He said 'Fuxx' so much that Wikipedia would probably have to list it as a proper noun. This fat bastard was the Bruce Lee of Verbal Judo, he could curse-kick the crap anyone to death.

However, it was rather difficult to grasp the concept of professionalism from this useless fat boy. Apparently, he had one redeeming quality; he could shoot as well as he cursed. Sgt. Foul-mouth's additional duties included marksmanship training. He always said, 'I guess those who could not be judged, you just shoot.' This was actually his one redeeming quality; I was beginning to like him after all.

I learned some basic tricks from Sgt Foul-mouth. When in doubt curse, when in trouble fight, then curse, when in danger shoot and curse simultaneously. Either way, someone is getting curse-kicked. The fact is I would rather get cursed out than arrested or slapped. Most people need both but quickly get in line once overwhelmed by verbal judo.

I was soon to find out that a good heartfelt 'Fuck you' is one of the most useful tools in an officer's arsenal (should be a holster for it on the gun belt). The phrase separates behavior. Either they calm down or we take it to the next level. Either way, we win. They walk away or you get to enjoy playing piranha with their faces. I leaned closer, 'Hey man, if you ever have to hit a criminal, try to put them in a coma, it is the same amount of paperwork, and it will save cops someday. Someday that piece of crap is going to face the men and women in blue again, they may not remember the verbal-judo, but they sure as hell will remember the day cops kicked the crap out of them.'

I later learned that the word 'Fuck', when used properly, can be as powerful as a bullet. You can only shoot the bad guy, but 'F' you(s)' are for crowd control, nosey civilians, stupid girlfriends and mommas, and co-defendants. I used the crap out of verbal judo, keeping the peace. Keeping the peace does not have to mean arrest.

The police solve many problems with a well-placed, well-timed use of profanity. For example;

- I will slap the 'Fuxx' out of you
- Shut the 'Fuxx' up!
- Sit the 'Fuxx' down!
- What the 'Fuxx' is wrong with you?
- I will 'F'ing shoot you!
- You are a stupid 'Fuxx'!
- Who the 'Fuxx' do you think you are?
- Stop; or I'll 'F'ing shoot!
- Don't 'Fuxx' with the police
- Don't ever put your 'F'ing hands on the police
- What the 'Fuxx' is wrong with you?
- What the 'Fuxx' were you thinking?
- Do I 'F'ing look like I am kidding?
- I'll hit you so hard you will forget your 'F'ing name
- Do I 'F'ing look like I care?

I used these phrases during my career far more often than I used physical force.

Some cops say they never had to curse or raise their voices to control the person. To them I say you are lucky, but somebody did. Somewhere in that person's life a mom, dad, teacher, or coach yelled or yanked a knot in their ass. You owe them a thank you, for everyone else, carries an ample supply of 'screw you(s).' They should have charged me with excessive force for my use of Verbal Judo; my Judo was ruthless. The use of excessive profanity was probably the first bad habit I picked up as a cop."

"Why do you refer to it as a bad habit?"

"Although I used profanity more than my gun or handcuffs, I trained myself to be more of a lion tamer than a horse whisperer. Times changed so quickly, many times I almost cussed myself right out of a job."

"Well yeah, the use of profanity is a sure write up nowadays," Walters responded.

"That is part of the problem, if you cannot curse them out and they don't want you to knock them out, how are you supposed to control them?"

"We are trained to talk and reason with people rather than use force."

"Then why do we both have 45 rounds, a Taser, pepper spray, handcuffs, and a baton? Sounds like I am just a relic, marked for extinction. They gave the Lions teeth but want them trained as Vegans." I stood up before he replied. "I gotta piss, all this useless crap around my waist, squeeze the crap out of my bladder."

"I don't think it's the belt causing the problem, old man; Old balls just can't hold water. Remember, there is a great power in words, if you do not hitch too many of them together."

I laughed but hurried along, the laughing made me spring a leak. Good thing polyester does not show pee spots.

3.5 Moot Court

I washed my hands and walked back to the holding area. Walters put his cell phone in his pocket, and I plopped down beside him.

"In the academy, they teach the use of detail in your affidavits and arrest reports. The reports should contain detailed notes and make sure the spelling is accurate. They even make you take spelling tests through the academy. Moot Court consists of testimony practice and telling the truth under oath. Man, the concept is awesome, you get to make quick decisions and if you make a mistake run the risk of being charged with Aggravated Perjury, and or losing your job. It seems like everybody wants to punish the innocent, while the guilty go free. I do not think this was the intent of the framers of the Constitution.

Despite the decline in morality and integrity in the world, people stupidly believe they can hold the police to higher standards, what is the standard? Which crackhead, rapist, or murderer, set that standard, and what is the basis? Should cops recruited from a decadent society be any less decadent than the society they came from?

It is as though stupid humans pay the police to stop them from becoming what they really want to become, the war is on eternally; and it is the age-old battle of good versus evil.

You also run into the dumbest of all questions lawyers ask about reports, 'Did you put that in your report?' The reason this is a dumbass question is that people assume that it must be true if you wrote it down. How damn stupid do you have to be to think that a person will not tell a lie on paper, hell we have an entire genre of literature based on lies, we call it fiction.

"Did you ever lie on a report?"

"I never had to lie in a report, because I always made the lie true. If you screw up; do not write it in the report, unscrew the mistake. Some crap you just do not want to admit to, so do not do it, and if you do something stupid, face the music. Besides, any court that does not realize that justice presents itself in just punishment is moot.

3.6 Diversity Training

"Something we can personally thank Rodney King for, is Diversity Training. Singularly, Diversity Training was the dumbest thing we endured in the academy. They sent a white guy, and an Indian woman to teach how to handle diversity. I remember back then , I was all about making sure there was equity, but I still felt a great surging, 'WTF!' when they announced the diversity class.

It was in this class that I first disclosed how I felt about women cops. It was also in this room that we realized that one of the cadets, an officer in the armed forces, (which meant he had college) did not know what Affirmative Action was (idiot).

On one particular day, we had to role-play. The white guy decided that the scenario was that my partner saved my life twice then told me he was gay. I played along, with the stupid scenario, until they decided that I needed to play the gay guy. I refused; I told them I was unable to play the gay. When asked why I cited that it would be like playing a monkey; I had no frame of reference, and no material to draw upon. The white guy asked me was I afraid of gays, and I said no I just did not want to play one and had no intention of playing or portraying gay. The Indian woman, chimed in, 'But it is their truth,' I responded, there is only one truth, at least on the stand, I wondered *if I could swear in like that. I swear to my truth, my whole truth, and nothing but my truth*, and it is not subjective. Either way, use someone else to play the games.

What I did not understand was why the Rodney King incident triggered diversity training. There was plenty of diversity at the scene of his ass kicking. There were both black feet and white feet up his ass; he looked like a zebra running away. Since the instructor was so concerned about his truth, they should have spun Rodney King, bent him over and tore his ass out its frame, shot the African American gentleman...then hugged him, sensitive enough?

One thing I learned is that you cannot make people like each other, but you sure as hell can torture them for hurting each other: the fact that they hurt each other should be the only testimony needed. This action occurred as a response to the suspect's behavior, is that not common sense.

We ran across a crazy dude one day, he fancied himself a Jedi. Stupid fool was out in the street in his robe with his metal pole using it like a light-saber. When we pulled up, my redneck partner called him, 'Toby-Won-Kenobi'. Yes, it was screwed up (not showing much diversity), but I laughed anyway because it was funny.

First, we tried the Jedi mind trick and attempted to get him to drop the sword, only to discover , not only is Jabba the Hutt immune, but crazy bastards are as well. It was not until we threatened to; stomp the shit out of him, stick a Star Destroyer up his ass and then bury him in the Death Star that he dropped his sword and surrendered.

Walters frowned, "No. we did not put that useful language in the narrative." I laughed, "But there is going to be plenty of diversity in hell."

3.7 The Gun Range

"Nearing the last phase of training, we went to the gun range, with Sgt Foul-Mouth as the instructor. Everybody boasted about how well he handled a pistol, and that he could shoot anything. This is a great skill for a fat man who did not do police work; at least we knew that in case of an alien attack, Foul-Mouth was there.

You know guns are not as loud as they seem, unless the idiot next to you on the gun range fires it too close to your ears. I learned how to draw and shoot quickly and proficiently. The pistol, though less powerful than the rifle is infinitely more practical for close-quarters conflict, less reloading and lots of bullets.

When I went to the academy, either you received a revolver, or you could purchase your own semi automatic pistol. The choices were a Beretta 9mm, Smith & Wesson 5900 series 9mm, or a Sig Sauer 9mm. I also learned that guns are expensive. New job, new cop, and a used gun; I went to a pawnshop and bought a used 5906 stainless pistol with the magazine (bullet holder) disconnect.

I loved the magazine disconnect feature, it is a safety feature, I believe all law enforcement pistols should employ the magazine disconnect. The magazine disconnect allows the officer to drop the magazine in case of being disarmed. When you release the magazine, the weapon cannot fire. The officer then can release the weapon, disengage from the suspect and transition to their alternate weapon, or club the suspect like a baby seal using their nightstick.

The first day I brought my gun to the academy, 'I got in trouble. I was practicing my 'Billy the Kid' impression, when officer I-Never-Arrested-Anybody (The idiot partner to officer I-Never-Made-An-Arrest) walked up to me and said, 'We do not twirl our guns here.' I should have asked her where could I go to twirl my gun? Instead, I held my tongue.

Man, cowboys did not have crap on me, I was a gunslinger! I never thought anything would make my crotch this hard, it was better than Viagra. Short of wearing Marine Dress Blues, this was the next most stimulating thing I had ever done. Now, I had two steel rods to run around with in my pants. I did not care which rod the women liked, whatever made them get naked, was fine with me.

I slept with my gun next to me the first night. I practiced safe sex, so I took all the bullets out. The second night we had a romantic candlelight dinner, and I gave my gun a name and a bath. I took 'Smitty' apart, oiled her up well then put her back together, man she went together smooth.

The first time I fired Smitty, she was loud and shaky, like the near virgin she was. I spoke to her gently and assured her it was only going to hurt for a little while, and I promised to be gentle. Bang, bang, bang, went the next round, and she took it well. Right then I knew, I did not only want to carry this dreamy piece of metal, but I also wanted to hit people with it. I wanted to hit them in the face, I want to make them never want to hurt others again, now; in my hand, was a Stainless Instrument of Correction.

"Cannot shoot everyone, again they prefer us to talk."

"How do you put handcuffs on with your mouth Walters? Cops afraid to go hands on, create their own monsters. Ask any former heavyweight champion; anyone can be knocked down or out. If you are afraid or prohibited from fighting, cursing, and shooting, why even respond to calls. This is why so many unarmed people end up with bullets in their asses, you 'Face book' cops got out of the habit of relying on hands and feet to be the most company used less than lethal options. By not slapping the taste out of someone's mouth, cops create inequity in the use of Force Continuum. The purpose of soft empty hand control and takedown techniques is to avoid needless escalation. But if dude won't go to jail, how are you gonna get him there, other than drag his ass there by the teeth? It turns out, I support gun control after all: My version of Gun Control is - do not miss damn the target.

3.8 Traffic Accident Investigation

"Yet another asinine part of the academy is Traffic Accident Investigation (TAI). This is a relatively useless police function. Stupid ass people are the cause of most Motor Vehicle Accidents.

- Speeding and losing control; Cause - Stupid Ass
  People
- Rear ending a car obeying the traffic signal: Cause -
  Stupid Ass People
- Traveling too fast for weather conditions: Cause -
  Stupid Ass People
- Letting your dog lick your face while you drive:
  Cause - Stupid Ass People

Since there is no law against stupidity, TAI really is not a police function. On the other hand, the only true traffic-related crime; DUI is a misdemeanor, and nobody really tries to do anything to prevent DUIs. Statistics clearly show that DUI is one of the leading preventable causes of death, yet the drunken, lying pieces of excrement, we call legislators do not provide for stiffer penalties and harsher sentencing. They are in it for votes; and sadly, drunken bastards love to vote for their right to drive into families drunk. Nobody gives a crap if you have a driver's license; I wager more MVAs occur each year caused by licensed drivers than unlicensed drivers."

"So you never had a drink at a restaurant and drove?"

"Of course I have, but that does not constitute a DUI. Stop finding fault in the primary mission of Law Enforcement. In case there is confusion, the meaning is in the title - Enforce the existing Laws. What the hell did you become a cop for? Dude, a tree never hits a car except in self defense."

3.9 Physical Training

"I found physical training to be the most exciting part of the academy. Not only did it improve cardio, strength, and awareness, the girls had to wear shorts and cute but cheap cotton t-shirts. I am not saying that I am a perv, but I sure as hell am not going to spend hours in the presence of bouncy 'C' cups and not notice (NOR DO I EVER WANT TO BE DIVERSIFIED ENOUGH WHERE I DO NOT NOTICE).

Understand; that as far as professional groups of women go policewomen, are among the ugliest. I do not know if it is the uniforms or common sense, but the pretty girls just are not signing up. I do not know why police stations even have gender-specific bathrooms; all the officers look like men most of the time. The young man teased, 'It's cliché I know, but as it is in the strip club Deja Vu there are a couple of pretty ones and the rest are ugly.'

The pretty ones usually are not known for their police skills; they take full advantage of the lack of competition. Less attractive women seem to make better cops, I guess it is because they are used to working hard, and not getting breaks. I love my mostly ugly sisters; they get in the dirt with us. Barbie's (of any gender) may look and smell good, but they aren't trying to get down and dirty...so we do not need them, but you can always count on ugly girls to get the job done.

I learned a lot as a cop. The single most important thing you need to learn is when to kick ass, to save lives. Quiet as it's kept, those who control their fear kick-ass, those with cannot control their fear shoot. Once I learned that pulling a gun out of the holster is more of a hazard than a help, I left mine safe. For most things, cops cannot shoot people. In terms of percentages, 90% of the crap we respond to we cannot use lethal force to resolve. This means the utility belt must-have tools and skills to deal with the 90%. There are not enough handcuffs, pepper spray, or Tasers to solve the world's problems, but you still cannot shoot the buttholes. Buttholes know it better than cops do, and they tell cops all the time. Since cops cannot shoot, then they damn sure better be ready to put feet in some asses.

In order to accomplish this reallocation of resources, one ABSOLUTELY MUST engage in some form of physical fitness. The only thing worse than letting a butthole get away is allowing or watching your partner get stomped or injured because you are too damn lazy to exercise to stay in the fight. Most fights do not last that long, but when the fight starts cops need to be 100%; because the ass saved might just be their own.

"You seem prone to violence, Andrews."

"No I am prone to survival and to helping people, the violence enters the arrangement the minute the criminal determines he refuses to submit to the authority vested in the cops. Anyone that determines that they are not going to be arrested invites, therefore; initiates the violence. I believe the police need to specialize in never backing down. Cops cannot afford to die, or quit. Too much hangs in the balance - innocent people need our help; they need our violence to save them from the violence of the world. Like the man said, "Sometimes you have to pick the gun up to put the gun down."

"Who said that?"

"Someone that knows the value of gunpowder; Walters, if you cannot carry your own lazy, fat ass, you are not going to do a great job helping someone else?"

3.10 The Law

"By far, the legal section comprises the biggest portion of the academy. Despite not having a Juris Doctorate, the police officer knows more law than anyone else I have ever seen. I guess the knowledge of the law is imperative to both enforcement and violation of the law.

Amazingly, in a society filled with criminal behavior, selfishness, and violence, the media portrays police corruption as the major concern. I put it to you if the thousands of rapes and murders and hundreds of thousands of domestic disturbances do not concern you then why should a grown man getting a blowjob while wearing blue polyester matter to you at all?

We digress; the Law as you know it is a hodge-podge of rules and principles both grandiose and inane; combined for the greater good. Lawyers may be experts in the knowledge of the law, but the police are experts in the application. This is why so many legal decisions made by those nine buttheads sitting on the Supreme Court often have negative results. The other thing we learned about the law is that, while it is without prejudice, society and the courts are not without prejudice. The only Absolute Certainty under the law is that if you are poor; you are screwed.

Cadets trudged through the books and the horribly boring classes. Man, I was amazed at how many damn ways there are to get arrested, lucky for me the police stay busy or I might have found my ass breaking rock somewhere in a screwed-up black and white jumpsuit.

I learned about domestic violence, (not sure if I agree with this law, I can think of a dozen reasons that beating the crap of your mate would make things better for society). I also learned about investigating homicides. Law class was actually the first clue that I made a grandiose mistake undertaking this profession.

The Law is the worst document in existence; it is the law that ultimately prevents justice. Where is the justice in returning murderers to society, yet we kill whales and tigers who attack their trainers? Where is the justice in cases where technicalities allow the victim no restitution or recompense? Where is the justice that there is no outcry for the fallen? Why is there no law that makes being a piece of crap a crime? Most criminals are not bad people, they are pieces of crap, and because they are pieces of crap, they commit crimes.

The law should be comprised of one very simple premise, which oversees regulation. Once society decides acceptable codes of conduct, the penalty for violating any of them should be the same.

- Sir, being found guilty of DUI - you are hereby sentenced to have your eyes beaten shut
- Sir being found guilty of theft - you are hereby sentenced to have your eyes beaten shut
- Sir being found guilty of assault - you are hereby sentenced to have your eyes beaten shut
- Sir being found guilty of rape, murder, or pedophilia - you are hereby sentenced to have your eyes beaten shut; PERMANENTLY!

Get the picture, if you leave home and act like an ass we make you wish you never left home, and make it so you may never leave home again. Regulation of in-home behavior is not necessary. You want to shoot dope ok, but you had better get it offline because if we catch you buying or selling outside your home. We are going to beat your eyes shut. Husband beat you do not call the police, set that piece of crap on fire at the family BBQ.

"That sounds barbaric Andrews."

"Is standing by and letting a man rape more than one woman, and not prosecuting him because his rights were violated, as if the victim deserved what she got. Like the rights of rapists should override common sense. The only reason these rights are still held out in such a ridiculous manner, is to help the rich and their screwed up kids. As far as burglars...screw them. Every burglary should end in a K-9 apprehension or shooting.

"That's extreme; After all it is just a property crime."

"Screw the 'It is just a property crime' credo, it is not just property; it is someone's property that people worked to own. Instead of saying, it is just property we ought to be saying it was just another burglar; bitten, shot, stabbed or set on fire. That is how you make a change, start with making criminals fear decency. If there is no fear, there is no order.

To believe that the human creature will continue to behave in a civilized manner is to ignore the Bible, news, history, and common sense. Stupid ass people are not from space, we make them. It may take a village to raise a child, but what the cliché neglects to mention is how many people we need to extricate from a village and keep the kids away from, to keep them safe. Every village has; molesters, abusers, thieves, rapists, thugs, cowards, whores and victims.

The problem is that in so many of the villages these molesters, abusers, thieves, rapists, thugs, cowards, whores are the leaders. Stupidly people hide behind these villains and expect protection. Expecting protection and decency from molesters, abusers, thieves, rapists, and thugs, cowards, and whores flies in the face of both common sense and safety? The reason they are villains is that they hurt people: how can any people ever be safe when their protector is a cannibal? We should not raise children that cannot or will not defend themselves, if we care, we need to prepare them because the world they face is screwed up, and in reality will devour them before puberty."

"The blindness of the law is supposed to reflect objectivity, not indifference, or oppressiveness."

"There is no law as long as the citizens are not free to be molesters, abusers, thieves, rapists, thugs, cowards, whores. However, why would we ever expect molesters, abusers, thieves, rapists, thugs, cowards, whores to abide by any law? You know in my studies of the law? As soon as laws are necessary for men, they are no longer fit for freedom."

3.11 Graduation

"I do not remember much about my rather unimpressive, unspectacular police graduation. At least in the Marine Corps, they do it up right, dress blues, Mameluke Swords, hard charging, blood puking, leathernecks graduating in a sea of pride. I do not remember who spoke, or what was said, but I do remember graduating.

The only thing that made my graduation memorable was that on the night I launched my police career, my badge fell off my uniform and broke. I graduated with a badge held together by tape, eagle head missing, pinned on my chest…perhaps that was the omen; the prediction of what my career would be like- a shadow of the real thing.

As I walked away from the stage, I heard a metallic clink. I looked down and there was my badge, the cheap thing broke already. I picked up the metal symbol of who I was to become, and it was broken. The eagle's head completely severed and popped off. A foreshadowing, of poor quality, the truth remained to be seen. Perhaps there was a statement made that I had yet to hear, perhaps I was the eagle, and the badge the silver-toned, path police officers swear to take."

"Talk about prophetic," Walters laughed.

"No I did this crap to myself. This was to be the omen of my career, for the shiny path was not to be had by me. The puerile, professional cop people dream about; that is not me. The milkman wears white because he does not have to get dirty, my job was to manage trash, how do you do that and stay shiny? The choice is simple, shine the brass, or kick some ass. One looks good the other makes the world safer. I learned to stop saying, 'Make the world a better place,' because no one wants that.

Even the crack addict agrees they want to do their dope in a safe environment. The music for my career was written at the moment I took off the binding of the silver plating, and killed the dead, stiff, justice model that caused the failings. It was time for this eagle to do what eagles are meant to do; soar high in the sky, use keen eyesight, speed, and power, and upon striking, aim to kill. If we buried the talons of the law into more criminal throats, our children could drink milk instead of appearing on the milk carton, and decent people could enjoy the fruits of their labor without fear of violence.

Instead, we hide ineptness behind tin; empty valueless tin. We hold up shiny monuments in the faces of victims that say we really do not give a crap. We are just here because we have a job, but we are not about to get dirty or break a sweat to help you. We ought to just make people file their reports online; on the website stuff WWW.The-Police-Really-Dont-Give-A-Damn.Com (Do not even make it '.Org', because we are just going to throw the crap in the trash anyway).

This is why the higher-ups wear brass because they are a tarnished image of what they should be. Like rust, Law Enforcement management eats away at the metal that makes and binds cops, so that there is no longer any tensile strength. Law Enforcement management transforms blue steel into aluminum, a metal that holds a shine no power. Brass is a soft metal, bendable and of little tensile strength, just like police administrators.

If people do not want to get their hands dirty, they should not take valuable, up slots in police departments. Law-abiding citizens do not need cops, neither do the criminals that turn themselves in and go to jail peaceably?

However, what do you do with the ones that do not want to get into the cage? You convince, coerce, or force them in, either way; cops have to use force to maintain civil order as well as they can.

Cops are like Eagles, we soar, we cast a shadow, we do not hide. As apex predators, our ominous presence should instill fear - but only in our prey."

"Apex predators, we are public servants, we do not prey on people, we serve at their will."

"So does the surgeon, he serves by attaining an expertise most do not have, using tools most cannot use and cutting away disease."

"People are not a disease," he interrupted.

"You are correct, they are infected, and many carry the disease. Even within the philosophy of medicine, prevention is better than cure. Shall I continue?"

He slumped back and pulled out his phone. He was listening, just not sure what to say.

"Sometimes I get involved in posturing, 'I'll admit, but for a man to attain to an eminent degree in learning, costs him time, watching, hunger, nakedness, dizziness in the head, weakness in the stomach, and other inconveniences."

Remember we chose to dedicate our lives to Law Enforcement, the highest of the Laws we enforce is that we should not violate the spirit of law by imposing our will on the people we swore to protect. This does not mean that the occasional child was not be spanked the occasional meal must not be taken away, the occasional adult not sent to bed without food. We in law enforcement have the task of enforcing only the laws that the people choose. The manner in which we enforce these laws has also been prescribed by the people. There's no room for interpretation, and professionalism should override bias and prejudice. In short,   the law enforcement professional should have more in common with a bus-driver than anybody else all we do is follow a route and pick up whatever is along our trek whether they be white or black handicapped drunk or obnoxious the bus driver's job is just to open the door and collect fair and drop them off along the route."

"You are starting to scare me," he mused without raising his head.

"That should have happened before you put on the badge. The minute they gave you 45 bullets to do your job, reality should have set it; maybe that is why we are here. I guess that got his attention, he looked up from his phone.

"We are here for violating the rules."

"We are here for not knowing which rules to violate," I laughed back.

4.0 ROOKIES

"Police business is a hell of a problem. It is a good deal like politics. It asks for the highest type of men, and yet there is nothing in it, to attract the highest type of men. So we have to work with what we get."

4.1
ROOKIES

"Once I escaped the deluge of ineptness at the academy, two wonderful things happened; I got a pay raise, and I got to carry bullets in my gun. Smitty was ultra-sexy now, not Fredericks of Hollywood, cheap sleazy sexy, I mean Victoria's secret sexy; soft, pretty, sleek, and voluptuous. The bullets were like her toes painted and pretty; ready to kick butt. A good gun is like Playboy magazine compared to Hustler magazine. Hustler hires anything that has breath (not necessarily a pulse) and displays their disease-ridden body for the entire world to see. Playboy, however, hires beautiful women to expose themselves tastefully with good scenery and props; this is the essence of sensuality. Playboy's layout leaves a lot to the imagination: my imagination.

Probation consisted of rotating between all three shifts and moving in three different areas of the city. I was one of the lucky Rookies, I had three good training officers, they each took pride in their work and were not afraid to be the police, they may have opened the door, but that which came through already existed on the other side."

4.2 Patrol Training Officers

"The Patrol Training Officer came online in the basic support role of Corporal. Patrol Training Officers filled in for Sergeants when excused, off duty, or on vacation. The Patrol Training Officer was the senior ranking officer on the scene where no sergeant was present. They could not discipline anyone, but they could recommend disciplinary action. They did not have the force of a Sgt, but they were definitely in charge when pit against officers of lesser rank.

The PTO had the ancillary duty of training new officers in the field. The academy taught concepts and rules, but the PTO used OJT (On the job training) to bring the rookie online. Policing is a hands-on job; you cannot learn it from a classroom. This is not due to the difficulty of the job; it is instead due to the stupidity of the human creature. You cannot police from an office or a room because only the criminal determines the criminal response. If we could police from the hallways, no cops need to die; alas, this is not the case. Hall Monitor Cops survive, while the patrolwomen and men die; by now someone should have noticed.

My first rotation took place on the second shift, in one of the richest parts of town. Funny thing is that the training officer I had was black, I mean gun holster black and he had a Jerry curl. I learned a lot from him. I had not personally seen a black guy speak down to whites, especially rich whites; it was different. I learned that rich people are just as stupid and annoying as poor people. Seems like middle-class people are too busy surviving to act like dumbasses. Rich and poor people prove that having too much free time turns out to be bad for the human condition.

Patrol Training Officer Curl was a little strange and he laughed at odd things, but he showed me how to love the many uses of traffic enforcement. He loved making the 'Jokers' move their cars or sign for traffic tickets. We rode around our zone and sometimes the entire district dolling out curl activator covered justice. He was fair but did not let the bourgeoisie push him around either. He also showed me how to be proactive in even the quietest parts of town

On occasion, when we were lucky or when the Sgt was feeling lazy we would collect the paperwork for the detail, this was Mail Call, and it occurred at the midpoint of the shift. All reports taken during a shift needed review and signatures from a sergeant, and then turned in before the end of the shift.

PTO Curl was the senior guy on the detail, so we often collected the mail. This meant meeting at the place we called the 'Office.' I loved going to the office, honestly who would not. Club Diamond (The Office), was a strip joint on the outskirts of downtown. After a long day or week of dealing with domestics, MVAs and generally stupid people on our beat, it was agreeable to see someone working their asses off.

PTO Curl would diligently wait to review, and complete all the paperwork before we left the office. There was nothing for me to do, while the paperwork accumulated, so I mingled with the employees. I guess uniformed officers hanging out in a strip joint may not have been the most prudent decision, but considering all the crap you get stuffed down your throat, a welcome escape from reality.

Club Diamond was so comfortable I started hanging out there when I was not at work. There was nothing good on television, so I pretended to collect mail several nights after work. Remember," I changed my tone, to a more friendly version, "Bad habits and decisions emanate and are cultivated, there is no one but self to blame."

"Get out of here; y'all collected mail in a strip joint?" I just smiled.

"Like it does now, a District consisted of several Zones, and each zone had a zone car and or zone officer, just like now. The coverage and size structure has changed. PTO Curl was one of the better officer's in the district and people looked up to him, perhaps because he was a PTO. Whatever the reason, when there was trouble, the district reached out to him.

As in every district, there were good, marginal, and crappy officers. Remember, however, the mark of a cop is not their personality, but the way they police. No one knows how stupid a person the chef is, we just enjoy the meal. A complete jerk or racist can be a great cop, and the best personality rarely makes good cops, they are too busy being nice. Therefore, the crappy officers are the ones who suck at policing, usually because they are lazy and/or afraid."

"How can a complete jerk or racist be a good cop? Don't be absurd"

"Walters, in time you will realize that it is not the racist that is the danger, it is the coward. Even in the Civil War, some northerners hated blacks, and many southerners who liked blacks. A man that picks up the badge and decides to be true to it treats all criminals as trash. Even the racist has to help victims they do not like. One of the best officers I worked with, hated blacks, but he spent his time in the projects helping those he could, arresting those he could, and never so much as even slipped out any racial slurs. The coward has no soul they only want to hide. Cowardice is why the brass overflows with tepidness; they intend to do whatever they have to stay off the street; even if it means screwing over cops. I would rather a man burn a cross on my front lawn than set fire to the floor I am standing on."

"Is it that bad? Is the backstabbing and shiftlessness really that bad?"

"Most of what you see in the news ain't racism, it is cowardice. A frightened man with a badge and a gun, is like a rabid wolf, no code, no friend, how can he that hides in fear and reacts from within the shadow of their own terror act with honor? That type of officer should continually be embarrassed by people who point me out as an example of what can be done without training."

4.3 A Female Perspective

"My second rotation was with a female officer, which was ironic considering that during the academy one of my infamous outbursts was that women could not perform the duties of a cop the same as men. This may be an unpopular view, but after twenty years, I can definitively say this is true, this is not a diminutive this is fact. Bullshit, that's caveman talk,' snapped Walters. There are weight classes in boxing for a reason, people of different stature have different abilities, in time however, we learned to stop putting the lightweights in the ring with heavy weights; we were harming our people.

Nonetheless, one of our first conversations was about the academy. We spoke about it candidly, Toni treated me with respect, and I treated her with respect. I can honestly say that despite her physical limitations she tried as hard as I did to be a good cop. Perhaps the measure of a good cop is not in the performance but in the effort? She was a good cop, but she could neither run nor fight worth a damn. As slowly as she ran, and poorly as she fought, each time I engaged she at least went with me, she was not a coward. Turns out, she was more man than many of the male officers I served with.

One day we got a call of a domestic, a call that cemented the main difference between women, men, and useless cops. We arrived second; another zone officer was there before us and waited for backup-prudent. The problem was that when we approached the screen door and observed the male suspect atop the woman clubbing her in the corner, no one moved to help her. I understand tactics, and I know one should be cautious, but there were other officers present with guns and vests, watching a woman being clubbed like a baby seal - WTF?

I jumped through the screen like a runaway squirrel. I went over to the corner after a quick scan of the apartment, I scanned long enough to see the area safe, and my two partners were still outside. I grabbed the club from the guy, threw it across the room, and then kicked him off the woman. I stood over him, making sure that the other officer (the male) had her under control of my female partner and I focused on the man. Get up! I ordered, repeatedly; but he refused to get up. I walked over and put a boot in his chest, repeating my instructions. He shouted loudly, 'I cannot, you threw my leg away!' Turns out dickhead was clubbing his wife with his wooden leg; crippled bastard!

We locked the idiot up and made sure the woman got the necessary medical attention. Then Toni and I headed back to the car, for more patrolling. Toni was big on patrolling and she made sure that I did not head to our zone along the same path of travel every day. Remembering that I was a soldier I did think her tactics lacked quite a bit of venom. Ironically, she thought I was too zealous.

As we sat in the car, Toni asked me for an evaluation of the event. I calmly said, 'Situation handled with no injury to the good guys.' Toni retorted that she thought I was too aggressive and that I could have gotten hurt. 'Me; too aggressive, never-but we had a job to do. I scanned the room when I entered, each situation is dangerous, but that is what we do. If not prepared to shed both blood and tears, one should not become a cop. But since you make comments, perhaps if my two partners had engaged, we could have maintained a larger margin of safety.' Toni, my new training officer replied, 'We have to make sure we survive long enough to do the job.' We pulled into our regular discount family restaurant to eat. As I exited the car, I said, 'If I do not do the job right I do not deserve to survive.' Then we resumed lighthearted talking and ate our bad, but cheap food.

"So you don't trust women and men the same?"

"Men and women ain't the same, but that isn't a bad thing. My belief that men and women are equal does not make it true. They are equally vital, but they have differing skills and capabilities. They both got to earn respect. My partner is family-not a step family either. We good for blood; or we ain't partners: brother or sister."

Then I joked a little, "Not all women are created equal, some become Law Enforcement Officers." He got the point.

4.4 A Less Than Humble PTO

"My third PTO, Jimmy was actually a lot of fun, even though we worked midnights. He was not overly anything, except comedic. He was more the speed of cop I wanted to be, balanced. He had a few hang-ups, one of which was to get on the radio around 0600 every morning and start his verbal Judo war with truck drivers over the CB. I am not sure what his deal was but he thought it was so funny, it actually was because we got death threats every time he did it. We scanned the frequencies, and when we heard talking zeroed in on the victim.

Jimmy used his attack phrase each time to try to get the dialogue started, 'Breaker, breaker, come back?' Breaker was the only pleasantry Jimmy shared with his unwitting victims. He then set in with his signature line; 'Anybody out there feel like sucking a dick?' Of course, if you know anything about truck drivers, this led to a stream of threats and unpleasantries from the truckers.

After about four or five minutes of ritualistic anti-gay banter between Jimmy and the truckers, always resulted in an agreement to meet somewhere and fight. Of course, Jimmy and I never showed up to the secluded locations chosen for the duel. I often wonder how long the truck drivers waited before realizing we were not coming to fight.

As fate would have it, Jimmy and I had numerous nightclubs in our zone. One rainy night we got a call, which must have been life's way of paying us back for the trucker wars. We got a report of a bar fight. Fights at bars are normal, what made this different was that this was a fight at a gay bar. Jimmy and I responded to this fight just like any other, no one said anything all the way there but there was considerable snickering in the car. We arrived on the scene to find about 12 guys out in the street, arguing, and one guy dressed like a French sailor sitting on the ground in the middle of the circle. The sailor was obviously the victim in the fight or at least the loser of the fight. I walked up to him and asked him if he needed medical attention, he said yes and he stood up holding his chest. I asked him if his chest hurt, he said no he was just crying a little.

We waited for him to compose himself, and then he told us that he just broke up with his boyfriend and when he saw his ex with a new beau, he was angry and confronted him. Apparently, the beau was displeased and asked the victim outside. The victim then added that upon arriving outdoors beau, slapped him in the face repeatedly, called him a silly bitch, and then slammed his head into a telephone pole. The victim then started crying again and did something else peculiar.

He turned his back to me then looked over his shoulder a few times at me as he shifted his position. It looked to me that he was lining himself up, but I could not figure out why? Then the answer came. As he fell, he warned, 'Catch me!' I did what any self-respecting cop would do when a person fakes fainting, nothing. He hit the ground (although not as hard as he would have if he really fainted), so now he really did need the medical attention. I looked at Jimmy to see what he would say about my not catching the guy, 'Hmm, must have needed a nap,' he joked, then, we arrested beau for bitch-slapping our fainting victim.

I guess officer I-Never-Made-An-Arrest was right; sensitivity was needed to be a cop. Oh well, I guess I screwed up because I did not care if dude banged his head all the way to the hospital. If you do not want to get your ass kicked, do not pick fights, and if you lose; tough crap, walk it off. Two grown-ass men; gay or not ought to have more pride than to involve the police in their squabble. Cops do not care about the stupid, just the innocent. Perhaps in time, I could learn to care about silly people, but that is not why I joined the police."

"So you do not think we should take time to try understanding the predicament of the offender? Sounds like you just want to scratch the surface of the problem. Systemic home failures, drugs, codependency issues, anxiety, and a host of other contributors make a difference, to how we should handle the person."

"Why; does McDonalds' have a special line for those with anxiety? I did not join the police to hold hands, I joined to kick ass. If I wanted to be sensitive and caring, I would have become a veterinarian. Regardless, keep those that influence you for the better close and never give them a reason to keep you far away."

4.5 First Encounters Of The Fake Kind

I looked at Walters and said something he finally agreed with. "It did not take long before I realized that much of what I thought about policing was just plain wrong. The first time I realized that much of what I learned was false, was when I encountered Officer Jack B. Nimble. To describe this man as Cro-Magnon would be inaccurate. This butthole was a friggin' cave-dwelling, knuckle dragging, Sasquatch. Nimble was the first police officer I saw educate a citizen on the difference between the Po-lice and the real police.

We backed up an officer on a traffic stop. When we arrived the officer had the suspect pulled over and was walking back to his car. We exited and walked up to his patrol car. 'You good?' we asked. He replied with the universal; I am ok police hand gesture, the hang loose thumb pinky wave. So we stood off and hung out until the traffic stop was to end.

While we waited, Nimble pulled up and exited his vehicle. It took him a while to climb out of his vehicle, not because he was fat but because he was (or at least looked), 11 foot 4 inches tall. He walked up to me, extended his hand, and said in the most uncharacteristic, 'What's happening my brother.' I shook Nimble's hand and we three stood around waiting on officer Now-What-The-Hell-Do-I-Do. In typical idiot fashion, the driver refused to sign the ticket.

Officer Now-What-The-Hell-Do-I-Do stood there waiting for the answer to drop from heaven. The citizen said, 'I am not signing, the ticket bitch.' Officer Now-What-The-Hell-Do-I-Do just stood there patiently, professionally asking the motorist to sign, but the motorist repeatedly and vulgarly refused.

Nimble stomached all he could, so he walked up to the motorist and towering over him said, 'Just sign the ticket, and go home.' The motorist looked up into the cloudy sky where Nimble stood and shouted up to him, 'Screw you too!' Nimble; very quick for his size, grabbed the man's head about the ears and pinned his head to the hood of the car. Then he replied in an informative manner, 'You must think I am the bitch police.' It was then that I realized three important things.

- There are two-kinds of police officers' (1)-bitch and (2)-non-bitch
- If you bounce a moron's head off the car enough times, he will sign anything
- The most important of all cop lessons; Cops do not take crap from the stupid, useless, inane people, it is dangerous

As I watched Nimble bounce the idiots head off the car from side to side-giving special to each side of the head as to not cause uneven amounts of swelling, I took a moment to look at Officer Now-What-The-Hell-Do-I-Do, and he was just standing there watching the show with his head shaking. I guess he figured his way worked better.

When the new hood ornament could speak, he gladly signed the ticket, apologized to Officer Now-What-The-Hell-Do-I-Do, and got in the car and drove away slowly. His head canted to one side like a dumbfounded dog, but he even used his seatbelt, I guess he learned his lesson, and it only took a few moments to learn how to behave in public when you are dealing with the police.

People need to understand that with authority comes the need for control. Without control, there is no authority. The authority to control people does not come from the chief of police, or the law it comes from the people. People ultimately decide about law and order.

The concepts of right and wrong are objective but the law of men is completely subjective.

Once the rules are decided, the police have the glorious task of maintaining both peace and order. Maintaining order is easy, you put up red lights, speed zones, no trespassing signs, etc. Keeping the peace is another story.

The dumbass who suggested not fighting fire with fire deserves several kicks right in the face. How else do you stop a man from robbing a bank, committing murder, or raping another woman? You make the penalty for such behavior so overwhelming the desire to be a piece of crap diminishes.

The Criminal Justice System is a joke, only poor people go to jail, and without the punitive sting of jail, there is only one last line of demarcation-the heel of a cop's boot. 'Might I remind you Andrews, that the police are public servants?'

Yes, the police are public servants, but they are not supposed to serve the public's whims, cops exist to serve the greater good, by KEEPING THE PEACE. A flawed concept in Law Enforcement - Community Policing was another major failing in police work.

Community Policing derived as a response to ease racial tension, it did not. Community policing gave rise to the Blue Ball Effect, where the Law Enforcement Community has become a swollen and impotent component of society.

"So you don't think being active in the community, and being nice to people helps ease tension?"

"Of course it does, not doing the job properly is what causes the tensions in the first place. Inner cities do not need baby kissers they need ass kickers who differentiate between race, finances, and trouble. If we police all neighborhoods equally and professionally, the effect would resonate unilaterally.

You cannot kiss enough babies to override corruption, prejudice, indifference, and disparate treatment. The police provide more than law and order they provide a sense of security. If people are afraid or distrust the police; then society cannot rest.

Society is a Democracy, which is why we elect officials. We all agreed to elect officials who enact laws. Once something becomes a Law we give it the authority to take control and affect our lives. This is the Blue Ball Effect; Police cannot be friends with lawlessness.

The very thing society needs to have, Law and Order, flies in the face of individual happiness. God led the way, He drowned all the people in the flood; cops just shoot a few but the intention is the same; cull the herd and deal with those that can observe some semblance of decency."

He slowly nodded and then slumped back on the bench. Body language speaks volumes. Walters said a plethora of things when he slumped back into the seat. Indifference is the worst thing that can happen to law enforcement professional.

Indifference leads to complacency, cowardice, and often resentment; in my opinion. I don't think the radical officers cause as much problems and the lazy shiftless, indifferent officers. The indifferent officer overlooks the victims' needs and drives by so they don't have to get out in the rain or the cold.

Based on his facial expression, I do not think the young officer saw things exactly the same way I did. "If you look at the number of complaints against radical officers, to include excessive force and bias; they are not statistically significant compared to the damage caused by officers, not responding to calls in a timely manner, neglecting to make arrests and call DCS because it's shift change. Moreover, there is a greater variety of ways to cause injury or at least allow it to happen; kids are most often the victim.

The problem with the public is that it places far too much emphasis on the concept of Criminal Justice. Due to Media input, and cagy lawyers the public believes that society should squander resources on criminals; at the expense of the victim. Apathy is the mutha of all police sins.

30-40 million people call the police in the USA alone, there a many that cannot call, cannot speak English, or their parents prevent them getting assistance. How many schools have had to reach out to Law Enforcement or doctors for victims that had it been left to their ability or access would have never been assisted? I know too many horror stories about people that were left to defend themselves against animals even the police would not want to fight alone. I have witnessed officers not make entry to check on the victim of a domestic because they were afraid to push the husband out of the way, to see if she was even alive.

Before you make a judgment, let me at least tell you my whole story. You should make a decision, you must make a decision but not until you have the facts.

I have been on this bench a few times, trust me, we got time, this crap takes all day."

5.0
PATROL

"What most people see is a badge, behind and beyond the badge is what they need to know...the person."

5.1
CHAPTER
WALKING PATROL

"The movie The Avengers gained popularity because they were a team of superheroes. The Avengers were rough, but fighting for the right side. Cop; real cops, not paper-pushers in costume, are the same way.

I learned how to police the old way: with a stick in hand. After all, how does one contend with idiot human behavior than to treat animals like animals? 'So we just act like Nazi's?' This is not why I became a cop. I wanted to help people. I soon found out that the only way to help good people is to rid them of the bad people.

It only took a few months before I realized that bad people were just like dog crap. They screw up a good pair of shoes, and even when you scrape crap off, the smell lingers. This probably scares people to think of the police as crap kickers, but that is what cops do. Cops do not go to birthday parties or Chuck E Cheese and beat up kids; cops chase bank robbers, rapists, and child molesters. One must wonder what happened to the world; so much so, that pieces of crap that contribute nothing and ruin life for decent people, have the protection of the people they victimize.

I drew walking detail when it really was walking detail. Walking detail consisted of getting out of the car and walking, no bikes, or Segways. One of the benefits of walking patrol was that you could sneak up on people and make more arrests. You also get to meet decent people and interact with them as well. We had three project areas we were responsible for, and we answered all the calls in those areas as well. It had three small cities of our own target-rich environments.

The team was a bunch of dudes and one dudette. She was a cool dude; she was actually from my academy class as were several other team members. There were also some older guys, most of which were lazy as hell. Craig was older but certainly not lazy. The senior officer, who was not lazy, turned out to be a piece of crap anyway abandoned his family.

Our days started like regular patrol officers, a boring waste of a meeting called roll call, then we went off to our merry task of finding victims. We split the Housing Developments (Projects) between us for the first half of the shift then worked as a group for the rest of the shift.

Normally, I rode with Susan, but today, I rode the range with a true redneck. At first, I thought Craig only hated black people, but I soon learned that he hated everybody, maybe blacks, and Mexicans just a wee bit more.

My redneck partner and I rode our zone looking for someone whose 'criminal rights' we could violate. You know unreasonable search and seizure, excessive force and best of all, no Miranda warnings. See, this is what being a cop has become, by arresting rapists and drug dealers cops are violating their criminal rights to be pieces of crap."

"People do have rights."

"Yeah," I snarled back, "The right not to be robbed, raped, or murdered. Although most criminal justice rights do not exist in the constitution, dumb-ass voters gave them rights. How can it make sense to throw out a case because the bad guys' rights were trampled? How did bad people get rights anyway, where does the constitution guarantee criminals the right to rob steal and rape?

For example, I was part of a walking detail, we actually had to get out of our cars and walk the Projects. This was actually fun because there was always someone to chase. Today was one of those great days, a day when some butthole decides he can beat two men with sticks, guns, and radios - you got love stupid.

We pulled onto Wesslor Drive, and there she stood our victim; a black girl, standing outside, in the freezing weather on the phone crying. When she saw us she got off the phone and ran to us. I got out first, seeing she looked more like me than my partner. The natives were somewhat particular about dealing with 'Whitey'; they felt that Whitey' did not always serve their best interest. 'Officer, he in there kicking her,' she said. She pointed to apartment 356, which was going to be our playground today.

I entered first, took enough time to make sure it was not an ambush. When I opened the door, I saw the so to be real victim standing up kicking a pregnant girl who lay in broken glass. The apartment was neat and clean, flowers and kids toys neatly stacked in the corner. Food was on the stove, and the floors mopped. The only disturbed furniture was the coffee table she fell on and broke."

The rookie officer raised his eyebrows because I called the guy a victim, the answer was soon to follow.

"It was obvious that our victim had body-slammed the pregnant girl and was still standing over her trying to kick the crap or the baby out of her.

I closed the door and he looked up. Before I got my one-liner out, he said, 'You going to have to take me to the hospital first.' This statement used to be a dream come true. We looked at him and replied, 'Anything you say.' This was one of those dream opportunities, like hunting the white buffalo, or Moby Dick. Here in civilized America, we found the most sought after prey in the Law Enforcement community: The Complete Butthole.

Since the door was already closed, and we did not want our victim to escape, we locked the door. I approached from upwind, stalking our prey. In domestic situations; in a home, there are too many potential weapons to mount a blind frontal assault. Therefore, we encircled our prey. Craig was from the good old boys' belief system. To him, there were only two types of people; Whites and everything else. I do not know if he got a special joy out of whooping black folk, but today he was going to get to let his whiteness shine through. I fully intended for this jerk to feel as though he was apprehended by a KKK lynch mob on the way to the party.

The public; (The three or four that read), do not realize what it takes to police effectively. They do not realize it takes more effort and more people to not harm a criminal than to utterly destroy one. Beating a criminal up is easy, we have guns, sticks, pepper spray, and cuffs. Trying to wrestle that criminal into a position to use your handcuffs takes more time because you are not trying to break off their arms and legs. If we treated everybody like crabs and snapped off their legs, I believe we either have fewer buttholes or need more handicapped parking. It would be no great loss to society because most of these crabs are of no social value; therefore, no one would miss their contributions.

Craig always went low because he was short, and I always went high. Once we had our criminal trapped, we launched our attack. Our attack was sinister. Craig had the infamous Maglite Flashlight, probably more feared at that time by criminals than guns. The 'D' cell-sized flashlight is about 14' long, black, and made of metal. Because it was metal and held the large batteries, it was heavy.

The little redneck always held out his flashlight like a club, he found that it got the criminals attention. I would then tackle them and slam them to the ground. If a suspect surrendered immediately I would stop the 'community meeting' if not we had a town hall meeting in the suspect's mouth. This fool wanted his meeting at the White House, so the presidential beating began.

This was no Congressional Caucus or party nomination beating. We beat this fool like an incumbent. You see, Mr. Stupid made several mistakes, not the least of which was to beat a pregnant woman. However, his attitude, the lack of remorse meant he would most certainly do it again. It was therefore incumbent upon us to highlight the error in his ways. In hopes that he would regret his aberrant behavior, and turn away from such; or at least spend the rest of his life looking over his shoulder, we beat him like mashed potatoes.

We commenced to host the election; we nominated that ass until we were tired. My favorite part of the election was when the victim finally got up out of the glass, stood on a couch and started cheering us on; Nomination, Election, Confirmation. Dickhead had done it; he made President of the I-Just-Got-The-Crap-Kicked-Out-Of-Me Club; a beautiful organization, every arrestee should get a chance visit the I-Just-Got-The-Crap-Kicked-Out-Of-Me Club National Headquarters.

Once we satisfied the taste for abuser blood, we were ready to take him to the hospital and then to jail. Satisfied, is a posture most bloodthirsty crap kickers never get to enjoy. Our brother firefighters are Smoke-Eaters and the boys in blue are not just peacekeepers but Crap Kickers. That is all we really do, move pieces of crap around the city. The fact of the matter is that there is no real way to fight crime because it is a basic human flaw to be garbage, so the best we can do is shuffle the pieces of crap around. We shuffled this duly elected club member to the hospital. This was the first lesson in this type presentation; this single lesson set the pace for my career.

When we got to the hospital, the ER people asked what happened to him. Yes, I agree with the need for the stupid ass question; but they ask it every visit. As though I am going to tell them that I just kicked the crap out of the arrestee. I told them, 'He was riding his bike without a helmet. They laughed, partly because it was funny, more so because they knew I was not going to tell them the truth. That is when I learned it; the way to be a good cop, do the thing, but make the presentation appealing to those who have to judge; in other words: Make your words or actions believable.

They treated Mr. I-Just-Got-The-Crap-Kicked-Out-Of-Me, with a few bandages, some stitches, and some aspirin for a headache. Then we took the new President to jail. When we got there, we charged him for assaulting the pregnant woman, resisting arrest, and assault on two officers for the injuries we sustained kicking his ass. The cowardly DA would not charge him for potentially injuring the baby so we put that on our tab. The baby may never know what we did for them, but it was our pleasure to give them a chance at a normal life, without a dickhead in their life.

Mr. President learned a valuable lesson that day or so I thought. I got wind several weeks later that Mr. President had put a bounty on my head. Imagine that, a price on my head for a free ass-kicking; irony at its best. We got a call at the girl's house again, but by the time we arrived Mr. President was gone, the coward. He was 'man enough' to beat a girl but not face a man. It is not like I had needed Craig, and I fully intended to go one on one with this guy.

A few weeks passed, no one claimed the bounty on me, but I did have a stroke of good luck. As I was driving past Georgetown Ct, I saw Mr. President sitting atop a wall with a group of guys. I parked my car, exited slowly and I would have put on my spurs, but they were not allowed, yes I did ask," I jeered.

"I walked through the group, or should I say dung heap up to my old friend and slapped the taste out of his mouth. He fell over backward and then tried to cower against the wall. The other pieces of crap stepped back; they too were probably only good at fighting girls. I stomped him like a bed bug, he tried to play possum, but I kicked him in the face-came right out of the coma.

I leaned over Mr. President and grabbed him by his ear, 'Look here, each time you put your hands on her I am going to stomp your ass again. I am by myself, so you know that I mean it. I do not have to worry about that price on my head because this pile of bitches here will not even help you. Do not make me have this talk with you again.'

Turns out, he left the girl and moved out; she was alone but he never beat her up again. She would not have had much luck with him anyway, what does a piece of crap really have to offer anyone?

I learned to love being a crap-kicker; it was an adrenaline rush each day. This is the difference between what police once were, and what they are now. Any quiet day, we made stuff happen. I loved to mix it up. There is no reason to put on the blue suit and gun belt, and not raise hell. The only person who wears more crap on their belt than the cops is Batman.

The infantry, a basic rifleman is the backbone of the fighting force; everything else supports him. Unfortunately, for decent people, the police department shifted from supporting hard-working cops to the political dog and pony show it is now. The administration runs the police department, but officers make it work. General Orders and other stupid rules, litigation, and disciplinary actions, do not keep the department in line, decency and honor are still the benchmarks of police work.

Cops leave Roll Call every day after being told what to do and where to go, then head into the darkness to find new victims. We wasted a few minutes at the Precinct fueling up and swapping war stories. Then we would get into the car and head out to our zone. At some point, we would have to waste 5-10 minutes arguing about where to eat lunch. 'Free' was always my choice, no matter how crappy the food was when it was free it was tolerable, but to pay for slop was never my choice.

The first stop today was The Whiskey Place. It was Friday, and that meant numbers payouts. The Whiskey Man was a pleasant enough fellow. We hit him one Friday paying out of his cash register and we took $15,000 from him for doing that. Now, every Friday around 5:00 pm, he set aside his numbers money in a separate box, and when we walk in he gives us what little he has left in the box after paying off.

It is not as if we got to keep the money, so it never mattered to me how much we took in, it all went into the property room but we made arrests. We walked inside the store, and several from our group walked around in the parking lot looking for other arrests outside.

Trash is not trash until someone throws it away. There is always someone's life thrown away hanging around any trash can they can find to hide in, or near. The Whiskey Place is just such a place; a trashcan, always looking for someone else to throw themselves into.

A visit to the Whiskey Place on Fridays always yielded cash and a few low-level arrests. However, we learned very early in our careers that an arrest is an arrest to The System. Administrators just want to prove they can count beans, that way they do not have to go out and make any arrests.

The next day they assigned us to Range Hill Projects. This particular crap hole had more clearly defined characters than the other projects. Most of the players hung around Cliffside. Today's assignments, same as any other day, seek out trouble and contain, to remove it. We watched Cliffside for a few hours to develop the pattern and we would see people stop near a tree, put money in the tree, and then pick up dope.

We stopped a few people and they had dope so we arrested them, and we were able to prove they were buying dope. What we could not figure out was who the hell was selling the dope. We converged on the area and searched the immediate area as soon as another sale took place, but found no one in the breezeways, nearby cars or vacant apartments.

Then I heard Susan yelling, 'Let me see your hands effing hands,' she was foul-mouthed. She was looking up into the tree. I walked over in time to hear Craig proudly proclaim that we had treed 'one'. He probably wanted to say 'Coon' but was smart enough to save that language for the Klan rallies he undoubtedly attended.

There the seller sat; treed, like Klan-man said, sitting on a branch. What he had done was climb up into the tree with his dope for the day and sat there in the shade of the tree, obscured by the leaves. Then all the guys on the ground had to do was make sure the crack-head dropped money, he dropped the dope.

We took about $750 out of the tree and invited the tree climber to end his sales for the day and come down. Like any good monkey sensing danger below, he stayed treed. Yogi decided that he would go up and make him come done. I had a better idea, an old trick for a young sloth. I ordered him down once more, and then threw a baseball-sized rock at him striking him in the head hard enough that he lost his footing and obliged our instructions to come down. He landed on his back, which means he winded himself and could not even protest as we cuffed him and took the rest of his dope. When he could breathe again, he cursed and swore he would complain. Who gave a crap, who would believe I knocked him out of the tree with a rock?

Back then, we did not have complete pieces of professional crap in Internal Affairs. The Internal Affairs people went after dirty cops and gross violations they were not all rats. The new Internal Affairs or Rat Squads are full of people with clean jackets, and few if any arrests. Because of limited policing, they have limited police mentality…just like common sewer rats. Most cops do not get in trouble for integrity issues, use of force decisions made in an instant however, often have prolonged results. The best way to help good people is to get rid of the bad people."

I cleared something up for Walters, "For the record, the good old days, back then and any other reference to the old ways always ended the day you joined the PD. Each time an old-timer refers to the old days, it is subjective as to what period they mean. That is what we real police call the industry, 'The Job'."

5.2 That Bitch?

"My partners and I worked in one of the most dangerous parts of the city, a darkened region of one of the housing projects called Harry Place. We got out of the car one day to investigate a female black who upon seeing us turned and walked away. We walked up to her and asked where she lived, over there she indicated. Across Charlome Drive, I asked? She indicated yes. With that, we told her she was under arrest for trespassing on Government Property. She tried to run. My partner grabbed her by the arm and escorted her to the car.

I laughed at the amount of trouble my partner was having with her. Although my partner was not the most macho man in the world, he usually did not have this much trouble with the women. When we got the car, I got a Misdemeanor Citation Book. When Skankasaurus saw the citation book she broke free from my partner's grasp and pushed him to the ground. I reached over and grabbed her dress, I also happened to clasp a handful of hair, and it all came off, not her clothes; her hair. That was when I realized that our girl was a guy.

Under normal circumstances, I would never hit a woman, but as this was not a woman, I slapped the horse crap out of Skankasaurus. I slapped Skankasaurus so hard that a palm's worth of make-up came completely off their face. Skankasaurus decided to turn to face me; she was actually going to man up to me. I loved it, a chance to slap this creature back into the Stone Age. When Skankasaurus drew back her man-sized fist, I hit Skankasaurus in the face-hard. Skankasaurus put his hands on the car; this dance was over.

I cleaned up all the makeup off my hands as we took the warrior-princess to jail. There were no further incidents on the way to booking. I turned them over to the jailers and went back to do my paperwork. As I was doing the paperwork, the jailers came out and asked who brought

Skankasaurus to jail. I walked over and told them I did. They told me that I had to go get Tuberculosis treatment because Skankasaurus was Tuberculosis positive.

I went to the hospital, and they put me on an INH (Leper) protocol. This meant that for 6 months I had to either get a shot daily or take a pill daily as a preventive measure. It also meant that when I went back to work the next day that my chair was over in the corner away from my partners. My teammates decided that I should ride solo for the next 6 months until I was no longer 'unclean' or died whichever came first.

We joked about it often but this was one of the lonelier times in my police career. Not only was I not interested in policing, but I was also worried about being a leper. This was a crappy way to go to work each day. I sat on one side of the squad room every roll call by my lonesome, while the others huddled on the other side.

After 6 very uneventful months, the protocol ended. Turns out, the test was a false positive, I had no more germs than anyone else did, but I learned a very important lesson. This was my first true look at human nature; this very type of behavior is why the world is falling apart. Those that were healthy were hiding in less space than they give the disease-ridden vermin.

Some butthole decided that enlightenment meant pretending that no one has a problem. Sick bastards and normal people should be separated. I am sure some bleeding heart also said plague victims should not be ostracized; I hope they died the next day.

"So what, we should punish people with problems, or mental illness, or issues from their pasts?" Walters asked, and it was a fair question.

I thought before I answered, "No, but I do not want to die of your disease either. Pretending you are not sick is not a cure."

I stood up, adjusted my gun belt, then that ballistic vest and looked at Walters, "Polyester sucks." Then I walked to the bathroom to urinate.

5.3 Balls Actually Were Made For Kicking

"The next adventure taught several things. My she-partner and I were riding our zone one day; I do not know why I ever worried about working with she-cops. Turns out, they can be cool; spending 8 hours a day in a car with a she-cop isn't the worst way to die. This crap was better than Viagra; bet you, I held an erection more than 4 hours plenty of days.

One day we rode the zone, talking about whatever dumb crap people stuck in a car talk about. We got some lame-ass call and responded. By the way, the definition of 'lame-ass call' is one you could handle from the comfort of either your car or the bastard. A lame-ass call is one where the resolution is to look all parties in the face and say in the most definitive police voice…Grow the hell up! Some Admin nightmare decided that it is better to send an officer to check on a barking rabbit than to save money and time and tell the complainant to eat a pile of crap.

After we answered the lame-ass call, my partner suggested we stay outside in the cold weather and walk through the housing project. It was cold, it was really a bad idea, and I really did not want to go; so we went anyway…ahhhhh, the power of SHE.

As we walked across this desert of useless humans called the Projects, we saw a dude walking away from an apartment, by himself. In our projects, no male over 18 is allowed, unless in the company of an authorized resident. Dude was trespassing.

We walked over to talk to Idiot 40 Plus. I made contact while Susan talked to some other crap-stick. While I was talking to 40 Plus, I noticed a knife blade sticking out his pocket. I asked him several times if he had any guns, knives or hand grenades, you know the standard crap. I also asked him where he lived, he could not answer."

"Why you call him 40 Plus?" Walters asked.

"Because that's how long he got in jail," I laughed back and continued the story. "With no warning, and no apparent reason, he pulled the knife out and lunged at me. I moved and was able to get the knife free from his hand. I yelled for him to stop as he started running but had to tackle him instead. As soon as we hit the ground before I even finished my roll 40 Plus was back up on his feet. I swept his legs out from under him and he fell again and bounced up again.

By this time, Susan had figured out what was up, and she engaged. I was proud of the little filly. She pranced up to 40 Plus and commenced punching it out with him. He had her hair, and she had approximately 1000th (a fistful) of his big ass afro. Since I was on the ground anyway, and 40 Plus was wailing on my partner, I punched him square in the nuts. In return for my affection, 40 Plus stomped me in the nuts and kicked me in the face. I guess I deserved it.

While I was busy trying to get my balls out of my throat, 40 Plus started dragging my partner through the bricks. Klansman later described the scene like something out of King-Kong. I wonder who one of us his considered the black ape; Afro-king or my female partner?

There I was lying in the dirt, in the world's stupidest leather jacket, trying to find at least one of my balls before I got back to my feet. I would have searched longer but 40 Plus was dragging Susan down the pathway hollering out for help beating the girl up. I heard about a lot of back-woods things in my life, but how screwed up is the world when a man, beating up a female; feels confident enough to ask other men for their assistance in her demise?

I limped my one good testicle over to Susan and tackled dickweed to get him off her. 40 Plus sprang to his feet like a spry little bunny rabbit and was off and running. As he ran, he threw what I thought to be rocks at me. I ran the drive chasing him and finally tackled him yet again. This time when 40 Plus leapt up, he stomped my jaw, and my hands then stood off ready to go toe to toe. I got up and drew my service weapon. My hand was jacked up so I had to hold it gangster style, with a sideways slant. 'Move again,' I said, 'And I'll put a bullet in ya ass.' Just as he moved, and I took out the slack, Susan ran up beside me and pointed her gun at him, screaming in what was mostly English. About 70% of her words were mutha…something or another, but the rest was English.

So much for shooting 40 Plus, two cops against an unarmed man would never sell. I did the next best thing. I pulled out my metal nightstick and chopped that bastard down to the ground. Hell no, I did not just hit his legs, and extremities: well I guess it depends on whether or not you call his head an extremity. Amazing how easily the scalp opens against a metal clubbing. I cannot read minds, even though looked like his brains were oozing out, but I lay good odds that each time I hit him, he probably thought so 'This is how a baby seal feels.'

PETA would have felt sorry for him; I beat 40 Plus until he could no longer move.

By this time, back-up arrived. I did not see her do it, but while dude was kicking my ass; I mean nuts. Susan called for backup. The boys were coming, the Blue Train was coming, and hell was coming with it. That is one thing I learned early in my career…you do not want any of the Blue Train."

"Blue-train?" Walters asked, squinting up his face.

"You probably never have seen it done, its old school. It's where everyone available runs blue lights to an ass kicking. By the time backup arrived, I was tired from beating the crap out of 40 Plus. I will say this, he never stopped fighting; his body simply could not withstand the beating. I beat each shoulder into collapsing then handcuffed each hand behind his back. 40 Plus never complained of any pain. Not even at the hospital when they stitched and stapled him closed. Probably had a great deal to do with the Lobotomy I just gave him. Funny thing is they did not even have to use anesthesia; he went to the hospital prepared.

While we were at the hospital, the rest of the mystery unfolded. Turns out, the reason 40 Plus fought so hard, was that he had a kilo of Cocaine under his jacket. We were able to verify that fact because of the wonderful outline, and content sample left on his black shirt. Ironically, if the dude had just gone back inside, he would have kept his dope. What idiot picked a guy (with the IQ of a mule) to carry his dope? I guess that is why they pick stupid people because they are expendable. Sadly, this jackass cost some other jackass in management about $35k.

Afro-king was one of my first trials, and he went to jail for almost 41 years. I think he got 1 year for the dope and beating me up, and 39 years for beating up a female, pulling her by the hair, and asking his Neanderthal friends to help him: some things never change. Unreasonable force is illegal. The force used has to be reasonable under the circumstances to protect the police officers and the public."

"So hitting a man in the head with a metal rod is reasonable?"

"It must be otherwise, why did they give us the metal rods? Sometimes you got to shoot a son-of-a-bitch, and sometimes; even though shooting may be justified, there are less than lethal options. So find a reason to justify the Use of Force!"

"Are you suggesting I lie of the Use of Force report?"

"No I am suggesting that you do the job right. Crack whatever heads you need to, shoot who you must, and talk to those that allow it. But before you put your foot in a fools chest: be right. Using force is not what gets most officers in trouble, it's is using the wrong force, or the wrong justification: or both. It should not be personal unless it is self-defense. Don't take the job personal. As master Yoda replies, that leads to the dark side.

Take pride in doing the best job you can, for the people you protect. The people we work for are not in jail cells, they are the ones, the ones in the cells victimized. So there is nothing wrong with using all of the force the people authorized us to use to protect them from human garbage."

"How do we know which ones are garbage?"

"Simple, other than stealing food – you are a piece of crap." The I raised my eyebrows several times in succession to add levity to my last statement.

6.0

UNDER COVER OPERATIONS

"We sleep soundly in our beds because rough men stand ready in the night to visit violence on those who would do us harm."

6.1
MAKING THE CREW

"The day arrived that somebody recognized that I was built to change the world. Speed and prowess earned me a reputation in the department; I earned the title Auto-Cop. I was fast, powerful and in my day, I sent more people to the hospital than STDs. As a result, I got a call one night from a sergeant in the street-level drug enforcement unit (Street Crimes Unit). He offered a job, a new job; undercover operations. How could I refuse?

I met my new crew; Wyatt Earp's new, Immortals: more lethal than Ness' Untouchables, and cooler than the Magnificent Seven. We even had a bald cop; country bastard could ride a horse and shoot though.

We met at a training facility and the greatest adventure in my cop-life began. We had a Sgt, two females, and 8 males; of course, I was the coolest of them all. Somebody else on the department thought as I did. I guess introductions are in order.

KEVIN - the leader of the pack was a veteran of the department, an old hand at U/C ops, and the progenitor of the new design. He was the mastermind of the crew and method responsible for thousands of arrests (and three times as many beatings). An older man, he was at least older than the rest of us. He was mild and seemingly soft-spoken, but he loved to set people on fire. He was a practitioner of the Me-Jack-You-Up style of karate, and he loved to practice. Under his tutelage, I later earned a black belt in Me- Jack -You-Up, Karate.

Yeah man, that was the crew; you would not believe some of the crap we got into and survived. Remember every one of these stories is true; I altered facts and situations slightly, to avoid jail, as well as embarrassment. This turned out to be the greatest adventure into the darkness ever recorded.

Most undercover cops have stories, but none of them have as many as we do, damn sure not as many good ones. As cops, we were the last of the holdouts, the last of the Peace Keepers; people like my team, won the West. People like my team, tamed Europe. People like us made the world a better place in which to live.

We did not get along all the time, and there was often friction, but we were true to the mission and to each other. I tip my hat to Blue Bloods everywhere, but I would give my shirt to my team…Always.

These dark knights did more than just a job, their exploits, later dubbed 'Operation: Be the Difference'. Being the difference took a toll on us all. No darkness ever stands alone. Inside of all of us hides the ability to be great. In others, we find the potential for evil. Throughout history, when the stars aligned and the wind was right, people emerged who turned out to be great at being evil.

The department split U/C Ops into Long-term and Short-term (street level) operations. Man, I just knew it was going to be like the television show Miami Vice, which was the ultimate training tool for U/C Ops; at least that is what I thought. Man was I wrong.

My first undercover car was a 5-speed hatchback, with a smashed windshield. Not only was it a piece crap, but also it was also hard to drive. However, that was its beauty, it was such a piece of crap no one cared what was done to it.

We went to another type of boot camp, which trained us how to testify in court, collect and secure drugs and drug-related evidence, and prepare high-grade voluminous case files. Those 40 hours revolutionized the department's approach to street-level enforcement. Those 40 hours brought to life, a program that would live in infamy within the department for the next two to three decades. This was the beginning of The Train.

The unit's primary function was to rid the streets of whores, pimps, drug dealers, and general creepy crawly-ness that accompanies junkies and addicts. Our supervisor wanted everybody on the same sheet of music since we all came from different parts of the department. Those 40 hours changed me forever, some good, some bad.

The primary eradication tool for this unit was the intricately dangerous mission op known as the Buy Bust. The Buy-Bust is simple, and that is what carries with it danger. The Buy-Bust occurs when you buy dope, and then bust the seller on the spot. This unit did several things to make the Buy-Bust mission as safe as possible.

- The person buying did not make any arrests
- The person buying had to wear a ballistic-vest
- The person buying had to train with, qualify with and use an Emergency-gun as well as their primary weapon when buying
- The arrest team was clearly marked

- All monies stayed readily available in case of robbery
- There was a covert distress code
- There was a separate takedown code, the undercover used during the drug deal to notify the arrest team to move in, even while talking to the bad guy

Before we could tackle this task, we had to learn how to be undercover. To be a good undercover, you have to be a junkie first and a cop second. You need people you can rely upon. You damn sure need reliable equipment, but most of all you need common sense. The fastest takedown team in the world still needs 1-1.5 minutes to complete the takedown. That is an eternity if you are shot, or getting mud stomped. TRY NOT GET INTO ANYTHING YOU CANNOT GET YOURSELF OUT OF. You cannot predict the future, but you do not need to take any unnecessary risks to buy $20 worth of crack.

Undercover training began with the savviest of suspects; whores. If you sell dope and you do not employ whores to sniff out your clients, you deserve to go to jail."

"Yeah one day I want to go to Vice or SWAT or something. I like training and learning new things."

"I understand young brother, but remember Vice and SWAT are tools of the trade, not the trade itself. We are here to keep the sheep away from the wolves, and the goats. Otherwise, we would not need Vice or SWAT. Do let those tasks make you, make them. I learned to put more trust in the nobility of character than in an oath."

6.2 Prostitution Enforcement

"Under certain circumstances, being in a car with a loose woman would be awesome, but not when you smell her twat before she ever gets into the car. Training began.

Apparently, there are different varieties of whores of varying smell and price. Starting with the lowest form first;

1. Crack Whore - This is the lowest form of Whore. Crack whore is a generic term; this type of creepy crawly will do anything for hard dope. She usually falls into three lesser categories;
   - Screwed up teeth
   - Missing teeth

- No teeth apparently Dilaudid, Heroin, Crack, and Methamphetamine do a number on your teeth as well and the rest of your whore body

2. Prostitute - Walks the street makes herself visibly a whore, usually has all front teeth. This is a crapshoot most are supporting both a drug habit and other types of demons like abusive relationships and homelessness
3. Dope Whore - More teeth, casual drug user but uses the drugs to get her in the mood and feed her habit, and need for rent money. Often the dope whore works somewhere menial
4. Massage Parlor Whore - Not unattractive, quiet, sits around all day to make a buck sometimes have a drug habit nut this one is the first money-driven whore
5. Stripper - Business prone, ironically the party scene affords her to be a drug user as well. Usually clean looking, and has a place to stay and a car. Often exist just above the poverty level financially; therefore, they have a semblance of a normal life, and usually at least one kid
6. Call Girl/Escort - Business prone, clean, good looking, all her teeth, prone to snort Cocaine, alcohol drinker, or Xanax; she makes too much off her body to look strung out, stays in shape
7. Mistress/Escort - Business prone, clean, good looking, all her teeth, probably no drugs. Makes her money selling the dream (GFE girlfriend experience). Smart ones know the dream makes more money than sex. Stays in shape, well manicured, and a good conversationalist

"Prostitutes are disgusting," Walters said.

"They come in all shapes sizes and colors; if they are the underbelly of society, what part of the animal are their patrons?" I queried compassionately. "I sell myself for the highest price. Exactly like a prostitute. There is no difference."

6.3 Picking Up Whores

"Working ho(s) was fun, but ho(s) are more cautious than most drug dealers. The Slut-buggy was always fun to prepare for the evening. Ho(s) get in and look at the car, they look for switches, wires, oil change stickers, and tabs on key rings with ID numbers for the vehicles.

After passing Phase One of the whore inspection, they move to Phase Two - Habeas Dickus, or let me see that dick. This phase is fun to navigate. You cannot whip it out; it is illegal and not smart. So; now you have to convince a whore that you just picked up for a cheap blowjob that you do not want to pull your dick out yet. The other downside is that Phase Two (see or grab the dick) is immediately followed by Phase Three - suck!

The 'not yet' stall works well most of the time, especially if you immediately rub her tits. Most whores do not want the police to stop the Slut-buggy for swerving and be found with a mouth full of crotch. They usually suggest a place or ask if you have a room. If they ask about a room, you got them, they are down with it, and it is just a matter of lines. One of the easiest lines consists of telling her you only have $X amount of money. Tell her the room is $X dollars, and ask if that is ok. The transaction is complete at that point, because her asking about the room proves she is a Whore. Once you tell her how much the room cost, and she does not get out, the balance is for sex."

"You can grope them," he looked interested for a change.

"You can rub anything they ask or allow you too, but no penetration. Of course, why would you want to stick your finger in a $10 rent-a-snatch? Various bacteria, viruses, and parasites, cause venereal diseases, (Sexually Transmitted Infections). Of the seven main types of STI: which burning sensation suites you best?

Once you slither through Phase Two, it is downhill. Once convinced it is safe to be a whore then all that is left is the deed (Phase Three). When they ask what you want tell them; intercourse, anal, oral, or half-and-half (oral and sex). Do not be shy; you have to work hard to offend a whore. Then is not the time to mention price, get her to commit to the course of action.

Once she has agreed to the deed, throw out the money part in some smooth way. Include the sex in the price of a room, tell her you need more money, ask for dope too, and ask is the money you have enough for both. If she says yes; that is great. If she does not respond, yet does not get out of the Slut-buggy; that is great. If she says no thanks, let me out, well then send someone else to get her, and repeat the steps you completed successfully and then negotiate a new route through Phase Three."

I adjusted my crotch, not because I was aroused, I switched from jockeys to boxers, and did not put it up right, and now it was uncomfortable. I hated boxers, actually hated that fact that after you pee no matter if you beat it to death, the minute you put it up it dribbles down your leg. What idiot thinks this is a good idea, and at my age, the dribble leaves me with wet socks.

"First, I must admit, I have rubbed, squeezed, and slapped some of the saggiest tits in the galaxy. Once; this whore got in and farted as soon as she sat in the car. Moreover, the trick stank. When her funky ass asked what I wanted, I headed straight in for the kill. I told her that I needed to stick something in her ass to help unstop that whore. She laughed as we drove down the street. I am sure she was thinking about the money she was going to make for a quick ass-rental. I was more worried about rolling down the window to abate the smell. Problem was that if I opened the window, the wire in the Slut-buggy would not pick up anything but wind noise.

I drove down the street, and as we did I said, 'Hey I am going to buy you some Tums, with this thirty dollars I earned in a card game, and then screw you.' She just kept laughing and I kept gagging on her funky ass fumes. Nevertheless, the drug deal was good, now I just needed to get her out of the Slut-buggy, and arrest her. I pulled over next to a takedown car and got out so I could breathe. Then they snatched Funky out of the Slut-buggy arrested her, and then we moved on down the street.

Our next victim was a halfway decent looking white girl. She walked inside a smoke-and-rob before I got to her. I walked inside to find her and she was not in the store. As I waited outside in the parking lot for her, a black dude walked out and started talking to me asking for a ride. As I spoke to him he said, 'Damn!' and shrunk away from me. As I turned to see why he reacted that way, I butted up against a .38 special. I must admit, the gun is normally unimpressive. I have seen the revolver in many pawnshops, but this was the biggest gun I had ever seen in my life. It looked like an aircraft carrier.

I was not sure what was up with this psycho-whore, but she had the upper hand for now. I took a moment to listen to the words she was mumbling, as she pointed one of the Guns of Navarone at me. 'Are you his friend? If you are, I am going to shoot your ass too. That is the last time this frigging man puts his hands on me.' It became clear that I walked in the middle of a domestic situation, damn! Well, I was in it now, up to my leaking kidneys. I switched into survival mode.

'Look, baby,' I said 'I am not down with no one putting their hands on a lady (whores either). I do not know him; he was just asking me for a ride.' With that, I pushed her gun out of my face; gently and then backed up a little. I looked at the dude and said, 'Handle your business, and you wrong for putting your hands on your lady.'

Siding with her bought me enough time to walk behind the car and draw a weapon, and clearly warn my team. They had been listening to the situation on the wire, but now I was out of the line of fire, I hoped she did not get shot, but she did have a big ass gun.

I heard the authoritative command, 'Police; drop your gun,' ushered from Custer's mouth. I stayed behind the engine block, hoping not to hear the Gatling guns, but I was prepared. Fortunately, she did the smart thing and dropped the gun. Custer arrested them both, and I went and peed behind the building.

The worst part of prostitution enforcement was picking up male whores, but there was no such thing with us as too icky or too sticky, icky and sticky is what we signed up to do. We frequented the areas of town where the male prostitutes hung out. With males, the contact was non-verbal. Most often, the man-whore stood or walked his corner did not flag cars, or whistle; they just looked in the cars.

What they looked for was eye contact, letting them know you were interested in their skills. Once they see that you are interested, you pull over, and they get in the Slut-buggy. Unlike the female that gets in ready to suck and grope, the male is more deliberate and calm.

In another adventure, we pulled up behind 10th & Saash, near an adult bookstore. The only fun part about picking up ho(s) is that not all ho(s) are girls. This area was nothing but man ho(s). I hate being the Ho-lice, and male ho(s) are a pain in the ass - no pun intended.

'Good evening,' dude said as he got in the Slut-buggy. 'You have any plans for tonight?'

'Yeah I replied I plan to screw you, and then cum in your mouth, is that ok? I got the room and $100 is what I got to spend.' Dude said nothing, but just adjusted his seatbelt, that meant we had a date.

This freak stood about 6'2", medium complicated, with a body sculpted like a statue for fitness. When we took him into custody I only said one thing to him, 'Man WTF are you doing out here sucking dick, have some pride; go rob people or something!' He just hung his head and walked over to the booking area. Then I jumped in the Slut-buggy to go find another one.

To make this ongoing process work, you have to change streets or cars, because notice you returning without their friend. It is easier just to transition, but if you can, the cover story, 'they left because I told them they charged too much' often worked.

'Hey man,' I said to my next guest 'I am not giving out free rides.'

'I know' he replied.

'I looking for some dick sucking,' I continued.

'Ok,' he replied, 'That's great; I'm game,' I queried, '$30?'

"That was something funny I learned about the whore game, men often charge more than women for that same sex act. This dude did something I was not expecting, he spread his legs and said, 'Prove you are not a cop'. WTF! Was the first thing that crossed my mind? There was no way this dude was going to tell people or testify to my beautiful virgin hands rubbing his dick as part of the drug deal. As big and healthy as he was his junk was probably equally impressive.

I had to think quickly, he did not have any tits; 'You first," I said as I spread my legs. I thought he would do a quick grab like the girls, but no, this trick must have been a Whore Trainer, he rubbed every single inch of me. Did not take him very long, my dick played Sumo wrestler and tried to go back inside my body to avoid this dick-smith's grasp. I soon realized this bastard was trying to make me hard.

He was going to have to rub the skin off to get a response from me. I wanted to kill this dude, you know how dicks are; they respond to attention. I had a surprise for him, I disconnected all synapses to my groin, you know, like married women do. It took what seemed like an hour and a half for him to unhand my groin. In fact, we only drove one block. He agreed to the $30, but when I pulled over for the takedown, he started to pull his dick out. 'What you doing?' I asked.

'How you going to suck me off if it is in my pants?' he inquired.

'I am paying you $30 to suck me off,' I responded.

'Oh no,' he said, 'No, I do not suck, but you can suck mine for $30.'

I do not know how we got the signals crossed, but it was still a prostitution deal. I dropped him off amidst the laughter.

I Jumped back in the Slut-buggy, and went looking for another Dragon to slay. None of the guys standing in the target area wore 'drag', they wore regular clothes. I picked up a tall black one. The last one was white; I liked to alternate the numbers-street rules.

'Get in let's go find some food.'

He got in, 'Good because I'm hungry,' he replied.

'I got something you can eat.' He was bouncing in his seat by now. That is until I started with the next line of information, 'I feel lucky.' I just had to get him to staging to make the arrest. 'I hope you like it rough,' I continued.

He put his hand across his chest in a most effeminate way, 'Oh my!'

'Yeah, bastard,' I said as I locked the doors, 'I'm going beat the crap out of you and put all kind of things in your ass.'

He started grabbing the door, and unlocked it, 'Aw no baby, wrong bitch!' he retorted as I locked the door again.

I sped up, 'Na bitch you keep that tight ass right in that seat.' He was panicking by now trying to jump out the car until I pulled up to the marked officers. He jumped to tell the police that I wanted to hurt him. He was right, what a bitch.

Last one for the evening, 'What's up dude, where you been?'

'Crap man, just hanging out,' He said as he slid into the seat.

'Man I am looking for something, vajango or something.'

'Shit naw, vajango make me itch, let us do something else.'

'Ok, some head will do, but I want a 3 or something."

We tried not to mix jobs because we wore different gear for ho(s) that dope. We wore light gear for ho(s) because it was easy to take off if we needed to change the undercover officer. Every once in a while we had to switch to takedown gear. We were picking up ho(s), but this was going to be a trifecta: one pimp and two ho(s).

The pimp directed me to Hotel Mallard. Hotel Mallard was a crap hole of course; nevertheless, Hotel Mallard was whore friendly. Someone named Patel ran the place.

'How much?' I asked.

He said, 'For two, a hundred.'

I was game, he made a call and said, 'Y'all busy, get together, I need two.'

A door opened and a small framed girl came outside and knocked on the next door. 'Follow that girl he said, but give me the money.'

I handed him the money and gave the takedown signal. Making sure to take the keys, I locked the doors and walked into the room.

As I walked into the room, I unlocked the car doors as the takedown team arrived. I walked into the room and started talking to my new friends, 'Ok who's on top and who's the bottom?' They laughed. I gave him the money the small framed girl replied, 'I know honey.' The second prostitution deal was complete; we needed the girls to agree to sex because we could charge them with prostitution if they said nothing; we could never prove they were consensual parts of the deal.

Now all we needed was the arrest. I gave the second takedown signal, and the takedown team moved in to arrest the girls. They knocked on the door, I opened it and walked out, and they took the girls into custody. What I did not realize was that they were still fighting the pimp out in the parking lot.

I looked over and Ike the pimp was acting like a fool, screaming and yelling. The officers shouted the required verbal commands, 'Quit resisting, you are under arrest.' It was hot outside, so I went back to the room, and sat down with the ho(s). The pimp was average, and he was not a whore, but they beat him like a slave. I am sure he would have rather taken a stiff one than endure the ride he got. Two ho(s) and one pimp later, we had two confidential Informants and a pimp with no hat, no fur jacket, no glitter shoes, and no teeth.

I moved on down the road and picked up another man whore. Dude had on a green shirt and blue shorts. He jumped in the Slut-buggy. 'What you doing he asked?'

I held back my laugh as I said, 'If I am lucky, screwing you.'

He settled back in the seat as we drove. Now that he was comfortable, he started asking questions.

'I just need $20 for a blowjob.'

I replied, 'I wanted some kinky stuff, but that will do.'

'What do you mean kinky?' He pressed.

'I was thinking about screwing you rough, I mean punching and kicking, and then I could throw you out the car.' I could tell by his facial expression, that he regretted getting in the Slut-buggy.

The more uncomfortable he got the more I enjoyed myself. When I locked the doors, he started whining and calling to the Lord. I pulled in behind a building where he tried to get out. I grabbed his shirt and started taunting him. He started crying and then the takedown team moved in and arrested him. He was so happy to be rescued by the police he did not even mind the arrest.

After we finished the paperwork, we got back out on the street. Unfortunately, there was another whore standing in the middle of the street, Ho-ing. I had the arduous benefit of picking up another, stank ho.

I pulled up to the girl and smelled her even before she got into the car. If there were some incense in the Slut-buggy, I would have lit it and stuffed the entire pack, burning end and all in her snatch. Under normal conditions, I do not smoke, but covering the rancid, burnt tuna melt mixed with onion smell in the car was the best use of cigarettes in human history.

The nicotine masked her wretched, stench, nicely. I was able to drive, gagging on just the smoke, not her rancid twat. I always wondered if there may have been some good excuses for poking ho(s); nasty, stinking, street walking, ho(s). After smelling this walking, can of rotten Tuna, with a yeast infection, I cannot fathom what would make a normal disease-free male talk to, pay, and stick anything inside a human that smelled like rotting flesh?

I am a professional, however, so I played along. As fate would have it this whore was friendly. She whipped out two Nat-geos (saggy-tits) and told me to touch them. I did, I tried to rub the nipples off them bastards. She pulled her tits away just before the nipples erupted in flames. Then next, she spread her legs to reveal a hairy, hazmat area of a groin. She grabbed my hand and did something, awful. She made me touch the Demon of Tuna. Not only did she put my hand on her snatch, but she also tried to rub my fingers across the great, slimy, oozing, divide. I looked at my hand, I was sure I was going to die.

If this had been a date, with a normal smelling girl, I would have enjoyed going from hello to second base this quickly, but I wanted this game to be slow pitch softball because I was getting sick. I was sick of her smell, her touch, and the impending social disease infecting my hand.

Despite all the horror, she subjected me to, I must admit; she was one of the nicer creatures I encountered. She was sweet, pleasant (not fragrance wise), and simply a nice person living a crappy existence. As we rode and spoke about sex, she asked me something that made me even more nauseous than her smell. She asked me if instead of giving her all cash could we stop somewhere cheap and get her something to eat. She was one of the only two people I have ever encountered that I regretted having to arrest. I wanted to feed her, I should have fed her myself, but I could not stop the whole team, while wired and buy her food. Even if I did, they would not allow her to eat it. I sadly gave the takedown signal."

"Sad, why? I thought you reviled all criminals."

"Sad because she was about to be treated like a whore. The takedown team moved in, and took stinky into custody. I walked over and took her to the side, I was going to arrest her, it was a dark deed, but I could still give her basic human respect.

As I arrested her, I said, 'Sorry I could not feed you.' She looked at me, touched my hand, and said, 'That's ok, you were only doing your job.'

Well, I disagree, if I was doing my job I would have fed her. I did arrange for her to work off her charges and have the charges dismissed. Sometimes you have to do the right thing, despite starting on the wrong side. The next time I saw her I fed her though. Never again, did I fail to feed someone that needed my help."

I leaned back and adjusted my posture because handcuffs are uncomfortable. "The next creepy-crawly we encountered was a 55-year-old. I remember her like it was yesterday. She got into the car, said good evening then squeezed out a massive, putrid fart. I do not mean a silent-but-deadly this whore blew one out. Then she looked at me and asked what I wanted. 'To open the window, you nasty beast,' I said, as I gasped for air.

Instantly I hated her.

'Hey, baby,' she continued, as though she was a playboy pin-up. Since she pissed me off, I went straight in. 'How much for anal?' I asked.

She said, 'Ouch that is going to hurt; $35.' I gave the signal, pulled over and got out of the Slut-buggy so they could arrest the fart-bag and I could move on.

We picked up whores for the entire first month. As we drew close to the end of the month, we lucked upon a building wherein, there was lots of space and chairs that were not in use. On this day we held, the Whore-Inquisition. At the Whore-Inquisition, each whore had her chance to tell her side of the story before we booked them.

The Arrangement; several teams went out to pick up whores, one officer acted as an undercover officer and three (marked) takedown officers. After each prostitution transaction, the takedown officers took the suspect to the Whore-Inquisition staging area and dropped them off so the games could continue.

I chanced upon a scene when I arrived. I opened the door to see a whore traveling down the hallway, being moved along by her hair. As she entered The Whore-Inquisition, another whore said, 'I will be a witness.' to which came a resounding; 'No! You just be a ho.' Before that trick knew what hit her, she was duct-taped like a mummy and sat in the corner in time out. This was some pimp type stuff.

On the down the road a bit, I saw a black female walking down the road, trying to look innocent, but she was a ho. This stinking creature got in and farted, yet another gassy ho.

'I'm gassy!' she said.

'Naw ho! You stink. Dammit, what the crap is wrong with you? They wash vegetables when they serve them. We wash chicken before we cook it, how the fuxx are you going to sell your snatch, and not wash it; EVER? Seriously, are you retarded?'

She did what any screw-slut would do when spoken to like a dog, hang her head in shame, and still try to sell the twat. She smelled so bad she agreed to give me a coupon, or in the case a Poop-on, five dollars off the ride in her outhouse. When she went to jail, I hope they made her sit on a fire hydrant.

One of the prostitution fronts we went into, (at least I did) was an establishment that modeled Lingerie. The complaint was that after the show,' if you spent enough money on the Lingerie, the girl came along with the purchase. I went in and saw this beautiful girl. She was smart, intelligent, and beautiful. Did I mention how beautiful she was? She was soft, like the petal of a rose. I did not want her to model, I just wanted her to sit there and be beautiful. It was not until my erection started throbbing against my biking shorts, that I came back to reality, and simultaneously realized I wore the wrong underwear.

When I worked ho(s), I always wore shorts, biker shorts, and underwear. It allowed them to grope, and me to cope. It also gave time to peel layers after we agreed on terms, giving time for the arrest could be made. The Law was that cops could not make penetration and could not get naked during undercover operations. All that was happening now was that the biker-shorts were acting like a tourniquet and cutting off the blood to my heads, this was the first time an erection made me dizzy. I made a mental note to investigate how my blood can safely redirect from my brain before damage occurs. I forgot to follow-up.

I paid the requisite price for the lingerie show. I am not Trans or nothing, but she looked so good in the lingerie, made me want to try the clothes on with her. Then it happened; a day I shall never forget. She turned around and removed her panties. As I watched her peel the panties off, and pull them down her long legs, over her perfectly shaped toes, all I could think of was I hoped she would throw them to me. She did, she threw me her drawers, and I caught them like an eager bridesmaid. I wanted to rub them all over my face, and wear them on my head, but I quickly remembered I was at work; dammit.

She bent over. 'Thar, she blows,' I said to myself, there it was my Moby, my pot of gold…Nirvana. This was, without doubt, a perfect vajango. It was small, shapely, firm, young, and happy looking. Reluctantly, I gave the takedown signal. I was furious at myself."

I did not realize I stopped talking and was staring into space. Walters nudged my knee with his, 'You ok old man,' he joked. I was but my groin hurt, and I could not adjust my pants in front of him; it would have been a dead giveaway.

I continued the story, the blood had returned to my brain by this time. "When the team came to rescue me they walked in and the girl was bent over, and perfect was on display. The first person through the door was a female officer, and like Medusa's gaze, she saw Perfect and froze. Later she claimed that it was because she was surprised, but I believe her crotch saw Perfect and turned to stone. I believe she could not walk because Perfect made her crotch hang it's beard in shame.

Then some Star Wars type crap happened. They came in to arrest the girl, to arrest Perfect. When they got close enough Perfect played a mind trick on us all, 'This is isn't; the vajango you are looking for.' Then I repeated it. 'Come on guys, this is not the vajango we are looking for!'

Perfect's crotch then said, 'Move along'.

Sgt was having no part of it, we wrote her a misdemeanor citation and walked out leaving Perfect, to rule her small corner of the world; shaved, perfect and alone.

The next trick on the strip was old; this freak was so old she had a comb-over, top and bottom. She looked like Barnaby Jones with tits. There probably had not been milk in those feed bags for a very long time. The hag was so old she did not even have to shave any more, the hair had stopped growing a long time ago.

'Hey, baby how much for some head?' I asked still in UC mode.

'For you?' She replied. Stupid whore, what did she think, I was ordering take out?

'Yeah for me,' *you ignorant prehistoric Ho* - I thought.

She said, '$20 with my teeth in and $25 without,' and she pushed her teeth out with her tongue, like that was sexy. A whore is a whore but who wants to screw a 90-year-old freak with no teeth and a comb over?

'Ok,' I continued, 'Get in we can go somewhere and do this.' 'No!' she said, 'One at a time; I do not get into a car with two dudes.' Sadly, the truth is that if she got in the Slut-buggy there would be three dudes.

'What the crap are we going to steal?' I asked, 'You do not even have teeth, and we paying for the vajango?'

"Sounds like you had a ball doing the undercover work. Ever get mixed up, and lose your way?"

I looked away and smirked; half snorted and then looked him in the eye. "I never really found the way back."

"What does that mean?" Someone walked past us in the hallway. I looked up; they were in uniform, a sergeant. They passed us both and did not even say hello.

"I am still working that out. I know one thing, when someone says prove you are a cop, it should be because you are out of uniform not because of your action, or lack thereof."

6.4 Minister Sling-That-Dick

"Today we patrolled our usual skank zones. We saw a clergyman walking the strip in full garb, attaché in hand. We paid him no mind at first. We saw him talking to the girls, but we were there to lock up some ho(s).

After approx. 2 hours we thought it odd, he was still trying to help these ho(s). We watched him from a parking lot. He was speaking to a girl and then he opened his attaché and showed her something inside. She shook her head and walked away. We waited for him to leave and then approached her and asked her what he had said to her. At first, she laughed, and then told us. She said, 'He asked if I believed in God, to which I said yes. He then asked had I been baptized to which I said no, I am not a Christian. It was what he said next that pissed me off. He said since I was not a Christian he could Screw me in the butt, and he showed me the attaché was a large jar of Vaseline.'

We left, and went to speak to brother Sling-That-Dick. I heard of the Spanish Inquisition, but never the Anal Inquisition. Apparently, his thing was to inquire of the unsaved whores, verifying their virtue by lubing them up and entering through the backdoor.

We pulled up and got out on Minister Sling-That-Dick, 'How ya doing?' I asked.

Minister Sling-That-Dick looked at me and said 'I am having a blessed day.'

I replied, 'I did not know Vaseline was used for a blessing.' He looked at me incredulously and asked what I meant.

'We saw you talking to that whore.'

'You mean my daughter, well actually child of God,' he retorted indignantly.

'Do you screw all your children?' I asked; 'We have a word for that.'

He acted offended, maybe he was, 'I am a man of God!' he started.

'Which God?' I asked, 'Because I am sure the one in the Bible does not issue butt-lube, what the hell kind of preacher are you anyway?'

Brother Sling-That-Dick replied, 'A man in search of a mission.'

'You mean in search of a turd,' I said as I moved towards him.

'You are under arrest,' we said and he asked for what? 'For attempting to pick up a prostitute, I mean a child of God.'

My partner looked at him and said, 'Sad that you are more of a whore than that prostitute.' He hung his head, low, but not low enough for me.

We wrote brother Sling-That-Dick a citation and made him throw away his Inquisition Lube. Stay off the street I said, or at least change your clothes. 'I used to really help the girls before I fell,' he said regrettably. Then he straightened his collar and walked down the street. I thought about feeling sorry for this pathetic man: Then decided Naa! Screw him."

"Yeah that's why I don't go to church, too much hypocrisy." Walters retorted.

"You're quite welcome to talk to a murderer try understanding their situation. The church is full of the same people you claim to want to understand and serve, why avoid them yet judge me for how I police?" I asked sternly.

"Because they have God, they are supposed to be better than that."

"And exactly what do you believe, what God do you believe in that makes it ok to judge some people and discard the rest - hmm now who has a twig in their eye? Stupid did remind me one something however; men never do evil so completely and cheerfully, as when they do it from religious conviction."

6.5 Prostitution Stings

"One of the duties of any good street-level vice unit is the prostitution sting, but it is a thing of the past as well. The sting is where the police put out an undercover officer; either she-cop or prostitute in the area known for real whores. Our whore-undercover officer then makes deals with Johns (Prostitution customers) and then the police swoop down and arrest the unwitting Johns. Most of the Johns go along without incident, but on a few occasions, we get to smash faces into the dashboard, we relished those moments.

On one such sting, we put an undercover officer out, the first time for her. There is a range of motion for the undercover officer we called The Stage. The Stage was the area within which the camera could pan back, forth, and see the undercover officer. All of the deals had to be on film for court purposes.

One of the things undercover officers have to remember is that the entire tape goes to court. This she-cop did not seem to understand what that meant. Her deals overflowed with references to her big hairy crotch, sucking, and a few other acts not commonly associated with street whores.

It was not until the undercover officer walked off the Stage and approached some dude who was vacuuming his car, did we decide to replace her.

'Hey there,' she said, 'Hey, would you like to screw me in the butt?'

Well yeah, he agreed (as if he was going to say no). Ironically, she never even mentioned a price, so we could not charge him, even if we wanted to. We did not want to entrap him that never goes over well. More importantly, we dare not play that tape in court.

Close Cover is an integral part of all Undercover Ops. For the Ho sting and innocuous beggar, or vendor of some type works well. As long as the close cover looks as useless as the surroundings, no one cares. On most deals I was the close cover, I liked it and I often got to kick ass in the line of duty. Besides, as much time as I spent as an undercover officer I understood the importance of close cover and vowed to never let the undercover officer get injured on my watch.

So here we are, whore central putting on a sting, and I dressed like a dumpster diver. We put a new undercover officer out; she was cute, though new to the scam and its nuances. The first dude pulled up and never asked for anything, he just whipped his dick out and beat it a little for her. She relayed the information; takedown officers followed him down the street a short distance, and summarily beat his eyes shut.

The next car pulled up and the white guy in it offered six dollars for sex. She agreed but later admitted that it hurt her feelings. The only value things have is the value we place on them. Everything in life is negotiable, but you know a person that is willing to sell themselves for $6 bucks probably has no feelings. Geoff was tasked to do the takedown, but as usual, he was yakking on one of his phones. He never acknowledged the takedown signal. Still dressed as Billy the trash-bagger I moved in. At some point, you have to lock the John up or he is going to start lubing up the girl.

The guy went inside a market to get a beer, to share with his $6 dollar prize. I walked up to him, showed him my badge him, and told him he was under arrest. He put his hands on the wall. For no apparent reason, he lowered his hands and asked to see the badge again. I obliged him. Remember if you look the part of a beggar, it takes a little longer to convince people that you are not a can-collecting bum you are actually the police.

After the suspect asked to see the badge three times, he decided to fight. He drew back his fist, but before he could fire his punch, I knocked him into the wall. Unfortunately, for us both (mostly him) the wall was actually the glass beer cooler wall. The $6 man went through the glass into the cooler. I reached in to grab him but the glass kept falling on him. I waited for the falling glass to clear, and then pulled him out. He was bleeding from a variety of places; his head looked like a pincushion. When I pulled him up, he was bleeding so badly I just dropped him on the floor. The blood from him pooled up on the floor. The store clerk called an ambulance for the idiot.

They whisked him away and wrapped him up like a mummy. It was scary, I had never put a human through glass before, and it was on videotape. I started to panic, what if, what if, what if ran through my mind. I was not sure if I needed a lawyer, or a priest or what the next step was when you destroyed a human's face over a misdemeanor prostitution transaction. I thought *what if I screwed up my disguise? How was I going to get his blood off?* All the panic subsided; I looked at myself and checked my disguise in the mirror.

Walters was laughing his ass off, so I continued. "If you're going to play a prostitute, you can't be too squeamish about that sort of thing. It's just part of the job, since the role requires it."

6.6 Club 'Sticky Twat'

"Whores come in all shapes, sizes and colors. White black, yellow, fat, red, and sometimes there is no other way to describe U/C work that DAMN! For today's assignment, the Coconut Moon pies (my boss he referred to most people in terms of their Moon Pie equivalent) decided to wage war on the seedy strip joints. This meant by default the black clubs since the sisters did a whole lot more touching than the white girls did.

This evening, they sent me into Sticky Twat, that was not its real name but that is what people called the place. At first, after arriving I thought the name was because you could put just about anything you want to put into the puss of the girls. Some guys even wanted to use one of the fat girls' twats as a locker and put his valuables in her for storage.

After a few lap dances, I knew why they called it Sticky Twat, you could not get the gummy residue of their juices off your hands without some of the orange goop mechanics use to clean up motor oil and grease. Man, what type of diet produces adhesive vajango glue? Moreover, how do they get their thongs loose from the flypaper? Anyhow, I signed out some (taxpayer) money, saddled up and drove down to Sticky Twat.

As in all deals, the issue was sex. The Supreme Court says you can get down to your drawers, but no sex. The problem is these whores do not fake. When you say blowjob, it is all you can do to keep your dick out of their mouths. When you try to slow it down, they get suspicious. The trick to picking up ho(s) is to be cool. Try not be the horny little spaz with a hard-on ready to squirt at the first touch. You need to lay back like it takes you a few minutes to get warmed up. Besides, remember that the Ho works for you; you hired her to suck you off, not the other way around. Occasionally, you had to threaten to slap a Ho to keep her in line, it is ok (to threaten) they are used to violence.

Sticky Twat was no different; a ho, is a ho, no matter what they charge, they are all hired for sex. I walked into this club, and like many seedy strip clubs, the strippers here look like battle scarred walruses. The dark lights cover their battle scars, but every once in a while they cannot hide them.

The other thing I never understood was why these freaks never shaved. I paid good money to see shaved action. All hair does is trap funk, moreover, nappy hairy never looks good on anyone and two more ideas, wash your arms, ass, and twat. If you are going to stick anything in my face it should be clean, you can sweat without stinking, can't you?

Nevertheless, here I was being paid to look at twats. So I looked; I looked hard, I took this opportunity to examine the full flower of the human genitalia. There were subtle differences in the girls. Like most aquariums, this tank had a variety of fish inside. There were small pretty fish, large mean fish, and of course, there were the ugly bottom feeders. This place accounted for all manner of fishy smells and texture, and most of them were not fresh.

You know you can tell a lot about a market by how it takes care of the items it has on sale. In this place, every part of the girls was being marketed, even the smell. When I entered, a guy was sitting on his hands, getting a lap dance. When the girl turned around and bent over, he sniffed, he inhaled as long and hard as he could...everything here was part of the sale; feet, hands, eyes, tits, ass, legs and hair, yes even hair...guys are pretty weird. When the clerk has crappy merchandise for sale, or in this case, a dirty, stinking ass that tells you a lot about the quality of the merchandise. I am not saying that all strippers are ho(s), but a woman who sells it ought to wash it, or at least a body mist.

Man the girls were jacked up. If you need to know what will take that fishy smell off your face out of your mustache after a lap dance; Jägermeister. That is the secret to their success; men will buy anything. The secret to selling vajango is the trappings; all girls are pretty much built the same, so they have to decorate. Pretty toes look good especially sitting around your shoulders. Tits (without battle scars) are especially nice, but should never adjoin armpit hair. If you are going to take the time to pretty up the toes do not put screwed up shoes on them. Ho shoes are ok, but spaghetti straps are always sexiest on feet.

Many women go the Fredericks of Hollywood route instead of Victoria's Secret route. Cheap, shocking colors are not sensual, there are slutty, and they leave no room for wonder. Soft colors always look best; because men, all men, still like a woman to be soft and pretty. This is why streetwalkers get paid less than call girls. The rough, toothless whore puts out, but she is not pleasing to the eyes. The girls that spend the money making their feathers plume, often get paid just to be close. Pretty birds, in nature, are not often songbirds, yet they attract the most attention at the zoo.

Here I was, scattered ass, shaved twats, lonely desperate guys, the smell of sex in the air, and I was getting paid to do this crap! Like any self-respecting dude at a titty Bar, I sat back and dutifully compared and contrasted all the T&A in the place, it was an interesting experience. Most of the girls had two tits; one had 3/4 of only one. She looked like a sea lion after a battle, I am sure that another sea lion bit it off in some battle. As big and fat as she was perhaps she bit it off herself in a fit of hunger. I gave her props though, took a lot of courage to load her fat ass into the hammock she used as a thong. She did have one advantage over the other girls, where they had to put effort into shaking their ass; hers would not stop shaking (ever).

Then her song came on, like any good circus animal she moved to the beat of the music. I expected her to mount on a ball and roll it around the stage; instead, she climbed her big ass on the pole: Kudos to whoever installed the damn thing.

Humunga bound her big ass onto the pole, she got about four feet up the pole before gravity and her massive tits pulled her back down. While she was up in the air, she spread her legs as far as she could, she had to open wide enough for the folds of fat to roll away from her glistening chasm. I learned that day that fat girls have fat twats, all sorts of other padding.

The song changed and the next trick out the cave wore a patch, I do not mean dark circles under her eyes; like Captain Hook, this chick had an eye patch. She was fierce, fierce enough to use the stage name Patches...I guess so, Captain Hook is copy written, and not as sexy. Patches strutted out in her black vinyl whore boots. She walked the stage, and despite a patch and an ugly ass face, she had a banging ass body. I often wonder *what most women prefer, a pretty face, or a nice body*? Patches turned around and backed her ass up; she bounced it pretty good, for a pirate. She laid down on the stage and spread her legs. The first guy put a dollar on her belly. The second guy stuck the money in her panties and rubbed her snatch a little as he moved past, she did not blink. Well maybe she did but I just could not see because she only had one eye.

The next dude put his face down into her twat and nuzzled it hard. I thought for sure she would smack him, but no, she moved her thong and let him get a few licks before she rolled over and moved away. I had heard of kissing booths but here you could eat vajango for a buck, not a bad deal...if you do not mind playing Russian roulette.

This went on all night, for the most part, I remained a gentleman, until this light-skinned girl came out. This trick looked good, not good enough to eat, but at least worth a lap dance in hopes she might fall in love with me (for tonight). When she came out her name was the same as the club, Coco. I see why it was named after her, she ran the place. I moved closer, to the stage, and got out my, I mean taxpayers money. The lap dance was twenty-five bucks; my boss gave me two hundred. I did not intend to give any back, what better way to investigate club Coco than to spend time with its star?

Coco stood about 5 foot 4 inches, and carried about 118 lbs. She had a thigh tattoo, her name of course, and the rest of her skin was without blemish. Her hair was chestnut and flowed naturally down her back, obviously mixed race, or used a perm in her hair. Two large beautiful brown eyes adorned her face and she wore small, non-stripper earrings. She wore panties and a sheer top that looked like a cape, and fastened around the neck with an open diamond running down her belly. The outfit was light blue, like the sky, and her toes painted the same color. She was a picture of what every man in the world wanted his woman to look like. It was not just her size, the colors, soft material, groomed feet, and hair, and the shaved un-pierced twat, made her devilishly alluring.

The love affair began right there, between Coco's legs. She came over and sat beside me, took off her shoes, to discuss terms. Some other lesser creatures walked over and asked if I wanted to buy the lady a drink. It took me a moment to realize she was referring to Coco as a Lady, I would not call her that, but tonight, at least for the next two hundred dollars she was my lady.

I bought drinks, ten dollars worth of Coke. Coco was sweet; she sat beside me and chatted for a minute or two. It seemed like genuine interest, but the truth of the matter is she could not begin the dance; our dance, until the song changed.

Our song began, it was a special song, I think. Coco told me to sit on my hands as she straddled my lap. She wrapped her arms behind my head and began to dance irreverently. Coco was the best sexual experience I ever had with my clothes on. This beautiful woman was sitting in my lap, totally focused on me. This was almost perfect, Coco needed just a wee bit of deodorant, but the dance went on.

She grinded her love against my lust, I do not know how she did not break my lust, as I throbbed beneath her. I know she felt the beat of my 'heart' pulsing through (hard as it was) synchronized with the song, one thump, one pump. I was totally feeling this girl, and she was definitely feeling me.

I never understood addiction, until I met Coco. I would never hook myself on a substance, but this moment, this dance, this girl was intoxicating. For the duration of the twenty-five dollars, I forgot everything. I forgot I was a cop, I forgot this was a paid dance; I forgot that she did this all night for anyone...this moment was all I wanted, forever.

There is not much else that I have encountered as inebriating as the gaze, body, touch, and chance of a beautiful woman. As I looked into her eyes, a peculiar thing happened. I forgot all the negative things about Coco, she was a working girl, she whored in a whore pit, and she allowed any man with $25 bucks to rub her lovely, sweaty, ass. Other than those things, she was perfect.

Dammit, I thought as the song ended. I could not let the love die, 'Wait,' I said, 'Do not go.'

She kissed my cheek and said, 'I got to go to work, honey.'

Work: that is right I was actually making a living verifying that this was a whore pit. To do that I had to make a prostitution transaction with a girl, or see so other infractions like the group oral sex: 'pus-eat-a-long'. Guilt showered my body, I could not do that to Coco, I could not disgrace her in front of everybody like that, not my Coco; but what to do I had a duty. I needed to think, but she was leaving, I had to stop her: What to do?

I got it; I pulled more money out and said calmly, 'One more dance baby, then I'll help you put your shoes on.' I got to speak to her until the next dance. I loved this job. Our next song started and she got back close to me again. This time she did not tell me to sit on my hands, this time she placed my hands on her hips, 'Roll wid me baby,' were her actual words, all I could hear was *I am all yours, this is all for you.*

As I sat there with happiness in my lap, I started to rub her back, as you would during a kiss; she never missed a beat or took her eyes off me. I never stopped looking into her eyes, I want her to know what I felt did not only exist between my legs. I wanted her to know that I loved her, at least for the rest of the song.

It was all about mutual love and respect (disguised as $25). When she saw me, I did not want her to see a customer but a friend. I knew halfway through the songs I would need one more dance to ascertain the information needed to make the deal. *Save another dance for me,* I thought as I dug into my pocket for more tax dollars.

It was time to make the hustle work for me. 'I got forty left for two dances,' I bartered. She took the money and tucked it into her clutch. She sat down and asked could she skip one song because her feet hurt. Sure, I said as any gentleman should. Why don't you let me rub them for you? She agreed and kind of rubbed my crotch as she placed them in my lap, she meant to do that.

This was the only time I could tell she spent a lot of time working. Her feet; as pretty as her toes were, were extremely rough on the bottom and the straps on her shoes hid her bunions. Not that I would have kicked her out of bed for them, but in each dream, a little rain must fall.

I was halfway through the money, and I am sure my friends outside were bored just sitting waiting to pounce. I needed to finish this moment (before I asked Coco to marry me).

A mean trick was next on stage, she was to be my target, and I knew she was a Ho. I waited until she finished shaking her rancid ass, then I made my move. Her stage name was *Candy*, and I am sure she tasted like black Licorice. I waited for her to get close then I flagged her over. Candy had no poise; she told me the price, took money, and then just stood there until the next song began.

I did not like Candy. She was not like Coco; she was just the average stripper, complete with attitude and whore tricks. I guess if you are ugly, you have to shake a little harder; this trick needed an earthquake. I let her grind on me and gladly sat on my hands. Candy stank, breath, ass, and armpits and need I say what else. This whore smelled like a pet store. Candy turned around and put her ass up. I did not touch her, so she grabbed my hands and put them on her ass. I smacked it a little. I was mad because now I really had to wash my hands.

As I sat there smacking her funky butt, I wandered off into health statistics from National Geographic's,

- *'Staphylococcus Epidermidis - Staphylococci are pathogens that inhabit the mucous membranes and skin of mammals, feeding on sweat and dead skin cells. Staphylococcus Epidermidis is the most common and numerous species of bacteria found on human skin. While this common bacterium is usually harmless, it can become harmful under certain conditions*

- *Corynebacterium - In humans, bacteria are the most common and numerous component of the skin flora. The sweat-eating Corynebacteria are regular skin flora, often found in the armpit, and can cause acne. The bacteria that feed on the nutrients in sweat and dead skin cells, is also found in the nasal mucosa as well as in the air, dust and soil*
- *Peptostreptococcus - The armpits contain many millions of bacteria per square inch, far fewer than the amount of bacteria found on the dry skin of our forearms*

These sobering thoughts brought me back to reality, and that reality was that being shot was the least of my worries; this girl was a Weapon of Ass Destruction.

I guess I was not aggressive enough; Candy put my hand on her, you know what. Then she grabbed my fingers, (as many as I let loose) and then stabbed herself with them. I closed my eyes as if I was riding Space Mountain (*Staphylococcus Epidermidis, Peptostreptococcus, clammy armpits, smelly snatch*). This ride was definitely more dangerous and going downhill fast.

Finally, the song ended and I retrieved my fingers. Now I was pissed. I had whore juice on my hands and had to wait to clean it off, hoping it did not eat the skin off my fingers. I paid Candy, and gave the takedown signal. The crew came through the door to rescue me.

I wondered *if would I be an amputee*, I need my fingers if, for no other reason, they were a matched set. I stayed by Candy, that was the kiss of death.

As it was with Judas, whomever I marked was the target for the police. They stopped the music and ran all the customers away. Candy sat down quietly after putting on her clothes. Then we heard some crashing in the backroom, and arguing, and then dragged Coco out of the backroom kicking and screaming. I was hurt; I would not have expected that of my darling Coco.

Candy was quiet, polite, and apologetic. I felt bad, had I led a decent yet stinky person to the slaughter? Did I trade a person that fell on hard times for a true Ho? I learned a lesson. We arrested Candy, and then filed all the reports with the necessary persons. I washed my hands several times over the next few days with antibacterial soap, I was never so glad they made me take a Hepatitis series of shots. I called the clinic to see if there was anything else I could get shots for, just curious if I could get an anti-STI regimen.

They said to use a condom, but wearing gloves to pick up whores probably would not work. I decided that day; when the feeling came back to my fingers that I was not going to die just to close a club. Next time I will stick a shoe in her ass, which would have accomplished the same thing, without killing me. Of course, we shut the place down and let the whore work off her charges, I dared not play that tape in court."

I leaned over smiling, "We been talking a lot about stupid crap but there are dozens of blue-idiots? I do not mean the Smurfs either, I am talking about stupid-ass cops' the world is full of them. One of the things that was actually surprising, was how many dummies wear a badge. Loads more spineless cowardly pieces of crap wear the badge, than there are, crooked ones. Crooked cops are not spineless, just dirty.

You expect a security guard to be a screw up. It turns out a whole lot of security guards are ex-cops or academy failures.

Cops and strippers are always a bad mix. Cops are cheap, greedy, egocentric people mostly, so free ass is right up their alley. Problem is that there is no such thing as free ass.

Although I have encountered some good ass for little to nothing, it was far from free, and I am lucky I can still pee standing up. As fate would have it, most strip joints would let cops in free, on or off duty. You will find that most smart crooks are friendly towards the police, why make an enemy of your enemy?"

"I guess that is why they don't want us to take free food and free rent, because it is really just a quid pro quo. People get police protection for free food. And the restaurants that charge full price rarely have cops eat there."

"Yes cops hang out where there is free stuff; they have to go somewhere. It is just the smart business that likes having cops hang out in their establishment; they tend to get robbed less. Instead of complaining, offer discounts or member cards."

"We are not supposed to show favoritism or accept favors. That is an executive order"

"Why should I hang out somewhere that costs me more to eat? Besides, aren't there sales and coupons for everything? Which way is right?

And Oh yeah, and never judge a whore by her beaver - shaved or not. There is so much more to some of them and less to others still. I met some really nice people, that fell on hard times and turned to the streets to survive. I do not know what makes them stay out there but they are not all money grubbing skanks."

7.0 STREET-LEVEL DRUG ENFORCEMENT

"To catch the bad guys, you've got to think like a bad guy - and that's why all the best detectives have a dark side..."

7.1
THE DRUG STING

"The Drug Sting was one of the most useful CI development, crime riddance tools, I have ever been a part of is the Drug Sting. Just as is to laundering money the casino, the Drug Sting is to sorting out human trash. My stupid Captain once argued that the only thing a Drug Sting did was identify junkies, how shortsighted. Demand drives the market more than supply does; of course, we need to know who the junkies are, they lead back to the traffickers. We had to remind the gold bar wearing genius, that burglary, car break-ins, pawned stolen goods, and commercial burglaries are almost the sole province of the junkie.

We did not know it then, but our brand of sting or Reverse Drug Sting as it was more appropriately called was destined for infamy. One of the things that made our style different was that unlike the bee, we stung multiple times.

- The first sting was the arrest, and that entailed the use of whatever force necessary
- Then we also took the car you drove up to the drug deal in, and the money used
- And after all this, we put your stupid face in the newspaper as a junkie

So you got your ass whooped and your crap took, what a day, what a job. What also made our cases great was that all evidence was both video and audio taped; here is how we did it.

I would walk up to the real dealer standing on the corner, and buy if I could. If they sold the drugs I gave the signal and the takedown team moved in and locked dude up for the felony. If he did not sell (but foolishly stood holding dope, or sold while I stood there), I started the ass whooping by, telling the close cover guys in the crew we had dope. I then pretended to walk away in humble junkie mode.

Once I saw the takedown team, I punched dude in the face, and then stomped the crap out of the dealer, and close cover handled his friends. Once the corner was clear, we opened the shop.

We set up the ESV (Extended Surveillance Vehicle) in a position to be innocuous, yet useful. From the ESV all videography occurred, and the 'Undercover Officer' was monitored and technically assisted. Once the ESV chief gave permission to proceed, the undercover officer exited the ESV and went out in the bush. With the phrase 'The undercover officer is in the bush,' everyone knew the undercover officers most suited to the area or type of drug, stood in the street wired, and pretended to sell dope.

Most of the street level deals were with black guys selling, so most of the time the black UCs did the undercover officer work, and the victims of their crime were mostly white. All-day, all the officers did was pretend to sell dope.

One particularly long day we were processing arrests like it was going out of style. It was so bad; we had to keep hiding the undercover officers to make the takedowns. 'Hey man was up' the UC said to the white dude in the car.

'Where Donte at?' the junkie inquired. It was not just that the junkie did not trust the UCs, the junkie also did not want to buy dope, and he had come to like the cut on Donte's dope.'

'Locked up, he violated his probation,' the UC replied. Honestly, who would not believe that a drug dealer violated his probation? 'What you need?' continued the UC. 'Junkie said let me get a $40.' 'Pull over,' the UC said, and he went into his potato chip bag and pulled out a dope pack. As soon as the junkie pulled over (Complicity shows furtherance of the crime) the takedown signal rang out over the wire.

The undercover officers stayed away from the vehicle, and on occasion, if necessary, made commentary on resisting arrest or evading arrest. If necessary, the undercover officer also narrated additional evidence or crimes occurred during the sale.

This type of operation pointed out two under-publicized facts known to Law Enforcement;

- Blacks were a major part of the problems regarding street-level sales.
- Whites are the major part of the problem regarding street-level drug usage.

"What does that mean? You saying white people use the most dope?"

"According to FBI statistics, numerically white people get arrested more for everything except murder and robberies; so yes they do more dope too.

Our job then was uniform, dare I say monotonous, ride around the city and lock up the black dealers one by one where they stood, and (not or) stand on the corner and let the whites deliver themselves to us.

The System never really talks much about the disparity; no one group is wholly to blame, but neither side wants to admit to their culpability; so screw-it we took them all. The Unit contained black, white, and female officers. Without any formal briefings or, memos, or emails (when we finally started using those); in the thousands of arrest, we completed there were no terms like niggers, spooks, honkies, crackers, cunts, or darkies thrown out, even by mistake.

Ironically, the people most responsible for the most clean arrests, use of force , apprehension of violent offenders, and servers of voluminous High Risk Warrants; are officers people often called dirty.

We filed fewer fraudulent charges, killed fewer armed and unarmed suspects, safely executed more search warrants, seized more cars and guns, served more outstanding warrants, than the 'professionals' people have come to know as Officers of the Law.

I do not know if it was because it is hard to get 12 people to agree to the same lie (although Congress and the Senate are proof this is not always the case), or maybe we were just too lazy, or maybe; we found a way to be whatever bad it took , to make good, without becoming bad.

I believe someone once said 'Blessed are the Peacemakers', the lifestyle did finally take its toll on our group, no one was unaffected."

Walter checked his phone. "No sooner than that set of idiots disappeared, another lurker pulled up. What a treat to see the baby in the car seat while daddy purchased drugs.

Amazing how fearfully the media portrays blacks, and how society maintains this mentality so that blacks are to be feared, yet whites pull up and purchase homemade chemicals, from groups of these dangerous dark-skinned ruffians. This is to maintain the lie, that the problem is not Eurocentric.

No drug problem in America is a drug problem until it affects the middle class. This is not due to racism alone, it is also business; the middle class is the tax and voter base.

On one deal, daddy of the year as he pulls up, 'Man man, quick gimme 2'

On this Day, we set up a Dilaudid corner. Different drug markets existed in different parts of the city; we always knew what the markets sold because of our Actionable Intelligence.

All of our action figures were intelligent, I joked. Want to know what the market, search the unconscious drug dealer at your feet, and see what he has in his pockets to sell - accurate, timely, intelligence.

The UC walked up to the car and noticed the baby, 'Man don't be bringing your damn baby back here in a car seat, what the hell wrong with you? You trying to get me jacked up.' The undercover officer said, informing everyone on the takedown team, that there was a baby in the car. 'Pull over man, let me get it.

'I feel lucky,' he said, as I stood right beside the car. The suspect never paid any attention. As he pulled away, the UC read his tag and gave the vehicle description. The UC also repeated the details of the agreed upon transaction so there was a concise record of what the suspect asked for, what money if any shown, etc. Consequently, there was evidence for both the civil and the criminal processes.

Daddy-dearest had his arm already ready, sleeve rolled up, in the ashtray area, a charged needle, awaiting the pill, and in the syringe, with a solution containing a little blood already within.

This piece of crap was back for seconds, had already shot up his low-grade Heroin, with a baby on board, driving high, and back for more. He was putting on his tourniquet when takedown moved in; another great photo for the family album.

After Daddy-dearest, there was a white chick; this one had a nice set of tits that were struggling to stay in her shirt. The rules said I could not ask for sex, but she could offer; I fully intended to breastfeed as part of this transaction. I mean, they were not skim or 2%, no buttermilk or cottage cheese, these were Acidophilus plus. The dipstick driving, at least had good taste in tits. I tried to be professional, but all I could think about was dipping them in my cereal every morning, both of them so I could have a balanced breakfast.

Dipstick, hollered (motioned to) one of the other undercover officers, probably because he was not used to seeing his dope dealers with a full-grown erection, drooling over his junkie girlfriends tits; screw him he's a junkie, who do they complain to?

'Hey baby,' she said, all I could think was, *come over here Fruit Loops, I'll serve you.* 'Come here,' she continued, 'Can I talk to you?'

That is street talk for can we make sometime of arrangement. I could not hear exactly what she said; I was tuned into WSM-ilk, broadcasting in stereo. All I do remember is the takedown signal ringing out and then they were in custody.

The arrangement; One $40 pill for her Teddy bear, $20 and a solemn (milk filled) promise to return another day with the additional money. Two adults and a car seized for a teddy bear's worth of dope. People would rather live in a community with unreasonable claims, than face loneliness with their truth." Even teddy bears have value."

7.2 Buy Busts

"What's your first buy-bust memory?" Walters asked eagerly. *I guess my stories were not so boring after all.*

"I pulled up to a corner, notorious for Dilaudid sales. As fate would have it, there was a prime target standing out selling to another drug using, piece of white trash. We could not refer to people in terms of color, so we made nicknames about them. Whites were Marshmallows, Blacks were Homies and Mexicans; well hell were just Mexicans.

As I drove towards him, I held up four fingers, which was Dilaudid slang for 'K-4' Dilaudid. Dude nodded in agreement. I pulled up and asked dude if he had any?

He said, 'No.' I asked him if he had Cocaine.

He said, 'No, again.' People may not know this but dope dealers reserve the right to not serve dope to anyone they get a funny feeling about. I then asked him if he had weed and again he said no. I had dealt with and heard tales of stupid people before and I had meddled with several in my time as a cop. This idiot was the poster child for stupid crap everywhere.

I replied, 'Then what do you have in your hand, gimme $20 worth of whatever the crap you are selling.'

Like the stupid jerk he was, he held his hand behind his back like a child and shook his head to say no.

Unlike licensed establishments who reserve the right to refuse service, I maintained the right not to be refused. I simply punched the soon to be felon in the face, and picked up the bag of pills he held behind his back. Now he had a busted lip to match his busted bag. We loaded him into a car and took him to staging.

One of the things we did for officer safety was not to stay in the area where the last kidnapping occurred. Once the deal occurred, and all the suspects and vocal supporters apprehended, we moved to a location nearby, yet safe to search them properly and do paperwork. This is what made us so productive, the division of labor. Whoever handled transport also handled searching and securing prisoners, as well as filling out the arrest report.

Someone handled property, another affidavit, and another, usually, the case officer wrote a brief synopsis on the case folder. When it was time to prosecute, since anyone can prosecute a felony, a team went to booking with the file and handled the case, while the transport officer dropped the prisoner and returned to the scene.

"Vice sounded cool."

"It was a different world from uniformed services. The uniform carries with it distinguishable authority, which means people know you are a cop. This affords a wealth of safety because hurting cops is just bad for business. In the non-uniformed world; there were no uniforms, no rules, just a mission- make the city safe. That was the world I wanted to live in, a place where you had to think, and there was always danger. That was a place where all my dark traits (violence, lying, deceitfulness, envy, unforgiveness, hatred, insecurity) became strengths. There, in the alternate universe codenamed: 'The Streets', where all that was wrong with me, made me great. All warfare is based on deception."

7.3 'Arr' Robbery

"We had more time, so I regaled him with more tales. I watched Peter Pan a dozen times but I could not believe that Griff was getting robbed by a guy with a pirate gun. Buy-bust is dangerous, especially when you buy from juveniles. Griff handed the kid the $20 trying hard to quell the foolish thought to go for his gun. 'Do not shoot me, man, here!' he said.

Cops pretend not to fear, but two things frightened me at this point. Firstly, the butthole had a pirate gun in Griff's face. It looked fake, but damn it would hurt and be embarrassing to get killed by Captain Hook.

Secondly, this was a juvenile and those little bastards actually would try. Griff did the next best thing; Griff let my crew know the guy was robbing him. Captain Hook had no idea what was about to descend on him…momentarily. As soon as Hook got the money, he started to walk away. Griff pulled the radio out, 'Male black, Christmas shoes, down jacket, and pirate gun,' sounded over the radio. Griff pulled out of the area to await the good news.

The news came quickly, it was not the good news Griff wanted, but we did catch Captain Hook. Griff hoped for a firing squad, but dude got a first-rate ass whooping. As Griff pulled up, Griff heard for the first time what came to be one of my favorite police related-lines, 'Beat his eyes shut!'

When the adjustments were complete, Hook needed a hook on his broken hand. We called MED-COM and transported him to a safe place. However, the bad guys should never feel safe around the police. After Griff recomposed himself it was back to buy bust for our diligent little band of marauders.

"I thought y'all want to shoot the crap out of everyone, sounds like a wasted chance, why they hell didn't y'all shoot him?"

"You miss what I am saying. Shooting people; especially kids, is not the mission; but it also cannot be an obstacle. Do not be afraid to kill; on the contrary be afraid not to protect life. Even at that, never kill if you do not have to. That is what training is for; to teach you when to kill, and it is different depending on skill. This was a violent encounter however: We used violence to resolve the problem without killing the thieving little bastard. It is not that he did not need killing or deserve to die; being professional means exhausting all reasonable means to apprehend someone, even though the human in you said set them on fire. I could have killed one almost every week, but then that would mean I was both afraid and incapable or controlling the situation. I was a part of the situation; we decided not to kill him. But I bet that's just one more story the media, and pissed off people will never tell you. It's weird but it is not the chains of some tyrant that robs us of freedom. Rather, it is the staleness of our attitude."

"Why did you refer to it as violence, not force?"

"Because if I said force, you would assume there was a box on the Use of Force form which covered what we did. Whooped his ass, is not on the form, but it damn sure should be. If we went by the book and the boxes, Dumb-ass-the-Pirate would be dead. How in the hell is an ass whooping worse than death?"

"But if we can kill someone justifiably?"

"Brother, don't kill no one you don't have to. There are so many things you can do to avoid killing people most of the time; but it takes timing and skill. I am not saying not force may be required, what I am saying is if you go ahead and knock a son-bitch out soon enough he won't need killing because he will be snoring. I believe often times waiting too late to go hands on leads to needless interactions."

7.4 Shotgun In Belly

"Buy bust was an adventure every 10 minutes. Perhaps 10 is stretching it, make it 30 minutes. All we did was go from dealer to dealer, lock them up, process paperwork, throw them in a transport vehicle and kept going. If you happened to be the first victim of the night, you were in for a long evening. We pulled down into the Edge Meade area. I knew this area well; it was part of my zone when I was on Walking Patrol. We pulled in the area we knew had the highest drug sales and I pulled over to the side of the street to holler at a fellow.

'What's up! You got some work?' Ironically, drug sellers have morphed the word work to cover their illicit lifestyles.

'Naw man, Fat Steve gat it,' he replied. I knew of Fat Steve, so I parked, got out, and walked around to the house.

More than anybody else in the unit, I got out of the car to buy dope. I did this for several reasons. We had to wear our vests to buy dope, it was a unit rule. We had a good supervisor and he tried hard to keep us safe. The vest worked well unless the person was standing higher and you were sitting in the car. The problem is that the bullet would most likely skip off the vest and down into your lap or the floor. If it landed in your lap that means it will strike the pelvic girdle or the Femoral Artery.

One was certain immobilization and severe damage, to the other, certain death. Rather than sit in the potential casket, I opted to get out and stand up facing my foe. I prefer a shot to the midsection, hand to hand, or even the potential to return fire than just driving away (again putting my back to the suspect with no cover). Tonight, more than any other in my dope-buying career, I would have the chance to try my theory.

I walked up to Fat Steve; he was leaning on a cane or stick. When I got close enough, I realized it was not a stick at all. I realized it was a single barrel shotgun when he stuck it in my stomach. Boy, it was at that point that I realized how dark it actually was in the alley behind his house. I realized how quiet night was, and how loud the people around us laughed. I looked around and wondered *would they help if he shot me, or pick over me like vultures*."

"What; did you just give up?" Walters asked sincerely.

"No, reality kicked in, Hollywood is the only place you are guaranteed to survive a shotgun blast to the belly," I replied. "I also realized a whole in my survival theory, a rather large hole, namely the space beneath my vest and my belt. Not saying that the groin had any protection, but heretofore I considered attacks from handguns and knives, I did not think anyone would be standing out in the street with a shotgun; they are usually difficult to conceal.

This fat bastard stood finger on the trigger with his shotgun in my gut, pressed just below my vest. The second ignorant ass thought entering my head was to go for my gun. I am not sure how much intestinal fortitude it requires to fire a pistol, but I am sure that once he discharged his shotgun into my stomach I would be missing whatever intestines I needed to shoot back. All I could do was think, the *takedown team was close, but if they rushed in and engaged, I would have been either dead or a hostage, and they risked injury.* I liked neither of those choices.

I chose the only option, I said to the fat pig, 'Man you going to shoot me or sell me some dope?' I was not sure if the message got through, until I saw my team trying to sneak up on the stick. I continued, 'Man take the shotgun out my belly and I will leave, screw the dope.' Then I saw the cavalry turn around and tactically regroup. The message got through; they knew now that the bastard had a long gun and an undetermined amount of ammo. I was alone again, but I did not let my teammates run into what is still considered one of the best weapons in the world for close-quarters shooting.

Fat boy then did something I did not expect, he asked what I wanted. To which I replied a twenty, meaning $20 worth of Crack. He broke out his Pack of dope and then sold me a large white rock substance. I turned and walked away. As I walked away, I reminded the takedown crew that he was standing with a rifle in his hand. This meant something to sensible police officers. I saw them turn around and go back to the cars. I knew what it meant and looked for cover. Because the team valued lives, especially (our own) we planned to make an arrest but prepared to be a firing squad.

This is part of the issue; the bad guy that people do not read about on the news when they bitch about brutality and excessive force. Men who trained with SWAT for years developed my crew and had the mindset, catch them if you can, hurt them if you need to, kill them if you must.

As with all encounters with the real police, the bad guy chooses which bed of three he sleeps in; jail, hospital, morgue. This eventually also meant that the squad reconfigured. As each had talents, we left the tactical crap to those with the skill, I am good, but some on the team were better at this type of tactical crap.

They surrounded fat boy and gave him his options. It turns out, he had walking sense, and he lived to tell another day. Instead of death, he found himself a CI, retaining all his teeth and mental faculties. We could have killed so many and they would have all been righteous kills, but for as much as we kicked ass, we did not take any more than we had to. That fat fool lived to eat another day.

"What is armor after all but a cage that moves with you? Another chance forfeited?" I smiled at him warmly.

7.5 Kid-Napped?

"Sometimes the boss was kind of a dick; he was too mission-oriented. Sometimes, people just cannot see the danger until the crocodile bites them in the ass. There were those of us in the unit who did not mind stomping a new butthole into people. Then others of us never seemed to make it to the takedown on time; Ever! One thing I learned from being in the buy car is how long the period is between the buy and the takedown. There is no excuse in the world for not busting your ass to make it to the takedown.

White people are 100 times more likely to be robbed during a dope deal, so when we went out we took special care to avoid situations when the natives were stacked too deep for us to safely extract the undercover officers. This was one of the innovative tactics this unit used, blending whites, and blacks. The white boys also had close cover, because it was easier to get the black officers in to hide nearby.

We wired up Griff and sent him out to face the dragon. We pulled into a black neighborhood commonly known for drug dealing (commonly called a crap neighborhood) and the game begun. The true hunters put the prey out for the jackals to crave. Griff pulled in and parked; the jackals took notice, they popped their empty little heads up to see the prey. When the jackals perked up to look at the prey, they made themselves known to the hunters. Some of the jackals looked around nervously; many of them had already learned that there were no free meals. Griff parked in front of a group of particularly ambitious jackals huddled near the mouth of their cave. Why the hell Griff pulled up to a group of 6 guys in masks, and big down jackets is beyond human understanding.

As soon as me and Tommy saw this idiot pull up to the Terror Dome we jumped out of our cars running and hollering. Sometimes, when the jackals are quick, they can take a few well-placed bites out of the prey before we can save it. These jackals had that in mind. Seeing the police running towards them they simply welcomed the new meal into their cave and closed the door to the breezeway behind Griff.

My heart sank, I was sure that was the last time I was going to see Griff breathing and in one piece. I thought of all the things they could do to him before we could save him. I wondered what type of funeral he would have (a least he was skinny and would be easy to carry in a wee little box.

We reached the mouth of the cave and Tommy pulled it open as we entered their lair guns drawn. It was worse than we feared, these were not jackals, and they must have been piranhas. Griff was gone, no bones, no carcass, nothing, only guns and dope flying around the breezeway like tumbleweeds.

Everything switched to slow motion, breathing, heart rate, words, and most of all time. I am sure we only stood motionless for a few seconds, but when your partner vanishes, that time wondering where he is feels an eternity. Griff and I were not that close, but he was family, he was my responsibility; he was in harm's way. I felt like crap, because I failed to keep brother Griff safe, someone had to pay, I guess we would be going Dutch since I screwed up, he was nowhere to be found. There simply was no more Griff.

The rest of the squad finally caught up, there we stood, a hand full of cops, dressed to kill, with no one to kill and no one to rescue. This was definitely one of the crappier days for me on the job and my first UFO abduction. That was the only thing that would account for the disappearance of Griff. Somebody had a wire radio in their hand. I breathed again, on the wire, as could be heard the voice of Griff and another dude.

I assumed the other person was humanoid, but where was the spaceship? We started to holler for Griff. He responded, but only in code. We knew then that it was not abduction, just a regular kidnapping. So we kept calling Griff, hoping his dumbass would figure out that we were looking for him, and reappear.

No luck, he stayed invisible. We went back to square one; knocking on doors in the breezeway. We knocked and Griff would say, 'Not it.' After knocking on half the doors, we finally got him to say, 'That's the one.'

Not knowing what situation lay behind the door, we knocked until someone answered. Just as we were about to kick the creature's ass all the way back into the Twilight Zone Griff said, 'Do not kill him he was trying to save me.' At this statement, we all stopped and looked, even the kidnapper sat down to listen. It was story time, we all had to hear this crap.

Griff began his story, 'I walked into the breezeway, and as soon as I did, he told me to come inside his apartment. I thought he was going to hook me up until he pulled out a gun and closed the door. He then told me to sit down and explained to me that they were going to rob me and he was trying to help me out. He understood that I just needed some dope, but continued to tell me that I should not take such chances, these guys were dangerous. He looked out the peephole periodically to make sure they were gone, but each time he did he pointed his gun at me while he was talking. He did not think about what he was doing, it was just in his hand when he was talking...the innocent.'

"That being the case, we took his gun, thanked him, and went about our business. Even though the dude was trying to help, he was trying to help a junkie so he was still part of the problem."

"So are the junkies the enemy too?"

"They are part of the problem, but they are more collateral damage than the enemy. The adage of justice is about guilty and innocent; the police are more often tasked with judging and controlling the stupid.

If people were employed at creating heaven on earth, everybody would be happy; instead each one is creating his own heaven by creating hell for others."

"And when they don't listen?"

"Call me."

7.6 What Kind Of Tactics Are Those?

"One day, we got a complaint about drug dealing going on at the Stuy Inn. The way this scenario worked was that dealers rented crappy rooms at crappier motels and sold dope there. That way if they got busted they only lost what was inside the room and the cops still did not know where they lived. This method was also a good way to stay near your target audience, so less chance of getting stopped in transit and losing the load. It was also a good way to maintain a healthy supply of whores, thereby increasing your profit margin.

My cousin wanted to ride with me this date, he wanted to see what the real police actually did. We walked up to the room. It was me, two other cops and my cousin. We approached two guys on foot and one of my partners dealt with them. We knocked on the door and got no answer at first. The clerk wanted the dude gone so after we knocked a while he assisted us entering the room. Upon entry, the suspect was asleep. I walked up to the bed and tapped on the bed a few times calling out to the suspect. I tapped the bed because most men react harshly to waking up to another grown man standing at their bedside; also, the bad guy could easily have a gun.

Dude looked at me and at my raid vest (Outer shell clearly marked with police patches and a badge.), then went back to sleep. I woke the dude again and told him to stand up. It took him a few moments to get right then he scooted to the end of the bed. Once at the foot of the bed, the suspect tried to grab something out of a bag at the floor of the bed, well the dance began. Despite Adrenalin and foolhardiness, I moved the bag first before kicking the crap out of the dude.

Common sense is a major part of tactics, only an ass tries to fight a man with a gun, so I had a choice; kick him, or move whatever he was after out of his reach. Since bonehead had gone to the next level, I joined him. I snatched the dude off the bed and pushed him to the floor and my partner checked his bag. There was no gun, so I eased up a bit. I told the idiot to stand up at which point he came up swinging. Game on.

As the suspect kicked at me I grabbed his leg and dragged him by it into the open areas of the room so we could finish our dance. The suspect was game. I punched him twice and pulled him back. He re-engaged with another kick. This time I dragged him out of the room by his foot. The suspect kept trying to punch me but kept missing just off to the right side. It was not until my cousin shouted; 'He's going for your gun!' that I realized what he was trying. I was not concerned because I had on a thigh holster, but now I realized that this little piggy wanted to go to the market. We were on the second floor, and the market was on the first floor. So I decided to make this little piggy go wee, wee, wee. I grabbed dumbass and shoved him over the railing.

Surprisingly as he flailed over the rail he was able to grab hold of my vest, and off to the market, I went too.

The suspect landed on the sidewalk, I landed head first in the hedge, it was an ugly green bush, but I was glad it was there or else my big ass head would have been a manhole cover. By now, my slow ass partner engaged, after running down the stairs. He tried to grab the dude as I climbed out of the prickly hedge.

The suspect broke free from my partner and ran. I chased him as I spit leaves out my mouth. I caught the suspect and tackled him. He was really strong and fighting hard. I rolled him over, tied him up in a full nelson, and grabbed his legs. So here we were, two grown men. Both of us on our backs, him sprawled open awaiting my partner's arrival. This was the first and only time I used the position and technique I called the Turtle. That is what this fool looked like on his back, belly exposed. My partner straddled him and commenced punching the fool.

After my partner dropped about 20 dum-dums (we called punches that because when applied correctly this is the way you act afterward) on him, I rolled him over to cuff him. This idiot still fought. I got one hand into a cuff and we kneeled in the parking of wrestling. During the scuffle the suspect bit my hand. His mistake; I bit the back of his neck near the Juguler and drew blood. It was like the Cujo and his idiot cousin out in that parking lot.

After the suspect stopped screaming, I stopped biting; or vice versa. I proned dude out and spread his cuffed hand out beside him. I administered several elbows to the head area slamming his face into the pavement, which at least got him to shut the heck up. It was not until I used his head as a battering ram against a brick wall did he stop fighting.

With all the fighting, my other partner had pulled his gun out on the other two guys from the room. We fought so hard he actually called my cousin over to him, gave him his gun, and told him to watch the other two guys. I am not sure who was more frightened the guy or my cousin. Fortunately, the guys did not move, cause I sure my cousin would have at least shot at them.

With help from the third officer, we were able to handcuff the idiot. We took him to the hospital and booked him afterward. It was not until we testified at booking that dude said he realized we were cops, he said he had a bad trip of angel dust and thought we were aliens coming to abduct him.

Funnily, the night court judge asked him if he thought Aliens usually dressed as Police from the Planet Earth as part of the abduction. He replied he did not know; after all, this was his first abduction. I would have laughed, but the night court judge laughed first, 'Sounds to me like jail is the best place for you, surely they won't break into a jail to abduct you, with all those guards.' He doubled the bond and I walked away laughing. Everyone that craps on you is not your enemy, and everyone that says they are going to help is not your friend."

7.7 Police; Search Warrant

Walters asked, "So did you ever cross the line or do something jacked up?" Fair questions since I held him hostage with my stories.

"Kicking around piles of crap never bothered me, I never locked up anyone innocent, but there was one thing that always bothered me. I never really thought about it at first, but it stayed on my mind. Probably the worst thing I ever did went unnoticed even by me for a long time. We used a CI and made a drug purchase. Within the requisite 72 hours, we got the search warrant signed and made ready for the entry. For what is sure to be the fastest search warrant in history, we made ready. SOP (standard operating procedure) type operation, requiring pre-raid surveillance, photographs, and all the safety devices we could carry.

We loaded up in the raid van and made our way to the target. Upon arrival, we open the flood doors of doom, and we sent in the clowns. We kicked the door off the hinges, and belled, 'Police Search warrant!' as we swarmed the location.

Once clear, we gathered near the center of the clean, but dark arid location. The only person we located was an older black female. She was lying on white sheets and weighed less than 100 lbs. As we proceeded to explain to her why we were there, she said, 'Do not come any closer, I'm dying of AIDs!' We left the warrant on the table, did not search, tried to repair the door frame, and then did a HAZMAT assessment of the location. It was funny at the time, but as I looked back on it over the years, we erred, I erred.

- Someone was selling dope out of her location, assumedly without her consent
- We kicked her door off the hinges, there was no way she could defend herself against intruders
- We never asked or offered her any help

- We laughed off her condition

Of all the crappy things, I am actually guilty of doing; this was the thing I was least proud of. In a career dedicated to helping, I failed to help one of the people I encountered, that I needed the most help, yet simply chose not to. I hope that this one thing does not overshadow all the good I did, but much of the pride over my accomplishments wanes.

I faced many people more dangerous and eviler than her but not many needier. I failed her because I could not conquer my own fear. I might survive stabbing or gunshot wounds, but who survives AIDs. I survived TB, and over my career would survive many more dangers; some foes you simply have to retreat from unless you are willing to pay the cost. That day, that fight, I was not ready for; for that, I am ashamed."

"Ever hit the wrong house with a search warrant? Ever forget to knock?"

"Yes and no. I have been on dozens of no-knock search warrants. All that means is that you don't have to knock, announce and then breach. The law has always required announcing. But the normal warrant requires cops to wait a 'reasonable amount or time for a person to answer the door' prior to entry. We normally used marked vehicles and the PA system to announce, that way even the neighbors will have to report that they knew that we were police because of the police car saying, Police: search warrant, do not resist. In regards to hitting the wrong house, well anytime you rely on second hand information from CI's and you have dealers that hang out in people's houses and sell dope to keep their homes safe, there will be mistakes made. Fortunately, my crew did a better job of quality control than most. Even at that, we hit the wrong door a few times. We fortunately ended up only having to replace the doors. I believe the marked car helped us as well, taking the time to use the equipment and training saves lives, even when mistakes are made. It changed me, it defined for me how easy it is to judge rightly after one sees what evil comes from judging wrongly."

7.8 25th and Overland

"Every new day met us with the same assignment, drive through the city and target every and anyone selling, buying or peddling drugs or snatch on the street. Little known fact; we spent thousands of man-hours in the black neighborhoods, not because of racism or discrimination, but because the National Black Caucus petitioned the government for help. Search American history. When settlers finally reach out for assistance with problems in their neighborhood the government responds with Problem-Solving Force. The NBC went to the Government and said they were tired of the tumult in the black neighborhoods resulting from drive shootings, vehicle pursuits, and drug sales.

The NBC did not go to them with the argument that no black people own planes, maybe they understood more about the Heroin trade and trafficking in the black community than this new generation, characterized by both access to more information, and use of less common sense. The NBC said we just want it stopped; they did not recommend leniency. Due to efforts by the NBC sentencing for Crack-Cocaine trafficking carried a penalty three times greater than the trafficking of Cocaine Powder. NBC called the Government and the Government sent us.

In the same manner in which the Patriot Act broadened powers after 911, The Office of National Drug Control Policy issued sweeping mandates against the crack trade. The government did not send the regular police, because they respond to a problem as Public servants. The response from the settlers' request was to send George Armstrong Custer, and hell that rode in with him.

Every day we saddled the ponies, strapped on guns; and then it was time to ride the plains again. Like the cowboys of old, we rode until we saw signs of hostiles. Dead bodies, fires, whore, and of course white people lingering around. The only thing as reliable as the Native (black) crack-head was the Junkie (white). Follow the trail of either and you would find real dope. We rolled down the plains until we ran up on the signs. The signs led us to a native, standing in the street serving a junkie. We did not need intelligence reports or field tests; we were looking at both.

We pulled down the street. I was driving. I pulled up and I looked at this man and it was obvious what he was doing but I had to ask anyway I said, 'Hey man let me get a 20 man' he said '20 of what?' 'Ready.' That's why people called crack ready because it's ready to use right then you do not have to cook it cut it short you just pop it in pipe and smoke) he said let me see your money' Same time I replied, same time. This did two things. One; it let my team know what part of the transaction we were in, we were almost done. Two; It also let them know that I was safe.

Once he supplied the crack, I started asking him for a phone number. This information let my team know the deed was done, without ever changing my interaction with the guy. 'I feel lucky,' I had dope, and so they came a whooping and hollering over the hillside like banshees out of hell. Something was different this time this time, this time the native did not run, did not flinch doing not blush. This time the native stood up, bore his chest, and just waited.

When you are used to chasing pray, something is unnerving when you encounter pray that will not run. Tommy got to him first. He grabbed our prey and everything looked fine until the prey grabbed him back. This was the first time and one of the only times when we watched one of our teammates thrown bodily down the street. I do not mean running fast or driving fast I mean the prey picked up the officer and literally threw him over his head down the street.

What does the lion do when the antelope knocks him down? Like any self-respecting other lion pride, we sent in more lions. This did not yield much better results, more antelope wrestling. More lions entered the fray against this one Antelope. As we took turns stomping the stripes off his four-legged ass, I thought, *this bastard would be a great addition to the team.* Alas; however, they did not send us to save, but to destroy the unsavory element; unfortunately; today, that meant him.

If this were an episode of Adam West's Batman, the sounds would be; TWACK, THUD, WHACK, and of course a whole bunch of HOLY CRAP BATMAN(s). This was not TV. Most of the crap inside the human body makes no noise when destroyed. There is a little-explored fact among 'civilized men'; anyone can be broken if beaten long enough. Severity in a beating can come from either veracity or endurance; this monster got a Gold Medal in both. We tagged out on him until we got tired, and stupid kept going.

Nearing the end of the ordeal (mainly because we were getting tired and frustrated), Custer put his weapon against Mr. Antelope's temple, 'Quit before I kill you,' was all he said. Mr. Antelope looked up at him from all fours where he was held hostage by the kicks of several of us and calmly said, 'Ok.' How perfectly gentlemanly of him, to agree to stop fighting, stop selling dope for the moment and accompany us to jail, by route of the City Hospital. If all our prey was this acquiescent, what a wonderful world this would be. Fortunately, for my macabre side, the world was full of trash and buttholes, fodder for the Calvary.

By this time, the natives were gathering, and the smoke signals were rising. Somewhere on the prairie, another butthole was being encouraged to stop selling dope. As the crowd gathered, it was apparent medical attention was required, not because it was needed but because it appeared to be needed. We called the ambulance because of the amount of effort put into bringing down Mr. Antelope. He fought more like Water Buffalo; his resistance warranted a medical response.

Actually, we should have constructed a hospital around dumbass, as much injury was intended. Mr. Antelope, however, just sat calmly in handcuffs, not sweating or out of breath, just waiting. Walters asked, 'What the crap was he waiting for his medal? Was he waiting for the ambulance or the public outcry?' No; he was waiting for his high to wear off, only then would the reality of what he endured kick in. I am not sure how much of his product he consumed or how long before meeting us, but he was a great advertisement for the potency of his crack.

Cocaine has a short life in the body and can be counteracted easily. Turns out a few hundred lion strikes was enough to screw up a good high. We got Mr. Antelope into the ambulance just as he crashed. Boy, there was a delayed reaction to the amount of force required to subdue him. He thrashed back and forth, and in my mind and maybe his, it looked like his body was reliving the 17 minutes prior when our feet were chin deep in his ribs. Then the time to be concerned arose. Notice I did not say worry.

Mr. Antelope fought hard and well, he made a lot of noise and so did we. It was obvious that we could not control him, that is why you got to remember to give verbal commands, for both the suspect and the witnesses. His face did not look too bad considering. No telling what the x-rays would say. As they drove him away, we stood and watched, both in anger, a little out of respect.

"Man sounds like y'all beat the hell out of a lot of people. That would never go over nowadays. People will not tolerate that type of policing anymore. They have too many rights now."

I reclined and stretched my knees, "News flash champ, they always had rights, we just cared more about the rights of the victims. I can live with every tooth I knocked out of bad guys' mouths because I never was afraid to stand between them and the innocent."

"Fear is not the same as using common sense. People don't want to live in fear of the police."

"I understand, believe me, it would make sense to cage the dogs when the work was done. Ask yourself if the amount of violence has changed since they decide to render the police toothless. Black lives do matter, all black lives. I just choose to focus more on the violence against blacks that does not involve the police. I wager far more people are killed by members of their own race, than the police ever have, man they blew the guy up in Dallas, he was black."

"Yeah but he was protesting police violence?"

"How many of those officers that he shot committed said name violence? Do not tell me that murder and violence should be condemned and then murder someone else, especially against those who are paid very little to protect the peace. That day was a good day to remember, to be reminded; anything in the jungle can be killed-even those claiming to be king."

7.9 Skeletons In The Closet

"We were definitely a squared-away team, but if you push any machine too hard, the strain will affect its effectiveness. The tempo we operated at was not human; it was insane. At one point, we were doing an average of 4 Dynamic entries per day. About half of our team was SWAT; this made it safer for everybody. One of our team leaders was a little fellow, but he meant well, and he took great pride in not having to hurt people needlessly, he was a true believer in using Special Weapons and Tactics to make a clean mission.

To be clear, the Dynamic Entry is defined as a tactic where surprise, speed, and domination are key. The dynamic entry is generally the fastest option for clearing large threats. The advantage of this style of dynamic entry is that it provides speed through the objective, especially when the location of your adversary is unknown. Speed in the dynamic entry, buys you surprise, and surprise allows you to neutralize your threat before he engages you. Vital to the Dynamic entry are two principles:

- Do not move faster than you can shoot.
- Overwhelm and dominate once inside the stronghold.

The other type of entry is the Deliberate Entry (Slow-Clear). The deliberate entry uses the same basic principles as the dynamic entry, but the tempo is much slower. The slower tempo is used when there are innocents, like babies known to be in the house or if it is barricaded. Hell, we did so many High-Risk entries, SWAT changed policies and procedures to keep up with us. We were definitely in harm's way. With my group, however, it was more like demonic entry than dynamic entry. We kicked doors off the hinges, set curtains on fire, blew fish tanks up, set a few people on fire (by mistake of course), and on occasion completely obliterated a colostomy bag, but we did all of this so we did not have to kill people.

I am sure if you interview the people we put our hands on, 100% of them would say they wish they had never met my team, 100% of them would also say they did not like the ass whooping, but would rather be alive. Violence; used properly, can save lives this may sound insane to you, but my team is responsible for thousands of arrests 99% probably resulted in violence but we do not have to kill 98.00 percent of those arrested.

After the door hit the ground, that little SWAT bastard went through first. He was about the same height as a hedgehog and twice as mean. He always entered first, because we trusted him to get us to the target and back safely. The little SWAT bastard could not buy dope or women for crap, but we put him on the end of a long-gun; wound him up and let him go each time; He brought back people to us, safely each time. Since we did so many warrants, people acclimated to certain things. Today was no different.

We entered the house, tore the doors off the hinges, and slapped the crap out of all therein. We planned the entry to ensure that the target of the warrant was home. It does no good to only torture the loved ones, when the head butthole, is away. The best way to make an impression is to do it in front of his family, piss his wife and kids off, go through his phone, and find pictures of other ho(s); you know turn his life into a liquid crap-pile. Taking dudes dope - good, his furniture - better, his money - best; his peace at home - HOME RUN.

Anyone that disturbs society's peace deserves none of their own. Dick-cheese was at home, so we had a long talk with him. There is a distinction between talking and torture; torture means the cuffs are on, talking means they are off. Either way, you kick their ass, but we spent most of our time talking, not torturing. Therefore, Mr. Cheese, where the dope we talked repeatedly about each time, we got no salient answer.

This went on for a while; it was not like we were just going to let him go anyway. As we sat still talking, one of my team members made a peculiar noise, then remarked, 'Hold on!' He got up, walked over to the open door, and moved the frame. When he moved the doorframe, everybody's heart, and balls dropped, well maybe not everybody, Mr. Cheese probably felt relief.

Mr. Cheese was the only one in the room that had any sense of relief because he thought he was safe. For a second; a nanosecond, he was safe because we were too surprised to move. This was not a door frame, it was a closet door, and if there is a closet door, there is a closet. If there is a closet, there is usually something in the closet. Well damn, when we opened the closet, we found the dope; it was on the floor between a guy's legs. Also beside the dope was a dismantled pistol.

The fact of the matter was that, while the dude was inside listening to all the talking, he had time to decide whether to come out shooting or to make himself as harmless as possible; fortunately, he chose the latter.

We were so distraught by the discovery, we allowed him to walk out of the closet and surrender himself, the weapon and the dope. When asked why he did not come out shooting, he said, 'Man I heard what y'all was doing just to find the dope, what would y'all have done to me if I came out with a gun?' We completed the warrant and the arrest without further incident, and with very little talking.

I went home, it was a very long drive, not because of distance, but because I had a very vivid lesson in complacency; a lesson that I never wanted to repeat. At the same time, he also reinforced the effectiveness of violence of actions and the usefulness of fear. Skill did not protect us this night, fear did.

We tried to laugh it off the next day, but there was nothing funny about the incident; except everyone's face when we opened the door. Instead of a circle jerk, this was a poop-face circle. He looked like a kid, sitting on the floor with his knees up and his face in his hands. Maybe he was trying to turn invisible; I sure would have tried. However, he had the best seat in the house; no harm came to him that evening. That was our way of honoring the fact that it could have easily gone the other way. Dude was smart; never interrupt your enemy when he is making a mistake?"

7.10 Is That Dirty?

We had time for more laughs so I continued my stories. "Eating lunch as a team was always a nightmare. 'Just how damn stupid are you?' I asked Hog Jaws. 'Exactly what is this crap we are eating?' 'It's Indian food,' he replied. 'Ok, I replied there are so many things wrong with that. First off, I am not a damn Indian. Secondly, this tastes like bonafide cow ass.' 'It's curried beef,' Hog jaws replied. 'Horse crap! I have eaten beef before and I never tasted or looked like this. And, why in the world would you buy beef from people that do not eat meat. How the hell do they decide what part of the 3000 pound steak, walking down the street will they serve other people?' I asked? 'I did not order Curry anyway.' 'Oh, I think I gave you mine by mistake, sorry.' He swapped food with me, 'This looks even worse!' I said. 'What is this, charbroiled butthole? I only ask because this tastes like crap.'

I guess that upset him because he started arguing with me. I am still unsure as to why you get upset when someone points out that he took their money and opted to purchase something for himself, he knew I did not want, but I guess that is why I have no friends.

Fortunately, blue lights drove by, chasing a car. *Thank God*, I thought; an escape. 'But someone owes me for this horse crap we just got.' We ran out to our cars and jumped in like the Dukes of Hazard. I am sure Hog jaws would have liked to slide across the hood like on TV, but he could not get his fat ass up in the air that high. I am unsure if the hood was designed to withstand that much weight anyway. I got stuck with Hog jaws. The Little sports car we rode in had flip-up headlights. He unlocked the door and I jumped in the car, without looking. A nasty smell came from my now wet ass. This ignorant fool put his spit cup in the seat. Now I smelled like mint Skoal chewing tobacco. I would have punched him, but by now we were flying through the city in the pursuit. 'Turn your headlights on,' I said angrily, 'Otherwise we look like a UFO, not a cop car, just blue lights floating along the city street; a great way to cause a car crash.'

We chased the car for miles. We were not even sure why we were chasing the guy car or who we were chasing. When there was an ass to be had, everybody tried to get a piece. I know you know, you aren't supposed to beat a prisoner in handcuffs, there is no honor in it, but as long as they are fighting and unrestrained, it's open season.'

"The Blue Melee?"

"The Blue Melee always used to follow pursuits. Like any other swarm, the melee allowed the pack, group, tribe, or whatever you call it, to get as many strikes in. The person who was inevitably blamed for injures was the arresting officer, or the officer initiating the pursuit on the radio. Remember," I cautioned, "It's your prisoner, whether you do it, or watch it done.

When I came on the job, EMTs and Paramedics were not bleeding hearts. Police, Medical and Fire all sort of worked together on the same sheet of music. They were interested in helping the innocent; to hell with the guilty or annoying. If you fought the police, no one took pity on you. Doctors never really asked questions, they did not want the police to have to lie. How else can you explain why dudes ears are missing, unless you lie?"

Even he smirked at my last comment, but I could tell he was not sold on the idea.

7.11 The Contract

"The story about the chicken crossing the road is a multi-generational limerick. What people misunderstand is that this must have been some badass chicken because we still talk about him.

Why did the police kick in 12 doors in two days? Cause some idiot lost his mind and put a contract out on a cop: one of my cops; one of my family. Many young upstarts threaten to put contracts on cops, but this one was real. Ironically, the contract was for 12 grand, and we kicked in 12 doors. I guess dumbass paid $1000 dollars per house we hit with one search warrant. One day, another stupid chicken decided to cross the road.

Hog Jaws was a butthole, a second rate butthole. First-rate buttholes intend to be buttholes. Second raters do not mean to be butthole, yet achieve butthole status nonetheless. Regardless, Hog Jaws was still family. So when the chicken decided to put a contract out on him because we arrested him, we decided to show that chicken, he crossed the wrong fricking road.

When some other piece of crap that we were locking up said there was a $12,000 contract out on one of my boys, we had to confirm the information. We did this the way we did everything: punched that bastard until we got the truth out of him. We confirmed that there was an actual contract.

In order for the contractor to understand the error of his decision, we opted not to speak to him, personally. We made a very, very, very, very special trip down memory lane for this piece of crap. We found as many aunts, uncles, cousins, boyfriends, and girlfriends as we could, and encouraged him to sit down with us at a summit.

We legitimately obtained a search for one address. I mean we did actually have one, the other 11 places; the price for crossing the road? 12 sets of doors off the hinges. Each door we kicked in we kicked the fool behind the door just as hard.

We hit the first door, what was behind door number 1? One baby mama, well she was not pregnant anymore so that made her fair game. We sat down with her and talked to her, 'Where dick head, what the crap are you thinking, and what do you know about it? Of course, we got a whole bunch of kiss my ass(s) and leave me the hell alone(s). How do you deal with a fool? You just talk to them in a language they understand.

We offered to use a translator, and slap that freak across the top of her lip and then drag the bottom of her lip over her nose. You know it is amazing how quickly we developed a rapport. She commenced to tell us where a piece of dog-crap boyfriend was and then he just was talking smack, he really did not want anyone to kill the police officer. She gave another address.

We saddled up and put all the stuff back in the car: battering ram and a crowbar, shotguns, helmets, and condoms. You know you need to take everything, because you never know what you will find on the inside.

Next address, number 2, was just one of his crew. This piece of dog-crap was holding dope guns and everything else. Anyway, but around 7 in that title match, the lookout commenced to tell us the truth about what was going on and it turns out it's a little bit bigger than we realized. Dickhead was in a gang and he was getting 12 Grand for the contract. Now, it was cops against them bastards. Chicken Hawks against Roosters, there were too many cocks in this game for it to work out well for anybody.

We went from house to house, one after another and it got later and later and later. You know it does get boring after a while kicking in doors and faces. Okay I lied; it never gets boring there is never enough time in the day.

We got the information from this last house to go to this other house number 17 Bloody Brook Road. There, we were supposed to find his best friend. We kicked that door off the hinges it actually came off the hinges fell on top of him so we jumped up and down on the door.

Once we got inside, we realized that the person we were looking for was the door attendant, actually the doorstop today, underneath the door. In order not to violate his rights, we opened the little window in the door; the little sliding window so we could talk to him. He could not talk much with the weight of a few men and the door on his chest. Alas, *I wondered if Atlas felt like this guy holding that globe.*

Gus, (that is we decided to call him) the doorman figured out the more we delayed, the more time he was spending under the door. Gus learned that although you may be able to hide behind the law and sometimes that is a good thing I guess it is never a good thing to hide behind the door.

We struck oil at the next house, we finally had information as to where to find Cheeky the Chicken. We drove to where dickhead was supposed to be hiding, and would you know, it is 2 o'clock in the morning. In a quiet neighborhood, not another soul for 10 blocks in any direction do you know we found that stupid SOB sitting out on the porch in the front yard. That day I would wager everybody within earshot, came to the realization that sometimes chickens just need to stay on their side of the road. Tommy saw him first, he bailed out of the van and did not tell anybody anything he just went where he saw a dude and ran up on him. The reason we were able to track him and the reason we were able to find him, was because we heard the first lightning bolt crack through the air. There was no real reason for us to help; we watched the house to ensure nothing came out of the house. It took about five, six, seven, minutes to convince him that he should not ever cross the road again.

Every chicken that crosses the road needs to have his dick snapped, wings broken, and have that little red thing hanging on his face ripped off. That is what we were in the business of doing breaking chickens; this chicken got a broken beak, two or three broken ribs. Most importantly; when you stomp the crap out of a gangster, and do not even bother to pick him up, but instead just left them in their front yard face down in the dirt, every other chicken that wants to cross the road will think twice before crossing on to our side.

There must be a price exacted for coming out of the darkness to harm those who do not wish to live in the shade with you. Just as the vampire fears these, criminals should be afraid to come out of the darkness, because we exist in plain sight; we do not have to hide what we are, or do."

He looked down at this phone; I lost him again. I could not tell whether he did not agree, or just did not want to admit defeat.

"I am surprised you lasted as a cop this long doing shit like that. I guess it is good that those good old days are gone."

"My friend, we were as far from the good old days as you could get. All those arrests, all those black people, all those white, people, and Mexicans, we did not discriminate - we took on all challengers to the way of life people wanted to live. What changed is what people wanted out of life. I believe the true measure of a thing, shows in what we do to protect it. If people no longer wish to protect their freedom and their lives then the question becomes what are they really worth to those people? We did not change; society no longer wanted a wolf pack. Domestic animals are easier to control, and they do not piss on things to mark territory, they belong to the master."

"So now I am a lap dog, because I don't favor archaic thinking?"

"When did fighting to defend those who cannot defend themselves become archaic? When did being free mean lowering your head? You remind me of the man that said, 'We die all the time to avoid being killed."

7.12 Blue Boys

I tried to bring the levity back by changing the tempo. "One of the dumbest things police ever got involved in was keeping 'Trophies'. Trophies were what we called gear that bad guys ran out of fleeing arrest. It could be hats, shades, shirts, tennis shoes or whatever they shed to be free. The problem with trophies is that they lead to bigger trophies.

The next phase of trophy collecting, I was introduced to counterfeit merchandise. Counterfeit merchandise has no value, and therefore belongs to no one; at least that is what we told ourselves. It was easy because the counterfeit merchandise was supposed to be destroyed, in favor of the real thing. Rather than destroy all the counterfeit stuff, we came up with a better use; Thug-drobe. What better way to move among the creepy crawlies than to dress like they did, and the stuff was free. No longer would I have to wear my own stuff to work, to get torn up, dirty and covered in creepy-crawly blood. I just use their Thug-drobe.

Thug-drobe soon leant itself to the occasional accusation. Once it was ok to use the Thug-drobe, it soon after, became ok to acquire property. It was no longer enough to wait for someone to shed items. Items seized in raids, or from arrests soon joined the ranks of the Thug-drobe.

As with all things human, selfishness crept into Thug-drobe, and required more. Nothing was real, mind you, but we wanted more, and required more. Where does one get more Thug-drobe, from Thugs of course? Search warrants soon marshaled themselves into shopping sprees. Nothing big, just clothes, shoes, CDs, bootleg videos, shades, jewelry, etc.

Of course, this gave rise to the non-discriminating palate. Things started appearing in Thug-drobe, that were not counterfeit. I did not stop Thug-drobing, until the day I met the Blue Boys. The last entry to the Thug-drobe, came in the form of money. Money had three mediums, cash, coins, or food stamps. When bad guys threw down dope or guns, they were always turned in. When we chanced upon a dice game, that cash was always given to the kids nearby, to purchase ice cream, or at least that is what I thought.

One day, I was invited to an expensive steak dinner, with a couple of the guys; with a couple of non-team member Blue Boys. The food was good and paid for with cash. They laughed, and one of them said, 'We can meet here after the next search warrant. I like the food.' I later learned that the host of the party was whoever had cash when we made the entry; none when we left. I shied away from paying for the meal, but admittedly, partook of a few choice morsels of Filet Mignon. It was not until two other events, that I left the Blue Boys Club.

One of the events was I saw a stick 'drop' as he was running, and it looked to be about an ounce of dope and some cash. I kept running but one of the Blue Boys stopped to shop. I figured the money would not make it back, but I was sure the dope would, especially since we caught the seller. To my surprise, the dope did not make it back. I figured that maybe it was because the seller would ask about the money. He also dropped the dope and it was easier for them both to disappear. I never got a straight answer about it leaving. There was a sneaking suspicion in my gut that the dope might not have been thrown in the trash either.

The second event occurred when I went shopping on a large operation. I had the spoils in my pocket and was about to go and put them in my car, when a drug dog alerted on my pockets. By alerted, I mean the dog did what it was trained to do, and that was bark and scratch when it smelled dope. No, I was not carrying dope, but greed caused me to forget that dope dealers stuff often contains dope residue. Contamination is the natural byproduct of handling both dope and thrug-drobe. Here I was, in a room full of trained detectives and observers, and no one listened to the dog. The dog, probably the most objective person in the room, had no allegiance to the badge, he had a bond with his owner, but he did not know how to lie, or walk the Thin Blue Line. I am not saying that his owner was dirty; I'm saying in a room full of badges, the only one on the job that day was the dog.

I played it off, and pushed the dog off me counting on my fellow officers not to pay attention to their trained drug dog. It paid off; I survived the event and was cured permanently. I left the Blue Boy affiliation, and never went back, but I could not say anything either. It was stupid, and I intended to use the stuff for work, but it only takes one tainted event to tarnish your word.

While I was learning from the Blue Boys, I discovered that the Blue Boy Network reached a lot higher than I realized. The Network was not so much an organization as it was an understanding. I soon learned that there is a lot more to Law and Order than law and order.

While the majority of the Blue Boy Network existed for gain and self-serving reasons, I also found that sometimes a rule had to be bent for the greater good,; for example, rescuing teens in distress. We got a line on a teenage girl, strung out on dope. She was living with a dealer, who kept her supplied and shared her with his crew. A citizen called in distress, and desperately needed their daughter rescued. A recent headline placed the dead body of another teenage girl in our city. The Network responded.

The Network decided that the rights of the victim, and the need to help, outweighed the Law. Legally, it was not rape or kidnapping, because the girl was 18 (at least by the time we got the complaint she was). The word came down - Get her out! We needed Probable cause to arrest the guy, or even enter his house. This could be done in one of two ways. Testy-lie to a judge, drag them into the event and have it play out in court (ill-advised), or TCB (Take Care of Business). We opted for TCB. Is a person in need of help not sufficient probable cause? According to the Courts, no, it is not probable cause. That is why Law and Order sometimes do not agree, decency is the ultimate probable cause, after all, 'Quod est necessarium est licitum, that which is necessary is legal' is a legal ideology.

When you are taking care of business, be prepared to ignore a lot of crap, as needed, and if needed, you might have to move a glove or two. Do not bring your own glove, but if crap goes south, move it enough to CYA (cover your ass).

We kicked the door in, wearing raid gear. We announced police, because we sure did not want to have to shoot anyone, considering we were there with information from an anonymous phone call, made from a pay phone. Under the law, we can suspend certain Amendments like the Fourth, to preserve life or evidence. Nevertheless, we needed that anonymous phone call, to allow us to work, within the Good Faith Exception.

How do you come up with an anonymous phone call? Do not tell them your name when you call it in. There it was, information we needed to act, a citizen in danger. I do not know if you have ever seen footage of a Seal hunt, well that is what this looked like. We were not interested in finding dope and not intended to prosecute anyone. We just clubbed the crap out of everyone that was home when we arrived. Anyone profiting from holding this girl hostage, had a headache for the next six months. We trashed the house, well at least we tried, but it is hard to trash a port-a-potty.

We found the girl and a bunch of homemade porno with her, starring in gangbangs. In the Armed forces, a crew-served weapon implies that two or three team members cooperate to make the weapon system operational. This victim was crew-served, but we took the movies and also destroyed them.

Sadly; there was a girl in the house we had encountered, during prostitution enforcement, and she did not even try to help the victim. She got hers when she fell down the outside stairs (legitimately). When she started down the stairs, she wore a robe, underwear, and hair. By the time, she hit the ground, one tit was dragging in the dirty, her weave was hanging off the stairs, and her already soiled drawers were stuck up her ass.

As for the host of the party, he would have fared better as the guest of honor at a cross burning. If you combine; Roots, the Good the Bad and the Ugly and Pulp Fiction, you have an idea of what happened. Actually, not Pulp Fiction, he got screwed, but not like that. After beating this kidnapping, raping, trick mercilessly, he was encouraged, not to provide party favors for any more teenage girls. Moreover, to show there were no hard feelings, we offered to clean him up. This ignorant butthole accepted the offer, so we dumped soap powder all over him and left him there, smelling clean and linen fresh.

We delivered the girl to a hospital and left her there with her family. We never asked her name or if she wanted the help. I do not know who ordered the rescue, but I tip my hat to them, that one was one of the best things I ever did as a cop.

The Network kept it all hush-hush, the bad guy complained but it was quashed. We did our job, nobody was happy, but it was the right thing to do. The butthole argues we broke the Law, but any law that would not help that child, lime him deserves to be broken and ignored, as does the butthole making the argument.

Many Blue Credits expired to accomplish the goal. We got a free meal at an upscale restaurant; The Network was happy. Undoubtedly, the forefathers of the Network were in the grey, but not this time, not always. Often Blue Credits helped save a cop that did right, but society calls it wrong.

Remember, however, Blue Credits are never free. There is always someone trying to cash in or exchange them, which means behind every internal move on the board, lurks the potential for owing someone or getting yourself put in check. I never found out who had the ultimate say, who called the Checkmates, but they existed. I believe Thug-drobe was a huge mistake, and the first stage in unraveling the pristine image and reputation of our Unit. What they should have reminded us of on one of our Unit Citations, was that there is no such thing as a little lie or a small theft.

"So you did cross the line? With your holier than thou attitude, I figure you were going to look me in the eye and tell me you never crossed."

I responded slowly, "I crossed but I did not stay. Why the hell you think we are having this conversation? It is easy to lose sight of the law and the rules, but before you do that you really have to lose sight of yourself."

"What do you mean there is more to Law and Order than Law and Order? Who are you Yoda?"

"If I was, guess where I would shove my light saber?" We both shared a well-needed laugh. "It is simple young man; there is no way to be all good or all evil. Many of the best men in history did evil, and many of the worst men did some good, how we determine these factors is contingent on what our values are now, but the actions examined, require examination under a time appropriate microscope.

Popular thought, or trial by media is not a valid measure, it is too full of opinion. A judge puts a man in jail that confesses to a crime, and it turns out that man is innocent; good or evil? A man rapes two women drunk one night, and the judge doesn't punish him for fear of messing up his varsity standing, good or evil? A cop makes a snap judgment and shoots someone that points a cell phone at him; he gets fired, no jail time? Good or evil? Same scenario, but the officer is white and the suspect, black, he goes to jail, good or evil? The law does not really exist for good or evil; it exists to maintain a status quo. Who knows, if you were older, you might have had to stop a little black girl from entering a school. Walter, there is sometimes a fine line between a cop and a criminal. What drives their personality may be the same, they have simply chosen different roles and professions to call their own."

7.13 The Punch Heard Around The World

"You gotta be kidding me, I thought as we heard the news, together. We did so much together, it was no wonder we did not really hang together off duty; we were hardly off duty." I continued my stories.

Another ignorant, insufficiently beaten, individual put out a contract on a team member; another dead or alive contract on a cop. Unlike TV, this was real life. Some bastard,, too afraid to pull the trigger on a cop, was out there hiding and hoping that a crack head or some other kind of idiot would ambush a cop, hoping to get paid. There is only one thing to do about a contract on a cop, make it the most expensive real estate in the contractor's life.

Tommy came to me one night after buying dope. He asked me for a little help. I was game, I knew it was probably not above board, but that did not make it wrong. Things are very simple if people are honest. If you want the world to be safe, simply remove dangerous things, and render the problems moot.

Evil does not fear righteousness, it fears something more dangerous; things like my teammates. People that had darkness inside, but learned to use it to make the world a better place. A killer is a killer, but change the target package and they become a hero. Some of the greatest heroes in history were men brave enough to control their own darkness, stand up and face down yours.

Tommy and I sat in his car doing surveillance, and discussing cover vs. concealment; honestly what the crap else was there to discuss. Tommy asked me about shooting through a house?

WTF? I thought, surely he was just wanting caliber information and weapon characteristics.

Tommy asked, 'Hey man you was a soldier, if you needed to shoot through a building what would you use?'

"A gun," I replied snidely.

Tommy said, 'I know that ass, what kind of gun?'

"Probably a 7.65 or 7.62 is what I would use," I informed him.

Tommy asked, 'What's that?' *And this fool was on a Tactical Team* I thought.

"It's what an Ak-47 shoots, that's why they are so popular. They are devastating, and will go through most things. Any particular reason you asking?" I inquired.

'You know they put a contract out on me.'

"Yeah?" I said, dragging the syllables out. "So what are you going to do, shoot up, a house?"

Tommy started, 'We,'

"My ass!" I interrupted. "We aren't doing shit like that." There was a line; shooting into a house was not what bothered me, who else might be in the house is what gave me pause. I am all about setting a castle on fire, but only to get the king, no random victims. Even if the sludge inside was dope-dealing scum; they deserved to at least see who executed them. "Man have you lost your mind, I ought to drive over your ass for even saying crap like that to me. Say some ignorant crap like that to me again; I'll fill the contract on you myself."

Tommy replied, 'My bad man.'

However, I knew he was not sorry he asked; he wanted a wheelman.

We did not talk much more about it, that day. However, a few days later, at the office, Tommy came to me and said, 'Man I need you.' I knew what that meant. Each member of the squad had a skill, mine was mayhem; I was like a zombie with a badge, not giving a crap is my specialty, why give a crap about people worth less than crap, to me that makes no sense.

Tommy had a major problem; we had a new supervisor;   Ted the Timid is what we called him. He fancied himself tactical, but his most practiced tactic was hiding. Tommy was not supposed to go anywhere unescorted until the contract was resolved. 'Man I am just going for a ride,' he contended with Ted. It was late, around midnight, *where the heck was he going* I thought. Then the worst thing for him happened, Ted decided to go with us and brought one other member of the division. This person was not even part of our team.

We loaded in the van and Ted drove. Tommy directed us to a familiar neighborhood. As we drove down the street, we saw a single male black sitting on the porch on the phone. Ted got excited, so much so, he tried to open the van door. I slapped his hand off the handle and looked at him, *seriously*!

It was too late; Tommy's blood had already rushed out of his head into his crotch. He wanted to kill the dude on the porch; and why not, this was the guy who owned the contract on him.

'Pull over Ted,' Tommy said calmly.

'Why,' Ted asked?

'I gotta take care of paying a CI,' Tommy lied. Ted pulled over, and as soon as he did, Tommy was out of the van.

I got out too, but not to go with Tommy, at least not at first; I went to Ted and closed his door as he attempted to get out of the car.

'What are you doing?' Ted asked.

I looked towards the direction Tommy ran off in, "I told you not to come, stay here."

'What are we doing?'

"You do not want to know, so do not ask again," I warned.

Then I disappeared into what some would call the darkness; I called home.

I heard Tommy before I found him. In the silence of the evening, the only audio were the words, 'You dope-dealing piece of crap!' Another guttural, deafening sound quickly followed. The guttural sound was Mr. Is-That-My-Kidney, as Tommy dragged him from the porch by his face and slammed it in his front yard. The other sound was the sound calcium makes when colliding with another hard surface. Tommy hit Is-That-My-Kidney so hard I thought he broke his own elbow, but it was Is-That-My-Kidney's jaw. There it was, the punch heard around the world.

I ran over to assist; not to help Tommy and certainly not Is-That-My-Kidney; I went over to help the story. Is-That-My-Kidney was a ragdoll when I arrived, but in order to sell the story, I put my hands on him; that way two of us would share the blame. Most of the time, I had my eyes closed, to stop the blood from splattering in them. I do not know why, but as the noisy spectacle unfolded, I sang a little ditty to myself, *The heels on this bus go up and down, up and down the heels on this bust go up and down, all night long. The sound that they make is smack, smack, smack, smack, smack, smack, smack, the sound they make is smack all night long. Then roll his body into the flowerbed, flowerbed, flowerbed, then we rolled is body into the flowerbed hope he would be there dead early in the morn.*

Yeah, stupid, I was not scared, I was bored. Tommy was like the Tasmanian devil; I could not really get in close enough to get a piece. Not just because of Tommy, but also because he had a bad habit of pulling his gun out and keeping his finger on the trigger, I really just did not want to end up shot.

We returned to, and boarded the van. Ted asked us what happened; I looked at him and closed both doors, his and the van's. 'I asked you what happened?'

I looked at him and replied, "Whatever you allowed to happen."

Ted looked at the female officer who was sitting patiently in the van. He understood what that meant, and he never liked me again, afterwards. He understood, that what did or did not happen occurred on his watch, he drove us there, and waited for us to return; the law calls that a wheelman. I did not intend for him to find himself in this mess, I was just trying to do damage control, no one told him to tag along. He was a supervisor, he should have cancelled the Operation, at least for that day, it would not have happened.

Tommy and I knew it would never come up as a complaint, as long as Is-That-My-Kidney woke up from his nap in the dirt. Ted was mad, because he should have never allowed it to happen; well at least he should not have participated. He was a coward and would have just as soon, had the contract completed, than do any police work - He was better suited for security guard.

4 more Blue Credits into the pot.

Suffice to say. We left that piece of crap in a pile; he looked like a lawn jockey. After we stomped the uniform off the lawn jockey, we really did just roll his body into his flowerbed and leave him there, sleeping with the daisies. In terms of the lawn jockey, the contract, and everything else, all I can say is that he was breathing the last time I saw him."

"Man he could have killed the guy, then what would you have done?"

"You mean would I have lied to cover up him shooting an unarmed man to death? No that would be wrong, besides we could never sell that story, I would not have let that happen. Everything was a game, and there is a line cops can't cross and still be cops."

"But if you could have sold the story?"

"No friend, that's not a story I would even want to sell. Revenge is an act of passion; vengeance of justice. Injuries are revenged; crimes are avenged. I still want to be able to look at myself in the mirror. I was rough, but I am a killer, not a murderer. Cops that murder, we can do without. But I realized my brother screwed me that night, I never gave him another chance to do so."

7.14 NFL Type Crap

"The thing that made our team so deadly, better yet, effective, was that we understood that policing is not a spectator sport. We loved mixing it up with people. Most of our takedowns and arrests were dynamic, therefore , there we lots of tackles, flying tackles, dropkicks, clothes-lines, stiff arms and dare I say stupid ass careless crap.

Tommy's fame came from the power of his hits; sometimes, however, we had to move out the way so his ignorant ass did not hit us. Unfortunately, one day one of us moved too slow, or maybe too fast.

'I feel lucky,' came across the radio; that phrase was like the bell at the Kentucky Derby, the horse came out of the starting gates with fire and vinegar in their veins. We had a clothing description and knew it was a male black (running from the police although not part of official descriptions, is what police call a clue).

We were then startled by the sudden confusion between Tommy and Griff. I kept trying to explain, as Bob and Bill tried to restrain Griff and dissuade him for shooting Tommy.

Remember the description of the suspect? Well, Griff is a male white, plus he was wearing police crap. What happened to him was some real NFL (Not Frigging Legal) crap. As someone chased the suspect into a bend, Griff never saw Tommy coming out of left field. As a result of not seeing him barreling down at full speed, Griff never had a chance to prepare for the NFL hit.

When Tommy hit him (and hit him he did), he drove Griff into a chain-link fence, through the fence onto the ground. Griff took the shoulder in his side low enough to bend him in half; all I saw was the - 'ice' left on his vest as he flew across the field.

He rolled out from under Tommy and came up enraged, drawing his weapon. I wanted to help Tommy but other than asking WTF, and dodging his weapon, what could I do. He tackled the wrong dude. To make things worse, it was a great tackle. It was the only friendly fire that got awarded. Full recognition from the team, as a great tackle, definitely one of the best tackles we ever had. It took a few weeks but Griff eventually calmed down, and things went back to our normal. Just remember, you no longer have back up if you are going to tackle your partner.

7.15 Tales of Aspirin

"Damn that hurt!" I said as I shifted in my seat. Sitting and or standing too long was now uncomfortable due to all my injuries. "Indiana Jones said it's not the years; it's the mileage that causes wear and tear, he was right. Ain't no telling how many times I used this phrase? I have been run over by bad guys and cops in cars, and dragged by a motorcycle. When you putting it down, bad guys get hurt, but so do we. The blue suit makes cops feel invincible we are not. Cops bleed just as quickly as the rest of humanity. Like Batman however, cops train and wear gear required to complete the tasks.

Let me tell you about some of the crap I screwed up. Kevin rode together again for buy-busts a lot; as always he was on the phone. The takedown signal came out across the radio. We moved in to make the arrest. We saw the guys running away from the drug deal into the darkness. I got out and gave chase. I ran after them hollering at them. Hollering served to let my partners know where I was, to announce to the public, if I had to shoot them and it helped regulate breathing.

I gave chase, into the darkness, I ran again. The good thing about chasing the bad guys is that it happens to them first. That is the secret to not being too afraid to chase them, as long as you can see them; most of the danger is covered. The bad guy encounters dogs, cliffs, snakes, aliens, and cannibals first, and his scream warns pursuing cops of any impending danger. Or so I thought. The one thing to remember is that you cannot see in the dark.

A flashlight is usually target specific, so you can see what you point at and a few inches beyond but that is all. I got close enough to one of the guys to tackle them, so I did a great dive tackle and took that Ho to the ground. I tackled him; I stepped on a plate, or bottle or something plastic because I heard a loud snap. I stood up to handcuff dude and fell over, as I felt pain seared through my mind.

When I looked down to see that my forearm dangling, anger joined the searing pain, and I looked at the suspect, and back fisted him as hard as I could as I said the words, look what you made me do. It was not until I struck him the third time, did reality set in.

I realized at that point that I was laying in the darkness, did not know where I was, holding a broken arm, with one bad guy on my gun side, and the other guy, somewhere in the immediate area. Now, for the first time since putting on the badge; for the first time since coming to this unit; for the first time in a long time, I was afraid. The thing I feared most was that I was alone, and might die alone; wearing a girl's bulletproof vest.

At the beginning of the shift, Beverly was buying dope and she has big tits. She could not hide her vest over her big-uns so we switched vests so she could have smaller humps. I was going to die alone and in drag. You would be surprised what kind of stupid crap goes through your mind when you are afraid.

I was fully prepared to let the suspect escape, but he was leaving empty-handed and bloody. I figured if I hit him fast and hard enough he would either run or give up. He gave up, and by the time Geoff arrived, I had stopped striking him because he was under control and apologizing for causing the problem. I was also able to tell the crew where the other one ran to and what he wore, so they caught both of the sellers.

As for me and my arm, well crap happens. Turns out, I landed wrong and broke my are to pieces. I knew as I rode to the hospital that this was not going to be good, and they had me strapped to a board, like laundry. They told me that it helps stop the bleeding, well, that is not true, the bleeding does not stop, and the blood just all goes somewhere else. I bet I could not even get a hard-on at this point. It was a compound open fracture.

Then, one time I had a broken nose. 'I feel lucky, I feel lucky,' relayed over the radio. That was confirmation of what we all heard over the wire so that all the takedown units knew that the drug deal was over and that we needed to move in and make the arrest. I bailed out of the car and took off after dude.

It was another fun foot chase, at least until my gun fell out of the useless holster I was wearing, and clattered down the street. I bent over and picked up my gun as I ran. I had to holster my gun and as I did, I took my eyes off the suspect. Because I did take my eyes off for that brief period, I did not realize that dude had stopped running and turned to face me. When I looked up I did not see a fleeing felon, I saw five of the biggest, blackest, ashiest knuckles I ever saw hurling towards me; too late.

They tell me that the automotive industry pioneered Crumple Zones, for vehicle collisions. pioneered Crumple Zones were invented right there on my face, as it crumpled, folded and wrapped around dudes face. Sad as it sounds, I could not do anything except apply brakes, and try to stop his fist from entering my sinus cavity.

Well, I backed up off dude's fist, so I could breathe. Everyone stopped, my crew, the bad guy, my breathing. Once I could breathe again, I said in my best Mickey Mouse sounding voice, 'Do not touch him he's mine.' It sounded funny, but I meant every word of what I said.

I commenced beating his ass, in the middle of the street. After I felt vindicated, I handcuffed him. We called him an ambulance, and I rode with him since my nose was broken. He looked at me and said, man, I do not know what made me do that, but I will never do that again. I just looked at him past my swollen nose, I said nothing. It is hard to threaten a grown man when you sound like Mickey Mouse.

Then another time, I had a Torn shoulder. We were off to the races, another foot chase, into the darkness. Here we go again I thought, *lions, tigers, crack heads oh my*. Dude ducked around a corner, so I went after him; I never really talked on the radio. Radio chatter takes too much time, and most of the time I did not know exactly where I was, I was just following the rabbit to his hole. So the bunny jumped a fence; not in the conventional sense.

This idiot just dove over this 4-foot fence head first. I put my hands on the crossbar and jumped over it smooth and in stride, except the fence gave way; so I went to the ground headfirst. Now I was mad, and my neck hurt. I got up and was still able to run butt wipe down. When I did catch him, I tackled him to the ground.

It was not until the handcuffing, that I realized I messed my shoulder up. I got my hand stuck behind my back; it caused excruciating pain to bring my arm forward. Man, I was tearing up crap that I did not even know existed; this time it was a shoulder.

Once, my clumsy ass cracked my tailbone. I'm fighting this crackhead in the bushes. I chased him after he sold dope. He jumped the fence, so I jumped the fence. He jumped a privacy fence I kicked the gate in on the mutha. Now, we are deep in the back of the bushes along the interstate. This was before they gave us Tasers and Pepper Spray, so all I had to offer him was a good old fashioned ass-whooping.

Being a gentleman, I graciously obliged him to an ass-whooping. The first course consisted of me punching him in the face repeatedly. He wanted to skip the soup and salad course, so he tried running again. As he ran, he fell down an embankment. As I was chasing him (far too closely), I too fell down the embankment. Turns out, life is the ultimate Kryptonite."

7.16 The Funniest Crap Ever

"Routine heroin purchases are not always routine. Heroin commonly is sold, packaged in foil or balloons, depending upon the source. For this amazing tale, the dope came in balloons. Balloons equal the risk of swallowing and death. Balloons and heroin equals Mexican dealers. Mexican always equals pre-slap language barriers.

- Small, expensive ass balloons
- Non-English speaking, illegal drug dealer willing to risk death to avoid jail, or having his family held hostage in Mexico
- A bunch of cops hollering you are under arrest
- Free healthcare (equals) a trip to hospital

I explained further, that the scenario is almost indefensible. Dealers know they stand a good chance of the balloons not rupturing, once swallowed. In the event the balloons do rupture the required health care is free; as either an arrestee, or if the police believe you, a drug mule, working against your will. Stopping the dealer from swallowing the balloon is entirely up to you.

Even with a powerful blow to the abdomen, or choke-hold, it is almost impossible to prevent the swallow. Because the world is so damn stupid, if a drug dealer swallows dope to escape jail, and dies in custody, they can sue. I say if they win, I say give them the dead body filled with dope, let them recover their drugs on their own.

So, if I have to go to the hospital anyway: surely, a man that swallows dope can stand to have the Guacamole slapped out of his mouth first. That is exactly what happened.

- We bought the dope
- We moved in for the take down
- Dealers swallowed the balloons as I watched
- I slapped some green shit out of the mouth of one of them
- We loaded them up and took them to the hospital

We thought the clown show was over when they swallowed the dope and got slapped around. Oh hell no, I laughed.

We arrived at the hospital and took them in separate rooms. Every so often, cops luck up in the ER and the right medical failure is working. This ER doctor was of the type ass or a foot doctor that has no patients, no office, and no breath mints. This incompetent butthole was perfect. If there was a GED equivalent for Medical School, this fool had two.

We entered the hospital lobby, and got rooms assigned. The doctor walked in, looked at the bleeding patient, and asked what they needed to be seen for. In his best-broken English, the suspect pointed to his face incredulously.

'The officer tells him, you swallowed some heroin, is that the case?' the witchdoctor asked.

Suspect 1 looked at him and said. 'No, no balloons.'

Dr Screwenstien repeated his query with suspect [#]2 in the next room. Suspect [#]2, spoke broken sign language as well, when asked did he swallow balloons, he said no but nodded yes. 'How many balloons did you swallow?'

'I did not swallow any balloons doctor,' his English was improving.

'But there are balloons in your stomach?' he said no, but nodded yes.

'Do you want me to take a look?'

'Naw, to hell with that,' he said, but nodded yes.

This was like talking to a child; and illegal, dope selling, dope swallowing, ass whipped child. The doctor decided he needed to take a look. So he started with an x-ray. The x-ray showed about 15 small items (balloons) in the stomach and GI tract.

The doctor came back into the room, 'Would you like me to remove whatever those things are?'

'Naw, screw that, I didn't swallow no balloons' he said, but nodded yes.

The suspect sweated profusely, and was obviously anxious. I hoped a balloon had busted. I always wanted to tick the box on the form that says 'Cleared by death of offender'. I sat back and waited to see what was next, I did not know the Mexican Circus was in town.

Dr Screwenstien walked back in an apron, with a tray and told the suspect to lie back on the bed and that he was going to see what he could do. He sprayed some numbing agent into the back of his throat, and then; then something awesome happened. Dr Screwenstien pulled out these two hoses, they look like the cord attached to the spouts at bars, used to pour sodas. He explained, one was a camera, and the other an 'Assist'. This idiot jammed both these things; down. Suspect [#]2's (now Victim [#]1) throat, and started moving them like puppet strings.

I had already peed a little on myself from laughing. Expectedly Suspect [#]2 (now a victim) tried to do crazy crap like breathe. He started fighting Dr Screwenstien who called for assistance from nurses, an orderly, and security. Security was for me; by the way, I was all but rolling on the floor, by this time.

Walters looked at me laughing, 'Man you are stupid.'

I knew something was wrong, Suspect [#]2 was gagging blood and spit, but no Heroin. Dr Screwenstien must also be a mind reader because, just as I thought it, he dug deeper. Suspect [#]2 gagged loudly, kind of like a roar from Godzilla. The smell of freshly evacuated bowels filled the room. Then there was silence. Suspect [#]2 stopped fighting: as well as breathing the son of a bitch was dead.

The first thing through my mind was trying to figure out how to get the dope out prior to the autopsy. Then it dawned on me, no suspect, and no need for dope. Alas, suspect 1 was still breathing. 'Code Blue' rang out as we rushed the corpse and Dr Screwenstien in his bloody apron, through the hospital. We sped by a large bald headed black guy jogging in the hallways.

As we wheeled by, the black guy asked what the condition of the patient was, Dr Screwenstien calmly said with a smile on his face 'He coded.'

They prepped Corpse 1 (formerly a suspect) for emergency surgery. The black jogger turned out to be the on-call surgeon; he looked at Dr Screwenstien's apron, 'What happened?' I cannot remember the name of the real procedure, but I referred to it as a Choke-The-Life-Out-Of-A-Mexican-Ostomy.

'What were you thinking; you did that in the ER with throat numbing?' The surgeon was not impressed with Dr Screwenstien, probably because he was still smiling.

'He still has the balloons inside,' Dr Screwenstien advised.

Suspect $^{\#}$2 had crap oozing out his mouth, he was lying in a pile of crap, his eyes were bleeding, and he just pissed on himself (not sure how you pee while dead but who knows)."

By this time, Walters and I were laughing loudly in the hallway. I wager this sound had not resonated within these halls for many years.

They got Suspect $^{\#}$2 breathing again, and his heart started beating again. While under sedation, the surgeon pulled the balloons out of his limp body and dropped into a bag that I held out.

15 balloons in all 10 grams of Heroin recovered, a job well done. Suspect $^{\#}$2, (recently back from the dead) stayed in the hospital for 48 hrs, under guard for observation.

Upon returning to the ER, Suspect $^{\#}$1 adamantly refused any medical treatment from Dr Screwenstien, and demanded to be taken to jail immediately. I did not blame him. We x-rayed him, saw nothing, and took him to jail. Both pieces of crap appeared in court 10 days later to face the charges."

"I once heard someone say, 'Cured of my disease, last night I died of my physician. Damn, was that not the best example of that that I ever heard?" Walters jeered.

"Yeah brother you learn a lot of things on the job, decidedly just how many things will cause your death."

8.0
THE SHOOTING
REVIEW BOARD 2nd Appearance

"I have been up here for this type of stuff before. The Shooting Review Board is always a drag. Probably because it did not have any real police on it, just a bunch of fat, old, company minded political hacks. I had to go because I had been involved in a shooting, embarrassingly enough, it was a vicious dog. This was my second dog shooting. Departmental policy changed, now any weapons discharge, fell under the investigative jurisdiction of the Homicide Unit. I wanted to make a good impression, so I made sure to lay the cheap cologne on thick and to put my company issue clip-on-tie crooked.

I walked in, and the FOP rep said hello, and took his position in a dark corner. Turns out, this would be the first in a series of appearances. Around the table sat a Deputy Chief, my Bureau Chief, My Captain, Internal Affairs, and someone from Homicide.

I got to go first of all the officers slated to appear. I had a simple story, no humans had been harmed in the making of my story (well they were not shot anyway). Assigned to the takedown team, I lurked down the street and watched the dope deal. I made it a point to get as close to the deal as possible, I always provided close cover when I was not the undercover officer. From that position, I could help bolster the information provided by the undercover officer. We always ran two police radios in the car during deals. One was dedicated to the body wires and it received only. We heard everything the undercover officer heard, but could not talk to them. The other radio was the talk around the channel, and it allowed us to update all actionable intelligence. 'Male, black, dreadlocks, about 40 years old, green pants and yellow shirt,' I confirmed the description of the seller over the radio. As soon as the takedown signal rang out, I moved in slowly so as not to startle the bad-guy, it also gave the undercover officer time to get out of the way.

When I emerged from my vehicle wearing clearly marked RAID gear, the suspect fled, heading back to the house. Although I gave chase, running blindly into a house is never a good idea. The gate nearest to the dope deal was actually on the side of the house, the suspect went around the corner first, and as I approached the corner, the corner moved. Admittedly, I was running fast, but not fast enough to hallucinate. I slowed down, just in time to realize that it was a 150 lb Rottweiler that was moving toward me at an angry rate of speed.

I broke, slid, back peddled, and then hauled ass. Expectedly I could not run fast enough. I fired three shots. One glancing side shot, one struck the hind left leg, and the third struck her about the temple, on the left side. It was to the third shot the dog reacted too. I believe it was the bright light and the sound that frightened her.

Other officers apprehended the suspect, I had to wait for animal control to come out and take her into custody because she was injured, but still aggressive and dangerous.

The investigators came out and the only thing that was a slight issue was that my bullets were mix-matched. The reason for that was when the Unit started, our supervisor made us get additional weapons, compact or revolvers for close cover UC work. The guns never came with any bullets, so we would acquire bullets from the property room slated for destruction.

There were no questions; I was done. That day's event was brought to you by the letters D and O and G."

"Bleeding hearts," I was shocked at Walter's comment, there was hope for him after all.

9.0
SMOKE SIGNALS

"Soon, several years into UC Ops, the stress of 30 plus hours of overtime per week, added to the existing stress of the job, started taking its toll on the unit. Flashy cars, easy money, and low accountability, is the breeding ground for all manner of Blue Woes. Friendships strained or ended, as did marriages. There was too much time together, and not enough time spent doing wholesome things. Besides, there was never anyone asking about the emotional health of the unit; everyone just assumed that we were all fine. I think the Administration knew we were not, but did not care, we got the job done. Not just any job, the jobs they wanted done.

"I remember one day, Chief Tubber walked up to me and Tommy. 'How you boys doing?' he asked as he puffed his cigar. He was much older than we were and had been a patrolman; of little note, apparently. He had played the cards right and got the job. 'I need you, boys, to do something for me, I keep getting calls about a house at 12th and Garden from the Mayor's office.'

He blew his smoke up in the air, obviously relishing his cigar and position. 'I need you, boys, to take care of it for me.'

'Ok, I said and turned to walk away.

'Hey Chief,' Tommy, 'What does that mean?'

Chief Tubber exhaled again, and amidst his smoke said, 'Just do what y'all do best.'

We walked away silently, commencing the planning phase. We pulled up to the location, and as predicted, people were out front selling dope. The UC exited the vehicle and made the dope deal. Once given, the takedown signal initiated the usual confusion. Upon our exiting of the police cars, the suspect ran into the house, which of course was our cue to follow.

Tommy and I got to the front door simultaneously. I flashed my light into a doghouse, saw nothing and then opened the screen door and held the screen so he could kick it in, what happened next blew my damn mind.

This moron discharged his weapon - twice. Bear in mind, we were close enough for me to hold the door for him. Both muzzle blasts crossed my right thigh, setting off searing pain. I did not know what happened, so I grabbed the muzzle of his weapon and pointed away from me holding his hand, pushing my gun into his throat at the same time.

'Don't kill me, don't kill me!' was all he could get out.'

As I squeezed the trigger, just before I shot back, the front door opened and the suspect was standing in the door with a gun in his hand.

Now I was screwed. I was not sure who to shoot, but I was damn sure that I was not going to die alone.

There is no telling what the dude at the door thought when he saw me with one gun in hand and the other at another officer's throat. I looked at him, 'Police, do not resist.'

At this point, I was not sure what to do or even which one I was speaking to. I could not get them both from this position. Tommy was not moving, he was begging not to be shot, and the other creeps were running around shouting commands, suspects running around the yard, it looked like the 100-Yard dash for the blind. The only thing not moving was my trigger finger.

'Just look!' Tommy pleaded, I figured he wanted me to see what was left of my thigh. I had pain; I did not know if I was bleeding. When I looked down, my jeans had powder burns across the thigh, and there were two black pit bulls at our feet.

The dogs were asleep in the dog-house and they were jet black so I didn't see them, but when we touched the door they went to work. Tommy had backed up to kick them, so he saw them before I did, but he did not have time, or maybe the words, to warn me before he shot.

My gun was still at his throat, but I spun and faced the suspect in the house, repeating my commands. He turned with the gun and fled through the yard. I gave chase with my partially fried leg, madder than a swarm of bees.

The radio was still chaotic. Reports of people throwing rifles and jumping out of windows trying to escape. I couldn't get the radio clear to transmit my pursuit so I just chased dude. Remember always watch their hands as much as possible. If they are going to kill or harm you they gotta use their hands.

I was running regular police chase drug dealers into the darkness with a gun speed; until a shot rang out behind me. Holy crap, someone was chasing me and shooting at me. That was the incentive I needed, I ran over the suspect, and we both ended up on the ground. I kicked him in the balls, then in the face, before he could find his weapon, and as I looked for mine.

Just as I found my weapon, and brought it up to face my pursuer, hands went up in the air. It was Stewart, 'I fired a pooper in the air.' He yelled as he skid to a halt

Ignorant dwarf fired a warning shot behind me, 'What the fuxx were you thinking,' I yelled?

I did not mean to run into the suspect, he got in the way. I went into Chubby Owens speed when I thought they were shooting at me and ran over his slow ass. You can run a lot faster when you think people are shooting at you, as opposed to trying to take one into custody.

When I got back, Tommy walked up to me and apologized. I was still burning, at least my thigh was. I was not mad at him, and I was glad I did not shoot him. He hugged me, and we went back to dealing with the chaotic scene.

As we walked around in the area, 'You were going to shoot me weren't you?' I just smiled a warm, yet answering smile, he knew I planned to never die alone; whoever sent me to hell, was going to hell as well.

We took care of the problems. Chief Tubber took care of the Internal Affairs complaints, and the City Hospital took care of the rest. Chief Tubber took care of us, however, no counseling, no psych tests, no drug tests, he even waived the required annual polygraph test - there was no need to waste money, we were all going to have to lie to pass anyway." We both laughed.

"Bur seriously, what do you mean handled Internal Affairs. Did they lie for you?"

"Not, adhering to the letter of a policy is not lying, it is playing by the rules. Chief Tubber, had a mandate from the Mayor to clean the city up. This happen if you let the sheep control the wolves."

"So y'all could do no wrong"

"No the deal was more like they changed the definition of wrong to suit their needs, and then empowered us to make the plan come true. With the understanding that if we were caught off the range we had to suffer the consequences. No trumped up charges, no planting dope, minimal collateral damage. That was the unofficial policy Du Jour - of the day. It sounds great but nothing is free. The old African proverb about magic came true for us. Those who wish to be served by magic often end up being its slave.

The liar's punishment is, not in the least, that he is not believed, but that he cannot believe anyone else. Eventually, the unit started falling apart and distrusting each other, despite which we never crossed the line; well most of us did not.

A couple of us ended up doing time, others were lucky to only get divorced, several got promoted and moved up chain of command quietly. ”

10.0 LONG-TERM INVESTIGATIONS

10.1
LONG-TERM INVESTIGATIONS

Things became hectic in the Unit; reluctantly, I transferred to Long Term Investigations. This assignment required less work and less trust. These guys were pretty lazy and well-taken care of. It was not that I did not enjoy the work; what we did required a level of trust that simply was no longer in the unit. Better to leave vertical, than stay and pray. Abandoning a sinking ship is not quitting, its reallocating resources.

No matter what we think of the Federal Agencies they represent the ultimate level in Law enforcement, simply put, they are the highest branch of the Enforcement community. I got the call. When you get the call, that your local efforts reach the ears of the national boys...it is a thing to be proud of. The Feds only want two things in a case, easy to win and easy to win. For that reason, the call is a good thing because it means you make good cases (usually).

I later learned that there is another reason the Feds call, because they do not give a crap about the real police, they just use us to further their careers. When I got the call, I asked them why they called me. It was a little of both. They needed someone not afraid to play in the dark, and they knew I could pull it off. Circle the wagons was the call, so we did.

My new team met with the Feds. They gave us the rundown. A group of guys wanted to buy hundreds of kilos of Cocaine. They wanted me to be the middle middleman. My job was to work with a CI and meet the crew. Arrange for them to see, test, and price the dope. They knew it was not my dope, and we knew it was not their money. I agreed, remembering that this was not my real crew and that you never trust a CI.

The dealers came to my fair city and we met. The first day was nothing but a meet and greet. We took them to dinner, and then for an after-dinner mint, they wanted to see naked women. People have no idea how much crime occurs because of a little piece of paradise. It must really be good everybody likes it; men and women. We visited several clubs and spent lots of money.

For the evening, everybody was caught up between those flashing legs. As I looked at the slender, glistening, often pierced bodies, I marveled at how different these girls looked from the street walking whores. Those street walking skanks, smelled and looked, awful. They charge for sex. What these girls charge, is to let you look. If I were a Ho, I'd wash my ass; put makeup on my track marks, and strip, damn walking the street.

I was so glad I was not out playing in the mud tonight. Vajango is vajango; I agree, but who wants a dirty, smelly one? Not only did these girls wash and shave theirs, they could make theirs look alive. When a man looks at a beautiful woman, he sees parts. When it comes to sex, you know what part that involves. When these girls danced, their parts danced too, their parts seeming to have their own personality. Their parts winked at you invitingly and without actually talking, saying, hello, I miss you.

Day two was a little more serious. We met, and I showed them 5-kilos. I did not tell them how much dope I was bringing. I showed up with three other guys, this way we avoided a robbery. I let them have their way with one of the kilos. It was real dope, but we do not pay for it, it was confiscated. They cut it open and then tasted the smell out of it. Once their tester-idiot was satisfied, they agreed to the price and said they wanted to see more tits.

Maybe these backward freaks do not have tits, where they were from. It is not as if they work and because of their shift work, did not have time to go see tits. It is not as if I do not like tits, but the more time we spent at the titty bars, the more likely it was, that I would run into a pair of tits that I had slapped the handcuffs on. I took care to go to clubs we had not busted a lot, but the pressure was on. When you got out playing with the idiots, there is a good chance that the idiots you arrested will see you and make a big deal; More eyes to beat shut. But it's a good way to screw up a deal or get killed. It is not like we searched these guys, or had any control over whether they were armed or had other fiends in the city. And of course there always looms the possibility of running it to uniformed officers that insist on being cordial.

We finally got tired of looking at tits (actually, I do not, honestly, who gets tired of looking at tits and ass…free). I took them home. The Feds provided the car for the next phase of the journey. I picked up my new friends and drove them to Texas, where they were supposed to have their money. It was a long ride, lying to three bad guys for all those hours. The recordings, taped in the car, provided hours on tape, of their dope and violent exploits. I was particularly interested in their violence; you know how I feel about beating their eyes shut. Yak, yak, lie, lie; for several hours that is all we did, everybody was happy.

When we pulled into the hotel, they had arranged; the atmosphere changed. They knew I had no dope, but could get it, and we were talking about more than a million dollars' worth of dope. That kind of money makes people do bad things to make a point.

The comment from the middleman did not help me. 'You have a gun?' he asked. Of course I did. 'That way there will be at least two of us against them.'

I thought about the odds, and decided against taking my gun into a room with 9 drug dealers. *I knew I could fight them off longer than I could survive a shootout against that many. I trusted my new team would rescue me in a timely manner.*

The Feds did not build my confidence; they tried to use a new piece of wire equipment, which they could not install properly. We had problems with the wire, so we had to use the old open microphone telephone trick. It was relatively safe to go into the room; they only saw 5 kilos and wanted more than three hundred.

If they were going to rob me, prudence demanded they wait until they could get the max bang for their buck. When I got to the door, they let me in. I walked into a room with a total of 8 guys, none of which were my friends. *If things went south, it looked like my eyes would be the ones beaten shut.*

The negotiations began. It was going to be a slow process. We haggled over the price until we reached one. When you are surrounded by bad guys and they all probably have guns, you negotiate with your mouth, but your heart thinks something else, 'My ass, my ass, my ass!' That what was really on the line here, not the drugs or money in question; my ass was on the line.

When you are negotiating the price of gold, you got to keep in mind, the most important thing Is, he gives a damn and it's not your money anyway. Second to that is, the negotiation has to be believable, you have to haggle as if it is your money even though you do not give a damn how much you spend. If you make the price too low, it probably gets you shot in the face. If you make it too high, you probably get shot in the face and then fired for wasting the money. You got to make it believable; he leads and sets a price, 'You setting a price for my product, I, am pretty sure you know better than that.'

Burtiss, the leader of the 'idiots', replied with a smile. 'Man you know where the money is coming from; all I am saying is that is all we got to spend.'

I sat down, confidently arranging this large deal, with 8 men that would just as soon rob or kill me. That is why, at the actual negotiation, there should be no drugs or money. Unless there is a reason to kill each other, the negotiation should be safe.

We finally agreed on a price; they were going to pay me $31,000 per Kilo. It was not a great price; it was about $3,000 below the going rate. These dumbasses decided they wanted to mess the deal up based on the delivery. They wanted to buy a hundred kilos at a time, break the city into quadrants, and have us to front a hundred kilos at a time and then they bring the money back. That was never going to happen; remember never have the dope and the money in the same place and you sure would never walk with a hundred kilos.

Now the real skill comes on the line. They made it understood the way they wanted to do business and now you have to figure out a way to unscrew this whole situation. That was a ridiculous breakdown, so I came up with a very good solution. I am not doing that horse crap, I told Burtiss, 'I drove down here for four hundred kilos, it's 400 or no kilos at all; doesn't matter who you know, it doesn't matter what you used to do it, I am not walking jack'. They walked across the room to decide what to do. I was left standing there hoping that they were not discussing where they're gonna bury my body.

At the same time as I was trying to plan how to get these fools and their money, and keep my scalp, I also had to worry about the jackasses that rode down with me, who were supposed to be providing back up. How were they back up, when they were sitting outside in the car, 6 officers deep, safe with guns, badges and condoms and I'm in the hotel room getting ready to get screwed, bareback by this group of ass wipes.

We digress, technical surveillance and electronic surveillance is just kind of curious. Take into consideration that if you go into the hotel room and the backup jackasses cannot hear me, then you cannot help me. One of the things that were unique about me and my old group was, we did not mind putting people in the hospital the old-fashioned way with gloves and boots.

I did not plan on having backup, something I always told my guys; do not get into something that you cannot get yourself out. If you have to worry about backup to save you, your ass is already had. I pretty much had cowards watching my back; they were just trying to make money now. I went out to go get something from the car. I checked in to see if they were listening and they were mostly sleeping. There is nothing as reassuring as knowing that the bastards who got your back, way, way, way in the back are keeping themselves safe.

I went back inside, no gun, no badge, no wire for a 400 kilo Cocaine deal. To run a big deal like this, there are supposed to be snipers, helicopters, and scuba divers. Some other SOB should be jumping up out the toilet, just in case you need them. I walked back inside and told those bastards, 'You saw the 10 kilos; you know I got the stuff. You messed around with the money and this is what we are going to do. I drive my ass back, and you can eat a dick until you get your money straight.'

They tried to pull a fast one. They tried to pay with funny money (counterfeit bills) and that is when we knew it was all a scam. The only reason they had not ripped us off, was because we never let them see all the dope. We never let them know where the rest of the dope was, so the most they could do is hold me hostage. These fools knew nothing about a 400 kilogram, $2.3 million Cocaine deal. If they did, they would have known that no one waits around sitting on 400 kilos of Cocaine, waiting on you to break piggy banks. About my cover on the deal, I say, the most dangerous thing in life is an incompetent that has been given a gun and a law enforcement badge."

10.2 Suspension Days

"Business went on as usual. Jacked up work shifts, crappy days off and free food. The problem with free foods is, it's all crap, but it is free. Anyway, so I go back to work right, and they give me a new assignment. My assignment is just as usual. Everywhere you turn, are crack heads, crack heads, crack heads, pill heads dope heads, weed heads, or heroin heads. Shift over; I head home right?

I come home, and there is a U-Haul parked in front of my truck. I am trying to figure out what the hell is going on because I do not have a roommate. Turns out it was just a crazy girl I was dating. She decided to buy a house, and we were supposed to move in together. Yeah, that does not work out so great for anybody. I was totally not going to move in with this crazy chick. It went downhill from there. She decided to come inside my house and refused to leave. What do the police do when somebody refuses to leave their house? Dammit you got to call the police.

I called the officers private work line. You use that line when you do not want to call the real police and have it recorded. I called and I said, 'Will you please come get this stupid ho out of my house, no threats, no violence. That was a thing back then, you had to say no threats, no violence as long as nobody put their hands on nobody you do not have a domestic. The police showed up. She left prior to their arrival because she knew this was not going to end well for either of us. Especially since both of us were in law enforcement. The Sergeant decided to send an officer back to my house to take a report listed as a matter of record/disorderly conduct. That screwed me; I do not know that until I showed up for work on Monday.

My boss says, 'Come here stupid, anything awesome happen over the weekend? I will let you know that the Captain recommended 10 days suspension.'

I went to my captain and tried to explain that it was not a matter of me lying, but actually, it was, because I lied about my address because I did not want the media to know where I lived. They were mad at me because they were supposed to trigger a full-blown departmental investigation.

Because no one answered the door at the address I listed, they assume I was attempting to hinder the investigation. We settled on 5 days suspension from my vacation. I thought I hit rock bottom when they told me I was getting suspended. This was about as slow as I needed to go. This is probably the one of the lowest points of my entire career. I figured that was not too bad, until they told me to turn all my crap in. They told me that I could not be a cop for three days; crap, crap, and crap.

As I was sitting in my room contemplating my 5 days of not a damn thing to do, it dawned on me like slap in the face, 'Man I can't badge my way into the strip clubs'. Now I was really pissed.

I went out to get something to eat and McDonalds was closed. I went back home, still nothing to do. I had some furniture to assemble; it together took me like 3 hours because some idiot put the instructions in Spanish. It is bad enough when the crap is only pictures, why even sell a product where the instructions are not in the language of the country sold? It took me forever to try to decipher it - crap, crap, crap, crap, crap, crap!

I did not have anything to do, and nowhere to go, so I did not bother putting on clothes. I sat in my drawers measuring, anguishing, and bored to death. I looked down at my watch and I realized it had only been 30 minutes. I was already suicidal. Holy crap, I thought to myself, how much longer was this going to take. I got up, cleaned up the house considering I was never home; that took another 30 minutes. I still had 4 days to go, suspension and regular weekends. I looked in the mirror at my underwear; no gun belt, no badges no gun, no pepper spray, and I realized just how empty my life was. I realized if it was not for that blue clown suit, I would have nothing to do

I did what any self-respecting man that got suspended did because he couldn't get along with his female friends would do; I picked up the phone and start dialing. I went down alphabetically and everybody I called was either married or happily married. I figured I would go through my list of phone numbers and start erasing people that have no interest in being around me anymore. That took another 30 minutes.

When I was done, all the names were gone. I tried to figure out what the hell to do next; strip joint or go buy beer. I went to the mall and walked around there for about 30-45 minutes realizing there wasn't a damn thing I wanted. The mall had a whole bunch of horse crap that nobody wanted, which was on sale or clearance. There is nothing worse in life than having money and there is nothing to buy but horse crap.

10.3 Operation Venereal Disease

"A tragedy occurred at the office one day. A civilian employee accidentally dropped a weapon, which discharged killing her. The weapon was a cheap pistol, wherein the hammer rested on the round and had a nipple like firing pin, affixed to the hammer. Because of the ancient design; when the weapon fell, it landed on the hammer and discharged.

Per policy, the division hosted a Diffusion Meeting (Counseling Session) because the death occurred in the workplace; they wanted to ensure that people felt ok coming into the office, after the event. A couple of professionals spoke, and then a few peer counselors and the union chaplain. The meeting went off without a hitch and the next day business resumed as usual.

The complaint came in, that, at The Social Club, there were people actually having sex with employees. I had completed operations in clubs previously, so they handed me the awesome assignment. I only had two questions;

1. *Why was that illegal?*
2. *Why the heck was I not a member?*

I got an answer to the first question and quickly rectified the second issue.

Employees screwing customers in a sex club falls under the prostitution statute, and there was a cover charge, so it is a Promoting (Pimp) issue, and then there are Adult Sex Club Codes violations as well.

My assignment was to go in and confirm they were having sex. 'So I have to get close enough to view penetration correct? I asked my Sergeant. 'Can I sample the merchandise?'

'Yes and get the hell out of my office,' was my Sgt's response.

I was happy. I walked over to my desk and pulled up porn sites; I was researching types of sexual activities common to swingers clubs. As I am a dedicated professional, I ensured that the other detectives underwent the Trainer program with me. I even gave out homework." Walters laughed again, he thought it was funny; the laughter was a welcome segway.

The day came, I got dressed for the part, no wire, no camera, no underwear. I did not take a weapon, because they searched you upon entry to the business.

I walked up to the door and read the membership application. Standard info, except, you had to sign a disclaimer, stating that you were not affiliated with Law Enforcement. Upon entry to the building, I noticed an old ass hanging out from under a mini-skirt. This hag was waitressing the table. After dropping off the drinks, she stood speaking to the people at the table, when a pudgy, little bastard walked up from behind, bent her over the table, pulled up her skirt, and simulated rear-entry intercourse.

I thought it was funny until the fat bastard turned around and his double-chinned, face turned to stone; it was the Union Chaplain. Good for him, I thought, and I walked on by. He just stood and watched me walk into the building.

I saw him walk out, and paid little attention to him except I noticed he walked over to the membership book and read it, walked back inside and disappeared down a hallway, which were all offices. I walked on in the club.

I honestly did not expect what I saw, the complaint understated this place. I was scared that Fire and Brimstone were soon to follow and I did not want to turn into a pillar of salt. The first room I walked into was called the Dungeon. I assumed incorrectly it was because of the old dragon working in the room. Whomever she purchased her lingerie from should come get their crap. She did not even need a bra; her tits were hanging within the belly portion of the outfit. They should have just put her ass out and let medical students try to explain what happens to snatch, when it exceeds 100 years or 3 million miles.

Some dude in a Social Club T-shirt had a bag of dildos; he was apparently helping some woman find the correct fit. Upon going further into the room, I realized it had a medieval theme, with torture, whipping, and tavern maids. In the corners of the room stood guys in matching t-shirts, I assumed they were security; they sure weren't the titty police.

I walked out into another area and we needed the titty police here too, there were all kind of felonies in progress. One saggy titted offender, had the kind of tits that gave both babies and grown men nightmares. You know the kind; the tit goes from the cleavage to the back of the arm.

This set up boasted office style cubicles, for exhibitionists. You and whoever occupied a cubicle, could engage in whatever sex act desired. Those outside, watched, every once in a while touched. This polar bear of a woman was on what appeared to be knees, (let us just say all fours) and she had a black guy behind her doggy style, and a white guy in front that she was performing oral sex upon. Similar things occurred in many of the 2 dozen cubicles.

I had the arduous task of detailing each act. I did this via voicemail; I simply called my desk phone and dictated details to be transcribed at a later date.

I encountered two other cops in the room, they saw me and left. That was the agreement, unofficial as it was. If you were some place and you saw a Vice detective you simply left, no questions asked and sure as crap no answers given. They honored the code.

Everything was good until I saw the pudgy chaplain bastard again. Friar Cop was standing near the bar watching me. His loss, I thought he needed to get his $40 bucks worth and leave.

I entered another room. The sign on this door, said couples only, screw 'em, I was lying anyway. In this room were younger couples, there were far fewer saggy body part felonies in this room. Wait, I spoke too soon, there were a few Federal infractions. The finest girl in the place, blonde and blue, and an awesome body, was sitting on a bench kissing some lucky bastard. The room only had benches built around the walls, so that the center of the room was empty.

Back to the girl; she was rubbing this guy's crotch so hard I thought she was trying to start a fire. Then she pulled something out of his pants; some Ripley's believe it or not type crap. This thing was so big; I almost called animal control to come to rescue her. Talk about the elephant in the room. Then that little flower, that picture of beauty, chomped down on that Narwhal. I was sad, I felt confident that she would be found dead in the morning; Cause of Death - Strangulation. I watched the spectacle a little while wondering *if I had a chance with her without Chloroform.* Then remembered the Narwhal, and reasoned that there would be no point.

I turned to see Friar Cop at the bar. This time he pointed at me when he spoke to the bartender. I was not sure, but it looked like he had just fingered me. (Not in the way this club would have encouraged), I mean identified me as a Cop. I was not sure, crap does happen after all when you party naked. I watched him this time; Friar Cop walked across the room to another security guard, pointed at me and said something.

This was the first cop I ever encountered, that I wanted to harm. Friar Cop; a peer counselor, a chaplain, and a police officer just compromised the safety of a fellow officer. What is so sad, is that the other officers were in there as well, we had all paid to get in the place (turns out he did not, he, badged his way in; so what the crap did he care who I was watching get laid?

I watched this piece of crap walk around the dance floor and point me out to three other guards. Then it turned 1:00 o'clock. I know this because the DJ paused the music and said, 'It's 1:00, you know what time it is; Start screwing, and use your damn condoms.' Like a trance, people started undressing and having sex on the floor.

This would have been a story for me to tell for ages except there were four men near a corner, they were not naked, they were not on the floor they were neither using condoms nor screwing. It was Friar Cop, two guards behind him and me. I could not hear what his fat lips were saying but in my mind, I knew it was, he's a cop!

The guards did not say anything, but my usefulness was diminished, hard to blend into a sex club with three guys following you everywhere. I waited for the guards to move; I only planned one shot. One shot, one kill, dead cop. I determined that day no matter if they set me on fire and ate me; I was killing Friar Cop. All this screwing going on and these idiots are staring at me. Friar Cop even spoiled my hard-on; all I wanted to do now, was watch him bleed to death.

We stood and stared for about 2 minutes, they made it obvious they were not leaving, and they wanted me to leave. Rather than get into a situation with them putting their hands on me, I left; slowly. I left slow enough to confirm that the lady bent over the table was an employee and that the guy with the dildos was an employee too. I returned to my car; thought about the blonde-haired person one more time then went to the office and completed my report.

Come Monday morning, I was called in to the Captain's office giving more details. Captain did not want details about the club; only Friar Cop. I had several meetings that day, people were hot, people were mad, at least three people were in trouble, and that fat little pervert was screwed. They made me draw diagrams and write explicit details. They wanted more information and a floor plan, so I got to go back again on the company dime. I had to take a female partner this time; she said she was embarrassed, I think she ended up using the supplements and information from the case to spice up her own sex life.

Turns out, Friar Cop was married, then they put it in the newspaper, and it cost him his job. Friar Cop used his wide ass as an alibi, but made the mistake of also mentioning the other officers present as alibis. They confirmed Friar Cop was there, and nullified his wife's lies. They were suspended for being in the club (not my fault by the way, reassured Walters, (Friar Cop screwed them too) the stench of his behavior angered me, but it was soon eclipsed. Must there always be darkness? To me, the thing that is worse than death is a betrayal. You see, I could conceive death, but I could not conceive betrayal."

"I guess that's why bad guys hate vice cops."

"Don't party naked."

10.4 Operation Little Big Deal

"Despite working at different tasks, I was still in the division with many of my original crew. There were always times when our paths crossed, today was such a day. Just as Little BigHorn was the last battle for Gen. George Armstrong Custer, Little Big Deal would be the last days of the reign of Kevin and his band of untouchables. Historically speaking, most Empires fall from within, in the Blue Game, earning Credits equals earning enemies. Sometimes there are just not enough credits.

On this date a large operation, Operation Little Big Deal commenced, and it required numerous officers from squads, many of us did not get along. One of the main issues was that the Favorite Squad, frankly, was a professional port-o-potty. Like any scathingly filthy, port-o-potty, floating in the blue sludge, were various sized and textured pieces of crap. This perfectly described the members of the 'Favorite Squad.'

The patron of 'Favorite Squad' was an unremarkable Captain, of dubious sexual persuasions. Under the leadership of Captain Bonne (As in Anne Bonne), I do not know exactly how she came to lead this band of pirates, but I believe her degree was in plumbing).

Although she did not pioneer the Blue Credit System, this squad was among the chief practitioners of The System. This was the veritable Blue Credit Bank. Who better to acquire Credits, than those tasked with monitoring the vices of the city? These butt wipes made money not doing police work, they just hung out and gathered dirt on people, to be used later.

Not everyone in the squad was a floater, but the majority of them were. The supervisors all were floaters, and there were the Three Stooges, a family of floaters. Embedded with the pieces of crap, were three decent detectives, who just wanted to do their jobs; sucked to be them.

This date, we met at the office, it was a Saturday. The weather was pleasant, and there were plenty of snacks in the machine; we were ready to go. The briefing started, it was my mentor, my old boss; ah, I thought, the untouchables ride again. The information for the drug deal came in via a confidential informant; hundreds of pounds of marijuana were coming in from another state driven by a couple of Mexicans. Normal scheme, normal set up, could anything go wrong. The logistics were in place, plenty of security, plenty of guns, a lot of dope, this was all over time (so that was awesome, hope this deal lasted all weekend).

It was not until the questions arose as to the credibility of the information and the informant, the hammer fell, my lips fell, and my overtime dreams fell. My dream weekend, overtime, drug deal, turned instantly from Heck Yeah, to WTF? Like WTF was he thinking using this CI. WTF was I going to do to distance myself from the deal. WTF jail sentence was I going to face after this was done.

I slumped back in my chair, but I was glaring at him, he knew. He finished talking and we walked out towards the parking lot. I, he, and Tommy stood in a small huddle in the parking lot. Geoff and we looked at him, and Geoff said what I was thinking, Why the heck you didn't tell us this was the CI before we got to the briefing; He replied, 'Because you would not have come. I need you; I don't trust these pieces of goat crap.' We were at odds on this one, probably for the first time. 'Only piece of crap here, is your CI, keep that bastard away from me.' Then for the only time I worked with him, I turned my back on him and walked away.

I disdained his plan, his idea, his concept, his operation, but never him. I trusted him, I knew him, he was my friend; but friends do not always agree. This was one of those times. Strange how you can have complete trust in a person, no fear to go through a door or into the darkness with that person, yet still have differing lives completely.

Off to the races we drove. The complex was a horseshoe, which made surveiling the exits easy. Hours went by with few updates, and then, as it is, with all drug deals, everything happens at once. 'The car is here, occupied twice, Green Toyota truck. They are pulling up to the apartment now. Problem one was that the vehicle information was incorrect. But the nightmare was only just beginning. We waited for them to enter the target apartment and then jumped into action. They were not carrying the dope, but we knew it was in the car.

Teams split the areas of responsibility; two teams handled the apartment and the suspects, and the other team, the vehicle. Before translator services were all the rage, the old method was simple; slap someone around long enough and anyone can understand English. There was no SAP (Spanish) button, ours said SLAP. It took a few moments, but they were speaking English with the best of them within minutes.

We acquired the keys and sent them down to the car team, opened the trunk, and viola! Not a damn thing, the trunk contained no dope. Apparently, we had been using broken English; we had to clarify the situation. A few more adjectives later and we realized that there was a major problem. The mules said they brought the dope, we expected dope, the car reeked of dope, these idiots had everything for the dope except a bill of laden; the only thing missing was the dope.

Obviously, someone screwed us, and only two people were in the bed; cops and the CI. Fortunately, the CI spoke English. They lied just as much, but it was in English. SOP on any botched deal; if the deal fails due to suspicious circumstances, you crucify the CI. All deals invalidated, and most often charges ensue from the botched deal. In this case, there was no missing buy money, we did not front any dope, and all we had to verify the dope was the 'acquired' word of two drug mules.

The CI was slowly running out of time. With each minute the CI lost support, until they only had one supporter; Kevin. Dammit! Now we were definitely on opposite sides of this fence. Unlike all the raids we rode together on, all the Lion paws, bloody noses, asses kicked, coma induced and even lives taken, this was the first time I was present when all the cops, and the bad guys were getting screwed, including the orchestrator of the deal.

It tore at my heart, I never thought we; he would get caught up in the game, and lose. Makes sense, however, if no man is an island, stands to reason that no man can beat the game forever. Like the naysayers on the Titanic, I was just sad to be aboard when we struck the iceberg,

Alas, wait, redemption, at least floatation, a plan emerged. Actually, the plan was hashed out amidst many, 'losers,' 'suck my junk(s)' and 'what the crap were you thinking(s)?' Kevin stepped in a pile of dinosaur-sized crap, in front of some of his worst enemies. The 3 turds were ecstatic and wasted no time informing Captain Bonne, the conversation probably sounded like this; 'Aarrgh Captain, these scurvy detectives need to walk the plank.' To which she probably replied, 'The booty has been plundered, how many pieces of eight, did we waste?'

No mention , of their exploits, and pillages, no reminder of all they have stolen, and made off with, the hundreds of thousands of dollars fraudulently acquired - just this deal, l they had the chance to burn Kevin on this one, and in the process, jammed as many of his crew as they could.

Sadly, it came to it, even I had angry words to offer, but they all came from respect and love, not betrayal. There had been only two betrayals that day, the CI (which is a given: CI 101- never trust your future and freedom to a CI), and Kevin betrayed himself. In betraying himself, and what he had learned in the thousands of drug deals, everybody got messed.

'Man, how the hell did you not see this coming, of all the crap we survived, how could you not see this coming?' I asked of my teacher. We exchanged a few more curse words, there were a few bullets thrown by hand, a gun disassembled and thrown in the bushes, and then we parted ways. I do not regret what I said, as I am sure he does not, I was right, I just wish I never had to say it. I knew there was to be a reckoning. A few screw you(s) between friends was not going to turn me against him, but it did leave us on opposite sides of the table; temporarily.

He spoke to the CI; at length, using all the finesse he could muster, both figured out the scam, and recovered the dope. The CI played us from the beginning. They never planned to give us the dope. They came to terms with the bad guys, it turns out they brought friends, and planned a middle occurrence (rip) unbeknownst to us.

Before we realized which car the CI's crew drove, they had already entered the parking lot and dropped the dope off to another person, who then left the parking lot.

Little Big Deal was beginning to unravel. Kevin's plan was going to bone everybody including the CI. He decided to drop the Bomb. Hundreds of pounds of Marijuana fronted to the bad guys brought to a location where there with 20 cops. Nobody was walking away clean.

'Ok, here it is, bring the dope back, or I'll burn you and dry screw you twice - no lube. I will tell Juan or Hector or which everyone you are screwing that you are boning a cop and you traded the dope for dicks and salsa,' Kevin said harshly.

This was the 'burn you' phase 'Then I am taking the dope, and not charging the dealers, but I'll put a Federal ICE hold on them, and then just let them go. They will end up dead, but not before they kill you. You have one minute to decide.'

The CI was not saying much, they knew their time was running out. Whether or not she feared CI combustion, I 'm not sure, but she knew he was not lying about the dope. No one was just going to walk away from losing dope, two mules and a car, yet not return the crap, the ass kicking,

I mean. The CI was not as stupid as we thought, she had walking sense, we got the dope back, and she got to live another day.

Little Big Deal ended with the dope in the property room, the Mexicans in jail and the CI(s) free. Part of the deal was to sign up the other person as a CI. I did not agree with the plan, but the most important thing was no cops, not even the 3 turds were harmed during the making of Little Big Deal. At least that's what I thought.

Monday is always a crappy day, it is a rehash of the weekend and a forecast of the week's goals and objectives; I knew this Monday would be different. This Monday included a T3 (wire-tap) briefing and the reading in and deconfliction. This means that they told us what the wiretap was based on and who the targets were, and the deconfliction was to make sure that all agencies agreed to defer to the lead agency and assist the ATF (alcohol Firearms and Tobacco) as it was in this case. There were 45 studs in the briefing room, and Captain Bonne walks up to, and puts her grubby fat hands on my knees and bends over between my legs like a scarred, battle-weary, she-walrus stripper.

Not only was it disgustingly distasteful and unprofessional, but it was also just screwed up. 'Tell me about Kevin, there are rumors and complaints that when he's off duty he...'

I interrupted, 'Captain, please get out of my lap firstly, secondly I prefer not to discuss Little Big Deal at this time, I turned in my supplement.'

She stood up indignantly, we spent quite a lot of time together due to the Friar Cop case, and maybe she thought we were friends. We were not. 'Come see me after,' she said as she slithered away into the briefing. Dammit; I knew I would be pinned down when she interviewed me; I had to make a choice.

After the briefing, I headed down the hall. Snivel Smith (Later to be Captain Smith) came out of the office; he looked smug, figured it was him that snitched. We are so bored, I told her everything.' I knew that he was always a cowardly piece of crap. I walked in the door and closed the door. I looked across the desk at this giant sea slug of a woman dressed in all polyester.

I had a choice to make, I made my choice. 'Sit down,' she said; I plopped down in the chair. Our relationship had always been agreeable, no friction and I did specialty assignments for her. This, however, would be different; the boss was going to ask of me something I was unwilling to do. 'Kevin,' she began, 'Tell me all there is to know about him. I want to know about Merchants Plaza, and what he does at the golf shop, and every bit of his extracurricular activities; I know y'all are friends.'

What she failed to understand, probably because she was fat, and the fact that the turds were her favorite pets, proved she neither understood the drug trade nor cared for her people. Kevin was not just my friend, he was my partner.

Snivel Smith and the turds laid him out like a filleted tuna, to dry in the sun. 'Captain, I will tell you anything you want to know about Little Big Deal, as for Kevin, this was by definition an internal investigation that meant I had to tread lightly, but I did check the rulebook about internal vs. criminal investigations. I had to answer honestly about Little Big Deal, but that was no sweat because there were 19 other people there, who were going to tell the story. I told almost everything about Little Big Deal, I left out a few details that did not help.

As far as Merchants Plaza, which was a security job, I had nothing but good things to share and stories of professionalism. She was not pleased.

I told her, 'Captain when I'm on the clock I have to tell you the truth and give you any details requested. As far as Kevin doing crap off duty, I do not know, you will have to ask him, I am not around him off duty, except for Merchants.'

She snorted back. 'So you mean to tell me that you approve of his personal life?'

'I am not a part of his personal life, we do a few things together like workout, but that's in a room full of people so nothing amiss there, I don't know what you are after. But I don't have it.' Then I sat back and awaited the tusks to come out and impale me.

What I know, heard or saw off duty, that was not criminal, I have no duty to report, and I would never go on a witch-hunt for my partners, we had shared too many adventures to start asking questions about what they did off duty. I could not face myself if after all the lion paws we shared; I worried about any stupid ass behavior off duty. She wanted a reason to screw with him; it would not come from me.

I called her a slug, I never said she was stupid, she asked about the CI. *Crap, crap, screwed* I thought before I answered.

'Yes, I know the CI.'

'Tell me about the CI, where you met, and what dealings he has with her.'

'We served a search warrant; she was present and had a warrant. She agreed to work off charges, and as far as I know, other than Little Big Deal, she held up her end of the bargain. I don't see her off duty, she is a CI.'

'Are you implying there is no personal relationship between Kevin and the CI?' she pressed further.

'That's correct she was searched on the deal, and wore a wire.'

'Did she have a gun,' she inquired further. Damn Snivel Smith!

'Yes but I had the bullets, and rendered it in operable, I believe she was supposed to trade it as part of the deal for the dope.'

'Do we trade weapons for dope detective? Is that something we are in the business of doing?'

'As far as I know captain we are in the business of getting dope, lying and scheming is what we do. There is no policy against using the gun as a prop. Even though a gun was present, the apartment and her purse were searched and we gave her an empty weapon as a prop.'

'There were 20 cops, on overtime, dragged into Little Big Deal; do you not see that as a problem in supervision?'

'Ok captain, the deal was jacked up, I agree, but that doesn't mean that Kevin was the cause. We got the dope; the bad guys seized the cars and some money and identified a new CI. Overall sounds to me like it was a dope deal.'

'Other officers said you two argued and disagreed about the deal.'

'Yes there are many ways to accomplish a deal, I did not agree with the way it was set up, but that happens about half the time.'

'What about this didn't you like?' Damn this beast was determined to bury him. How many damn credits is this going to take, I pondered. The truth was not that the deal was messed up (it was) nor was it the fact that 20 cops were there.

Turns out this whole barrel of monkeys was the Blue Dick at work. Somebody higher up wanted the contract for Merchants, and the 3 turds wanted all of us gone so we could not observe the cannibalistic underworld behaviors, which Captain Bonne protected. She used the turds to gather dirt on cops; they didn't even have to make dope deals. One-half of her drug squad did not handle drug deals. Not to mention 2 of the turds were husband and wife.

The married turds worked on different squads only on paper, and as far as we could tell, they must have had an open marriage because the wife was always with another detective, sitting on his desk and always in close quarters. The turds actually kept away from the rest of the division, because they were hated and untrustworthy. They were floating pieces of crap and they snitched and monitored and recorded as many things as they could, just for leverage against their evil deeds.

'Well, I would never do a controlled buy in a horseshoe. One-way in and one-way out seems like a good idea, but I believe it leaves you open for a crossfire. In addition, I would have made the CI sit at staging with the Tech instead of inside the parking lot, and then we could have better monitored everything they did, and might have avoided the rip. I certainly would have had a translator on board, and I never would have done a takedown in an apartment. The bad guy knew the location; the CI is fully exposed at that point?'

I kept it tactical, I kept it professional; I kept it the way I wanted to explain the deal. Little Big Deal was just another event in a long line of crap that we needed to maneuver around, but our days were numbered.

As fate would have it, our number hit. Of the 20 officers, more spoke against Kevin than for him. The Blue Dick marched him out of the building, like the dude on the western called Branded. Of all the reasons to go after a venerated detective, the mastermind of thousands of successfully executed dangerous felony operations; it was because someone wanted to take his extra job away so their greedy ass could cash out.

The day they walked him out, I walked out with my brother, in spirit. That day, Captain Bonne broke the back of the Reign of Justice and Aggressive Enforcement used to make the city safer, and a better place to live, for all the hostages we rescued and the neighborhoods we cleaned up. Street level and buy bust was never the same again.

After Bonne the Slug shipped Kevin, she separated his people into different squads to make sure they never pissed in her pond again. At least that was her intention.

The Day the Turf Stood Still was a scary day. This was the day I realized that whatsoever Blue Credits we acquired were no longer valid. Crap, I had to behave like one of them other cops. You know the ones, the cops afraid to make arrests and to knock peoples' dicks in the dirt. I resigned myself to walking out to pasture, and remaining under the Blue radar, but the times they were a changing, my exile did not last long.

I would have used all my credits to save him, like American Express, some places just do not accept Get Out of Jail Free Cards."

"Why didn't anyone save him?"

"Sometimes doing the right thing sheds light on other people not doing their jobs. I guess it rubbed many people the wrong way, that this little tribe of officers, were able to make such a difference, make so many felony arrests, deal with dangerous felons and situations, contend with harrowing situations resulting in fewer fatalities per capita than any unit in the Department (probably world history). Jealousy is a son of a bitch."

10.5 Desk Jockey

"They say into every life a little rain must fall; well it started raining one day. In front of the Police headquarters, the chief stood smoking his cigars. We knew each other well as the squad made him happy, and had done all the things he asked to be done. I did not know it at the time, but Captain Bonne was in for a surprise. 'Afternoon Chief, you got one of those cigars for me,' Chief Tubber exhaled and smiled at me.

'Renarde,' he called me by my first name always, I like to think it was because he respected and liked me, more than likely it was a subtle sign of showing ownership, as though I was his pet.

'What have y'all been doing? The Mayor has been calling; people are standing out selling dope again.'

'Nothing I can do I'm not even street-level anymore, there's nothing I can do from where I am.'

Another puff, then he dropped his ashes off into the planter. Then another puff, 'I took care of that.' I was not sure what he meant, but I had an idea.

'I couldn't save Kevin, he won't be back'

We stood there for a moment, and amidst his smoke, said, 'Y'all get back to it.' Then he turned his back and finished enjoying his cigar. As I walked away, *I wondered how many credits this assignment came with.* Exile was over; I was back.

I was back to street level enforcement again this time they asked me to train. Buy-bust is the staple of drug enforcement. Where there is no street-level enforcement, there is no real interest in controlling crime. According to the American Federal Bureau of Justice, a high percentage of all crime is drug-related. According to the FBI, offenders were under the influence during the commission of these crimes:

- Crime of violence - 24.2 percent
- Rapes or sexual assaults - 30.0 percent

- Robbery - 23.3 percent
- Assault - 24.1 percent
- Aggravated assault - 26.2 percent
- Simple assault - 23.5 percent

These numbers do not reflect the crimes committed to get drugs or drug profits. Some of the numbers are higher or lower in specific categories like college campuses versus violent crimes, but 90% of burglaries are drug-related, and often, it's repeat offenders. Ever wonder where, how, or when offenders get their drugs? They get their DRUGS ON THE STREET!

This does not mean that the sellers are all standing on the corner, but they have to meet and exchange somewhere, and that requires low-level interactions. Even Kilo drug deals, have to involve the street; transportation and distribution all occur on the street. That is why it takes a certain commitment to crime fighting to do street-level enforcement.

For the new assignment, they made two squads. Much to Captain Bonne's chagrin, the squads contained 3 of the original, tainted members, not her turds; real cops. Two of the supervisors were from my squad, Tommy, and Bill, home sweet home. They sent a turd sniffer to ask me to go to SLU (Street Level Unit) and train. Imagine that, the man who did not sell his friend out, did not betray the craft , and did not want to work for Jabba, was invited to come out and play; with the blessing of the chief. Holy crap!

They tasked me to train the new officers. We had classroom time, which I instructed, and then it was time to get them out in the bush. The new team was different; they were all laid back cool guys that looked up to the old team. Some of the UC-Rs had worked assignments with us before and they were well aware that this task required stealth, sleuth, and a great deal of heavy handedness;

As I was trained, the first thing we did was pick up ho(s). Ho(s) are just convenient, they are fun for everyone. Item one; they had to wear the gun either on the opposite side or not at all. Like most cops, this concept was met with resistance and disdain, but if you wear your pistol, the whore will feel it. They search you in three ways, remember. A few botched deals and they learned to move their weapons. So many guys go into UC work, for just the plainclothes status.

If you do not want to do UC work, do not be a UC. The main job, the constant, in real UC work is varied; you are going to always have to be something else. Item two; the other benefit to whores is they never want to go to jail. Turns out it is not fear of incarceration, it is harder to get dope in jail, and while locked up they cannot get their fixes as easily. Consequently, they are almost always willing to be CIs and buy dope.

Batter up I said, to the first UC-R (undercover rookie), remember you can grab her tits if she asks, and she is going to rub your dick, but that is all you can do to prove you are not a cop. If they do rub your crotch, then put those facts in the report. Hard to claim you just wanted a ride when you get in and rub a dick asking if the driver is a cop.

I heard all manner of stupid excuses for not having sex in the car. Hard to sell that you are looking for a blowjob, and then refusing it. Therefore, we trained them to always say they do not want to get pulled over, and they want to enjoy it so they would park. There were a few, I have no driver's license, no smoking in the metro vehicle, no I'm working as security that's why I have a handcuff key or gun, my wife's pregnant, my wife's a bitch, and even my wife is dead.

Once the prostitution deal occurs, the actual arrest required no force, but a crap load of care. Whores carry all manner of crap in their purse, NEVER PUT YOUR HANDS INTO THEIR PURSE; dump it out. It is hard to get rid of hepatitis, AIDS, or any other blood borne pathogen. Once you encounter a sharp contaminated item like a needle, or crack pipe. Here is a partial list of crap you seldom find in a street ho(s) purse;

- Soap
- Toothpaste
- Douche
- Vagisil
- Ky jelly
- Breath mints
- Dental floss
- Clean socks
- Deodorant
- Toothbrush

We practiced on the whores until the UC-Rs were comfortable and better equipped to do mass arrests, lie, and manipulate people. The added benefit was that arresting whores brings in a vast number of Informants and Intel.

You know what I learned from picking up whores and walking In their shoes?"

"What, condoms are important?"

"The human race is a monotonous affair. Most people spend the greatest part of their time working in order to live, and what little freedom remains, so fills them with fear, that they seek out any and every means to be rid of it."

10.6 Sometimes Mistakes Happen

'Ok he's getting it from a guy in a KFC uniform, he just showed up. Make sure you grab KFC,' was the information broadcast over the radio. 'Move in!' I did as normal, hunt my target down, and apprehend. The guy took off running and I gave chase. He ran into a dead end and suddenly turned to face me. I drew down on him, and he put his hands up.

As I closed the distance, he thrust his hand into his right pocket, as though he had a weapon. By this time, I had closed the distance enough that I kicked him in the stomach, sending him to the ground. Then I rolled him over and handcuffed him without further incident. Story over right? Nope, not by any means; this story would not end for another 9 months.

I dragged the carcass back to the area designated for paperwork. When I arrived; the voice, the man that initiated this capture looks at me and says, 'We do not need that one anymore; we got the dope and the money.'

'Dammit' I replied, 'Hunter you asked for him, here he is!'

'Well I do not have anything to charge him with,' he replied.

'Well, what the crap am I supposed to do with him now?' Just as we begin discussing this young black man's future, he started complaining of feeling dizzy. I kicked him in the stomach, nauseous I understood but dizzy? 'I got shot in the head, I get dizzy sometimes when I run, and can I have some water?' the suspect explained.

My Sgt walked over and said three words, 'Now we're screwed!' and walked away.

A candid and unfortunate conversation with the team ensued about charging the suspect with something. I said, 'With what, he ran until I said stop then put his hands up. He's ignorant, but he has a job and you put him in the dope deal, I am not throwing a charge on anyone.'

Whilst we were hashing out his future, someone snatched him up and took him to jail. Upon arriving at the jail facility, the transporting officer called us back and asked what his charges were? WTF? Was the unified response, how did he get down town? Ok, so now we're really gonna get bent over.

I never planted dope, a gun or threw a charge on anyone; a source of personal pride. Yeah, I done sent more people to the hospital, than smallpox, but they were in the game.

Soon, it was determined not to charge him and to bring him back home. 30 minutes after patrol dropped him back off to the unit; Humpty Dumpty (the suspect) went home and requested an ambulance saying his abdomen hurt (ok that one was mine). We got a phone call; from EMS stating that he requested an ambulance, and said that the police had beat him up and then let him go (you would think he would be grateful, we let him go).

Ok Sgt was right; this was going to be a hassle. The Sgt also reminded us of the adage, if you put your hands on them, take them to jail. That was the prevailing Blue Law, but my law was higher. My law is, if you man enough to play in crap, learn to deal with the smell. This came along with the job, sometimes you get the bear, and sometimes you just get bent over (no lube).

Was I to blame, well yeah. Although my ignorant partner started the whole thing, it really was not his fault. He just reported what he observed. The suspect created the problem by acting aggressive. It was my choice to handle Humpty Dumpty, now I had to face the music.

Another call came down the pike, 'Take his crap!' that was it, they took my stuff: my sword and cape, suspending me and putting my ass on a desk duty answering the phone. Like I said, I was bent. Humpty Dumpty said I whipped his ass, and not only did not arrest him, but never filed a use of force report - yeah bent over.

The order to take my crap soon turned into; and put it in a box. I had received separation orders. No chips to cash in this time, too many heads would roll if they did not burn me. It chapped my ass, that after all the hard crap I did, this is what I was on the bench for, letting a turd go that we never should have grabbed.

If they were going to can me, I was ok. No other officers were sucked into my black hole, I was glad about that. Because no one tried to screw it up, it just worked out that we broke one too many eggs. Screw Humpty Dumpty.

What I did not know was that three days after the first call, Humpty Dumpty went back to the hospital and was now in ICU, after bleeding internally for three days. His stomach hurt, he was bleeding internally. *Vindication, at least I broke something* I thought. I was on the crap list, but at least my karate was still good, I had doubted myself.

Humpty Dumpty stayed in ICU a month and lost all kinds of internal bowels. It was during this time that Chief Tubber; we spoke often, one of the byproducts of my job skills.

I placed only one call, it was to the chief 'It's just me Chief, I'm alone, no one else goes down for this.' It was not that anyone else needed attention, but they were looking to blame someone, because they knew a lawsuit was coming, Screw it, I hit him; blame me, and only me. Chief signed off on that, which also meant that he would not be able to save me if any saving needed to be done; I burned a Credit and accepted my fate.

While waiting, the bell began to toll, I knew for whom it tolled. Internal Affairs came hot, they came hard, and they came fast. They sent my case to the Criminal Investigations Division; the Department did not want to pay Humpty's bills, I was a kite whose string had been cut.

Ironically I was not bitter about the treatment, I was accused of a felony, what else could the Dept. do Walters? 'They could have had your back; sounds like they gang banged you.' I smiled, 'Look man, my jobs was to be a terror in the dark. Politics is a huge part of Policing. The department could not afford to admit to sanctioning people like me. I could not make this go away, too many moving parts, and too much documentation from the hospital. When they could they hid me, I got caught with my hand in the cookie jar. All they could do was put down their rabid dog.

I was not upset, until an Armed Robbery detective came to see me. 'I heard about Humpty Dumpty. He is a piece of crap. He did not have a gun; he was messing with you because he thought you were an Armed Robbery detective.' I leaned a little closer, 'We been watching him for a month, we knew y'all were in the area, he's a suspect in about 13 armed robberies. If it makes you feel any better we are going to burn him. Sorry, you are getting banged.' *Dammit*! I thought, a career gone over a piece of crap, but I was still glad I did not throw a charge on him, and then I would have been a Blue Dick.

I spent many months on the desk answering the phone. I never realized how many idiots lived in the service area; holy crap. Mental giants inundated the Station with calls. It was disgusting; I had to install car seats for an even dumber stage of moronic, people too stupid to figure out how to install car seats correctly. They should pass a law if you are too stupid to know how to care for kids you should not be allowed to have any. Seriously, the box had pictured instructions, what the crap!

If parents can't understand neither the written instructions nor the pictures, how are they going to do stuff like, help the kids read, order from the menu, or heaven forbid microwave a meal. I wish they needed help figuring out which tit had milk in it, that I would not mind teaching. Both of us laughed at the last comment. Yeah I am a low-life.

Over the months I got legal advice from fellow officers like you should have lied, you should have thrown a charge on him, and my favorite; why not plant dope. Even the higher-ups sent messages, like look for a new job, never put your hands on someone, and let them go. For the first time in my career, I wondered what being a cop meant.

Obviously, to most, it meant CYA (cover your Ass), when you make a mistake, apparently, the thought of apologizing or admitting a mistake never entered their minds, even though the Good Faith rule allowed for mistakes. Nothing allowed for planting dope, falsifying charges or lying; but that is what I was advised to do. Up until now, I will admit, I have slammed many heads into the wall, but those heads had it coming. Dude was a piece of crap, no doubt, but I still did not have a charge.

But wait there's more! These bastards charged me with violating policy. They said I violated three policies. Now I have to go give a statement to these underlings about men's work. Damn, having to justify men's work, to individuals who do not do men's work is not only demeaning, but also difficult. What do we have to talk about?

Then they really took my crap. They took my badge, my gun, my ASP (expandable batons), my cuffs, and stupid as it seems, my Class A hat because it had a hat badge and my ID cards. Not the ID cards, that; said Police Officer. That was it, humility; they stripped me and walked me out of the fort-like in that western. If I had a sword, they would have probably broken it - I was now a civilian *persona non-grata*. Screw me!

I was not a virgin at the Internal Affairs counter, but this was different. This time The System was not on my side, the bean counters wanted me gone, so they could avoid the lawsuit. What is more, many years before, I had filed a complaint against another officer regarding a domestic incident. There was no love in my heart for cops who abuse their families, no love at all. Owing as well to the fact was, that the law had changed, and mandated reporting; I was not only going to report it because the officer was a pile; I sure as hell wasn't going to sustain an arrest for failing to report, to cover his useless ass. However, he had friends; Tick friends.

The woman beating officer's Blue Tick friend Captain Butt-Kisser-Cockeyed-Bastard was the presiding official over my disciplinary hearing, and he was out for blood. Because of my domestic report, he promised me that if it took the rest of his career, he would donkey punch me. Even from an ugly policewoman, this phrase would not have been so bad, but this was a dude!

Another official on the board would be a dirty detective. I worked a case against Nevada, and tried to get him fired. Now this garbage pail was also to judge me. I lay in wait and prepared for my days in the interview room. I knew what to say, and how to say it, it was just different now. These were cops; (allegedly), this was supposed to be family. It is different when the people judging are the same people that are supposed to have your back.

The whole Thin Blue Line, is a merger of blues, the Line is only as blue as the officers who stand on it. Corruption, domestic abuse, and planting charges and dope have no place on the line. Being rough during an arrest is a no brainer, but the Line exists for a reason; justice is the reason, not just-us.

I thought about it each day I answered the phone, watching the officers in their uniforms, my uniform, go by. Look how far I am from the glassy-eyed rookie, no longer innocent; but now a true believer. I believe that people should be safe; I believe that bad things should happen to bad people, and most of all I believe that the only purpose people like me exist in the world is to stop the darkness overrunning it all. Is it not the Mongoose that has become famous for fighting the King Cobra? Mongooses have a special skill that enables them to fight and defeat the snake; they have immunity to venom. I too am immune to venom, all the years of working in the darkness, I did not become good, but I stayed there, right at the line. I may never be awarded for decency, but there are thousands of kids and people that have thrived, in the safety I helped foster.

I am immune to Tick venom. I straightened my back and waited, not for the bad guys, but my guys; I waited for the police to come to get me and judge me. Months went by, and nothing happened. One day I received the letter, it was on Blue paper, how telling. It formally charged me with Excessive force and Failing to Render Aid. I laughed;

no, it was not so much funny as ironic. All the hides and horns displayed in our office wall, I am hauled before the Council of Idiots for this crap. I summoned my Union Lawyer and we went.

'Sit down Detective,' Dickhead the Tick said. I sat down. 'We need to make you aware of your rights that are listed in the (Tick) letter we sent you.'

'I read those, my lawyer and I signed off.'

'Good,' Dickhead, the Tick continued, 'then you can dispense with these forms. Now you received a charge letter so you know why you are here, you also read the policy on truthfulness correct?' I nodded. 'This is being recorded so please answer verbally,' the detective retorted. I wanted to reply, *Yes Dickhead*, but I left the latter portion off.

'Just tell me what happened Detective?' I have attended too many interview schools and testified too many times to fall into that trap, never answer an open-ended question. However, there was nothing to hide, no matter how they tried to spin this I did not screw up. The culprit did not get raped (kicked yes), and no one was violated; A criminal did something ignorant and was apprehended. I stand behind what I did, so I told Dickhead the Tick the story.

After completing the story, Dickhead the Tick asked questions? How many times did you kick him, what was he charged with, and what did you do after, were the big three he repeated. I was charged with three violations, so they had to address each one separately.

After the second round, Dickhead the Tick started to get testy with the questions, implying wrongdoing. 'You know the handcuffing policy don't you detective?'

'I do, 'I replied, 'It also includes a useful section on unhand cuffing. I took the guy into custody for what appeared to be involvement in a drug deal. He ran from a clearly marked officer, investigating a felony. Then he motioned as if retrieving a weapon, and was knocked down using the get back kick. It is not as if I kicked him in the head. He lunged forward like had he a knife or pistol, I needed the extra room to shoot. He did not thrust his hands into his pocket until I moved close enough to handcuff him. Creating the distance was what the kick is designed to do. Then I gave him some water to drink. I had nothing to do with transporting him to booking. He was not processed into The System, he was released from booking.

Dickhead the Tick continued, 'Do you think you know how to handcuff properly, are you not supposed to handcuff the suspect while he is standing upright, or bent over a car, why prone him out?'

Indignantly I replied, 'I handcuff as I see fit, based on the situation, that is the difference between the real police and people like you. Bad guys tend not to stand still and let you handcuff them; the prone handcuffing position is what is prescribed by Agency training for felony arrests.'

I hoped Dickhead the bastard was mad. He was mad. 'I handcuff people; you do not know what I do?'

'Yes, I do unless you eat those you handcuff, where do you hide them; you were never at court or jail, so why are you even handcuffing anybody?' Then I crossed the line, 'Do you even qualify to ask me questions about arrests, have you ever made any?'

Dickhead the Tick replied incredulously, 'I went to the same academy you did' difference is I am not the one being investigated. Shall we continue?'

"Side Note: It's probably unwise to piss off the cop who is investigating you. Not only was he investigating me, Ticks stick together.

We wrapped up the interview, and as a result, they slated me for a Computer Voice Stress Analysis (CVSA) (lie detector test). That did not bother me, my job was to lie, so I could pass regardless, but I was not lying this time, so I had no concerns. I passed no problem, the only thing left to do - disciplinary hearing; another Council of Idiots.

Not all of the idiots on the council were my peers, some had made arrests, one had graduated the academy with me, one had supervised me, none had done drug work, and none had done my job. One piece of crap was that black Michelin tire looking cop from Club Tip Top, Det. Nevada. Captain Butt-Kisser-Cockeyed-Bastard stacked the deck against me; he planned to see me gone.

I had a lawyer, but to hell with him, it was my job on the line, I prepared my own defense. I studied the policy, line by line, studied my charges, and found the loopholes; what I did, was not covered by any written policy - I had a fighting (fighters) chance.

Captain Butt-Kisser-Cockeyed-Bastard started the meeting by having the charges read against me and introducing the 'jury', I mean the board of officers. I knew everyone there, but they asked if there is anyone on the board that you object to, adjudicating the case. I did not want one of the guys, Nevada; he was a dirty, piece of horse-trading crap. I did not object, I was ready to go to task on this one.

The dance began; they asked me what happened, and I told them. Captain Butt-Kisser-Cockeyed-Bastard started his questions. 'Why did you kick him, let us get to the heart of it, we are here because you used force against a person and failed to arrest them?

'That's true, but there is nothing that says I have to arrest someone just because I put my hands on them. I have discretion. Turns out, what he did, at best, was a misdemeanor, and therefore, I have complete discretion as to whether to arrest.'

Captain Butt-Kisser-Cockeyed-Bastard replied, 'What about your duty to the company?'

'I didn't think I had a duty to lie to protect the company.' Butt-Kisser-Cockeyed-Bastard had no response.

Captain Butt-Kisser-Cockeyed-Bastard continued, 'Let's deal with the fact that you failed to render aid to this man.' That was the second horse crap charge.

'Regarding that matter, no one knew the guy had internal damage. It is not like I used a karate kick, I simply kicked him back off me. He never asked for anything more than water. And he said he had a preexisting medical condition, and he said the remedy was to drink water and I gave him water.'

Captain Butt-Kisser-Cockeyed-Bastard and I argued for at least 10 minutes about whether I rendered medical attention, I am not a damn doctor. Then we went on break, it was time to make a determination as to my guilt.

I knew what Captain Butt-Kisser-Cockeyed-Bastard wanted, he was told to fire me, to avoid the lawsuit. In addition, Captain Butt-Kisser-Cockeyed-Bastard still planned to fire me because I did not help the officer on the domestic. As if I would help a piece of crap cop that puts his hands on a woman - TO HELL WITH HIM, THEM AND ALL COPS THAT BATTER WOMEN, I will never help them."

I leaned closer to Walters, 'And you better not either.' He said nothing.

I continued with my story. "Outside, little Miss Lady walked up to me."

'You know they want to fire you, don't you? They have orders to cut the strings.'

I knew that they wanted to, the ignorant suspect, lost some guts, and some organs after I kicked him. I did not say anything about the case, we just talked.

We resumed the tribunal. We put on the next witness in my defense, the departmental Use of Force Trainer.

Captain Butt-Kisser-Cockeyed-Bastard started, 'Sgt Babbs, tell me. What is the current departmental training on the use of force, documentation and Medical attention?'

'There is no medical attention required. We teach the method, and there is no reason for medical attention, it is not supposed to cause injury. It's not that type of kick.' Since there is no injury intended, there is no paperwork required, in terms of a use of force report,' replied the departmental Use of Force Trainer.

Captain Butt-Kisser-Cockeyed-Bastard was pissed; he was fuming in his seat. He just knew Sgt Babbs was going to devastate my story. *Ha-ha* I thought, *screw you trick. Even though we were friends, Sgt Babbs was not there to help me, he was a SME (Subject Matter Expert), and nationally recognized. Sgt Babbs taught the techniques used, so he may have been covering his ass too, either way he punched the main hole in the prosecution's case.*

Then Captain Huscon spoke up. He liked me, I had worked for him before, he knew I was squared away, plus he liked me, 'Well, Andrews, didn't you say that you gave him a glass of water, and that's what he said he needed for his medical condition? That's rendering Aid isn't it?'

Captain Butt-Kisser-Cockeyed-Bastard took another blow to his vengeful attack, changing his victory into a humiliating defeat.

It was over; I won. Doing the right thing, being honest, not framing the kid, despite all the Departmental critics, and attempts to disavow, was the right thing to do (as I knew it to be). Captain Butt-Kisser-Cockeyed-Bastard had one last trick up his sleeve. 'The Board voted to exonerate you, over my objection, you may return to your assignment, B detail in Patrol, with Tuesdays and Wednesdays off.

He did it; he pulled a Hail Mary out his ass, and screwed me. No longer a detective, no more weekends off, no more over time. This glump gave me the crapiest assignment he could find. I would say at least I left with my honor intact, but Captain Butt-Kisser-Cockeyed-Bastard would not even know what that phrase meant."

"No lesson this time, what did you learn from this adventure?"

"Well years later, that detective apologized and said he was under orders to railroad me out of the department. I didn't like him much, but I understood, and thanked him. More importantly, do not be afraid to do the right thing, even in the face of ridicule, or the loss of something more valuable; honor has value."

10.7 Enemy In The Wire

"I adjusted my posture; polyester has a way of making your groin sweat, I did not want to tug myself in front of him, but I was wrestling with a wedgie that I was going to have to address shortly. I felt like Rip-Van-Foreskin. I had been out of uniform for so long, I had to purchase one that fit. I did not have any more money on my account, crap; I had to spend cash. I hoped Captain Butt-Kisser had two heart attacks, the first one, and then one when he got to the hospital and revived him.

I reported to work my first day. Who the hell really goes to work at 1500 a.m., what idiot devised this shift? I was blue again, people spoke to me now. The same stupid bastards that walked past me every day when I was disempowered, now recognized me as the dude from all the Lion Paw stories (Lion paws is a nice way to describe kicking peoples asses).

I went to the detail Sgt, and asked Sgt Moustache if I could ride with someone for a few weeks, until I got my bearings. It had been years since I was in uniform. He agreed, despite his reputation of being a dick, I never had any trouble with him.

I had my respect and reputation back; many of the younger officers looked up to me and remembered me from the drug classes I instructed in In-service. What they liked best, however, was that I was not a lazy, doughnut eating hack like so many had become after a few years on the force. Many of them could not even keep my pace. I started setting standards and made fun competitions to make the week hurry by. It turns out Patrol was not terrible. I got a zone soon thereafter and my days off changed to Thursday Friday, mostly due to my work ethic. Patrol was not bad, once you escape roll call. Couple of BS calls, and then we got to go playing.

We would get together and go to the hot areas, and look for trouble to get into. Cops have to seek out the darkness and bring light to the situation, otherwise crime spreads, and decent people live in fear. It is our sworn duty to make criminals as miserable and uncomfortable as possible at all times. If you do not like the duty, to hell with you - get a civilian job then.

Things were good, I was happy. I was leading in warrants obtained; I was solving crimes, albeit bull crap stuff, but I was making arrests. The Drug and Gang Unit at the Precinct reached out to me periodically for help with search warrants, and drug busts.

While I was disempowered, I made friends. I became unofficial Mayor of the screw-ups. Numerous officers got into trouble and sat with me in the timeout corner. I spent nearly a year disempowered. One of the guys in the corner was an ex-Army Ranger. Will Storm was not alright, he was not ok, he was not even a little off - he was jacked in the head. I befriended him; but I knew crazy when I saw it. I figured, better to be on good terms with him when he decides to go on a killing spree at the Precinct.

One evening, we had mail call. Sgts, meet officers out in the field, and go over paperwork to make corrections before the end of the shift. Will was there, as well, arguing on the phone, as always. Then, 'Well fine then, how about when I get home I shoot you in the face?' he yelled into the phone. Mail call ended. The officers tipped off, as if they did not hear the utterance. The Sgt truly did not.

Sgt Juliet was eccentric; he had the personality and temperament of an alcoholic. Always loud and off color, he was pleasant though. I walked over to him and asked him what he was going to do? He replied about what, I just pointed at crazy-ass Will. I was not trying to snitch; but you know how I feel about domestics. I also did not want to leave Sgt Juliet alone with a sack full of crazy. Sgt Juliet inquired, and I told him what was said, the law had changed; failing to report could cost me my job and freedom, not to mention some girl's face.

Sgt Juliet and I walked over to Will. Will threw his cigarette down and jumped in his patrol car; then this nut job turned on his emergency equipment and took off. We jumped in our cars and followed him. He drove around the mall access road three times with lights and sirens blazing. People probably thought we were a carousel or something, a carousel of idiots.

When Will the Nut job stopped, he rolled his window down, and went in his sullen, Full Metal Jacket crazy, trooper mode. I walked up to him, and took up a tactical position to back up Sgt Juliet. I was prepared to protect Sgt Juliet. I did not leave home this day, ready to shoot another cop, but I was not about to let crazy kill one either. Who knew I would be training to protect a cop from another cop.

'Will, are you ok?' Juliet began with a stupid ass question.

'Yes, I'm just thinking,' Will responded, tapping his fingers on the keyboard of his computer.

'What you thinking Will?' I knew that was the right question to ask, I just hoped Will would not answer.

'Thinking about killing myself,' Will said

Damn! A suicidal Army Ranger; I had been in the service, as well. He had more Armed Forces training than I, and I had more Tactical Police training. He was trained to kill; I was trained to save lives. But at this distance, even he could not get us both from a seated position I thought. We had already blocked Nut job's car in, so crazy would have to run on foot from this point.

'Will, is that the same girl that wrecked your car?' I chimed in trying to de-escalate, better to out think this idiot, than shoot it out. I relied on the time we spent on the desk, to give me some advantage. Fortunately, it did; just a little. 'Come on man, let's go sit down over there and talk. I pointed to some outdoor tables nearby at the mall. I wanted to get him away from the shotgun and extra duty ammo as well. I was sure he was running the scenario in his mind, as to how he could maneuver into a firing solution against two shooters on higher elevation. I guess someone could accomplish the feat, but Nut job had his seatbelt on (thank heaven for stupid people), I suppose he did not want to wreck without a seatbelt before a shootout with two cops. I shrugged my shoulders and Walters laughed. Cops are like that, we find solace in cynicism.

As soon as Nut job stepped out of the car, I grabbed his wrist pinned it, and disarmed him. It was a useful stunt, one of the UC techs showed in Vice. This was not really a technique, one showed as a gag, to practice, when we had down time, to see whose weapon you could snatch from behind.

By the time Will realized the weapon was gone, so was his career. We transported him back to headquarters. He was my friend, he let me handcuff him, and take him to the Precinct. Felt crappy putting cuffs on Will, but he was under control and safe, why screw up a good thing. Putting rounds in his head, groin, and chest would not have thrilled me either. Only thing he said the entire trip was to ask what I thought they would do with him, 'Get you some help buddy,' I replied.

At the Precinct, I took Nut job to the bathroom and unhandcuffed him. 'You think they will fire me?'

I thought, *No crazy, we need more suicidal homicidal people on the street. They are going to give you your gun back, so you can go home and shoot the girl; do not be late to work tomorrow.*

'I don't know Will. I am sure it will be alright when you calm down,' I lied; I was standing toe to toe with a trained killer.

Ok so get this, I continued, as I touched Walters's arm; this crazy son-of-a-bitch, spent less time disempowered, than I did. These damn idiots wanted to fire me for kicking a piece of crap, but they just gave Will, the Nut job, back his badge and gun. I was so thrilled to see my friend, the Army Ranger walking the halls of the precinct again.

'Why?' Walters asked surprised.

'Because if they fired me, I would sue, and they would have to admit their Psyche profile did not work. Internal Affairs shied away from him as well. After all, it was still a domestic, overheard by several cops; most of whom they never interviewed.

As fate would have it, about a month later, I walked out of the bathroom at the Precinct, and Nut job was standing in the hallway of the precinct practicing his draw-stroke. The Precinct is basically a box with a box in the middle, when you come out of the bathroom, the hallway in both directions dead ends into a wall. Behind the walls, are interview rooms, and the Detail Sgt's squad room. I waited until Nut job finished practicing his draw stroke, and holstered. He then calmly walked into the roll call room.

I walked into the Sgt's room and walked up to Sgt Moustache who was both of our Sgt. 'You ain't gonna believe this crap,' I started, and told him the facts.

This time, I decided to leave it alone. They called Nut job back into the office and took his badge and gun again. As ridiculous as it is, they gave the lunatic his gun back, and had to take it a third time.

Finally, they fired him, and put out a statewide safety bulletin, warning all cops to avoid confrontation with him, listing him as armed and extremely dangerous.

Well hell; Blacks lives matter is new, but who in the hell's life matters to the Department, when you keep putting a deranged killer on the street? Who is truly safe from a crazy Army ranger with a badge, gun, and uniform? By the time anyone could raise the alarm 'enemy in the wire' how much damage could he have done, and to whom?"

"What does he have to do with BLM?"

"Man, nothing we do, stands alone. You cannot believe any lives matter, when you send a baby seal killer out there to club cops and crooks. You can't tell what matters, and to whom, by the training and the discipline of the department. In politics, only votes matter, Administrative abuse and indifference drives people to the edge."

"The edge?"

"There is no honest way to explain it, because the only people who really know where it is are the ones who have gone over."

11.0
SHOOTING REVIEW
BOARD PART _{4th Appearance}

"I know "I answered, "Which shootings did I skip? Why, you don't think I am going to tell you all my secrets do you?" I laughed; he paused, as well. I suppose he wondered what I had to hide, nothing, another dog, and another human. Just did not want to deal with them today.

Shooting people is something cops must be prepared to do, if not you, risk death, or worse, cause someone else to die. While all my shootings were righteous, I do not really think they should be boasted about. I also did not want to answer too many questions about how it felt.

If you think shooting a dog is a hassle, wait until you pull the trigger on a human. Main reason, dogs do not sue! There is no great morality to what police officers do; not too long ago, they enforced slavery and discrimination. Europe did not outlaw rape until the 14th century, and it was for purely economic reasons. Morality exists in the law, and in our hearts, this is the fallacy of society: the same hearts that overlook human suffrage, write the laws. With that in mind, yeah, I shot the bastard dog, more than once.

Oh look, Flying Monkeys, I thought, as I walked into the room. The walls seemed tall, compared to the small people in it; it was like Alice in Wonderland. 'Come in and have a seat Detective, the Chief's designee requested. I disliked Dept Chief Sheppard, mostly because he was a dick, nothing special, just a dick. I sat down. Flying Monkey 1 continued, 'Up next is item 7 Officer Involved Shooting.' *Now I am an item, I mused, I wish I had shot Flying Monkey 1.* I pulled my notes out, so as not to contradict my original story. 'We have several questions for you.' Before he could espouse his stupidity, 'If I may, it is easier for everyone if I tell the story, then you ask questions, then there will be less confusion.' They agreed. Running your ass is always dangerous, but as Mark Twain said, 'If there is a story to be told tell it, never let the truth get in the way of a good story...if there's a good story, let it be, don't spoil it with the truth.'

'I responded to a call of a man chasing people with an axe. I assumed incorrectly, that this was just another bull-crap call, or a domestic. Either way, I anticipated the suspect's disappearance prior to my arrival. On this hot day, no clouds in the sky, light traffic, kids away in school, Chris the Psychopath, decides to chase people, with an axe.

Chris the Psychopath preceded the event, by hacking a cat into pieces. This did not go well with the witness, so they called the police. Before the police arrived, however, Chris the Psychopath, decided to chase the witness, with the axe. A passerby, seeing the lady being chased by the axe murderer in training, jumped out of his car, and intervened.

The lady fell while running and Chris the Psychopath closed in but could not get to the witness because Mr. Good Citizen intervened. 'Get up, get away, call the police!' Mr. Citizen yelled, as he threw his shoes at Chris the Psychopath's face.

Chris the Psychopath, responded with hostility to the interference of this stranger and turned his rage towards him , and chased him instead, with the axe. We were on the way, as fast as the policy allowed. Prior to arrival of the first car dispatch radioed that MED-COM was on the scene, (someone was hurt) but they staged until such time as Chris the Psychopath was rendered safe. I sped to the area; I wanted to help with the rendering.

Computer Aided Dispatch (CAD) relayed another update, male white, striped shirt and khakis, standing in the breezeway bleeding about the head and neck.

By the time I arrived, the perimeter was already established. I exited and ran into the breezeway, the silent breezeway. As I ran into the breezeway, I observed Mr. Citizen receiving first aid. It appeared that Chris the Psychopath, had struck him in the head, using the axe. After striking this victim, Chris the Psychopath barricaded himself in an apartment. The Sgt, on the scene, Sgt Moustache, decided that we needed to make forced entry, to ensure the safety of anyone inside (rightly so).

I discerned several problems with his plan. The rationale was correct, but the execution abysmal. High-risk entries, and high-risk warrants require training; preservation of life comes first. There are many reasons to kick in a door, but only one way to do it correctly:

utilizing as much care as possible. This would not be the case; currently there were crossfire issues galore. Since I possessed the most extensive level of training of anyone on the scene, I undertook redeploying the men. The Sgt on the scene maintained the mission, but had no problem surrendering to superior tactics and training.

The Sgt devised a plan to engage the suspect, secure the apartment and rescue any hostages (with a little brush up was not too bad). The apartment complex gave us a hard time over assisting in opening the door; they actually refused to help. They told us they prefer we kicked in the door (To this, I smiled. If they did not mind the police kicking the door in, they were going to be thrilled with what we did to the rest of the apartment).

Once set, the Sgt gave the go ahead. His plan consisted of three stages.

- Stage 1 which was that officers cleared all the apartments on this particular level. Sgt Moustache was to deploy Pepper Foam Dispenser; standing in front of the door, preparing to foam the suspect upon contact, even if Chris the Psychopath was with his axe
- Stage 2 consisted of me, and another officer on the non- hinged side of the door. I surmised that, the Mule-kick or any type of forced kick entry, into an unknown hostage situation against an axe-wielding maniac, was not a great choice. I readied myself to pry the door open slowly at the lock, sounding like entry with a key. The plan was not to panic Chris the Psychopath anymore than necessary, hoping that the opportunity to hack at another human might titillate him. Upon exit, Chris the Psychopath would receive one verbal warning to drop the axe, and then I was to neutralize Chris the Psychopath; he was mine to deal with alone, the secondary officer assigned, I had worked with before: I was on my own
- Stage 3 was to occur immediately upon engagement or neutralization of the subject. The other officers were to flood the apartment and look for hostages. I was to provide any required medical attention until MED-COM took over

I pried the door open, and as soon as the latch gave way, Chris the Psychopath snatched the door open. I was to the left of the doorframe. Mr. Chris the Psychopath stood about 6 foot 2 inches tall, glasses, a collared flannel shirt, and a very large, knife. Sgt Moustache gave the first verbal command, 'Police, Drop the knife!' he then immediately dispensed Foam. Chris the Psychopath, simply wiped the foam away, and then instead of lunging at Sgt Moustache: he turned on Stage 2 probably because we were closest, and his greatest threat.

My partner NEVER engaged. I pushed him back, but Chris the Psychopath was moving forward faster than I could back away. The plan was to neutralize him inside the apartment, but I was still tending to my objective. With Chris the Psychopath out of the apartment trying to stab me, the apartment was clear, and I yelled for the other officers to clear the apartment.

After one similar verbal command, I neutralized the subject with two rounds, center mass. The subject fell to the ground bleeding profusely. I did not want to render him first aid, but it is required, so I applied direct pressure to both wounds, until MED-COM arrived and stabilized him. Stage 3 gave the all clear from inside the apartment indicating there were no hostages. Once relieved, I went to a private location, and prepared to give my statement.

'Then the inquisition began. We are glad you made it safely. We have a few questions.

1. The subject was barricaded correct? What is
   policy about a barricaded suspect?
2. What do you mean, the officers were in a
   crossfire, did they shoot at each other?
3. Why did you not use a battering ram?
4. Why didn't the Sgt shoot him as well?
5. Were you in fear for your life?
6. What special schools or training did you
   obtain?
7. Do you feel you made a good tactical decision?'

I adjusted my positioning to get comfortable and prepare to reply to the barrage of questions. 'Departmental policy on barricaded suspects is set up perimeter, and hold in place until SWAT arrives, unless to prevent immediate loss of life.'

I decided that since we did not know who was home when he ran into an apartment, and he already attacked two people with his axe, that we had a duty to make sure he was not inside killing other people. Moreover, I did not make the decisions, Sgt did, I agreed with the decision, and I added tactics to it, but it was not my decision.

I reconfigured the officers for optimal deployment due to potential for collateral injuries. The breezeway is not as wide as you might believe; maneuvering an axe and a shotgun would prove to be difficult. Since I led Stage 2, I could not deploy a shotgun from that angle effectively, I would have been too close, but the pistol can transition into the holster, rather than sling arms, leaving me to go hands on.

As far as the crossfire no, they did not shoot at each other, but the configuration they set up, placed them in each other's fields of fire, so I intervened. Overlapping fields of fire tend to cross if the subject moves. In such close quarters, if Chris the Psychopath started running, the searching or traversing fire covered the officers within the hallway, making the situation unsafe.

We did not use a battering ram because we did not have one, most cops do not carry one of their own. As far as to why neither Sgt Moustache nor anyone else fired their weapons, it is simple; I engineered our response, to have fire in only one direction, which was out in the parking lot, which we had rendered secure prior to entry. We could not have a bunch of officers firing back into an apartment complex, the potential for damage and loss of life was too great. I did not tell them, my partner never engaged; I just said he was not in a tactically sound position. In the crossfire way is never a tactically sound position.

'Was I in fear for my life? No.'

'Then why did you shoot him?' asked the moron from Internal Affairs Division.

'Because he was trying to kill me with his knife,' I snidely replied.

Another Zombie Tick spoke, a Captain appointed to sit on the board, 'How do you know he was trying to kill you?'

I am sure the look on my face said far more than my words, 'Because that is what the normal outcome of being stabbed by a large knife is - death. It was deductive reasoning. I was well within the Use of Force Continuum. The suspect escalated both the danger to the community and to Law Enforcement.

Despite the actions already taken by the suspect, less than lethal force occurred, first. The plan was to use less than lethal force to contain him; he resolved to change the dynamic. Had he not tried to kill me, I would not have had to fire my weapon.

As far as special schools or training, I received High Risk Warrant Planning and Execution, High Risk Raid Planning and Execution,

SWAT, Tactical Entry, High Risk Arrest and Takedown Procedures, and a host of Non Tactical schools, as well as Combat training and tactics from the United States Marine Corps.

I used my training the best way I knew how, to ensure the safest resolution to all involved; society, law enforcement, and the suspect.

Zombie Tick spoke again, 'Why was the suspect's safety placed last?'

'Because he was the threat, he had to be rendered harmless, before safe: that was his choice. We emptied all the surrounding apartments and the parking lot adjacent so that the backdrop of where we had to shoot was cleared of people and roped off. We could not shoot into the apartment, because we still had no information as to who was inside the apartment.

We finally learned who's apartment the suspect was in, and the bloody victim stated that he believed the person in the picture inside, on the wall, was his attacker, but there was still no certainty as to who the occupants were in the target apartment. If the man is running around, chasing people, trying to hack them up, who is to say he didn't take a few people home to hack on?

It turns out; it was Chris the Psychopath's apartment, but we could not verify that until after we cleared it. Stage 2 had carte blanche to the door at a 90-degree angle, and no officers stood on the side. Setting the fields of fire in this manner enabled Stage 2 to provide either suppressive fire or offensive fire as needed. It turns out that it was suppressive fire; we were not shooting in defense of Sarge.

As far as my tactics, they were literally by the book, so yes I feel I made a good tactical decision? I believe this is justified by the results that only the suspect was injured.

The suspect had ample time to drop the axe or halt his attack; he did neither, even after the first shot, he continued to attack, after the second shot, he attacked, and he kept trying to get the axe after he fell to the ground.

I kicked the axe away, but he tried for it until I restrained him... With all the confusion and the shooting, I was still able to direct Stage 3 into the door safely, and then render first aid.

This operation would not have gone as smoothly if Sarge, had not put preservation of his men, and innocent lives first, and let his ego get in the way. He should be commended (I believe he is the only person I ever recommended for commendation for Inaction).'

'Detective,' Sheppard started again, 'what could have been done to avoid this situation?'

'There is no way that this could have turned out better, had we made entry with a key, it would have been a medley of confusion, and crossfire.

Chris the Psychopath did not even die: how it could have worked out better. We used the minimum force allowed by the suspect.' They asked me the same stupid questions for the next hour, and then we final parted ways. There is no way to avoid crime; it is dictated by criminals. We plan and train, but they act when inspired. Otherwise, there would be no crime.

The review was intense, and necessary, but not for the reasons I believe. I believe, that the most important thing which could have come out of the review, was improved tactics and officer safety.

I am glad no one important got hurt, no officers injured, weapon discharged, all bullets in the target. I looked at my badge and realized that day, had I died, the review would have occurred regardless; I just would not have been the guest of honor.

I believe that insufficient force leads to excessive force. Sufficient resolve as the first response will neutralize either the situation or the suspect. Failing to do either, requires more force and places people in harm's way. Once in harm's way; fear or malice give rise to excessive force.

My entire career, I wanted to shoot a few pieces of crap, until I did. It was not fun, it was not a rush, all my shootings were righteous, but they were all based on tactical decisions, never emotion. Taking a life would be a cold calculated decision, easier to live with easier to justify, and facts are not opinion.

12.0
THE BLUE DICK

There was a reason the Government outlawed Law Enforcement Quotas, because they screw the System up, worse than it already is. Lady Justice is supposed to be blind, not stupid as crap. How can you mandate LEO actions? What are cops supposed to do, text the bad guys and offer them fuel rewards, if they commit crimes and let cops catch them?

Quotas make liars and criminals out of the police. The guaranteed way to destroy public trust is the Quota system.

From the quota system we get;
- Racial profiling (Messing with minorities)
- SES Profiling (Messing with poor people)
- Excessive force (innocent people tired of being messed with)
- Agencies and cases lose integrity (releasing guilty people)

Someone once said that 1000 guilty should go free, before 1 innocent should suffer. Well this flies in the face of the quota system, because cops have to create the guilty, which means cops invariably *screw the Innocent*. The same people who elect Statistics driven, public officials, are the same ones that do not want to be messed with."

"So who are the police supposed to harass?"

"The newest system of raping of the Less Fortunate is COMPSTAT (Computer Comparison Statistics). It is the epitome of idiocy. COMPSTAT is both the brainchild, and the cave, wherein the Blue Ticks hide."

"What is a Blue Tick?"

Man do I have to teach you everything? "Blue Ticks are the cowards, liars, and politicians that drink the blood of the True blue officer. They claim credit for all the hard dangerous work cops accomplish, yet hide in the dense polyester forest of lies called 'Policies'.

From behind these lines of lies, they protect the rich, the greedy, and the elected. Let's not pretend the high crime areas receive help due to altruism, high crime directly and negatively impacts property value. The Dicks did not release us to make the city safer, they released us to tame the west; to get rid of the hostiles and make way for Progress.

Do not get me wrong, I love walking my family at night without fear of victimization; but I never lose sight of what we did, what it took to get here. It's not just the blood, and bones of the evil strewn throughout the city. Many innocent victims fell prey to policy, and had to wait for the ass whooping to become problem enough for The System to get involved.

See, brother blue blood, The System has many parts but it lacks a heart. If you disbelieve, go to the jail docket (this is the court docket for people that could not make bond) and see how much time is dispensed to the poor, versus the probation given to those out on bond. There is a simple sinister equation at work; those who cannot make bond usually don't pay taxes.

In most cities, people with 'ties to the community' often get out of jail free, Released on their own recognizance. Ties to the community, actually means 'tied-to-the community', they have vested reasons, not to leave, like property, family, businesses, and jobs. From these 'ties' The System generates revenue.

Before we anal-eyes the Tick Colony, lets understand one thing: There is no way possible to make more arrests, and the crime rate go down. Truth in sentencing is the only thing that can fix the crime rate. If people are in jail, they cannot repeat offenses. Otherwise, how do you reduce crime, when the population is growing and the police, more vigilant? It is a simple equation, more arrests = higher crime rates; unless you lie about the numbers.

This lie is part of a Federal Process, The System uses, where Agencies can reclassify crimes. In this manner, the statistics show a reduction in crime even though the jails swell. This process is the equivalent of the lies, Petroleum companies told the government, in the first years of the Obama Administration. They said they did not gouge fuel prices, yet one such behemoth posted a $12 billion profit for the same period in the year following their new policies. How is it possible to do the exact same thing, sell to virtually the same number of patrons, and yet post a 12 billion dollar profit, above the already large profit from the year before?

The truth about COMPSTAT, and for that matter, most crime reduction statistics is that they are lies. COMPSTAT serves no purpose, except to maintain the dark shroud Law Enforcement has cast over the public, to ensure them that they are safer. 'Tuna Row' was the result of

COMPSTAT type policies.

It is funny that you asked me about Tuna Road. Firstly, it was not Road but Row," I laughed. "When we were putting in tons of work, people in the LEO (law enforcement community), started complaining. Officers started complaining because it lengthened the amount of time they spent in booking. Supervisors complained because the officer stayed in booking thus delaying response time to calls for service. Jail complained because they did not have enough beds, and Night Court complained because of tripled time to obtain warrants.

The Criminal Justice System cannot handle the real volume of business; their solution; Release more criminals. This ridiculous solution serves society right. Anyone stupid enough to release a criminal deserves what they get. WHAT IN THE HELL DO YOU THINK CRIMINALS ARE GOING TO DO WHEN THEY GET OUT? THE SAME DAMN THING THAT GOT THEM ARRESTED IN THE FIRST PLACE. People are not criminals because they get arrested; they get arrested because they are crime-committing pieces of crap; ergo, criminals.

We used to lock up so many ho(s), that before we could return to booking, to process a new batch, the other ones already secured release. This is where the logo Tuna Row came from, the slimy, smelly trail of fish sellers, leaving the jail, walking back to whoredom.

One pimp and two ho(s) later, they were back on the street continuing crime. We therefore had to arrest them again, to be released again, only to be arrested again. This is another reason it is IMPOSSIBLE to lower crime rates by releasing criminals, because the numbers keep going up.

Ticks come up with new ways to tell old lies. The method used by the Ticks, is sneaky. Ticks reclassify the crimes to new categories, thereby falsifying the true nature of failing Criminal Justice efforts. Burglaries become vandalisms, attempted homicides become aggravated assaults, DUI becomes reckless driving, and assaults become disorderly conduct. Stats and Quotas pull officers off the streets, and their new job is BTDC (Blue Tick Damage Control); they sit at the station and lie.

Where is the integrity in Law Enforcement, when Departmental Policies rely on lying to survive? The Mayor decides that there are too many rapes in the city, how do you reduce the number? Well the best way is to set fire to the rapists, but too many people would complain about that, so we lie. We have to lie, bastards did not stop raping; what happened to the reports; can you say Matter of Record. We take the report, but do not classify it as a sex crime unless there is a known or identifiable suspect. We just let it sit in the corner of miscellaneous crap until we can close the case. Sure, we assign it to Sex Crimes detectives and get the victim help, but you ever wonder why Sex crimes have so many Matter of Record cases assigned to them? Do they find missing lawn mowers as well?

Once a week, the Ticks convene and smear the layer of crap, thicker. The lies have gotten so bad that society does not even scoff at the scent any longer. Over time, hidden truths morph in the dark soil of deceit into something much worse.

Now criminals have neither fear of jail nor incarceration, at least, before, they used to fear the police. I may not get you anytime in jail, but the time it took you to re-grow your frigging teeth and hair, counts for something after the arrest. More arrestees need to look like cancer patients; hair torn the hell out, teeth, falling out and tubes coming out their asses. Society needs to see what happens when the police get involved; police are the last line of defense.

12.1 The Other 'Tics

The Tick, the Blue Dick and those that hide behind the badge, are cousins but there are distinct differences. In every Law Enforcement agency in the world exists the same types of cops;

- Smart-ass cynical veteran - self-explanatory
- Smart-ass cynical FNG (F'ing new guy) - usually trained by type 1 and becomes a purveyor of the environment
- Lazy veteran - one-step above government employee, in that they will rise to any standards set, but nothing extra
- Lazy new guy veteran want to be - lived around cops and pretends to want to be part of the good old ways 'Roid-ragers - pseudo boy builders, angry small minded individuals who use the badge as a power trip, often ill -intentioned
- Cowards who will not engage - officers who either for sake of altruism, or sheer stupidity cower from confrontation
- Cowards engage from fear - officers who are afraid to fight
- Government employees - Does just enough to get by, average or below average performance

- Hard-worker - Takes pride in the job and the work they are doing, somewhat of a risk taker
- Decent - Average to above average worker, not a risk taker.
- Should have been a security guard - Just want the badge and gun, they enforce obscure laws on safe people.
- I just need a job to support my habit or hobby - In between government worker and lazy, this is just a job to them they try avoid conflict both internally and externally
- Ex-military (Just needed a job, should have been a security guard, hard worker, smart ass cynical veteran) - Ex military group consists of many subsets, except the ex military is more disciplined in their approach; due to training and experience. Therefore, whatever category they fall into, are at the top of that stage
- Well-intentioned - Chance takers, often taken advantage of and trouble prone
- Cowboys - Risk takers, glory hounds, adrenaline junkies
- Blue Ticks - Lazy, cowards, that started coasting as soon as they left the academy, they will do anything to avoid real police work (fleet managers, Precinct keepers, property room)
- Blue Dicks - Most often identified by the phrase, 'As soon as they got (promoted, made detective, became Community Affairs OFC etc,) he became a dick.' A commonly mistake belief; much like the effects of inebriation, promotions, or assignments, do not make the dick, they allow the dick to come out of hiding. Like an uncircumcised penis, the Blue Dick is just beneath the foreskin of the promotion or new position, waiting to come out and flex in front of the world.

While the Blue Tick has no problem throwing other officers under the bus, the dick makes a career out of it. The other distinction is that only Ticks and Dicks are a world unto themselves, because no one else respects them. Our entire political system is financed by wealthy private interests buying politicians and making sure the rules are written in their favor."

13.0
TOXIC SHOCK SYNDROME

"The misuse or prolonged wearing of a tampon, allows for irritation and bacterial growth, possibly resulting in TSS. Though considered rare, TSS can be life threatening. Both the Ticks and the Dicks need blood to thrive. In the political arena, blood-leaching is a common occurrence. Between those willing to shed their own blood for a parking space, and those willing to shed other people's blood for a parking space, there is blood to spare.

The Mayor; the ultimate parasite, lets government leaders suckle from the nipples of The System, and receive whatever morsels thrown out to the vermin. The Chief of Police is no less a parasite, he just wears a uniform associated with helping people. It was not until I was sucked into the vortex of the area, did I realize that there is more politics in policing than policing. Voting citizens make the law, by electing their Tick (That is why it is called 'Tics, short for Politics). Once the elected officials determine their choice of meal, they set policy.

It is in this Toxic environment, that Ticks and Dicks find their calling. The Mayor finds a Tick they can trust (control), that will not do what is right, but will do what the Mayor wants and this is the person, most likely to become the new Chief. The ultimate sacrifice is where the Mayor, Chief, and District Attorney General are all bloodsuckers; beneath this Triad of incompetence and malevolent indifference, decency has no chance. Whatever the prevailing 'Tics' are for the moment, the officers that transgress receive punishment.

Because of this TSS (Toxic Shock Syndrome), the environment amongst First Responders, in general, is cynical, oppressed, and demoralized. How foolish, to overly burden those who keep society healthy. People that are drowning, find themselves dragging others down into the depths with them. This is why these three jobs are plagued with suicide, chemical dependency, and domestic violence? Add to the difficulty of the job, the toxicity of Government, it is amazing that there is any longevity amongst First Responders.

When is the cop off duty? Never! Headlines simply say 'Off-duty cop'. Ever wonder what your dentist, priest, or electrician is doing when they are off duty? Why is it that people pretend like the man who drinks on the weekends, cannot stop in time, to report for their shift? Is everybody in the country reporting to work under the influence? Surely a man tasked with taking a life, knows when to take the last drink.

How can people, plucked from amongst the sinful, not sin? Sure cops fall, and they always will, but many; too many fall more from TSS than external violence. This is what happens when cops face murders and rapists, and are afraid not to take action, but more fearful of which action to take. Too little action, the cop dies, too much action, the cop goes to jail or gets fired. And who gets to decide on the appropriateness of the Action; Ticks and Dicks? People have fled, having to make this type of decision their entire career.

As the TSS worsens, the toxicity forces its way into the training regimes, so much so, that the academy and the hiring process become the filter for Ticks and Dicks. Rather than pick honest people willing to make the hard decisions, they prefer people willing to do the will of The System."

"How does this differ from your relationship with Chief Tubber?" My young friend asked.

"Simple buddy, he was a different type of man, in a different time. He and the Mayor had a crap-pile of a city, and wanted it cleaned up. Now that it is clean and sterile, they have no need for Wolf Hunter Packs; even though wolves (criminals) still prey on the sheep.

Once the homesteaders move in, lost sheep simply become part of the cost of doing business. Developers move in and gentrify the city after the Mayor allows the Chief to clean it up. Once the rich and affluent move in, they pull the wolves back, they do not want Wolf Hunter Packs on the street because they see too well. Rich and affluent do not want a good DUI or Drug Unit near an Ivy League school.

If there are Wolf Hunter Packs, the rich and affluent stay busy on campus, and the Endowments move to another city. The rich contact the Mayor and determine that they want campus security to do the job of duly sworn officers, and the Mayor tells the Chief to back off.

Every year, rapes occur on campus, with known suspects, and nothing happens because the police, those who could help, are never involved in the story. The Chief knows, the Mayor knows, rich and affluent know, but no one says anything - bad for business.

Sadly, the Ticks and Dicks rarely fall prey to the TSS they

promulgate, because they stay clear of it and look out for each other. How sinister a city that allows innocent girls to be the fodder upon which they survive. Think how many illicit trades, other than the sex trade, stack atop young girl's backs. Date rape, and date rape drugs, club drugs, Morning after pills, the liquor industry, the entire spring break industry is based on young girls getting drunk, and getting naked.

I may be a bastard, but I am not a piece of crap. I never covered for a rape, domestic or assault against a woman. I kicked in a crap load of doors, and if all I could do was whoop the ass of the guy inside, I NEVER left a young girl in the crap hole. If she went back, that is not my fault, but I saw to her freedom, before I left. This cost me, because I had to learn to survive the TSS. I am ashamed to say that if I had not collected dirt on Cops, I would never have been able to help as many people," He sat back astonished.

I looked him in the eye, "Do the job right or quit. We took this job to help those who could not help themselves, regardless of what jacked up situation they got themselves into. This job is all about going into the underbelly, and pulling people through, not wearing the clown suit. If that was the job, to stay safe at the Precinct and Starbucks, why the heck do they give us badges, guns, bullets, ballistic vests, and a radio to call for more? This is an honorable job, one of the most honorable there is, don't you be the mud on the badge that stains it for us all. Do not fall for the lies of the administration about morale, being your responsibility, about transparency, about accountability, and about whose job it is to make sure that everyone's truth is accounted for.

Do the job, apply the law equally without biases, learn the policy, and document every violation you can from the Ticks and Dicks; believe me one day you will need them."

He shook his head, "Naw, that's some snitch type crap."

"Ok, but when you go to a house and the 16 year old step daughter is beaten and raped by step dad, and you clean his clock. What you going to do then? Do you believe that you should have shown restraint, take him to jail, just to post bond and then return to do it again. Or should you stand between her and that man and say to him as he resists arrest, after your ribs, jaw and concussion heal, if you touch her again, I will finish what you started? I chose the latter, your day will come.

I would rather answer to a Tick for helping a sheep, than live knowing that I left that child at the house to get fingered some more.

If the police will not help her, what chance does she have?"

With that, I stood up, and headed to the bathroom. I had to pee more often than before, I hated getting old. Not just because no matter how hard I shake, it still drains down my leg now when I leave the bathroom, but because I cannot get in the fight as often any longer.

I shook my leg as I walked down the hallway, trying to rearrange my junk, and avoid the dribble. Getting old sucks.

"So what should I do," asked Walters?

"It breaks my heart to think of how many children will go to bed tonight hurt and afraid because of mom, or dad; and there is no one there any longer for them to reach out to.

Why has teen suicide and drug use increased? Because the police no longer do their frigging jobs, I pounded my knee; this was a subject close to my heart. Even the guys in jail disdain people that hurt children. The kids are just trying to medicate the bacterial infection caused by the Toxic environment the Ticks and Dicks protect."

I softened my tone, I was angry but not at him. I was angry because so many cops go to sleep every night having made no effort to make the world safer. What cowards the officers must be, that they do not even tend to the safety of their own families.

"Every day you are a cop, crack every head that needs to be cracked, save every life you can save, walk away when you have to walk away; most importantly hold your head high and do a work to be proud of."

"You act as though the Administration is full of cowards and liars. Is that because you are angry because you are being mistreated?"

"I assure you I have not been mistreated; I have done enough for more than two lifetimes. I can tell you that they are dark, and disloyal because I hold many of their secrets, I did many of their dark deeds, and covered many of their cowardly actions and deceptive words. Just because something isn't a lie does not mean that it isn't deceptive. A liar knows that he is a liar, but one who speaks mere portions of truth in order to deceive is a craftsman of destruction."

Then I smiled, and scratched my balls, and plopped down on the bench. The wood made the grinding, etching noise consistent with the handcuffs digging into wood.

"So many cops I know have vehicles interiors replete with scuff marks. I recommended that you use a t-shirt wrapped behind you to save your leather interior.

"Don't know why you assumed I sprang for leather,' he laughed.

14.0
PRECINCT DETECTIVE

14.1
PRECINCT DETECTIVE

"I did my time in patrol and a Detective position availed itself. Make no mistake, patrol is honorable and damn awesome, moreover it is necessary, but I wanted to do something else. The problem with patrol is not the criminals, as with most jobs in the department, the problem is Blue Ticks and Blue Dicks, the family of pests, the cowards who go inside to avoid work not to improve conditions for their people.

It is hard enough to deal with stupid people; sometimes the crap necessary to fix the problem (not patch) is to put a bastard's eyes out. Blind people are not out robbing, raping, and stealing. If the blind want to commit crimes, then push their blind asses into traffic, or down some stairs - problem solved. Blue Ticks and Blue Dicks do not see law enforcement this way, they see it as an administrative task, and they try to legislate gang activity and rapes.

I figured I could do a precinct defective job. I applied and got the position, a new position. I anticipated training, instruction, guidance, motivation - nope: Not a damn thing. I did not even get a manual. Undercover OPS gave us 40 hrs of classroom before we ever ventured out into the field. Kevin with his faults and dogma cared more about his people and the criminals, than the department; they left it all to my discretion.

I sat at my desk the first day, and they gave me some Offense Reports and told me to do something with them. I did; I moved them to the other side of the desk. WTF else was I supposed to do, they did not specify.

After about a week of WTF and watching TV, someone took me under their wing and explained the ropes of the new job. Most important, however, was that I had weekends off again.

I was a precinct detective now. I answered my reports, filed my garbage supplements, and listened to the radio. I soon found myself doing what I knew how to do best, look for bad guys. I rode around, backing up patrol officers on calls and looking for criminals. Did I mention I got no training?

What I did have was a badge, a gun, a car, and a lot of frigging bullets. When I was not playing pawnshop repo guy, I rode the territory and looked for crap to get into. People always said I had a death wish, they were wrong; I really wanted to help other people's death wishes come true. With all the training, the department gave me to investigate crimes and be a Precinct detective; what did I learn? Not a damn thing."

14.2 Who's Screwing Whom?

"I got a real call, a rape/stabbing. I figured that meant dude must have had a really, really large penis, not so. Patrol responded to a call and decided that a detective needed to respond. Like doctors, the authority to say that someone is dead, the precinct detective is often required to put the official Horse Crap Seal on a case.

I walked into the apartment, after greeting the officers. I liked to be friendly to the uniforms, after all they were my backup, my shooters on the grassy knoll; another thing that emphasizes the difference between blue ticks and the real police. I realize because of my duties and the danger, was that I needed the Blue family. Blue Ticks and Dicks did not give a crap because THEY NEVER PLANNED TO NEED BACKUP, ONLY REAL POLICE WORK REQUIRES HELP. What does the Precinct car cleaner need a Taser for other than to get an erection?

The apartment (crime scene) was a dump, two Mexicans and two white girls lived there. I know what you are thinking, fat white girls from the trailer park right? You would be incorrect. The victims were some good-looking girls, nice asses, tits, and relatively nice bodies; yes, they were whores. As with all stories, there were three sides, the real story, and the half-truths told by both sides. Since the girls were naked, the guys were already in cuffs when I got there. One of the girls was blonde, the other brunette. Turns out these two sluts were actually cousins, (some Deliverance type crap). Blondie did all the talking. These were not the toothless hags I was used to dealing with; they looked like someone picked them up in a club.

I did not realize how selective my hearing had become, I was hearing all manner of crap as she spoke, and we met the (lucky ass guys) at Jeueros Cowboy Bar. This is our apartment, and after a few drinks, we came back here to watch TV, and chill. Once we got home, *brunette* and I decided we wanted more beer and that is when we sent him (Lucky suspect #1) to get some. (I wondered what type of beer blonde drank; I would like to bathe you in it I thought.) As good looking as she was, she had terrible breath. (I wonder what you have to eat, or how many dicks you have to suck for your breath to smell like hers, I was forced to deduct 3 points). When lucky suspect 1 came back, he went into the room with brunette and they were watching TV, (I noted in my report the lack of a TV) and I heard brunette screaming.

I jumped up (off lucky suspect #2's lap) and ran into her room where I saw suspect #1 raping her, so I stabbed suspect #1 (with the free-floating knife I found, laying around brunette's room. Well at least now we knew why one of the guys was bleeding from his left side. I now had to speak to the other lady, because it turns out that now she is a sexual assault victim.

Brunette was even better looking, she had pretty feet, but she wouldn't say much. Blondie kept telling the story and shouting about the Mexicans, but the rape victim was expectedly silent. Once the of rape allegation surfaced, we took the suspects outside and let them sit in the ambulance. I had to talk to the brunette.

'Ma'am, I will be investigating this matter. Is there anything I can get you while you are here? I have to ask you some questions, but I can request a female officer if you prefer.'

'No, I am ok,' she replied quietly.

'Ma'am, this other officer is going to stand right here in the doorway with us ok, (I wanted her to feel safe, it still must be embarrassing to have to tell men, the details of your humiliation).

'We met them (the suspects) at a bar; we came back, and suspect 1 and me went for beer. When we came back we came in here to have sex, and that is when suspect 1 raped me.'

'Please clarify, how or what he did that violated you, you said you intended to have sex with him. By the way which one are you talking about?'

'George,' she said.

I had already amassed some preliminary information quickly like the names of the suspects. I looked at my pad, maybe she was confused, she described the suspect (suspect 2) that was not bleeding by physical description and clothes (greet shirt, jeans cowboy boots), then added, 'You know the one that's bleeding.'

'Ok please continue.'

'I kept telling him to stop, but he wouldn't so I took his knife off his belt and stabbed him. Then we called the police.'

I called the CSI dweeb in and asked him to have the suspects put his clothes on and take full body shots of them and their clothes. As they did this, I went outside to confirm what she was saying. The guy she described (Marco) had on a green shirt, jeans and cowboy boots. The other guy, (George), looked like Roy Rogers, big ass hat, short with wagon wheels on it, black pants, a giant belt buckle, and on his right hip, a scabbard for a knife. I was starting to doubt my little fillies, 'Whose apartment is this?' I asked.

'Ours,' she replied.

'And where do you work?' I asked.

She replied, 'I don't.'

'Then how do you (*whores I mused silently*) pay the rent?'

'My cousins pay the rent,' was her cool answer. *That is funny* I thought as I looked down because she listed unemployed on her report.'

'But Marco was raping you and you stabbed him correct?'

I walked outside and asked Marco, who he had sex with and how much it cost?

He was honest, he said, '$200.00 with the girl.'

'Which girl?'

'I don't know her name, the pretty one.'

'Then why is she saying you raped her and why did she stab you?'

'I didn't rape her, we paid them to have sex, and we have paid them before.'

'So why did she stab you.'

'Stupid whore got mad, because I did not use a condom and I came in here.'

'Ok, well buddy you gonna have to go downtown, we will let them figure this out.'

'But she stabbed me after I paid her,' Marco added. I was getting irritated, the story was obviously wrong and I was still not sure what transpired. I felt compelled to do a show up at this time.

A show up is where you take the suspect and stand them out for the victim to see, it's not like TV where they are in a separate room, I usually sit them in my car, (so they feel safe) then stand the suspect up. A funny thing happened on the way to the forum, the whole story fell apart.

Roy Rogers (George) started chattering like a monkey. 'I screwed her, he said pointing at the blonde, and I didn't touch that girl.' I asked

Marco who he had sex with. He pointed to the brunette.

'WTF!' I reached my BS limit, and looked at the most verbal of the group, the blondie. 'You stabbed him right,' I said pointing at the stabbed guy, 'because he was raping her right (pointing at brunette).' I looked at brunette, you stabbed him right (pointing at Roy Rogers) because he raped you she said yes. Then I asked Gorge, who were you screwing then, he pointed at brunette. Now it made sense.

I took the brunette back inside. 'I cannot help you if you lie. Is that why you don't want to do the rape kit, because you screwed the other guy?' She looked at me with no real expression, 'Or did you?' Something happened, and someone got stabbed, what happened.'

'The guy who got stabbed, did he rape you?'

'No,' she whispered 'Did you stab him?'

'Yes,' she whispered 'Why did you stab him?' He raped her (the blondie)'.

I rubbed my clipboard, 'Tell me what happened.'

'We met them and came home to have sex, I was done first, then I heard them arguing. When I walked into the room, they were standing up arguing, and she (the blonde) said, he had raped her, so I stabbed him.'

'Where did you stick the knife?'

'In his side,' she replied.

'Show me,' I requested.

She re-enacted herself stabbing him in his side, his right side because according to her reenactment, she walked up from behind and stabbed him in the right side. I did not have the heart to tell her that he was stabbed in the other side.

I walked into the other room, 'Ok blondie, tell me the truth. Who stabbed dude?'

'I did, she exclaimed, he raped her (brunette).'

'But if he raped her (brunette) why did you stab him, and not her (brunette)?' I walked in and he was on top of her (brunette) raping her, screw him.'

'So this has nothing to do with (the stabbed) dude ejaculating inside you, after paying $200.00?'

'I am not a whore; he owed me money for rent.'

'Sure, sure, I understand...I never called you a whore, but where did the knife come into the story?'

Blondie whispered, 'I told you I stabbed him.'

'Good enough for me,' I said standing up, 'Officer, unhand cuff the guys.' The males were un-handcuffed, and then I turned to the ladies, 'You two are under arrest for aggravated assault.'

Blondie got irate, 'I get raped and have to go to jail?'

'I thought you said it was her that got raped.'

'Up yours!' she said. *Well we know someone got bent over* I thought.

Since the girls both claimed to have stabbed him, and he had been drinking, and was not sure who stabbed him, I took them both to jail. I personally believed Blondie stabbed him, but I did not want to charge the wrong person. When they are both claiming it, somebody is obviously lying, but no one here is innocent, so; to hell with them; On to the next case. Remember, there are two lies to every story.

14.3 Habla!   Poor Bastards!

"The next case was truly tragic, and screwed up. I responded to a shooting, in the most ethnically diverse area of the city. Five people got shot, sadly, 2 did not recover from their wounds - shotguns are like that, not very forgiving.

My Spanish was not going to be good enough for this case so I had to call in help to translate. A whole bunch of lunch talk (that is my level of fluency in Spanish, because I order at Mexican restaurants a lot) we figured out the jacked up story. A white dude and a black dude robbed 5 Mexicans. The white dude had a shotgun, and the black dude had a pistol. They ran up on the Mexican dudes and demanded their money. Apparently, the conversation went like this, 'Freeze! Gimme your money. Anybody moves, gets shot.' Three unfortunate things occurred after the verbal interaction.

- The white boy obviously had the jitters
- Only one of the Mexicans spoke English
- The black dude never wanted to be free again

When the Mexicans panicked and ran, the white guy blasted two of them, and then the black guy shot the other three. That is a damn high average for robbers. Maybe the international venue necessitated robbers have more firearms qualifications.

Yet, in all, they got about $75 bucks. 3 shot dead for $75. Hell, I would have given them that to save these poor bastards lives. The five amigos were all illegal. During the summer, illegal's get robbed all the time, because they get paid cash, and don't speak English, so getting help takes a little longer.

Even if they snuck across the border, and do not pay any damn taxes, they didn't deserve to be laying dead at a car wash. I truly felt bad that these poor fellows died because they do not have an SAP (language translating) button. I would make a cruel joke here, but innocent people died so I will forgo the typical police humor. Walters nodded his assent, maybe there was hope for him after all. The case eventually ended up in Cold Case. The Precinct did not have the resources to investigate it properly.

Remember Walters; avoid miscommunication. The price you pay for it is horrendous."

14.4 Are These Bastards Ever Going To Run Out Of Bullets?

"This detective crap was not half bad. When I was not stuck at the Precinct doing crap reports, or recovering lawn mowers, I sought out whatever high-speed, low drag cases that came across the radio. Tonight turned out to be a *Bobsled* night. That is a night where you are going from call to call, chasing bad guys.

El Salvador must be Spanish for 'Gigantic Piece of Crap' because they produce a whole septic tank full of people that migrated to other countries. .   What is sad is surely, some decent people live in the country, it seems like they just do not visit our country.

First call - 911 hang up, clerk shot during a beer run. This occurred four blocks from the police Precinct. Upon my arrival, the clerk was en route to a trauma center with a .357 pistol slug in her chest. We looked at the store video, and waited for the owners to get to the location. According to the video, the female clerk was standing at the counter when two Latino males walked up. The shorter of the two had a 24 pack of beer under his arm. The clerk taps the counter as it became obvious that they do not plan to pay, and then he walked up to the counter and for absolutely no reason, other than he is a cowardly animal, he shoots her point blank on the chest. Then he walks out of the store the parking lot. She was stable, and hopefully would survive the attack from the first two animals.   When the owners showed up, the place turned into a petting zoo.

Two other pieces of horse dung, two older white males (gas station owners), came in and only wanted to know when they could reopen. I asked them about the care for the clerk, they said they would pay her bills if she asked, but otherwise, she would have to pay her medical bills herself. I made a point of helping file her Workman's Comp and labor complaints against her bosses. She survived thank God, but she moved out of the area, actually I think she went back to Somalia, where it was safe.

Second call - While standing there with these two capitalist animals, a shooting came across the radio, invoicing four Latinos. The location was not too far from me, so I saddled up and headed that way. I was not finished with the other crime scene, because the video was not complete, but I had to respond to this scene. Scene 2, was an intersection of Tuckwin Dr and Picktell Pike. According to the passenger in the vehicle, his friend was sitting at the red light playing some loud ass music when a red Toyota truck pulled up beside them. Without warning, the passenger pointed a revolver out the window and fired one round striking the driver in his head. The witness could not see the tag but recognized it to be a Georgia tag. As I was standing there, listening to the witness explain the event, I received a call from the patrolman at the last Precinct. The vehicle description from the first shooting was a red Toyota truck with a Georgia tag. *Dammit* I thought, *I hope I run up on them and get a chance to even the score.* It was going to take a scorecard to keep tally this night. The witness described a large silver revolver, probably the same .357 from the Somali chick.

Third call - A bolo (be on the lookout), went out, as I was standing in the intersection. 'Red Toyota truck' involved in a shooting about 4 miles away. One of the guys must have an IV drip, because apparently these frigging idiots needed more beer. How much beer do these idiots drink? Can they not get coupons or sponsors, and why did they need to keep shooting people?

I zoomed up to the next scene; it was the two devils from earlier. This time someone saw an El Salvadorian flag on the truck and got a partial tag. At least we were getting closer; hopefully the boneheads were out of bullets. I pulled up to the next stop-n-rob. They were not even robbing the places, they were just shooting people. The witness, an Indian clerk, was not shot, but his Indian coworker was not so lucky. This incident was almost the same, except the clerk with the bullet in the shoulder was not behind the counter. The clerk behind the counter yelled that the guys were stealing beer, and when they tried to leave, the younger clerk tried to grab the beer back, and got shot for his trouble. He was on the way to the hospital. Fortunately, all the victims went to the same hospital. This would be a first for me; three victims, same suspect, and same hospital.

This time, the store video got a good facial image of the shooter and his giant tear mark on his left cheek. This time, we got a picture of his face, he slipped past, but now we knew who we were looking for, and they made one other mistake, they sped away from the scene of the crime, and brought attention to themselves. The older clerk described the gun; it was a silver revolver, large, presumably, unless they reloaded and was out of bullets)

At the hospital, I made my rounds. Victim $^{\#}2$ was in a coma, victim $^{\#}1$ was ICU, and victim $^{\#}3$ was in stable condition. I asked him a few questions, with the most important question being, whether he was going to prosecute? 'I have to, or they make me pay for the beer,' the poor sap let on.

'What?' I said.

'Yeah if we don't go to court we have to pay for the beer, but they don't pay us to go to court.'

'Well, hell I would damn sure not be wrestling nobody for beer. But I can't understand why you tried to get the beer back.' Each one of these robberies was for less than $30 but left two people fighting for their lives and another one, shot. I also helped him file a Labor Law complaint against his boss.

Time to end this maybe a statewide ban on beer sales, or maybe we would get lucky. We did. I just did not know it yet. The next day, I sat at my desk, putting all the paperwork together, and typing up reports etc. I knew they were not done; it would just be a matter of time before someone shot back. I hoped it would be me doing the shooting, but at least they had not paired up with the Oreo shooters (black and white guy) from the other scene.

I stacked the usual crap reports in the corner, I did not plan to even look at them, I had real work to do. About 3 hours into my work, a patrolman came over to me, 'Hey detective,'

'Remade,' I corrected. I never cared to separate myself from my fellow officers, although detective is a grade above him, I was not above him, he was blue like me.

'We had a hit and run the other night with all that was going on; I did not get a chance to run this by you.'

And there it was, our lucky break, the Red, El Salvador hell wagon, bumped someone in a parking lot, and they got the tag information.

'Damn,' I said as I stood up, I'll call you when we find them.'

'Thanks Renarde,' 'No thank you, be safe.'

I sat down, he had a piece of paper attached to the report, he had already run the tag, and affixed the address to it. I grabbed my radio, and walked out to my car. I put my ballistic vest on, got my rifle out of the trunk, and headed out to find them.

I did not give much thought to arresting them, otherwise I would have called it in, I told myself I wanted to make sure they were home, and I did not waste anyone's time. Truthfully, I was angry about the Somali girl, to watch the store video of her hair blown up in the air because some animal shot her over beer. To add insult to her injury, she worked for animals.

Somali needed a knight, someone in her corner. I pulled out of the parking lot, committing to one recourse; push the fight, create the exigency, and force their hand. I am not a back shooter (unless you turn around after threatening me with your gun), besides, I wanted them to know who sent them to hell. Negating morality, it was exceedingly difficult to convince myself it might be ok shooting someone in the back.

I rolled through the city, on patrol. I did not want to miss one single opportunity to make the world a better place by removing trash. They say that murder is not part of the job description; sure, there are rules of engagement, but didn't society give me a badge and gun to do that which you could not or would not. Did you not empower and ask me to make a safe place for your kids to play and your dogs to crap? Cannibals even eat other cannibals, they do not go to the salad bar, they do not eat tofu, and cannibals do not crave any other dish. What then do you do with a cannibal? Either feed them meat, or put them down. Society provides the innocent meat, and society asked me to put the Cannibals down.

Maybe there was more cannibal in me than I realized, because I wanted to eat tonight. Maybe Dexter had the right idea, abide by a code, to avoid capture. Dexter did not use a moral compass; but instead devised a way to remain a cannibal yet walk among vegetarians. I forgot, there is a word for that Training; and I endured months, years of training to do this job. They wanted it done better and faster, and cleaner, so they trained me to do it from the shadows, completely being able to withstand the light. Tonight, I would bring my skills back to life, back into the darkness of the light.

Dammit! I thought, as I swerved to avoid not 1, but about 6 cars. Holy crap, a vehicle pursuit, the pursuit looked like Smokey and the bandit. Wait, wait a damn minute, there was a special guest star starring in the pursuit. It was the murdering pieces of crap from El Salvador and my red truck. *Hot damn* I thought, as I waited to turn around and follow suit. There would be many witnesses, but since they already created the situation, now I could justify using all my ammo, it was old anyway and my weapons probably needed cleaning.

Down through Corridor Street we sped. Luckily, no one was out, it was an older neighborhood, better for us. By Departmental Policy, officers must stop the pursuit, if too dangerous, or if the suspect starts endangering the bystanders. Departmental Policy also requires that once a marked car joins the pursuit, any unmarked vehicles must slow down and drive like regular humans."

'Left, we went left on Haymaker Rd,' the second car in the pursuit bellowed out over the radio, 'Speed 45, light traffic.' 'Continue,' was the one word response.

"This is how we protect the sheep; Departmental Policy places unbelievably restrictive rules on officers so that innocence is not shed.

Undeniably, the rules need to exist; I would hate to run through a school zone, to kill the bastards; that would make me worse than them, unless they were bad kids. But seriously, the rules have to exist, which is why they train us to be better. Undercover training instructs on how to get around the rules to do societies' real biding.

As quickly as I had joined the race, 'He wrecked out.'

It was over; the bastards might be arrested. I tried to get up to the front, close enough to run over anything that fled from the vehicle, but like most slime, the occupants simply slid to the bottom of the truck and laid there. Irony, irony I say. Murderers, looking to the cops, they just ran from, for mercy and justice; patiently waiting until their next meal.

Man, I wanted to shoot into the truck but by the time I got close, it was too late, too many eyes, too many lies to be told, too many cops in the crossfire. It was over. Damn, I only recognized one occupant in the truck. For now, all I could do was to interview the devils. Turns out, they were running from the Gang Unit. I probably would have known, if I had reached out to them about the suspects, except, I did not want their help (interference).

They brought my tattooed friends to the Precinct, and put them in an interrogation room. I met with the Gang Unit Sgt in the hallway. Sgt Kingman was not interested in working with me, frankly, I shared his feelings, but this was not the time to allow our petty territoriality to get in the way.

'Hey Sarge,' I began, 'I got him on three shootings, two of them are critical.

What you got him on.' 'He's just one of the group that we been watching, but they are responsible for a lot of crap. So how do you want to play this?'

Just then, I got a phone call from a number I did not recognize. 'Hey Donaldson, this is Special Agent Zuentes, do not question him, and I want your file!'

I guess he said something else, but I hung the phone up so I did not hear it. I should have recognized the 'Dicknumber', but it had been a while. A dicknumber is a cell phone number of any punk ass Federal Agent. This particular dick worked for ATF (alcohol, tobacco. firearms). Did I mention that Special Agent Zuentes was a dick? I only know this because I met him at the last briefing and have worked around him. I did not have him in my contacts, and every cop knows, you put every Fed you meet, into your contacts, because they can be useful.

My phone rang again. I ignored it, while Kingman and I stood looking at the stacked piles of crap they had rounded up, this evening. Amidst all the cases we were about to overlap, I had the best three. My case had some video, so I could make the cases without the benefit of other members of the group identifying him.

Dammit my phone rang again, dicknumber again, 'Hello, this Andrews,' I answered intending to annoy.

'Hey man, you hung up on me,' he complained.

I did not appreciate the way he spoke to me. 'I want your case file and stay away from Nury.' I paused to make sure I said only the necessary things.

'I would curse you out, but I am busy. Since there is no letter giving you my case, and since I neither work for or with you, I am sure there is a screw you, in the immediate future with your name on it.'

Sgt Kingman smiled, 'I am sure we called him.'

I really did not give a damn, 'He drew first blood.' I said as I laughed with Kingman.

This time, Kingman's phone rang. He worked with Special Agent Zuentes all the time, so he was a lot more cordial and probably has shown more respect.

Kingman hung up, 'I got to go let him in the building.' Then he walked towards the sally port.

A few minutes later he and dick-head came up to me. Special Agent Stupid, started to say something, so I walked off.

Kingman stopped me, 'Hey Renarde, we gotta do this together, so we can get them off the street for good.' He was right; I just dislike smug federal buttholes. For the scope of authority they have, Feds do precious little. Turns out, the three of us had overlapping cases. My case had the best video, and was the lynchpin of the ATF's case against the revolver. Kingman's case involved a bunch of Gang related drive by shootings that this murderous idiot may not have been involved in, but certainly had information about.

Kingman took us all to a small conference room. I still had nothing to say to dickhead. But, I did have a plan. It was not that I was smarter than the ATF Agent, nor had more authority; nevertheless, I devised a legally sound method to make all three cases. In typical Federal fashion, Special Agent Stupid kept trying to take over everybody's case. This was precisely why I did not want to work for or with him, but I did want his jurisdictional power.

'I have the gun,' dickhead snapped.

'Actually, it's in my building and I am the only one that can put it in anyone's hand.

'No one cares about your cases,' he whined further.

'That is something else you are wrong about, I do, and my victim's do; what I don't care about, is you, what you say and what you want. You want the case; go through the proper channels. As for my file, good luck without it, I'll shred it before I give it to you,' (I would not do that to my victims) I reassured Walters.

"I think he finally got the point, 'What's your suggestion?'

'Simple; you know the weapon is stolen, and the serial number filed off because the Gang Unit called you otherwise you have nothing.'

"They just called you in, to use a Trigger-lock case. (This is what we called a Federal gun case. A habitual offender convicted of two prior felonies arising on different occasions. The offender must serve the maximum sentence, day-for-day without early release. A life habitual offender has two prior felonies, one of which is violent and has served at least one year on each. In this case, a life habitual offender must serve life without parole. Enhancement means doubling the penalty for a drug charge because of a prior drug conviction, or possession or sale near a church or playground).

"I simply have the best chance of getting this done. I make all the cases, and everyone wins. All I have to do is get him to admit to, or discuss one of my cases, and both of your cases are made. It's simple, let me do the heavy lifting,' I looked at ATF, 'And you stay out of the way.'

We all agreed that the plan not only had merit, but also was the safest. If my plan did not work, they could still try to get their cases resolved on their own.

I walked into the room. I knew a little bit about pissing people off. I also knew that bravado was high on the list of cholos' behavior. The first thing I did when I sat down was put my finger on his green teardrop, on his face. He sat back obviously irritated: Point for me.

'Ok dude, your name is Numpy.' He spoke some English.

'Nury, mi name is Nury.'

'Okay Nuvy, let me read you your rights. Can you read?'

'Nury, my name is Nury and yes I can read.' He raised his voice a little: Point for me.

'Picture books or real books, you look like kind of a farmer or something, did you even go to school.' No answer, he slumped back in the chair: Point for me.

'You have the right to remain silent,' I began. He had a little trouble with a few, so I did the rest in Spanish. When he understood, and signed the waiver. It was time to apply my craft. Having laid the groundwork by pissing him off, he now thought I was an idiot.

'De que pais ? (Which country are you from) Mexico?'

He laughed and said, 'No El Salvador.'

I wrote it down. 'Es usted cuididano? (Are you a citizen?)' We both laughed at that one. We figured out an address for him, date of birth and full name. 'So why are you here in the country? What brings you into this fair land?'

'I wanted to work?'

'So you have a job? Where and how long have you worked there?'

'I have not found a job yet.'

'But it's been five years. How have you survived, do you get government benefits.'

'No,' he answered, matter of factly. I think he was proud not to be on welfare; go figure.

'Then I am confused, if you came here to work five years ago, why have you not found work? And you did come in through Mexico, correct?' He nodded his head. 'So when you get deported, we will just send you back to El Salvador.' This was the first time he showed disdain; he did not want to go back home. 'Do you not want to go home?'

'No send me to Mexico, I cannot go back home.' Why not child support?' I teased.

He laughed, 'No Sombre.'

He meant El Sombre Negro (The Black Hand), a government hit squad, consisting of specially trained troops, sanctioned to do only one thing; hunt down and kill MS-13 gang members.

'El Sombre? What they got to do with you? Are you MS? Is that why you have a tattoo and left El Salvador?'

'Yes, I was MS when I was there. I don't really hang out with them anymore.'

'Weren't you with them today, and tonight?'

'Yes, but they are just my friends.'

'Do they feed you and help you with rent? How can a person get out of the gang?'

'Yes sometimes, because I don't work. It's for life'

'So they pay you to hang out with the gang and you just go along with them when they do bad things?'

'I go along but I do not participate, like tonight I was just riding in the red truck and the cops started chasing my friend. We had not done anything.'

'Then why did your friend run?'

'He had a gun in the truck and he's illegal.'

'It is his gun?'

'Yes, no mines, it's too big for me.'

'So your prints won't be on the gun at all?'

'Not mine, I do not like guns.'

'Then what's the tear for? Doesn't that mean you killed somebody?'

'No, this, (he motions to his face, and waves his hand across his cheek) this is from a girl that broke my heart, that is why I am crying.'

'Quick question, do you recognize this truck?'

'That's my friend's truck?'

'Other than tonight, when was the last time you rode in it?'

'It has been a while.'

'Have you ever been to jail?'

'Once' was his lying response, 'Here in this country?'

'Yeah they said I robbed.'

'Ever shoot anyone?'

'Me, no I don't like guns.'

'Well can you explain what this is in your hand (showed him a picture from the last robbery) and what you are doing with it.'

'That is not me.'

'Look at his face, he has the same big nose, and the same teardrop on the eye.'

'I see that, but it's not me, maybe my friend.'

'This is when y'all stole beer from the Esso and shot the clerk, were you there, do you remember?'

'I remember that I was not there, but it was my friend, he came back with some beer that night, and said he had robbed. I was scared and told him to go back and pay for the beer.'

'Did your friend shoot the girl too, and the dude at the red light with the screwed up music. I understand why you shot him.'

He just smiled, 'That was my friend, and he's crazy.'

What he did not know was that the witness had picked him out of a photo line-up. Moreover, his friend Carlos, had already confessed to being there for the girl, but not the other two. He told us that he was scared from the first shooting and went home, and described the crash he caused. He said that he stayed home because he was scared and gave this genius the truck and told him to go hide. Carlos already agreed to testify for a deal.

'Anything you can tell me about the church shooting last week, was it your guys. You know where they went to the church in Madison and pulled up and told several young men to join. They didn't so there was a drive by shooting, 4 people.'

'That was not me, I don't go to church, but I heard about it. Those were Mexicans that shot up the place, Brown Pride.'

'Why would Mexicans try to recruit Salvadorians into their Gang?'

'Maybe they want some good food, I don't know.'

'Hey butthole,' I said standing up, 'Someone described a big ass silver revolver being used. What you bet, your stupid ass was on the other end? I have already talked to the DA; you are not going to jail, or Mexico. I raised my hand and spread my fingers, so that it cast a black shadow on the table, El Sombre!'

I got all the way to the door, 'I didn't shoot at the church, but I was there. Don't send me home and I will tell you who shot.' 'It was you and the other MS members with you at the church?' 'Yeah man,' he slumped in the chair and I walked out. Checkmate.

It was done. The slovenly victory was ours; he did not admit to shooting in my 3 my cases but:
1. He admitted to being an active MS-13 member
2. He admitted to his group using his gun in a hate crime
3. Being at the Esso robbery
4. Being convicted of a prior felony
5. Conspiring with a group in acts of violence

Not too shabby, I thought as I left. I walked up to Kingman, and ATF, 'He'll never be free again!' Then I walked away. At least I knew where to find the piece of crap, when I needed to charge him.

"That's it?" Walters asked, "What about the other two victims?"

"Headshot found me several months later, more than a year, and asked why the guy was never prosecuted for shooting him? The sad truth was that the guy was left for dead at a hospice, and we failed to check on him. His prognosis was terminal, but he was lucky. I prosecuted Nury for that too.

I had a hard time prosecuting him for the headshots because a lying whore of a DA complained on me. You are not going to believe this horse crap. I was so surprised to see headshot when he walked up to me. He asked to see a detective as I was leaving the precinct. I did not recognize him, I only saw him incubated and comatose. He told me what happened to him and then I remembered. He updated me on his medical condition and I plugged him into some victim services.

After speaking to him, but while he sat at my desk, I emailed the ignorant ass DA. Everyone called her Bottlenose. She was not as intelligent as a dolphin, but sounded, moved, and was built like one. She had the case in her division. I told her the details, and that I had a suspect. I then gave her the name and prison number of the suspect, explaining a little about how he came to be in my custody. She replied quickly, 'If you have the PC, go ahead, charge him.' I did just that. I did not even bother to indict dickhead, I took out a warrant on him, while my victim stood there, and then I gave him a ride home.

About 8 days later, I stood in front of the Lt, as he contemplated a resolution to this new complaint on me. Bottlenose complained to the Chief of Police that I jumped chain of command and all protocol and haphazardly charged the suspect. In doing so, she maintained that I ruined a murder investigation, the suspect was cooperating. I was aghast, that this girl was so stupid. Ignorant fool, did not even discuss it with me, she ran straight to the Chief. Lt allowed me to read the email, and then asked me WTF? This was one of the times that doing the right thing, the right way, worked out as it was supposed to.

I asked Lt if I could have a copy of the email. I probably should have warned him what I was about to do, but I did not. I drafted a very short email, to Bottle-nosed and CC'd everyone she had emailed, included. The list was somewhat lengthy.

My response lacked poise, detail, and tact; but the crap was on point. 'Dear General (short for District Attorney General) Olivet, it has come to my attention that an investigation has been compromised. This is a pity; however, next time you intend to accuse someone to massage your guilt, READ YOUR DAMN EMAIL! Please see attached.' Then I hit send.

'Andrews, get in here,' resounded from the Lieutenant's office. He had a half smile, half curse written across his lips. 'Chief's pissed; you cursed in the email, don't do that crap again. Get out of my office.'

"It was over. Isn't it amazing how something like an email chain can make a difference? I attached the emails we sent, I always save emails in the case file. She failed to bother to look at the name of the suspect, or look into his history, or anything, if she had she would have remembered she was working a deal with him. 'Screw her,' I said adamantly, 'Trick,' I said looking down at the floor.

The Somali girl got out of the hospital and the country. I got a plea on that one too. See you are starting to understand me, it is always about helping the victim.'

As I sat here talking, I began to remember how much crap came from within the halls of justice. As I put a voice to my story, I realized how tiring the job of a cop is, because you catch shots from both sides. I realized that the crap I felt for the job, was not for the badge, it was for those who hide behind the badge, to make a career; all the cops, DA(s), jail personnel, and even the meter maids. The entire Law Enforcement came to exist to make society safe, and orderly; what the hell attracts the bleeding heart, anti-law, and enforcement people into the uniform or the DA office? By default these should be the people whose hearts seek only to objectively, yet strictly, enforce every law on the books, and get the stupid laws removed. It is hard to walk the straight and narrow when these tasked with defining the straight and narrow themselves are violators."

14.5 Investigating Family

"Damn, damn, damn, damn, damn, damn, damn, was my response when I first got the news. This was the crappiest first day back from a weekend, on any job in my life. Sometimes being good at a thing, means you have to do crap you do not want to do.

I found out later, that I had a reputation and a name within the department. Apparently, my brothers in blue dubbed me The Terminator, because if I was on your case, you were screwed. All the years of working investigations, made my path cross many officers. If they were innocent, or at least justifiable, I helped, but not the ones that crossed the line. Someone told the Ticks, and one day they sent for me.

Sadly, the people I hated more than Sticks, the Blue Ticks, had a use for me. I received the call from a Deputy Chief. Sit Down Renarde. We knew each other, prior to promotions and we got along. We need you to look into a complaint. As a precinct detective, I could not imagine why Deputy Chief Tom (Short for Uncle Tom) needed to tell me this personally. By the way, if you missed it, Deputy Chief Tom was one of those, spearheading the lets fire Andrews team, after the kicking incident.

'We have a complaint on an officer,' he began. 'We have an assignment that requires special skills.'

As he gave details, I silently seethed about his intent. There is more than one-way to screw an officer, this was a good one. He was going to make me a pariah. I did not want the job, but no one ever asked.

This was not the first time, dealing with allegations against cops in vice, you see everything. However, this time it would not be happenstance, I would be hunting cops. This time, he sent me adrift inside the family, not to clean house but to make me so hated, that I would be forced from the family.

Family quarrels are bitter things. They don't go according to any rules. They're not like aches or wounds; they're more like splits in the skin that won't heal because there's not enough material."

14.6 Club Dog Pound

"Club dog pound was the first time I hunted cops. There were always rumors of peripheral complaints going around, but most allegations were too vague, ridiculous, or unsustainable to handle. In this case, there was an allegation from a CI that two cops were working in an after hours strip joint. The two cops were black, and the club was black. The allegation was that they were working the door, searching people and taking the cover charge. What I did not know back then was, that somebody used a Blue Credit to save Nevada, but he hated me, not for that, but because I was not like him.

Club Dog Pound was a regular Port-a-Potty. The entire building was just a series of rooms and spaces, painted black. This building had not passed codes in years, and the only reason any one would be caught there, was for the fringe benefits. According to Intel, the strippers here were prostitutes, and you could buy guns and dope from this place as well.

I had a complaint, a CI and a physical description of the officers involved. I put a line up together, and included officers matching the demographics. To my surprise, the CI picked everyone on the page. This normally would be funny, and I was laughing until the CI informed us, that two of the officers were taking money at the door, and they were present when drugs and guns were sold.

'Man, they dirty. Many times, the guys in uniform would come in and do an inspection, those guys at the door, were either holding the guns or dope, or guys were hiding guns under the table, because those two dirty cops were using the police radio, to listen, they warned everyone when the cops came to do the inspection. So there were cops in the room, where other real cops were working and they didn't even warn them that the guys had guns and dope. Plus most of those girls weren't even 18.'

If it pissed this CI off, you know how I felt. Another allegation, I had to take seriously.

The CI met with us on the days, most likely to catch the involved officers. I sat in the parking lot and took pictures from outside. Occasionally, the CI's narcoleptic ass would go inside. The CI was supposed to be watching and talking but when he started snoring; I would call him and wake him up. I had back up, but due to the allegations, and not wanting any other squad members dragged into what was sure to be a crap storm, I let them park around the corner and listen, but not see.

Once I gathered enough evidence, I put a search warrant in motion. The process took a while. I had to do a series of Plain View dope purchases, where the CI bought dope in plain sight of the officers and used that information as PC (probable cause), to show their involvement, and dereliction of duty.

The investigation did not last long, maybe a couple of weeks. No one rushed me, but I figured it was important to get it done quickly. The Captain required weekly updates, but no urgency existed. Once I got done with my investigation, Kevin and I, laid out the plan. We developed an Ops (office of professional standards) Order, and ran it up the flagpoles.

The old adage about keeping secrets, when one of the two people, were on their deathbed, was never truer. This was the first bump in the road we encountered. The plan started getting push back, the moment it went upstairs. Fortunately, Kevin and I made the decision early, to leave the names of the targets off reports that were sent up the chain of command. The Captain knew, because she gave me the complaint, but that was all, as far as we knew. However if she knew, then her three flunkies knew, and if they knew, that was four people too many.

Oddly enough, there came requests for more information from up stairs, and pressure came, in terms of Requests for details from Internal Affairs. I ignored them, because I could. I just did not answer the phone, when they called. This was a criminal matter; IA could get the file afterwards.

I got the call from the Chief's office, telling me to reach out to Internal Affairs. I did as instructed and cordially reminded them that this was a criminal matter, and that the case would be available, if there were any developments.

In order to acquire the much-needed help, I went outside the Division. I did not tell anyone but Kevin and the Captain, which means that everybody probably knew. I reached out to an old co-worker, another undercover pretender, Sgt Ted. We got along ok, I guess I had no respect for him, as a cop, or even a man, for that matter, he always came across as a well-dressed coward. He disguised his cowardice, with what some would call 'polish'. Ted provided some support, people to do surveillance and gather random information on the club like real estate, demographics, utilities, ownership etc.

The search warrant briefing started with the typical BS disclosure that we had a complaint, and developed .C. (probable cause), for the case. After that, it went downhill from there. Once we told the audience that the suspects were cops, there was cynicism and derision, moaning and groaning. For some reason, even cops that are not dirty, get an attitude, when the police go after the police. I am not sure why, I never wanted to be associated with, befriend or protect a dirty cop. I know some officers think that what my squad did was dirty; but that is because they did not know what we did, and the people that were dirty, they assumed were teaching us their ways.

There is no denying that we were rough, some might say brutal, but what we did, saved lives, made neighborhoods safe, and made cops safe. People need to have respect for the authority of the police force. People empower a cop to keep them safe; that is what it is called a 'Police Force'. Remember always, cops have two jobs, both given by society; one job uses a whistle and handcuffs, the other a gun.

You ever wonder why society arm cops with guns? Because there are just some buttholes that need to be removed from society (shot). Society makes the laws and determines what they are willing to stomach. Is a cop a lawman, judge, and jury? Yes they are, otherwise take their guns away. Hell even judges do not use guns.

I had to listen to the standard crap, 'You working for IA now, snitch, Serpico etc,' I listened for a while, and then started my portion of the briefing. 'Yeah, well I don't get down with dirty cops, I would assume you felt the same way, maybe that's part of the problem. If you have a personal reason you would like to excuse yourself, do it now, before I read the Probable Cause statement and give you the names. Hopefully, these names are not your friends, or maybe this time, I missed your friends, either way, I do not need a whole bunch of horse crap from the peanut gallery.'

I paused; no one moved. 'That being said, this is a group effort. Here with us today is Long Term, Street Squad, Intelligence, and the Municipal Compliance Team (Codes). There is an allegation from a CI that two cops are working in an afterhours strip joint; Club Dog Pound. The two cops are black and the club is black. The allegation is that they are working the door, searching people and taking the cover charge.

I had a complaint, and a CI and a physical description of the officers involved. I put a line up together and included officers matching the demographics. CI informed us that two of the officers are taking money at the door, and they have been present when patrons sell drugs and guns. The CI states many times patrol does tavern checks and patrons holding either guns or dope hide their guns under the table. The suspects use their police radios to listen and warn everyone. According to the Intelligence Division, who also has a complaint on the place, the strippers here are prostitutes and many under aged, and you can buy guns and dope from this place as well.

The entire building is just a series of rooms and spaces painted black. This building had not passed codes in years. Considering the allegations, SWAT will do the execution. Once SWAT clears the building, they will maintain interior and perimeter security. Aviation will assist with entry as will patrol, who will close the street off just once we get on scene.

After the location is secure, all patrons will line for searching, then be marched out the door. Upon exiting, Intelligence will use a video camera to get a name, DL photo, and age of each patron. We will pull still shots later. All weapons and drugs recovered leave them in place, untouched, for fingerprinting. MCT (smart cop), will inspect the building once the patrons vacate the location.

Any cops located within the building will be disarmed, and placed separately in a patrol car. Chief has already authorized the immediate disempowering of the officers as well, and the seizure of all Police weapons, cuffs, radios, and badges; pending the formal IA investigation. This part is important supervisors; DO NOT ATTEMPT TO INTERVIEW THEM OR ASK ANY QUESTIONS UNTIL AFTER I INTERVIEW THEM. If they violate the law, they violate policy, not vice versa; let's not screw this part up.'

There was a silent drum roll in my head, 'Danny Nevada and Paul Christopher are the suspects named primarily in the allegation. Also identified as patrons, not principals are Steve Wootin, David Oshcarman, and Carl Stephens.' There was a little murmuring, then silence fell as my Captain rose to speak. 'I have Command of this incident. If I find your phone number in their phones, as of now, I will have your badge. Supervisors, everyone answers to me tonight, whether they work for you or not. Are there any questions?' There was one good question, 'Are we talking cops to jail tonight?' I did not like Captain, for various reasons, but I liked her answer, 'If we make any arrests tonight, they will no longer be cops; cops would not be found in a place like this.' The briefing was over; time to get the show on the road.

I admit to getting a relatively hard woody, when I saw the parade of police cars, en route to the club. Swat pulled out with their Armored Personnel Carrier and black van then patrol cars, UC cars from Vice and Intelligence, and an ambulance and finally, yet importantly, some Ghostbusters looking, cars from MCT. In all, about 21 cars caravanned through the city on the way to the search warrant. All this manpower and money wasted because of a few useless cops.

Five minutes out, four minutes, three minutes (I was about to mess up the front of my pants. I hoped I was not fully engorged when we arrived, or it would be hard for me to run). Two minutes, one minute, the marked cars deployed to block the streets. Aviation's Helicopter, swarmed in and hovered nearby, until entry. SWAT was in the parking lot, and there it was; the spot light in the sky, the helicopter's speakers giving commands.

Due to the target being both a business and a nightclub, we had to go with the slow clear option. Dynamic entry into a nightclub with blaring music smelled of disaster. It only took one person's inability to hear the 'Police Search Warrant! Do not resist,' for this to go lethal. That is why the helicopter also used its spotlights to shine into the building, hard to say you neither heard, nor saw, when the lights blaze into the building.

We had no prior knowledge of who else would be in the club, but the targets were there. SWAT was present for anyone feeling the need to die of lead poisoning. SWAT made entry, and the first course of business was to find the owner or manager, get the turned music off, and the place illuminated. Ripley's Believe It Or Not! They did not have crap on us; this night, the first target, opened the door and was all-eager to assist. Nevada identified himself, and then led SWAT to the owner and offered any other assistance. SWAT cordially invited Nevada to speak to me.

I waited outside, per OPs Order, until SWAT gave an all clear. Since Nevada, the dimwit, wanted to help, I let him.

'What's up Andrews,' Nevada said as he walked up. 'We was looking to serve a warrant, the guy is a witness, but he isn't in there.'

I knew that was some bull; the other officer did not work in personal crimes, he was in property crimes, and they were not working a case together (I checked). Not that they could not be, they just were not. Then the CYAs (cover your ass), started.

'We come over here about once a week, and stand in the door and check IDs to see if we can find the guy. Man, all kinds of drugs and crap go through this place,' Nevada continued.

'Yeah, I know, that is why we are here, lots of complaints about whores and drugs. Any word on who the pimps are?'

'No not really,' Nevada says, 'I guess the whores belong to the club.'

I smiled, and walked away. Nice try I thought, as good a lie as any, I would have a time, trying to prove they were taking money and not just checking IDs.

We video interviewed the people as they left. Three girls were under age, the youngest, 16 yrs old. I referred them to Child Sex abuse. In all, we spent about 5 hours at the club, got about 5 ounces of Cocaine, and a dozen guns. I submitted my reports, ran the findings up the chain, and waited to see what they wanted me to do next. Several citations were issued, and code violations levied, but not much against the targets.

I got a call from my Captain, 'I read your report, there's not much here against Nevada and company. What do you want to do now?'

'Now that they know we are on to them, and that they really should not be there, I say we go harder this time, develop a few of those arrests into CIs and let's see what I can develop. If nothing else; buy from the owner and shut it down.'

'Very well, go ahead but do not take too long, or spend too much money,' captain instructed.

The next call I got was from Beverly, I knew this would be interesting. She started her tirade, by informing me that Nevada walked up to her in court and told her to tell me to back off the club; otherwise, he would reach out to his friend the Chief. He reminded her that he, the

Chief, and one of the suspects were all from the same city, and he would ensure that Chief opened all my old Internal Affairs files and run a fine toothed comb through them.

After a hearty laugh, and a good deal of time telling her not to worry, if they could touch us, they would have; I replied with a three-word response for him, 'Eat a dick.' That pretty much summed up what I both wanted him to do and what I thought of him professionally, and personally. Then I drove downtown.

Upon arrival, I spoke to the lobby guards, and then pushed the top floor on the elevator. I was going to the bottom of this; it just so happened that, the bottom of this, was in an office on the top floor. Chief was pretty laid back, since we did so much work together, it was not unusual for me to drop in to his office unannounced.

I spoke to his secretary, 'Morning, he in today?'

'Sure; are you up here to sign your Use of Force reports?'

I laughed, 'Reports, how many are there?'

'Six,' she replied. I would probably have blushed, were I embarrassed, but I had no shame about what I did.

I signed all the reports, never even bothering to look on the reverse of the reports to see what determination the supervisors turned in to the Chief's office. If there was a problem I would have known by now, otherwise, it was business as usual.

I walked into Chief's office, 'Renarde,' he said as he looked up, 'What do you need?'

I replied less politely, 'You sicked your lap dog on me Chief?'

He looked up from his desk, whatever unimportant thing he was doing to look busy he stopped. 'What are you talking about?'

'Nevada sent me a message, that you said to back off Club Dog Pound, or you would come after me, and he reminded me that y'all are from the same city and implied that you are his protection.'

Chief laughed, 'First of all I do not need any help, coming after you, and secondly Nevada and I are not friends. So I would not worry about it, if I were you.'

'I figured as much, but I thought you should know he is handing out threats and trying to orchestrate cases in your name.' I walked out of his office, got on the elevator and went back to doing the voodoo that I did so well.

Back at work, reality set in, one of the treacherous Trio in Vice walked up and handed me a file. 'We had that complaint for several weeks; we just didn't do anything with it.' He smiled and walked away. Dammit, it was over, the case was not blown; it was doomed from the start. He was the Captain's way of telling me that it was over, someone above her, either called her off the case, or used their get out of jail free card. In this club, we found under aged strippers, officers, drugs, and guns. No prosecution ever occurred; they took the case from me, reassigned it, and buried it.

I used up considerable professional collateral, and burned a few bridges trying to do right in a vacuum. People never understood why I was angry when they took the case.

"Is it because it made you look bad for nothing?" Walters asked innocently.

"No it is because people do not understand the true power of a dirty cop. Media is so stupid, they have people believing that dirty cops are cops that slap the hand cuffed, fix traffic tickets, use drugs, target minorities, and drink all the time. These are not dirty cops; these are just undesirables. Dirty cops have the power to write bad search warrants, seize property, take lives, plant dope, make warrants appear and disappear, bury criminal cases and hide with impunity. To plant dope, is a singular action, and yes, that is both ban-jacked and dirty. To fabricate or bury a case requires help outside the department, like in the DA(s) office. You have no idea. I know, because this is where I spent years, operating in this grey area, except, I never used my power to allow the guilty to victimize or use the innocent.

It cost a lot, but I personally have arrested and made criminal cases against more cops than anyone else I know. The case may have had some chicken crap components, but they were not chicken crap cases. Chicken shitting someone is when you find obscure, minor issues to charge someone with...Sometimes you have to do this, to make the Internal Charges stick, but I never chickened anyone, all my cases were righteous criminal cases.

Still, it does not seem to matter to some cops, many still hold a grudge that I ran pieces of crap away from the department, making it safer for them and everyone else. I will never understand that mentality. However, I did modify my behavior in my own arrests, to erase the suspicion that I was a dirty cop."

"So what then?"

"I don't have all the answers; just don't sacrifice good people over stupid crap."

14.7 Weed Anyone?

"Once I earned the reputation as a cop hunter, all manner of complaints rolled across my desk. One of the most chicken crap cases I worked was against a cop. The complaint was that this officer wore his uniform to parties; where under aged girls were drinking, doing drugs and having sex. I did not mind working that case because there were kids involved. Fortunately, the complainant wanted to feed live Intel, as to when the cop was at the parties. The complainant also stated that the cop drove them in and out of town to transship Cocaine. Seemed credible, why else would this complainant tell the police he is around dope.

After several attempts to confirm the complaint, I had to unfound it. None of the dates lined up, when the guy said the cop was at the party, there were worksheets showing him at work, and I followed him to and from work, several times when he was allegedly at one of these minor mixers. That too was crap; I followed the cop at work and watched him duck calls all night. Lazy as hell, but nothing indicated that he was dirty.

I learned that if a person complains long enough, the Blue Ticks will just about chicken shit anyone. This turned out to be just such a case. My new Captain was a career Tick. He had me go to the cop's house and try to prove that his wife was using dope. I resisted, and pointed out that the wife smoking pot was not enough to indict him as violating policy unless he saw it happening, it did not seem to rise to the level of associating with known criminals. Captain Dick-tick also made the legal argument, that if she is smoking and or storing the dope at their house then he is in possession (This argument I could not defend against).

The two ticks giving me the task were lawyers. To add insult to injury, the tick continued, 'We want you to pull his trash and let us know what you find?'

'I cannot pull his trash, because he keeps it on his porch.'

'Then go get it,' 'I cannot, he too has 4th Amendment rights.'

'Look this is Internal, so it does not matter,' said Captain Dick-Tick 2 (How underhanded).

'Internal, Then why am I here? I only do criminal.'

'Look just go pull the trash,' replied Captain Dick-Tick #1.

'That sounded suspiciously like an order, in which case I decline, but if you want to put it in writing, I will take care of it.'

Neither Dick-Tick looked happy with my response; I did not give a crap.

I was not about to break Federal Law, to prove misdemeanor crap we do not even prosecute on a daily basis. Captains Dick-Tick left it where the conversation ended. However, the undertone was that they wanted me to get a search warrant. I wrote the search warrant based on legal PC acquisition and then met with the Ticks. This time I took my supervisor.

If the Ticks were going to order me to do some underhanded stuff, I wanted a witness to my redress. It is like the tree falling in the forest, a good screw you or gag on one, is wasted without a witness. Of course, they were less likely to say ignorant crap in front of another witness, but they definitely wanted me to pull the trash regardless. I pulled the trash another legal way, and found barely enough.

We sat down in the office, and updated the Captains. 'I found a little bit of weed.' Although I had done search warrants based on the same amount of drugs, I did not want to railroad the guy, because it was his wife, but a deal is a deal. When he took the job with the Department, Officer Stupid, agreed to stay clear of trouble. Some crap you cannot avoid, like use of force complaints, crashes etc. Then there is other stuff, DUI, domestic violence, being married to a pothead, is completely unavoidable.

It was a tiny amount, but it did give us PC to write a paper. I handed over the Search warrant; the Probable Cause section was sufficient, to get a signature from a judge. I knew this to be the case because it was already signed. I also knew I was going to have to serve the warrant; they were not backing off this guy. As stupid as he was, he was a freebie. Dude was white, young, no civil service and no protection; he was perfect.

Even Ticks realize that periodically, the police have to clean house, to maintain both credibility and objectivity. The public cannot feel that the police are immune to prosecution, and the police certainly cannot afford to give in to this belief. Dragging this guy out in the spotlight and throwing his ass in the fire, saved face, and allowed protected people to continue to escape. Not a great solution, not even a good solution, but this is the way The System works." I looked Walters sternly in the eyes; I hoped he understood the implication.

"Captain Dick-Tick [#]1 and Captain Dick-Tick [#]2 read the warrant, like I was actually going to change it anyway. Then things got dicey. I was ordered to snatch the guy up, at roll-call, and take him into custody. Again, I resisted, but Ticks do not understand. Because Ticks do not plan to do police work, they do not need backup. No matter what a cop does, it never goes over well to drag him out of roll call. More importantly, one should also remember that the person dragged away from a job, and to a potential jail sentence is wearing a pistol, a bullet resistant vest and carrying at least 45 bullets. Crap like that, needs to be taken into consideration, it sure as hell was listed in the Operations Order.

I drove to the precinct, my squad in tow. The stupid ass supervisor, Turd #1 (one the captain's flunkies) and I, got into a heated discussion in the parking lot pertaining to what to do next. I was not dragging this cop out of roll call. I was ambivalent about charging him anyway; it was such a small amount and not really his.

It was not until Turd #1 (arguably one of the largest pieces of crap; Ever) spoke, that I knew I was right for feeling wrong. 'Don't you think that the police should be held to a higher standard?'

It hit like a ton of bricks, he was another epiphany for me, and this case was another epiphany.

Hypocrisy can slap you and make you feel helpless. I realized for the first time, what ho(s) felt like, when their pimp spoke. I realized that this time, in this case, in this spot right now, that I was one of the two ho(s), the other cop my supervisor represented the System which is the Ultimate pimp. I felt cheap, used, and dirty. I would have taken a shower but it takes too long to take all the crap off I donned for this operation.

After all the crap I did, those who cannot remember their birthday because I kicked their brains loose, or cannot crap because my boot caused permanent blockage when I kicked their ass, the ones thrown down the stairs, or for that matter, thrown up the stairs. Damn, I felt like chicken crap for this case. I let many civilians go with this amount of weed, even Cocaine, because it was just not worth the hassle. This poor son of a bitch, no mercy for him; I felt like a cannibal.

I decided the best way was to call the Soon-To-Be-Ex-Cop into the lieutenants' office, and let the lieutenant disempowered him. In doing so, in a routine manner, it disarmed this Soon-To-Be-Ex-Cop, so that no suicide happens, while I stood in the parking lot.

They called Soon-To-Be-Ex-Cop in, told him some horse crap story, while I stood outside like a good whore. Turd [#]1 was all smiles and proud, looked like he was in the middle of a happy-ending (damn that would mean I was jerking him off).

Why this corn-filled piece of crap was pleased at the demise of a young cop far less dirty than he annoyed me. I never really considered before what turds felt like when flushed. I guess the last one down is hoping the cycle ends before he slides into the swirling abyss. I guess that is how Soon-To-Be-Ex-Cop felt, like the last turd he waited eagerly for his turn - hoping toilet ran out of water before he slid.

They led Soon-To-Be-Ex-Cop into an interview room, 'Sit down Officer Soon-To-Be-Ex-Cop let us talk.' He sat down looking all doe eyed. I worked with this idiot several times in the past; he transported people for me, to jail, and asked on several occasions if he could join our squad. Well now, I can finally say yes, he could be a CI.

'This is not an internal investigation, I reminded him, I only do criminal matters, do you understand?'

Before he could answer, another supervisor burst into the room, 'If you lie we will fire you!'

Possibly the only time ever, Turd #1 and I agreed. We both looked at the genius, and simply shook our heads.

I looked at Soon-To-Be-Ex-Cop, 'Please ignore that outburst completely, let me remind you of your rights. You have the right to remain silent, anything you say can and will be used against you in a court of law,' I paused; Soon-To-Be-Ex-Cop had no response. 'You do understand that you have the right to remain silent?' Again, he made no response. 'You have the right to have an attorney and to have that attorney present with you during questioning.' I had a camera and room full of eyes on me, there was little I could do.

I kicked him under the table, 'Yes I understand,' he replied dryly.

It was now in his hands, I gave us both a way out, if he had walking sense, 'Do you wish to give up these rights and speak to us now?'

I prepared myself to pack my pads, and walk out then it happened, this ignorant cocksucker spoke, 'Yes I will speak to you now.'

Ignominious is the only word I can think of to describe the defeat I felt when he threw away his career.

'Do you know why you are here?' It was obvious by his response he was clueless.

'No not really, they told me I was disempowered, based on a complaint but did not tell me about what.'

'We received a complaint about you at parties with under aged girls drinking in uniform, and about you smoking dope and helping people traffic Cocaine.'

He sat back, 'I don't do dope.'

'Think before you answer my next question.'

If he lied, termination was automatic, if he told the truth he was both a criminal and unemployed. 'Do you or anyone that you know use drugs?'

'Not Cocaine,' he replied. 'And as far as any girl underage drinking, the only party I been to in uniform was at Pratt's house. I got off that night and went to the house to see if my wife was there, she was not, so I left. I did not think I needed to change, to walk into a party and pick up my wife.'

'You do, if there are drugs present. Were there drugs present?'

'Probably, they use sometimes.'

I wish he had exercised the right to shut the hell up. 'Clear something up for me then, if you don't use drugs, but you went to pick your wife up at a place where they use drugs, does she use drugs.'

It hit him; finally, he realized he should have shut the hell up. He finally realized he was destined to be the milkshake guy at McDonald's the following week.

'My wife,' he slumped in the chair, 'My wife is the cause of all of this.'

'Sort of,' I replied, 'you bear responsibility too. I have a search warrant for your house that I have to execute. You may feel free to consent to the search and show us where the dope is, if there is any at the house; however, here is a copy of the warrant to be executed regardless.' I was not being spiteful, there was no reason anyone investigating a dirty cop wanted to lose, due to a faulty consent search.

He glanced down at the search warrant, and then to complete the humiliation, he added, 'There is a little weed at the house.'

Aghast, I looked across the table at Mr. I-Am-No-Longer-A-Cop-As-Of-Right-Damn-Now, took a deep breath then said, 'Let's go, I won't walk you through the Precinct in handcuffs.'

I patted him down in private for drugs or the second weapon, training dictated we look for. Finding none, we walked out of the building. We drove over to his house; Mr. I-Am-No-Longer-A-Cop-As-Of-Right-Damn-Now was in my car with another detective. 'Look man, if I have to arrest you anyway, the way I look at it is that I should give you a chance to help yourself as much as possible. You cannot save your job but if you shoot straight with me about where the dope is, and whose it is, where it is from and how much y'all are moving, I'll take care of you the best I can.'

'It is not mine. She smoked while we were in college, I kept telling her to stop, but I knew. I haven't smoked since I joined the department, but I never made her stop. We are not selling it; she gets it from some black guy that comes to the house. I do not know his name, but she buys a ¼ ounce at a time, and that will last for about a month.'

'You let a dude come to the house and sell dope to you and your wife?'

'I am not usually there.'

'Is that supposed to make it better or worse?' I asked.

He continued, 'I don't know anyone that sells drugs and since it won't save my job anyway, I don't want to work for y'all.' I understood his reaction, I would not have cooperated this far.

At the house, we made a soft entry, having placed him in cuffs before leaving the precinct. The house was clean and orderly, so we left it that way. He showed us the cliché shoebox with weed, rolling papers, and a glass pipe, which he said belonged to his wife. I tried to get the Ticks to allow me to write Mr. I-Am-No-Longer-A-Cop-As-Of-Right-Damn-Now a Misdemeanor citation, but they would not hear of it. I had to indict him, on 2 grams of weed, and drug paraphernalia. I hated the whole ordeal, but he was of no value to the department anyway, and destined for compromise.

I remembered a call from the Media Officers that started, 'The Department needs your help.' I was asked to create an official lie to cover the Department's ass when a news story broke about officers in uniform in sex clubs. I figured the Department needed my help again.

Captains Dick-Tick wanted to parade this guy in front of the news, bad for him, worse for me. I did not want this chicken crap case dangled around my neck forever. I gave the guy the wrong time to turn himself in, on the warrants. In doing such, I arranged for the media to arrive 2 hours after I booked him quietly and let him skulk away into his new

French fry filled life.

I ruffled a few feathers in the media, and the PIO was pissed. Oh well, that is what happens when you play the game, sometime you win sometimes you lose. Nobody won that day."

"Why did you try to help him?"

"I was not trying to help him, I was doing my job. The allegations were unfounded, he did not smoke dope, and he fessed up. If we fired every cop that had a piece of crap kid or spouse, half the force would be gone, they sacrificed him because he had no 'Tics, and no Civil Service. They sacrificed the little red herring, to take people's eyes and ears off worse problems in the department like Nevada, nepotism, theft, sexual harassment and other types of corruption higher up like gambling and promoting prostitution. See; I know the difference between heavy handed and dirty."

"You regret the Job?"

"Best thing I ever did. Choose something to do or enjoy that will not get you fired. More importantly, utilize the right to remain silent."

14.8 Polygraph Who?

"In a futile effort to get the 3 Turds removed from their assignment in Vice, some dimwit, complained after failing to get their job, that they had not taken the mandated polygraph test in a while. The inconvenient thing about the complaint, was that since whinny-ass complained of a policy violation, the mandate (as it should have), moved across the division. The policy mandated bi-annual polygraphs.

I was a seasoned liar, it was my job, I did not fear the test, but the tester had discretion to pass or fail you, and this was a great opportunity for the Ticks to witch-hunt, or say, use the pimp hand on a disobedient ho. I received my notification of date and time to report for a poly. The appointment showed 30-minute appointment duration, longer than a street deal or prostitution deal, but less time than a delivery or UC Operation, this would be easy I thought. I continued to think it would be easy until I read the name of the examiner, Lt. Hibiscus, my snide attitude hiccupped.

Lt. Hibiscus; aka Blondie, an old teammate and I worked the streets together a long time ago, not so long ago that memories failed. Yet another problem with secrets, they linger, even after the deed is long done, the effect can still overwhelm. I pulled up at HQ, and walked into the lobby. After signing in, I made my way to the assigned location. There she sat, she looked the same, same smile, same demeanor, hell, same hairstyle. However, it was different; we were on opposite sides of the table, with a robot in between us. I walked up and gave her a hug, warm as ever.

We sat down, 'How are you Renarde?'

'Fine, this is a waste of time.'

She smiled at me, 'You received your letter, please sign it in front of me. Standard Internal Memo, reminding me that if found to be deceitful, termination is automatic.'

Her professional candor and lack of casual response made me leery; I had to assume we were being monitored. She witnessed and notarized my lie.

I wondered if that made it a truism, I planned to lie about everything; easier that way to establish a baseline. Even the base line question I lied about, at least that is what I told myself, I reminded myself that my UC identity is who I am really, now therefore, my real demographics were all fallacious.

'You remember how this works, I ask you a series of questions to establish a baseline, then I will ask you the following questions, to which you will answer with either a Yes or No, no other responses count. Not answering is not allowed.

1. Have you stolen money?
2. Have you used illegal drugs?
3. Have you lied about facts during an investigation?
4. Have you planted evidence?
5. Have you ever struck a suspect that was handcuffed?
6. Have you ever not turned in property?
7. Have you ever used confidential funds for personal use?
8. Have you ever failed to act when a suspect was being assaulted or witnessed the assault of a suspect?

As I listened to the questions, two more questions crossed my mind

- *Do they want anyone to pass this damn test?*
- *Is this graded on a curve?*

She must have read my mind, 'Do you consent to the test?'"

(Like I had a choice), "The test, yes, the tester no."

"What is your objection based on?"

"I can beat the machine,' I started, "That is not my problem. Questions 3-8 are my problem."

"Why is that?" she asked. I knew then, we were not being recorded. I could not ask if we were being recorded, that was a red flag, but she could not control my answer, a chance she dared not take.

"My objection is that you know that I am lying because you were there, with me, or me with you, depending on the situation."

She sneered, which meant for her, that she had already considered this eventuality between us, I was still unsure of whether that was good or bad.

"Let's look at each question one by one and see if your concerns are valid. Have I stolen money; No that is an easy one, same for illegal drug use. Have I lied about facts during an investigation? Well I never lied, unless reconfiguring the facts is a lie."

She did not reply, I wonder why (she taught moot court when she was training me.)

"Have I planted evidence, now, that I've have not done. Did I ever strike a suspect that was handcuffed?" She raised her eyebrow, this even she did not want me to answer.

"Yes, I have had to wrestle, hobble, and or spray handcuffed suspects."

"Other than that?" she asked.

"Nope," I answered.

"As far as, have I ever not turned in property?" We both laughed at that question. We used the drug pipes, and food stamps, or whatever accoutrements frequented our craft, and of course thug-drobe but never guns or drugs.

We continued our debriefing, "Have I ever used confidential funds for personal use. No I have not," I said, while crossing my fingers. The prevailing methodology was to utilize whatever money was in hand, including confidential funds and then make sure that the money was back in the fund by the close of business at the end of the month. Apparently, this informal policy was not right.

Finally, I got to the last question, "Have I ever failed to act when a suspect was being assaulted or witnessed the assault of a suspect?" This one, I used, to ensure that she was not recording, or had not gone all the way to the dark side of the force. "Only the ones you hit or we did together."

She sat back in her chair with an incredulous look on her face; I shrugged one shoulder and smiled a crap-eating grin.

I would never throw a partner under the bus, however I'll be damned if I let someone drive the bus over me.

I passed the test, turns out it actually was not that difficult. When I got to work the next day, I was surprised to see the Director of IA at the office. It turns out that so many people from the division failed the question about using confidential funds, that it was determined beneficial to remove it from the battery of questions; Go figure."

"So you can beat the machine?"

"Yeah, they trained me to. It is easy to beat the machine, but after a while, even you cannot remember the reason for telling the lies."

14.9 Where You Ever A Lawman?

"I would like to say something cliché, like it was the best of time and the worst of times, but the truth is, sometimes criminals are so frigging stupid, it begs the question: Is this a joke ?. However, when the stupid people are cops, then the questions changes to; are you frigging kidding me?

My phone rang? 'Hello, this is Andrews.'

'This is Dr Gooch,' the voice on the other end of the line replied.

'Detective, I received your number when I called the police for assistance with a pill case I have.'

I agreed to meet with her. CIs are great, but when the witnesses are professionals, like MDs or PhDs the effect is awesome.

I rolled over to the Doctor's office. We sat down, she was pleasant, but what impressed me most with her, was her diligence.

'I was covering for another doctor, when I came across an employee file (this was to be an internal criminal matter) which I found to be of concern. While meeting with an employee, Cindy Guneman, in the office for her annual physical. The employee listed no drug use, in their profile, but when I spoke to her, she stated that she used Hydrocodone. To ensure that the information in the file read correct, I checked her information in the State Controlled Substances Database.

Within the Database information, it was clear that the information provided, by the officer, was not congruent with the level of pharmaceuticals shown. I inquired as to her physical condition and she explained that a work related accident caused an injury. She further explained that the reason her boss sent her to the company clinic was because she got into an argument with her supervisor about carrying a weapon, and was told that she could not carry a weapon and she could not work.'

'Sounds reasonable,' I added, trying to figure out how I come into the scenario.'

'I just came right out and asked her about the use of the Hydrocodone. She replied that her doctor told her that she had to get the prescriptions, if she wanted to sue, so he kept writing them for her. She added that she and her husband both got prescriptions for opioids, from the same doctor, but neither actually used them, they just threw them into the toilet. She later told me that her husband David Guneman worked for the department as well.'

I figured that was the worst of the problems, but the saga continued. 'I then called her husband back in, after reviewing his file, it too read, nothing like the Controlled Substances Database (Nail in the coffin [#]1). His file also annotated no prescription drug use of any kind. I reached out to their doctor and asked about their medical conditions. The Doctor, already under investigation for over prescribing, shared with me that they were seeing him for pain management, for various injuries.

David told me, however, that he was being written prescriptions that he did not want, and the doctor refused to stop writing them, so he just filled them and threw them away.'

To think this witness, this doctor, was a podiatrist; she put this case together like a detective. The rest was up to me.

I had two suspects, two conflicting medical professionals, paperwork, and a database with their names in it, signature logs from pharmacies and with my training, more incriminating evidence was sure to follow.

I collected data, a lot of data, interviews, medical records, pharmacy records, eyewitness statements, voice mails and a host of other bits and pieces. I learned how to think like a Tick, and get rid of the problem, even if it's chicken crap."

Walters shook his head, "It's just prescription pills man, no big deal, and they were cops."

"Were cops, is correct," and I added a hearty, "Screw them two. People do stupid crap I understand, but these pill popping pieces of crap were using copious amounts of dope, so much so, that they had to be coming to work, under the influence. Do you want to go through a door with a frigging junkie, and have them, behind you, with a gun?"

Walters nodded his dissent.

"See brother, it is easy to see the faults and weaknesses in other people and we choose to cover each other, but only a fool makes allegiance with their own demise. Trust me, I know, only so many secrets stay in the dark, then when they hang you out to dry, there is no love or forgiveness left for you. People trust us to do the right thing, sometimes that's to take a life, sometimes to give a break, but sometimes it is to slap a set of cuffs on a cop.

This is not like the other cop, he was just passively stupid, these two were pieces of crap, trading their badge for dope.

After compiling the data, it became clear that both of these buttholes suffered from a severe case of Stupid-As-Crap-Itis. This disease, though not rare, if left untreated, often proved fatal. In the case of cops however, it could be both fatal and lethal. I did not plan to see collateral results of either, on my watch. I took keeping the innocent safe seriously, I did not spend years bending the crap out of the law, to sit by and let cops break it, especially those that hurt people. Dummy $^{\#}$1 and $^{\#}$2, unlike No-Longer-a-Cop, was not just watching his wife smoke weed; they were abusing their power and Narcotics (this is not the 70s).

According to policy, I needed to inform IA about the case; however, since it came across my desk from the higher ups I operated under the assumption that they undertook any notifications. As such, I did not feel compelled to report to anyone except my Captain and immediate supervisor. For the most part, they both left me alone, not that I was special, it was easier to streamline the process and kept it as quiet as possible, if you did not involve everyone.

The first thing I did after amassing the data was develop a timeline of violations. Unlike having dope in your hands, in pill cases, the dope is usually gone. There are a few things in pill cases to look for, owing to the fact that there are not as many laws governing the personal abuse of prescription drugs. The main violations to look for are;

- Obtaining a Controlled Substance by Fraud
- Forgery
- Identity Theft
- Doctor Shopping
- Insurance Fraud

I set to task proving as many violations as possible, not to screw them as much, as to ensure they left the job.

Making the cases, started with the contention that the cops were not just getting drugs for her accident and lawsuit scam (which is not a valid reason by the way - I cautioned), but then why is the husband getting the pills? The answer manifested itself, as soon as I learned the prescribing physician's name. I knew Dr Piercel, all too well, in fact along with 7 other investigators and the Media, had a case against him for all kinds of alleged stuff. That was what I needed, to convince me that this was no coincidence, and that maybe the cops had assistance in their scam. There was only one other thing troubling me. Either the Dumbass cops were using crap loads of dope, or selling the pills. They were dirty either way, of what, I was just not sure: yet. The only way was to leave my tower, and go talk to the doctor.

On the way, a nail for the coffin [#]2 landed in my lap. Apparently, the doctor's girlfriend was also his nurse and had filed a complaint with the Medical Board about the doctor's prescribing. Part of the complaint was a voicemail, 'Let me tell you about a doctor and two dirty cops. They provided security for him at the clinic. It's not even a clinic; it's more like a Crack House with all the patients sleeping in the lobby waiting around to get their fix.'

With this information, I changed the game plan; I went into surveillance/verification mode. It was not that I did not believe the corroborating sources, (I had the Controlled Substances data) , but I needed to know exactly what I had dropped into my lap. It is not a habit to allow anyone to slip through my grasp, certainly not going to start with two junkie cops.

I sent CIs in, several times, to just sit in the lobby, and get a prescription filled. The scripts were easy to acquire, and the zombies were both in and outside the office, this was not a legit operation. The video evidenced the goings on, and strengthened the other agency's cases against the doctor.

The next step in the investigation was to; see what the staff and the files said about the two idiots. Nail for the coffin [#]3, was that the female officer had two files; one in her married name and the other her maiden name. This was the Subterfuge portion of the statute for both officers, and also proved beyond a doubt that this was not an inadvertent occurrence. The staff also confirmed the doctor's relationship with the nurse, and that the officers hung out in the lobby in uniform, maintaining control over the zombies. The staff believed that the officers received pay, because they provided security at the office, but could not verify any checks to the officers from the book keeping software.

More and more, the barter system was in play in this clinic, the two cops were at the clinic to get drugs, and the doctor took care of them, in return, they provided security for his ongoing drug enterprise. It is not uncommon for a Drug Trafficking Organization to use cops as security, everyone one wants to feel safe. Why you would feel safe with junkies on the job is beyond me, but I am not a trafficker.

Next, in the list of things to do, was talk to the girlfriend. Nail for the coffin $^{\#}4$, she provided details of the officers getting their prescriptions off site or in the parking lot, from the doctor, having not had any further examination. When I questioned this, pointing out the examination notes, she admitted that she was the person that entered the data, and it was false. Although she was involved, she was getting the whistle blowers deal - C'est la Vie.

I returned to my tower and dug into the paperwork for Nail for the coffin $^{\#}5$, and $^{\#}6$. The chicken crap issue was that the cops did not have permission to work extra at the clinic. The other issue derived from their files. Their files definitively listed no physical problems and there was no drug use, for the prior year as well as the current year. This morsel, violated by policy and the law, under the subterfuge and fraudulence portions, as the officers told two different stories to the doctors.

The nails were adding up, and it was looking more and more like the two junkies stumbled into a supplier and traded their badges for pills. It's cliché, but how many pimps and whores live in one city? Another pimp controlling two more ho(s), this time not with slaps, but with pills.

The officers were so far out of control, they placed their careers in the hands of zombies, to keep their secret. A doctor and his real whore, maintain their lie, supply, and each other, for all of the above. This was their undoing, ironically not the zombies or the whore, just a partner with loose lips and no ability to think on their feet, sunk their ship. Sad, they sold themselves so low; they became street walking, ten-dollar whores, no values, no discretion, no value to society.

Time to call the rats back to the cage; I would waste no cheese on these two. They were about to determine what they wanted written on their professional tombstones.

I met with David first, I figured he would be the most difficult. 'Sit down officer, let's talk. This is a criminal investigation, but you are not in custody and you are free to leave.'

He sat down, and looked at me. 'I am trying to clear up a few issues; maybe we can avoid any misunderstandings. I did not read read Miranda warnings, he was free to go. I started, 'Are you in pain management and if so for what?'

'I was, but that went away, so not anymore.'

'So in your file, where you wrote, no Narcotic use, is because the problem abated?'

'That is correct.'

'Then please explain why you are still getting narcotic prescriptions filled, or are you the victim of ID theft?'

'No I am not a victim, I just never got the prescription cancelled, and the doctor keeps writing them I do not know how to stop him.'

'Why keep paying to have them filled, your insurance carrier might be less than happy about that fact.'

'I just did not know how to stop him writing them.'

'Do you pick them up yourself at the pharmacy?'

'Sometimes,' he replied.

'You and your wife pick each other's pills up?' He nodded his head yes.

'Which name do you use to pick them up for her, married or maiden?'

Smiling he replied, 'Both.'

He was not smiling because he was happy he knew he was caught, he was just being friendly. 'What do you do with the pills, you fill for yourself? You pop them or sell them?'

Replying indignantly, 'I would never sell them, most of them I throw in the toilet.'

Remember the disease Stupid-As-Crap-Itis can be fatal. Why show up for a voluntary interview, and tell the truth. He could have lied to me all he wanted, and it would not have really affected his employment. The Department would have complained, but he could have survived. However, to show up, tell the truth about lying and committing felonies was not a brilliant move.

'Have you ever picked drugs up for her in her maiden name?'

He nodded his head in agreement, again. I am not sure if it was too much, or not enough narcotics, making him so stupid, but he buried them both.

Next up was, Idiot [#]2.

Idiot [#]2 walked into the office with one of the stupidest grins I have ever seen. I instantly hated her. Too much of anything is bad; too much stupid is jacked up. She was messed up, her attitude was not cavalier, it was more like she was mentally deficient. I do not mean retarded (although an IQ Test might have been warranted).

Idiot [#]2 propped herself up in a chair, and introduced herself. Maybe she did not realize that her picture was on the table in front of her. 'Yes ma'am, this is a criminal investigation, but you are not in custody and you are free to leave.'

'I know, I am here to clear my husband. I think I got him in trouble (*no crap*; I thought, *were it not for you he could be somewhere patrolling the streets stoned out of his mind*).'

'Why are you under that impression?'

'He told me he spoke to you the other day, and you asked if he knew that I was getting two sets of pills. He didn't, the day he picked them up for me, I forgot to remind him that I used my maiden name, because I did not have my ID with the married name on it, and I planned to go get the prescription, I just could not, at the last moment.'

'Ok I will just document that, and that should fix that problem. And you are in Pain Management correct, for your back?'

'Yes, I got hurt at work.'

'Ok and why do you have two files at the doctor's office?'

'They just never merged the files; I have been going there since before I got married, I will have to remember to get them merged.'

'Anything else, you want to tell me, to clear up?' She stood up, said no; she then slithered out of the interview room, leaving a slimy trail and aura of stupidity.

I compiled my notes and went back to my lair, from wherein I planned to strike out and remove them as quickly as possible. Little did I know how much of a hassle this case was to be, I planned on push back from the suspects, disdain from some of the family, chicken crap support from the Ticks and lots of paperwork; I did not plan to run headlong into a fight with the District Attorney's Office.

I was not a great fan of the District Attorney, actually I thought Stacy was a bit stupid (and he had a girl's name). I never thought him to be corrupt and gullible. Not long prior to this case, we had occasion to cross swords; I won. Some pill-popping aristocrat felt the weight of my pen when I charged her with 25 felony charges. Stupid ass District Attorney General Stacey Jones received a call from Madam Aristocrat, whilst she was still in jail. After the Madam Aristocrat called the DA, from jail, he called the Magistrate to arrange for her to be released without bond so she could attend a funeral (had it been her's I would have agreed).

The Magistrate did not to want outright refuse the DA, so he muddied the water and made her ineligible. Once Madam Aristocrat bonded out of jail (she could afford the bond), I received a call from the DA personally requesting some concession in the case, to which I professionally and cordially declined. The DA's Office recused themselves, and turned the case over to a Special Prosecutor.

On this date, the limp wristed, underbelly of society in the DA(s) office, claiming to represent the citizens of the jurisdiction called about my cop case to which she had been assigned. Assistant DA Tree-Hugger voiced her personal objection to pill cases. She decided that the case he cops admitted to and to which had irrefutable proof had no merit, at least, not by her pot smoking standards. The arguing with DA Tree-Hugger led to several volatile meetings with my chain of command, and that finally led to a meeting at the DA's Office, with Stacy.

Ironically, the DA General weighed in on my side, citing personal ideology had no place in the DA(s) office; the office DA(s) was in place to enforce the existing law; which was ironic considering he just tried to help his friend. Sometime later DA Stacy and I clashed again. This time the unindicted suspects served Federal time.

Since DA Tree-Hugger had nowhere to go officially, she tried an end run. The requisite determination by the DA was, 'If' a law had been violated it was to be enforced. She attempted to nullify the validity of the case and the charges. This, DA Tree-Hugger did by way of setting up a meeting offsite to discuss the case. What DA goes to the Defense Attorney's office to discuss a case? This useless vegetable, that's who.

Upon arriving at the meeting, my Sgt and I, sat across from the defendants; Ironically DA Tree Hugger, sat with the suspect across from Law Enforcement. This set the tone, 'We are here to discuss the case and get things out in the open, I don't plan to indict, but I want this resolved.'

I looked at her and said, 'That being the case, we can stop here. I am a criminal investigator. I will charge this matter via warrant, if I must. If they are not prepared to give a statement, then why are we here?'

The defense counsel did not even argue, but DA Tree Hugger did. She argued that it was her choice and she was not going to charge the matter. I stood up. Having prior dealings with me, the defense team knew they had won the battle. They were however about to lose the war.

DA Tree-Hugger could not stop me; the law and her Office were both on my side. What defense counsel did ask me was that I did not make any information from the meeting available to IA. As much as I hated IA, that was not an option, both, by policy and common sense. I refused.

The idiots told their stories, and I made notes. After fairy tale time ended, DA Tree Hugger tried one last time to help the villains. 'I still do not see what law they violated. I think this was a good session, but no violations.'

Anticipating her stupidity, I handed her a line item synopsis of each violation and the section of the Law it violated. She had nowhere to run this time. The case was in black and white, she would have to pull the JFK bullet out her ass, to save these two.

'I don't need you to tell me the law,' she snapped after she glanced at what I handed her.

'Not tell you counselor, reminding you, I was not sure if you knew the Law. If you don't like the law; quit or move.' Then my Sgt and I walked out. It was time to put this baby to bed.

While I could not get the dirty doctor criminally charged because he had cooperated, and technically had paperwork showing he had been lied to by the couple; I went after him civilly and via regulations. I hit the crooked couple with a combination of about 45 Felony charges, and numerous internal charges.

I knew DA Tree hugger would try to help them out, so I filed a complaint about her behavior to her team leader, and she was assigned (competent) help on the case, resulting in convictions and terminations for both Law Enforcement professionals.

I did do one thing for David, because he asked. 'Can you help me out, cop to cop?'

To which I replied, 'Were you ever actually a Lawman?'

It was not just his drug use, and involvement in peddling, there are things cops are required to do

- Answer calls
- Direct traffic
- Work crashes
- Help people in general
- Make decisions
- Take guns from people
- Respond to high risk calls for service
- Render first aid
- Take lives

While I may not like the manner in which you complete these tasks, as long as you do, I have no problem with you. What I do not understand is, how you accomplish these things and still find the time and desire to beat your wife, drink heavily, or casually use drugs.

Many officers went to prison or were terminated, during my decades on the Job, but never for doing the above listed 9 things. When I asked David was he ever a lawman? It was not so much a question as it was an opposition to his self-description, as a cop.

"I bet a lot of cops hate you," Walters cut in.

"I am not the butthole described by many officers. He asked me if I could help him avoid the Press, who had arranged with the Ticks, to film when I arrested him. We simply moved the arrest time up by an hour." I wiggled my eyebrows up and down to indicate to Walters this was an activity I enjoyed. "I called the Ticks and stated he showed up early, so I booked him."

"If he was as loathsome as rumored, why help him at all?"

"I told you I am not a complete jerk. I did my job, but look at how many people tried to save him from his own actions. Doctors, nurses, and his lawyers were at least getting aid, but also assistant District Attorney. Not everything is always black and white.

I did not need to parade him in front of the camera to do my job, I am a Shadow Creature by trade remember. My best work occurs in the darkness. Like pesticide, I can kill things already inside the house but a better method is to stop their entrance. This pest was already inside, I got rid of it, why do you need to see the rat struggle in the trap - I thought you hired pest control to get rid of the problem, not enjoy its suffering.

Besides, we must always remember that the police are recruited from the criminal classes." Walters looked puzzled, he may not understand the complexity of what I tried to explain, I hoped in time he would understand, or at least not fall victim.

14.10 KPG Gate

"They gave me a case on several of the guys from my (old) unit. Let me clear it up." I said to Walters, "My unit is always the first street unit I served on. The others were Units as well, but none like the fist group. I read the allegation, and decided that they did not need my help; they needed someone to throw the bastard in the trash pile.

It was not that they did not stomp a few butts, it was that the butts that got stomped started the fight and were arrested. This was not a criminal case. The Department did not like my answer, and took the case away from me (as usual, I was never a Tick or a Dick, so I didn't play politics with my charges).

My supervisor was a Blue Tick and wanted to do anything he could to bust a cop to appease his Blue Dick boss; even two good cops. Not on my watch.

At a staff meeting, Det Blue Tick, the new detective on the case reported to the Sgt B.Tick that my friends (the suspects) would not talk to him, would not return his call, and were thereby refusing to cooperate with an Internal Investigation. The Det Blue Tick and the Sgt B.Tick got permission from a Blue Dick, to dis-empower the suspects.

I made a call, 'Hey,' I said 'They are coming for y'all with some jacked up case. Get off the phone, call Geoff and both of you call to make an appointment.' Craig started to interrupt me, 'Just make the damn appointment. When you get there invoke Miranda and leave. That will back this crap off you.'

Amazingly enough, Sgt B. Tick reported that both suspects called and made appointments to come in for an interview. They walked into the interview, requested lawyers and left. Not that they were in any real danger, but when you have DA(s) like Tree Hugger and Blue Ticks, anything bad can happen to good people.

It ended there, the entire thing died. There never was a crime committed by my friends; the crime was in giving some of the other investigators badges and the title - police officer. I was beginning to understand why criminals hated Vice Detectives so intensely; they hate betrayal. A bad friend is worse than an enemy, an enemy you can see and avoid, but to detect an insincere friend is hard."

15.0
LOOK WHAT WE BECAME

"But the statistics show and the department says we are doing a better job of policing now than 10 years ago."

I looked at the young officer, doe-eyed and eager, and missed those days in myself. I missed the days when cynicism was not in charge, and bitterness had not seeped into that small space between my badge and my heart.

"Social trends have taken a downward spiral in the last 10 years. Teen suicide, military suicide, domestic violence, self-medication, over doses, and mass shootings are all on the rise. About the only thing that is not on the rise is goat screwing."

"Why is that?" Walters looked at me and laughed as he adjusted his vest for the 47th time since we have been sitting here.

"Why do you keep adjusting your vest?" I knew the answer but asked anyway.

"Because it itches, and it sticks to my chest."

"Then why wear it?" I continued, again already knowing the answer.

"It keeps me safe."

"Yeah, like the truth, it fits awkward, and is uncomfortable, but it keeps us safer. They hunt down puppy peddlers and goat lovers and jail them, but people that harm humans, get probation and judicial diversion. The FBI reports the following crime statistics for a particular year;

- 17,284 murders {approx 40% are domestic related}
- 99,856 reported rapes {1 in 3 women and 1 in 4 men have experienced a sexual assault}
- 803,007 Aggravated assaults
- 1,000,000 DUI
- 1,000,000 DMV
- 319,356 robberies
- 715 police officers arrested

Although 715 is a ridiculously high number of screw-ups, yet it still only accounts for 0.0000014% of the 5,229,635 reported crimes that year. The 'tics, Ticks, and Dicks by agreement, distract the population from the alarming amount of violence prevalent in the country, and focus on the minuscule amount of crime reported and charged against police officers. Why are Ticks and Dicks not held responsible for not doing crap about the other 99% of the crime?

Left out of most Crime Rates tallies, is also information on the number of crimes associated with religion, medical malfeasance, teachers, and crimes against Native Americans and illegal immigrants (which includes human trafficking).

The insidious national practice called Uniformed Crime Reporting is a way to downplay the actual crime rate. Those who lie to us, thereby preventing proper preparation and caution, are not doing this to protect us; they are doing this to protect themselves and their careers. After all, who would elect a mayor that allowed crime to run rampant? Then-again, who would re-elect a mayor that lied about the crime or refused to admit how dangerous the city is, and did nothing about it?

In excess of 1.5 million crimes committed annually are completely preventable; DUI is just another substance abuse issue we refuse to handle effectively. Ask yourself, if I am a bastard for fighting crime and hurting those that seek to harm others, what is the piece of crap that makes money off them?

Truth in sentencing is the most simple of all legal principles, yet the one most frequently abandoned. If the sentence fits the charge and the person duly tried, is found guilty, how hard is it to put their goat loving, cigarette smoking, car-jacking ass in jail for the requisite period of time?

There is no civility in not punishing the guilty and allowing the innocent to live in fear; how is that just? If Black Lives Matter is true, then why is it that, black people keep protesting and arguing about arrests and not the incarceration of blacks? What is a hate crime? Surely you got to at least, dislike a person if you murder him right? Then there are all those crimes, like human trafficking, that no one wants to touch; why?" I kicked his boot, "Because **poor people do not buy ass**. Who the hell has $5000 or more, laying around to pay to screw a 15 year old, other than rich guys? Human trafficking is expensive, because humans cost money, they need food, clothes, transport, to be hidden, and controlled. Like most consumer businesses, the need drives the market.

Something else I learned about street walking whores; they do not sit idly by and watch kids be abused, they tell the police. So if the trafficked girls are not on the street going to the seedy hotels, where are they going? Upscale places, places the rich and affluent people go. No city with a trafficking problem, does not know where to find the victims, 'tics (politicians), Ticks and Dicks say nothing because they keep that a secret. The secret is not the whereabouts, the secret is that we know and do nothing.

I have slapped the crap out of so many people; my hands feel like leather now, screws up date night. I laughed. I assure you each one, if asked, would readily tell you that they preferred the slap to Taser, or gunfire. You cannot un-shoot someone, but the slapped face stops stinging almost instantly. Why do I need a body camera? So you can watch the cops on video. Does this help stop the behavior? Hell no, of the 715 cops arrested, how many of their crimes were caught on tape? Only the completely demented would commit their crimes on tape.

Ask yourself however, how many necessary slaps or screw you(s) went undelivered? With all those slaps I delivered, I rarely had to discharge my weapon, because the slaps controlled the situation. When you tell a man to catch a snake, but limit his options, he fights differently. I learned fight skills, and on top of that, I had a team that had my back; no matter what. Rather than abuse it, I used it, and watched my behavior, not because of the camera, but because of the team. I determined that no one would get hurt on my watch (outside the arrest), and I never allowed bad guys to be abused either.

Black lives, White lives, Mexican lives, but none of them matter when blue lives are threatened. Like the man said, 'I like everyone, but when it comes to being killed, I am downright, bigoted.' No lives matter, when the 'tics and Ticks play the numbers game, for votes. The only time they amend the numbers, is when they can lie about a crime reduction. FYI, there is no way to reduce the crime rate without removing the pivotal element; CRIMINALS. More arrests, equals increased crime rate. More residents, and immigrants, equals increased crime rate, urban growth and renewal, equals increased crime rate. As long as there is crap to steal, there will be thieves.

As long as there is no punishment for theft, people will break into your home and take stuff. 'Psst,' I leaned in, pretending to whisper, the crime rate naturally falls due to population growth. The number of bastards in the country grows constantly, so that per capita, even without the police, crime can be shown to be on a decline, because there are more people in the equation. Numbers always lie.

There was a time when putting on the badge meant walking into the darkness and being the light for decent people. There was a time when people were leery of cursing at the police or fighting with them; no longer. With the non-pursuit policies, remedial gun range, training for pointing guns at people and termination for questionable actions, how can blue lives matter.

If cops do not feel safe, if society takes away their vests and guns, then how can they stand in front of the world and do their jobs without fear? Today, now; I fear the victim because I cannot trust them. When people call, they have already decided how they want the issue resolved. The victim has become the lawman, judge, and jury.

"So are you saying that cop's hands are tied?"

"Political corruption works by having an equally corrupt legal system to protect it. Between trial by media, and politics, cops find their hands tied, only the criminals are winning. Telling cops to stop protecting the hundreds of millions, and prevent or investigate the millions of crimes because of the 715 is absurd. I wager a lot more that 715 new crimes will be heaped on society this year. Which one of the reports or activists are going leave home and respond to those calls for service? By the way use powder with cornstarch for that issue with the vest."

16.0
SADDLE TRAMP

Slumping back against the bench both of our handcuffs made the distinct grinding noise they make when they dig into wooden benches. "Where does that leave us?"

"Here I am, 20 years later, a saddle tramp, too much cop to go out to pasture, too old to shut up and just take shit. Some dumb ass admin nightmare decided that Narco work leads to corruption, no research, to determine the real causes of corruption amongst police.

Obviously, we still do not consider cowardice corruption, and it fills the ranks of the upper echelon. Sadly, those who were never the real police, write policy for those who do real police work. Here is the truth, when the police no longer need you, and when the administration no longer cares about the lives and families of its officers; they are just little blue pawns. Nothing says as little about a leader than a lack of concern for their people.

Some argue that I should be happy about the lack of danger, and responsibility. To them, I send a hardy, kiss my blue ass. If I was afraid to face the darkness, the danger, and the crazy, I would have done something else with my life. Policing is not for the faint at heart, but sadly, it is a dying art. In the face of cowardice, lethargy, and sheer stupidity, the new police are of no value to citizens in distress; they only exist for traffic enforcement and alarm monitoring.

These dimwits actually think it is ok to write another cop a ticket, screw another cop's wife and or daughter, and snitch on another officer, because he slapped the taste out of the mouth of some slime ball criminal. Why would society want their police to be afraid to draw blood, what the hell do you need when your house is being broken into or you are car-jacked? It is not always hit and run, the hospitals and morgues are full of people who need real cops on their beat, but had to settle for Mayberry's finest donut thieves. Sad that policeman sleep at night, knowing that they have done nothing to make the city safe, on their watch; to them their shift was just another donut outing."

"So what did happen to the team?" inquired Walters.

"You mean the family, the last of the holdouts? As with all families, we broke up.   Some went inside as detectives; others received promotions and stayed the course. Some never made it back from the dark side, and a few joined the administration and bought into the lie."

"How does that make you feel?"

"Lonely brother, it was a great adventure but it was lonely. I never got to really dig into the Blue, because I spent my time in the grey and in the darkness."

It was my turn to face the Disciplinary Board. I walked in and sat down. There were old faces and new faces, but no friendly faces, no Blue faces.

Before they said a word, I knew time; my time was up. They read the charges, and explained why my behavior amounted to termination. I smiled and looked at the calendar; it was the first day of Chicken Shit Season.

I stood up, adjusted my gear and looked at the faces around the table. In the room, there were six faces; not a cop among them, not a badge in the room except mine. There were professional cops, the ones that hide behind the police work of others and pretend that their decisions make a difference, or make the world safer. Marines may make blood flow and grass flow; but it is the cop that makes the city a safe place to live.

The only thing I was ashamed of this day, was that we all bore the title 'Cop', and people saw me and thought of them. I walked out silently, there was nothing to say, no one in the room would understand anyway.

I walked up to Walters, "Well brother, this was my last dance in The System." He stood up and we shook hands. It was not the firm business handshake, more like a parting connection. I was reaching back through him, and he was saying a respectful goodbye. The kind of respect you render to a retiring hero, a warrior made obsolete by politics and time. It was a goodbye, permanent in its sincerity, reminding me that the day would never come again that the people would admit they needed me, and my team. They might call upon us, but they would never again admit the need existed because that would be an admission failure.

"What does that mean?"

"It is simple; The System pays your bills, and feeds your family. The System gives you vacation time and can take it away. The System is going to buy you a boat, diamonds, cars, and braces. That same system is going to put innocent people in jail because of the color of their skin. One judge will put them in jail, and then another judge will let them out. The same System that will lock my kids up, for a DUI, will allow me to make a few phone calls and get it taken care of. The System helps everyone even if only for a short time, The System is you and me; The System is people.

This System requires retirement and then makes the cost of living too high to afford, but then it will give my kids money for college and jobs. The System is how we all survive. Sometimes The System needs you to lie, sometimes The System needs you to kill. Sometimes The System demands you break the law. It is ok though, because the law is made by The System, so we use euphemisms for The System.

We cannot beat The System because we are The System: all the lies, theft, deceit, and reprehensible behavior is who we are. The System is just the name we give our darkness; The Brass lives in the shadow of cops: because of their tarnish, the badge's brilliance darkens further.

If I drag a wanted felon, behind a building, handcuffed and kill him; what is that but a murder? Yet The System can sanction it, as being necessary. That same activity, if caught in plain sight, is a detestable occurrence and The System comes down hard on you. It is not because The System cares, it is because The System controls people by giving them Bread and Circuses."

"When did The System begin?"

"Before I was born," I said then I turned and walked away.

"Man that crap just isn't fair, you help make this place safe for people, and for officers."

I turned and looked at him. No one even said come back, or stop, or even bye; it was just another day in The System; my last day in The System; actually it was The System's last day for me. It was time for me to go; actually, my time was no more.

"The age of the real police was at an end. Now what people get are cops afraid of doing their jobs. Surgeons afraid to cut, watch dogs afraid to bite. The city has moved into another age, the age of the Law Enforcement Professional.

It is not racism, but fear and ineptness we see now on TV. Reason and rhetoric cannot stop a man from stomping his girlfriend's face in…but I never seen a dead man; do anything criminal."

I stood up to walk away and turned to him. "You cannot beat The System son, no one does. Some learn to work with it, some learn to to profit from it, but most just survive it. Either way, you cannot beat it, so it makes no sense to get mad at it."

"Man that's screwed up!" Walters said releasing my hand I took my badge off and handed it to him.

"It's just life brother, no one survives it. I did my job, I told another person how to be a cop; how to take care of the victims, how to take care of sisters and brothers in blue, and how to take care of himself.

In this way, if you pick up the mantle, the work continues, the bad guys do not go free, and those lives you do touch, do not have to live in permanent fear of the dark. The Dicks and Ticks wanted me gone, society wanted me gone, it was just time for me to disappear."

The only thing in the world worse than a vigilante is a coward. The vigilante fights for a cause, even if wrong. The coward will not fight for anyone or anything, even when right. I learned that the cowards of this world breed vigilantes because people respond out of desperation, when those tasked and empowered to protect them, are too lazy, corrupt, cowardly, or indifferent to do the job.

Whatever Walters was when he met me; he walked away knowing a cop.

17.0 PROLOGUE

I walked out of the building that I learned to call home. I looked back and quickly thought of all the things that had happened to me in this building. Good, bad, happy, sad, this building was where my family lived. A family I now had to leave.

When I walked away, I knew I could never live here again; there was no room for an estranged brother from the shadows.

I walked to a nearby bar. I no longer had a badge and a gun, although I was still in uniform. This must be what Ticks and Dicks feel like. I looked like a cop, but no longer had the power or authority to act like one, just a figurehead. I took my top off; I was still Blue and did not want to embarrass my family.

I ordered a drink then stood up and spoke loudly, "I would like to thank every officer in the world that is worth a crap. The ones with the drinking problems that come to work sober, fair, and honest to face their demons in silence. Thanks to the officers that do not steal, even when crap at home gets rough. I would like to thank the ones that work their zones, lock up the guilty, and befriend the innocent, and helpless. I would like to thank each officer that leaves home every day and leaves their family, in the care of another officer to make the world a little bit safer for everyone. I would like to acknowledge that just cracking heads and making many arrests is not all there is to being a cop. Often it is taking the woman and her kids to a place of safety, or helping the overdosed parent get help, so their kids will not be helpless.

Some days, it is just being in the right place at the right time so the robbers go elsewhere, or the domestic in the park does not happen. Sometimes being a cop is taking a child away from their useless parents, or giving them stickers, and feeding them out of your pocket while you wait for DCS to do their jobs. Maybe being a cop means going by and sitting in a basement with a man and his dog, and letting him tell you his stories, as he waits to die alone in an armchair.

I tip my hat and badge to you. I am proud of each of you that does not hide from danger, does not leave the unarmed citizen to do our job, or stands on the wall and says, 'I'll handle it for you, leave it to me. I love you all, I respect you all, I cannot be one of you any longer, but you will never have to look over your shoulder and wonder if I am near."

I downed the glass (tasted like crap, I was cheap…I was a cop remember) and went home.

I walked in, sat down, and put my gun in my mouth. Just before I pulled the trigger, I remembered something someone once said about suicide. "Death is easy. To live, is the most painful thing I could imagine, and I'm just weak and no longer willing to fight." She was right. I did not want to die, just, not to live without my badge, but I had to push the fight. This was just a different fight. Moreover, if I pulled the trigger, some cop had to do a BS report. Fortunately, I am not that selfish.

I put the gun down, picked up the remote control, and turned on Looney Tunes.

My last life overflowed with tears, graves, lonely faces and faint glimmers of the badges that time forgot; I decided to start this one off with laughter, a try to find something else to fill that small space in front of my heart, where the unmistakable impression of a once worn badge lingered.

"Life is hard. Then you die. Then they throw dirt in your face. Then the worms eat you. Be grateful it happens in that order."

True

Blue

For

Life

"Almighty God; whose great power and wisdom embraces the universe; Watch over all officers; everywhere.

Protect them from harm in the performance of their duty to stop crime, robbery, and violence.

We pray, you help them keep our streets and home safe, day and night.

We recommend them to your loving care because their duty is dangerous.

Give them strength and courage.

Protect my brothers and sisters, Grant them your almighty protection. Unite them safely with their families, after duty has ended."

Thanks to the following persons whose statements were used by permission in this book.

- Nicholas Klein
- Barry Eisler
- Ralph Waldo Emerson
- Truman Capote
- Malcolm X
- Antoine de Saint
- Mary Wilson Little
- Josh Billings
- Woody Allen
- Pythagoras
- Miguel de Cervantes
- Raymond Chandler
- Shannon L. Alder
- Criss Jami
- Donna Brown
- George Orwell
- Solon
- Klaus Kinski
- Blaise Pascal
- Paula Malcomson
- David Videcette
- Craig D. Lounsbrough
- Elizabeth Gaskell
- Napoléon Bonaparte
- Rebecca Solnit
- Dr. ML Rapier
- Samuel Johnson
- George Bernard Shaw
- Steve Magee
- Swami Sivananda
- Hunter S Thompson
- Patti Callahan
- Michelle Alexander
- Shiv Khera
- F. Scott Fitzgerald
- Gore Vidal
- Bangambiki Habyarimana
- David Gerrold
- https://ucr.fbi.gov/crime-in-the-u.s/2018/crime-in-the-u.s.2018/tables/table-43, 2020.